The
Unfinished Garden

The Unfinished Garden

BARBARA CLAYPOLE WHITE

HARLEQUIN®

entertain, enrich, inspire™

Recycling programs
for this product may
not exist in your area.

ISBN-13: 978-0-7783-1412-7

THE UNFINISHED GARDEN

For questions and comments about the quality of this book, please contact us at CustomerService@Harlequin.com.

www.Harlequin.com

Printed in U.S.A.

First printing: September 2012
10 9 8 7 6 5 4 3 2 1

For Larry and Zachariah
And for my parents, Rev. Douglas Eric and Anne Claypole White

Many things grow in the garden that were never sown there
—*Thomas Fuller*, Gnomologia, 1732

Worry gives a small thing a big shadow
—**Swedish proverb**

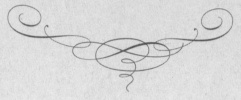

One

Tilly leaned over the railing and prodded the copperhead with the yard broom. Nothing much scared her these days other than snakes and hospitals, which she found oddly depressing. You needed jolts of fear, little hits of adrenaline, to appreciate the buzz of life.

A tailless skink scurried past her gardening clog, and a pair of hummingbirds chittered as they raced to and from the feeder. In the forest, the hawk screeched for its mate.

The venomous snake, however, refused to budge.

Growing up in the English countryside, the most terrifying creature Tilly encountered was a Charolais cow. Isaac, her child guru of everything indigenous and nasty in rural North Carolina, had stared, gobsmacked, when she'd shared that gem five minutes ago.

The porch vibrated as he pogoed up and down, no doubt rehearsing the pleasure of bragging to his chums: *My copperhead's bigger than yours.*

So what if she didn't belong here, any more than that manky elderberry hiding behind her tropical plants? This was

Isaac's universe, and she would never rip him away from it. She had failed her son three years earlier. She wouldn't fail him again. Although, once in a while, it might be refreshing to breathe air that wasn't as congealed as leftover leek and potato soup.

Tilly panted through a sigh. The heat had sprung early this year, sideswiped her without the gradual warming of late spring. August weather in the first week of June? Bugger, her summer was set to revolve around watering. She should have been watering this afternoon—not trying to outwit a comatose snake. Or repotting perennials. Or planning to fire her assistant. Of course, firing Sari meant finding time to interview a replacement, since the business had been twirling beyond her control long before Sari had appeared as the opposing force that stops an object in motion. Isaac had been reading *Newton! A Giant in Science!* lately. Inertia was his topic of the week.

If she'd paid more attention on the day Sari torpedoed into her life like a Norse berserker on Red Bull, Tilly would have realized Sari wasn't applying for a job; bloody woman was prowling for a cause. Just yesterday, she had tried to persuade Tilly to meet with some wealthy software developer about landscaping his new la-di-da property. Landscaping, really? Piedmont Perennials was a wholesale nursery. Besides, design clients would expect plans revealed in drawn-to-scale diagrams, and Tilly couldn't compile a functional grocery list.

Isaac stopped bouncing. "What's next, Mom?"

Damned if I know. Killing the snake was neither a thought she could follow nor an example she wanted to set for her critter-loving son. And no way could she find the courage to shovel up Mr. Copperhead and toss him toward the creek.

Tilly grinned at Isaac. Sticks of flaxen hair poked out like scarecrow straw from under his faded cap, and the front of his T-shirt was caught in the elastic of his Spiderman underwear. As usual, his pull-on shorts rested halfway down his hips. He was small for an eight-year-old, and every time Tilly looked at him, she saw playground bait. Which was the real reason she kept him at the private Montessori, not the math skills or his inexplicable passion for science.

"I'm fixin' to find that varmint a new home," she said. "'Cos he sure as heck can't 'ave this one."

As predicted, Isaac giggled through her English-accented Southern-speak. His laughter gave her precious seconds to think. No time to allow him to doubt, even for a millisecond, that his mother was able to handle every situation that rocked their lives. Except, of course, one involving snakes. And hospitals. But she wasn't going there in her mind, not today.

"What about calling that wildlife guy from the school field trip?" Isaac said. "Doesn't he rescue unwanted snakes?"

"Angel Bug, you're a genius. I guess I'll have to keep you around."

She expected him to puff up with pride. Instead he frowned and looked so like David that Tilly had to bite her lip.

"What do you think Daddy would do about the snake?"

Tilly no longer instigated the what-would-Daddy-do game, even though she screamed silently with memories: David waking from a nightmare, his voice full of need, "Promise you'll never leave me, babe"; David reaching for her with hot breath, greedy hands, and whispers of "Jesus. You make me so horny." David asleep on the sofa with baby Isaac tucked into his arm.

Isaac was only five when David died. How many of their child's memories were regurgitated stories she fed him? Did Isaac remember his father's passion, his contagious energy, his insistence that she sprinkle mothballs around the sandbox to bar snakes? David had loathed the bugs and the snakes. Mind you, he'd hated everything about life in the South, although not his status as the youngest distinguished professor in the University of North Carolina system.

A memory pounced, and Tilly smiled: David teetering on the sofa as he hurled an academic tome at a creepy-crawly moseying across the floor.

Her husband had done nothing without panache.

"What would Daddy do?" Tilly scratched the burning itch of fresh chigger bites under her arm. "Pitch a wobbly, then insist we move to snake-free Manhattan."

And once David chose a course of action, there was no U-turn.

"Daddy would have made us leave? That's awful."

But was it? Tilly stared into the forest that isolated them at night behind a wall of primal noise. This property had been on the market for two years when she and David bought it. No one wanted the unfinished house that was falling to ruin, the overgrown creek clogged with decades of trash, or the forest littered with refuse from a builder who abandoned the site after his money ran out. And yet the first time Tilly saw this land, she fell in love. Wild jack-in-the-pulpits poked through the forest floor, and untamed beauty whispered to her. But she left England for one reason, and that reason no longer existed, despite the Daddy game.

Tilly never talked about David's death, but the fact of it kept her company every day, like an echo. The ICU doctor had given her options and then asked how she would like to proceed. *Like,* a word that suggested choice. Funny thing, though, she never considered the choice was hers. One second of blind, misplaced faith, of assuming she knew what her husband wanted, of uttering one short sentence:

"David has a living will." That's all it had taken to destroy both their lives.

The phone rang inside the house, but neither Tilly, nor the copperhead, stirred.

The forest smelled different on hot evenings, like an oven set to four hundred and twenty-five degrees and cooking nothing but air. Tilly sipped her gin and tonic, closed her eyes, and listened to the pounding of the basketball on the concrete slab.

"Mom?" Isaac stopped shooting hoops. "Are we expecting someone?"

Please let it not be the chatty wildlife bloke returning with the copperhead. *Please.*

A silver convertible—*Alfa Romeo, fancy*—swung into a flawless turn and stopped under the basketball hoop. Damn, too late to sneak back inside, lock the door and pretend no one was home. The bearded driver tugged off his sunglasses and sat, motionless, his fingers pinching the bridge of his nose.

"Who is he?" Isaac whispered.

"Beats me," Tilly said. "Haven't got the foggiest."

The driver opened the door but didn't emerge.

"He looks like Blackbeard." Isaac stepped behind his mother.

"He's most likely lost. Don't worry, Angel Bug. I've got this covered." She tottered forward, trying not to spill her drink. "Can I help you, sir?"

The stranger, dressed in black jeans and a black T-shirt—*in this heat?*—didn't reply. He had retrieved a backpack from the passenger seat and was fiddling with its zipper. Gradually, as if the movement were choreographed, he turned.

"You're barefoot." He made no attempt to hide his disapproval.

She glanced into the driver's-side footwell. "And you aren't." Blimey, not so much as a sweetie wrapper on the floor of his car. Now *that* was impressive.

"James Nealy." Nealy…was that Irish? James Nealy, a name you snapped out with a click of your tongue. A name, like James Bond, that meant business.

He scowled at her, and she tried not to gawp. But really, he had the most stunning eyes. They were dappled with layers of light and dark like polished tiger's-eye. "I have a six o'clock appointment."

"You're the software developer? Bugger. I thought I canceled you."

Isaac tittered.

"Is that so?" Was there a hint of amusement in those eyes?

"Sorry. I meant, oh dear, my *lovely* assistant was supposed to call and cancel. I'm a nursery owner, Mr. Nealy, not a landscaper for hire. Can't help, I'm afraid."

That was it. Sari was so fired.

James emerged from his litterless car and slung the backpack over his shoulder. He definitely had that piratical look, although his beard seemed more like week-old growth. And his grizzled hair, which was straight and floppy at the front where it hung to his eyes, yet a mess of curls at his neck, was too short for a buccaneer. For some reason, she thought of contradictions in weather—a downpour through sunlight or the clear, bright day after a tropical storm. Maybe it was the result of speeding along in a convertible, but his hair gave the impression of having recently broken free from a style. Could he be growing it? If so, bad decision. She stroked her damp nape. Hair *that* unruly needed to be tamed or snipped off.

He turned to close the car door, pausing twice to tap a silent rhythm against his thigh with his index finger.

Isaac sidled up to her. "He looks like Ms. Lezlie does when

we're bouncing off the classroom walls. As if he's bursting with yells he can't let out."

"Hmm," Tilly replied.

Insects droned through the forest and the compressor grunted to life.

"Isaac, love." She inhaled thick, syrupy air and imagined the humidity clinging to her like an exhausted two-year-old. "Time to do something cool and quiet indoors."

"Awww, Mommmmm." Isaac's basketball fell to the concrete with a gentle *boing,* and James trapped it with his foot. Isaac glanced up, unsure.

James cocked his head to the right. "Tar Heel or Duke fan?"

"Tar Heel, of course," Isaac said.

"Good man." James winked.

Isaac beamed and then skittered into the garage to put away the basketball before bounding up the front steps two at a time.

Okay, so James Nealy had been nice to her son. That bought him five minutes.

James straightened up and towered over her. Well, most people did when you were five foot two, except for David. David had been the ideal height.

She swiped her palm down her cutoffs and extended her hand. "I'm Tilly, by the way. Tilly Silverberg."

James twitched, the slightest of tics, and his hand darted forward, touched hers and darted back. David always shook hands with a firm, double-handed grasp, drawing you into his space. But James's palm was cool, his loose handshake more of a dismissal than a greeting. His face remained impassive while his fingers flexed as if he had a cramp.

"Your assistant mentioned $25,000. I'm willing to double that."

Sari had discussed a figure with him? *Wait a minute.* He was offering her $50,000? She could redecorate, buy a new truck, go on a cruise—not that she wanted to. Since the crippling bout of seasickness on her honeymoon, she had avoided boats. And exactly why had she agreed to go snorkeling off the Great Barrier Reef when she hated snorkeling? Because it was always easier to say yes to David.

But widowhood had taught her to say no.

A crow cawed deep in the forest, and Tilly shuddered. Actually, it was more of a full-bodied spasm. Fifty thousand dollars, but at what price? There was a reason she hadn't expanded into retail despite Sari's best efforts; there was a reason she let Sari deliver customers' orders. How could she find the oomph to engage in other people's lives? Hanging on to Isaac's and her own was challenging enough.

And Isaac, her pint-size sage, may have been right about James Nealy. He was all wound up with nowhere to go, his fingers writhing with more nervous energy than those of a philandering priest waiting to be skewered by lightning. She should back away, right?

James flicked his hair from his face once, twice, and tossed her a look that was almost a dare, that seemed to say, "Go ahead. Ask what invisible demon snaps at my heels." And she nearly did, on the off chance it might be the same as hers.

She sighed. "I can recommend an excellent landscaper in Chapel Hill."

"I don't need a referral." James scanned the forest, first to the right, then to the left. "Your property has this controlled feeling, yet the borders speak of nature rioting. Breaking free, but in an orderly way. Your garden by the road is organized bedlam."

Tilly screwed up her face. Was that a compliment?

"The plants all grow into each other," he continued, his

speech speeding up. "But they're balanced in height and color, contained by shrubs shaped to fit. Individuality within structure. It's perfect." He cupped his long, thin fingers into a chalice. "It's perfect."

"Thank you." *I think*. Did he really believe there was a thought process behind her garden? She worked on instinct, nothing else, and after thirteen years of hard slog, had barely begun. How could this man, who was in such a rush that he had extracted his checkbook and a pen from his bag, understand?

"Shall I pay half up front and the balance when you're done?"

"Listen, flattery's lovely, but I have no experience in garden design."

"No experience? What do you call that?" He pointed to the woodland path that snaked through arching sprays of poet's laurel and hearts-a-bursting to open up around a small border edged with fallen cedar limbs. Mottled tiarellas wove through black-stemmed maidenhair ferns; a mass of Indian pinks with tubular flowers embraced the birdbath she'd rescued from the dump; the delicate arms of native Solomon's seal and goldenrod danced behind.

"Instinct," she said.

"Fine. I'll pay $50,000 for your instinct."

She would laugh, but the heat had siphoned off her energy.

"Mr. Nealy." Tilly leaned toward James and gave what she hoped was a firm smile, like opening your door a crack to a stranger but not letting him inside. "I appreciate your willingness to pay such a large sum for my *instinct*. But Sari told me that you're building a house." Tilly pulled back. "You should be searching for a landscaper, not a nursery owner."

James picked a single, dark hair from his black T-shirt. Was he even listening? Mind you, offering to double his payment without so much as a peeved expression suggested more money than sense. According to Sari, he had made appointments with every local business listed in the yellow pages under landscape architects, landscape designers, landscape contractors and nurseries. That was beyond thorough and not the behavior of someone she wanted to work for…if she were wavering in her decision, which she wasn't.

"I don't have the right qualifications for this job," Tilly said. "My answer has to be no."

His hand shot to his hair, then jerked down to massage his shoulder awkwardly. "You have a gift, and I'm willing to pay for it. How are career definitions relevant?"

Tilly swiped sweat from her hairline. No perspiration rolled down his face, no damp splodges marred his slim-fitting T-shirt. She had no eye for fashion, but Tilly understood cut and fabric. That simple black T-shirt probably cost more than her weekly grocery shop. Certainly more than today's red tank top, which was one dollar's worth of the thrift store's finest.

James cracked open his checkbook.

"People don't say no to you very often. Do they?"

"I need this garden." He clicked the top of his pen then repeated the gesture.

Interesting. Need and *garden* in the same sentence. Now he was talking her language.

"I *need* this garden." He grew still like the eye of a storm.

"Yes, I rather gathered that. Shame it's not for sale."

Tilly caught the scent of gardenia, that finicky little bugger she had come to love for its determination to survive. She braced for an outburst, but James surprised her with a smile. A warm smile that softened his face of angles and shadows and touched her in a way his handshake had not. If he were some fellow shopper queuing next to her in a checkout line and he threw her that smile, she might be tempted to give him the once-over. Not that she eyed up men anymore.

"I'm sorry." Tilly flicked a dribble of sweat from her pitiful cleavage. "This heat is making me cranky, and I don't mean to be rude, but I can't help you."

"You prefer rain to this interminable heat?" James scrutinized the sky.

"God, yes. I'm a rain freak. How did you know?"

"English accent."

The hawk drifted overhead, and Tilly watched it disappear into the forest. "People tend to guess Australian, since my accent's such a hybrid. English lilt, American terminology, although I swear in English. I'm not sure my voice knows where it belongs." And what did she hope to achieve by confessing that?

"The rest of you feels the same way?" James studied her.

The polite response would be a shrug. The impolite response would be to say, "None of your business." Tilly chose neither. Longing stabbed her, longing for Bramwell Chase, the Northamptonshire village that anchored her life. Longing for Woodend, the four-hundred-year-old house that breathed her history. Haddington history, from before she was Mrs. Silverberg.

"Some days." *Bugger.* Why did she have to cripple herself with honesty? Other people told juicy little fibs and fat whoppers of deceit all the time. But with one baby truth, she had shoved the conversation in a direction she had no desire to follow. "You're clearly comfortable, though, sweltering in the nineties." Her mouth was dry, her throat scratchy. She swept her tongue over her gums to find moisture. It didn't help.

"I'm familiar, not comfortable, with this weather." James returned the checkbook and pen to his backpack, but Tilly sensed he was regrouping, not conceding. "It reminds me of childhood summers, and childhoods have a powerful hold over us. I'm sure you agree."

Tilly didn't trust herself to answer. A thrush trilled from the mimosa tree, but she imagined the music of the blackbird's lullaby at Woodend. She pictured the paddock rolling toward fields dotted with clumps of bracken and the ancient trees of The Chase, the medieval hunting woods, looming beyond. If she closed her eyes, she might even smell her mother's lavender. Tilly wasn't aware of starting to walk, but she and James were sauntering toward the forest. Anyone watching might have assumed they were friends out for a stroll, which proved a person should trust with her heart, not with her eyes.

"Where's your childhood home?" Marvelous. She meant to terminate the conversation, not prolong it. But when was the last time she had a bona fide *I'll—tell-you-mine-if-you'll-tell-me-yours* chat with anyone? Just last week, Rowena, Tilly's best friend since they were four years old, had written a snarky email that started, "Answer this or I'm giving you the boot." And yet Tilly had discovered an amazing truth in the last few years: the further you drifted away from others, the easier it was to keep going.

Had James not heard her question? "Where—"

"Rural Illinois," he said.

Aha! *That* was why he wasn't sweating. "Farming stock?"

"I've tried hard not to be."

Tilly fished the remaining shard of ice from her gin and tonic and crunched it between her teeth, dampening the crescendo of cicada buzz. "Look, I'm melting faster than the ice in my gin, and I have to start supper. I apologize for wasting your time. I should have made it clear to Sari that I had no intention of taking the business in a different direction." Actually, she had stated it every which way and then some. Sari, a dean's wife with a master's degree in communications, had understood just fine.

"If I took you on as a client, I would be rushing helter-skelter into something new, something I can't handle right now. I appreciate your interest in my work, but I can't help you. We all need things, Mr. Nealy. We rarely get them."

"I'm curious. What is it that you need?"

Tilly rubbed her left hand across her mouth, jabbing her thumb into her jawbone. "Peace," she replied.

"In the Middle East?" He dipped toward her as if to catch her words.

"Peace from others." She held his gaze and felt the remnants of her bonhomie sizzle up in the heat. "I need the world to bugger off and leave me alone with my thoughts." *And my guilt.*

Sinew jutted from his neck. "That's a dangerous place to be, alone with your thoughts."

Tilly gulped back *why,* because she didn't want to know. Her thoughts were like tender perennials in a greenhouse, and she didn't need some stranger to crack the glass.

He blinked rapidly, and his mottled eyes filled with an expression she recognized. She hit a fawn once, driving along Creeping Cedars at dusk. Sprawled on the verge, the poor animal lay mangled and broken, its quivering eyes speaking to Tilly of the desire to bolt, hampered by the knowledge that there was no escape. The same fear she saw now in James.

Vulnerability, the one thing she could never resist.

A burst of sunlight caught on James's small, black ear stud. A black pearl?

"Please," James said. "Please show me your garden."

She would have agreed even without the second please. "On two conditions." She slugged her gin. "You understand that I'm not agreeing to take you on. And I fix you a drink while I freshen up mine."

But James didn't answer. He was wandering along Tilly's woodland trail, his index finger tapping against his thigh.

Two

Faster. James floored the gas pedal, even though faster was never fast enough. Twenty-five years ago, he would have been tearing across farm tracks on his Kawasaki H2, a motorbike that had earned its nickname of Widowmaker. Tonight he was racing along some county road in his Alfa Romeo Spider with the top down and the Gipsy Kings blaring. He conjured up his favorite scene from *Weekend at Bernie's* in which a corpse water-skied into a buoy, but couldn't even rustle up a smile. Movie slapstick was his happy pill, although obviously not this evening.

He glimpsed his reflection in the rearview mirror. God Almighty, some stranger could zip past the Alfa right now and have no inkling of the horror festering inside its driver. At worst, he looked like a guy trapped in a killer hangover and the black-only fashion dictum of the eighties. No one would guess that he was, quite simply, a man trapped. James had read somewhere that life was about how you lived in the present moment, which might be true for millions of people without obsessive-compulsive disorder. But for James, living in the moment was hell. And he never got so much as a day pass.

Would he ever find peace, or would he always be that kid terrified of the boogeyman hiding in his own psyche?

He could feel germs mutating in the soil. Soil Tilly had transferred to him. Why, why had he shaken hands?

The Alfa screeched onto the gravel in front of an abandoned gas station and James leaped from the car, leaving the engine running. He grabbed one of six bottles of Purell from the glove compartment and emptied it over his hands, shaking out every last drop. Terrific. Now his palms were sticky as well as contaminated. Cringing, he rubbed them together until they throbbed.

A squirrel shot in front of him, rustling dried-up leaves as it disappeared into the forest, squawking. Smart little rodent. *I'd run from me, too, if I could, buddy.*

Shaking his hands dry, James glanced up. He needed big sky, Illinois sky, not this wimpy patch of cerulean obscured by trees. Even in Chicago, he could see more sky than he could in Chapel Hill, where the forest closed in from every angle. And at night, the roads were dark like pitch, trapping him, blind, in purgatory.

Was it too late to reconsider this whole move? Yes, it was. He had started down this path the only way he knew how— with absolute commitment. There could be no running back to Illinois. He had made sure of that by selling everything— the farm, the business, his apartment on Lake Shore Drive. Everything but the Widowmaker and the Alfa.

He had moved south with one purpose: to be part of the exposure therapy trials at Duke University, and finally, *finally* learn how to reclaim his life from fear.

A rusty white pickup truck lurched down the road, an animal crate on its flatbed rattling against restraints. His father had offered to cage him once—a drunken joke that wasn't remotely funny. Regret rose in his gut, and James hardened himself against it. Back then no one, not even James, had understood that his bizarre behavior and repetitive thoughts were caused by an anxiety disorder. And his dad? His dad died believing that his only kid was damaged beyond repair. But James was going to prove him wrong. *Hell, yes.* He was going to prove his dad wrong. OCD had nearly destroyed James's life once. And he would do whatever it took to become that guy, that normal guy, who could shrug and say, "You know what? Once is enough."

The original plan had derailed, but he wouldn't turn back. Not that he could even if he wanted to, since he'd never been able to walk away from anything. OCD was behind that, too. It was the root cause of every success, every failure, every gesture, every desire, every thought…every thought.

This was his amended plan, 1b. No! 2a. Odd numbers tingled through him like slow-working poison and jinxed everything. This plan held the promise of freedom—freedom from the nightly window and door checks, freedom to sleep past the 4:30-a.m. treadmill call. Freedom to expose himself to the minefield of unallocated time. Doing nothing was akin to unrolling the welcome mat for every funky ritual his short-circuiting brain could sling at him. It was beautifully, impossibly straightforward, his plan: face his fear. And not just any fear, but the mother lode. The biggest fucking fear of all. Dirt.

James's pulse sped up, and his heart became a jackhammer pounding into his ribs. He swallowed hard and tasted panic, metallic as if his throat were lined with copper. The voice inside his head that wasn't his own drowned out everything as it chanted over and over, "You're going to die, die from disease in the soil." He started rocking. Movement, he needed movement. The voice told him to twist his hair, told him if he didn't, he would catch cancer from the soil and die. But he didn't have to listen! This wasn't a real thought. This was brain trash, right?

Or he could just twist his hair twice. Then twice again and twice again. Six was a wonderful number. Soft and round and calm. But rituals were cheap fixes. Compulsions only fed the OCD monster. It would return, stronger, unless he fought back.

He thumped his fists into his thigh. *Don't cave, don't twist your hair. If you can fight for ten minutes, the urge will pass.* He counted to forty and stopped. Ten minutes? Hell, he couldn't make it to one.

Was he crazy to retire at forty-five and abandon work, the only distraction that restrained fear? There would be no more relabeling irrational anxiety as the stress of running a successful software company. No, those days were over. Now he was free to follow the lead of his faulty brain wherever it led.

Me and my fucked-up shadow.

James tapped his lucky watch. *Tap, tap. Tap, tap. Tap, tap.* Now he'd contaminated his watch.

Panic gnawed at his stomach. Germs were mutating in the soil, breeding like bunny fucking rabbits, but he was not going to twist his hair. James sucked in a breath to the count of four. He held it for two seconds then exhaled. *One, two, three, four. Repeat, James, repeat. Slow the breath, and the heart and mind will follow.*

Everything would be okay if he could just hire a landscaper—Tilly Silverberg—under the pretext of beautifying his new ten-acre property, when really, he would watch and learn from a professional. She'd made it clear no amount of money would change her mind, which was intriguing.

Not that he was cynical, but money talked. There had to be another way. *Did that bring him to plan 2b?*

James concentrated on slowing down his breath, winding down his fear, and reliving the moment he had seen her garden on the edge of the woods. His pulse had slowed, his thoughts had fallen silent, and he'd known, just known: whatever lay at the end of that driveway held the key to his plan.

Piedmont Perennials had been his final appointment at 6:00 p.m. Six, a sign that everything would be okay, except for that god-awful honking. James glanced up as a skein of geese flew over in textbook formation—an imperfect, imbalanced V with one side longer than the other. Symmetry soothed his fractured mind, but the lack of it….

James jerked around, searching for a focal point, a diversion, anything.

Stop. Please, just stop. And a picture of Tilly dropped into his mind. She moved with the elegance of a prima ballerina, albeit one in a scarlet top and frayed cutoffs. Scarlet, she was a woman of bright colors who could spin through life laughing, gin in hand. But there was a sadness in those huge, pale eyes. Yes, she was beautiful, but beauty held no meaning for him. He was attracted only to women who were as screwed up as he was, even if they hid it better. *Fuck. Not good, not good.* Eighteen months celibate and focused on one thing—fixing himself. Fighting terror sucked up enough emotional energy. How could he salvage any for the mess of love and desire? Besides, being alone was his default button. Best for others, best for him. And yet…Tilly had made him smile.

His insides were heaving with fear, and she made him smile.

Her feet, poised for a pirouette, were so small, so vulnerable—so bare. Bare and dirty. And covered in soil. Soil on her feet, soil on her hands, soil she'd transferred to him. Soil poisoning her, poisoning him.

Boss back the thought, James. Boss it back.

Bossing back, the most basic weapon in the cognitive-behavioral therapy arsenal, sounded as easy as flipping on the turn signal. Don't want that thought? Toss it and change direction. And yet summoning those three short words, *boss it back,* demanded enough focus to cripple him.

Why, why had he shaken hands with a gardener, a woman with dirt under her thumbnail? He must get to the rental apartment and throw everything, even his Pumas in the washing machine. Scour himself clean and then scrub the car inside and out.

Lose himself in time-consuming routine, his comfort and his curse.

But first, vomit.

Three

The ache in her right shoulder blade, an old symptom of her scoliosis, continued to throb to the cacophony of spring peepers. Or had they already become bog-standard tree frogs by early June? One of those Southern things Tilly could never figure out. Read-aloud time, that most precious part of the day, had slipped by unnoticed, so she'd promised Isaac he could come back outside in his jammies to catch fireflies.

The phone rang and Tilly picked it up on the first ring. "Piedmont Perennials." She swallowed a yawn.

"Tilly? James Nealy." His voice was deeper on the phone. Or did she mean sexier?

Bugger it. She really must start checking caller ID. "Seriously?"

"Seriously." He paused. "Listen, I realize you're probably doing bedtime with your son."

At least he was aware of that fact. Half a Brownie point in his favor.

"And I'm sorry, I'm sorry...I know I took up enough of your time yesterday evening, and you've made your position perfectly clear. Perfectly clear. But I'm—" he hesitated "—obsessed with your garden, and sadly for you, that won't change. Name your price and conditions. I'll agree to anything."

"How about agreeing to find someone else?"

"Not an option." In the forest, a blue jay jeered. "It has to be you. Your garden speaks to me."

She laughed. She had a gardening groupie? Was this how David had felt every time a grad student drooled over one of his lectures? Not a bad sensation, really. "Are you always this sure?"

"I have good intuition, Tilly. I wouldn't be retired at forty-five if I didn't."

"Lucky you, because mine is crap." One irreversible mistake, that's all it had taken to dull her intuition into nonexistence. Tilly shivered, despite the clawing humidity. For a second she was back in the cold, white hospital room. Some days she wasn't sure she'd ever left.

A carpenter bee looped past, searching for a place to burrow. It would, no doubt, drill a pretty little hole in her cedar railing. One bee, one hole, meant nothing, but small things had a nasty habit of becoming big things. And she didn't want to think about the damage a colony of bees could inflict.

"So there is a chance for me?" James said.

Obviously, she hadn't mastered *no* quite as well as she'd thought. "You know, I really, really want to dislike you."

"Yes, I can have that effect on people. Although they tend to skip the *want* part."

Tilly smiled. If he kept this up, she might have to change her mind. "It's late, and you're right. I'm in the middle of bedtime."

"Can I call tomorrow?"

"You're pushing it."

"Sorry, sorry."

"Do you always apologize this much?"

"It's one of my more annoying habits."

"You might want to work on that."

There was a sharp intake of breath on the other end of the phone line. "I'm trying." His voice was lower, quieter.

"Good night," Tilly said, and hit the off button before James could reply.

She scuffed up a dusting of red clay with her gardening clog and imagined rain. English summer rain that pattered and pinged and smelled fresh, clean and cool. James's talk of childhoods the day before had unsettled her, left her with an aftertaste she couldn't nix. A quick fantasy blindsided her— running home to her mother, her twin sisters, Caitlin and Bree, and of course, Rowena. Tilly may have changed her name and citizenship, but she was English at heart, just as she would always be a Haddington.

Isaac, who had been searching the edge of one of her shade beds for who-knew-which disgusting creepy-crawly, rose and yanked up his pajama bottoms. "Thinking of Daddy?"

"Nope." Her eyes followed a vapor trail toward the stratosphere.

"England?"

"Busted." Bugger, she was a pitifully easy read. Thank God she never had secrets to keep. "I was remembering gloriously wet summers when I was your age. Snakeless, too."

Isaac recoiled as if she'd driven over skunk roadkill with the truck's windows open. "Are you going to drag us back?"

"Wow. Why would you ask that?" *Avoidance, smart move.*

"You think everything's better in England." Isaac twisted his foot, and a hunk of guilt constricted in her stomach. "But I want to live here, in our house, for ever and ever."

"I know, my love. I used to feel the same way about Woodend."

"Do you still?"

Not a fair question. Woodend was the place that caught her when she fell from life, and it always would be. Isaac continued to wait for an answer, but a sugarcoated one she couldn't give.

"Woodend is a place of memories. I was born there. I met Daddy there…." Tilly stared at the dogwood tree they had planted on the sixth-month anniversary of David's death.

"This is a place of memories, too, Mom. Yours and mine and Daddy's."

But the memories here were polluted with grief. Once again she had shared too much and disappointed Isaac. Yes, he was old in intellect, but emotionally he was far younger than eight.

"You're right." Tilly swelled with love. Sometimes just looking at Isaac made her chest heave with the imagined horror of a thousand what-ifs. "I'm sorry. I'm a little lost today."

"That's okay, Mom. I have lost days, too. Hey, I need to pee. Want me to do it by the cold frame to keep the deer away?"

"Please. But watch your aim." Tilly turned toward the beat of a hummingbird's wings.

"Mommy?"

"Isaac?" She spun around.

Pajama pants shoved to his knees, he was clutching his penis. "I have a tick. Near my willy." His free hand agitated as if he were shaking a maraca. "It's latched on."

"Piff. I can get that sucker off." Finally, a problem she could fix.

A groan of thunder tumbled toward them as the edge of the

forest retreated into darkness. How had she failed to notice the towering storm cloud banked over the upper canopy? The sky exploded with a boom that rattled through the window casements and through Tilly. She jerked back into spider thread, the kind you never saw, and then *blam!* You were wrapped in goo, snared by a teeny-tiny, almost invisible, arachnid.

An arm slipped around her waist, breath tickled her neck and familiar fingers teased the sensitive spot above her hipbone. The blades of the fan sliced through the bedroom air, and tree frogs serenaded with the noises of the night. "I love you," David whispered in the soft mid-Atlantic accent that masked his Brooklyn roots.

Tilly tried to turn and touch the ridge of scar on his right cheek, but her limbs remained weighted to the mattress. The mockingbird shrilled from its nest, and David's arms retreated.

Don't go, my love, don't go. It can't hurt you. It's just a bird.

Tilly jolted upright in bed, her heart thumping. She glanced at the ceiling, but there was no creak from the room above to suggest that Isaac, who slept on the edge of his bed in deference to his plush lizards and snakes, had, yet again, fallen out.

Dawn was creeping around the blinds, sneaking into her bedroom with a fresh reminder that she was welcoming another day as a widow. And her phone was ringing at—she squinted toward David's space-age alarm clock—6:00 a.m.? It better not be James Nealy again, unless…dear God, no. No. Her breath quickened; her mind swirled in memories. Was it four o'clock on a black November morning with rain pounding the deck, the air crackling with a late-season thunderstorm, and her mother's voice, quiet but solid, "Your father's fading. Come home"? Or was it 12:01 on a balmy May night with spring peepers jingling in the forest and one of David's inner-circle graduate students crying as she whispered, "David's been rushed to hospital"? Why did life boil down to phone calls in the middle of the night? Who this time? Her mother, one of her sisters, Rowena?

Tilly yanked the phone from its base. "Yes?" Her voice raced out with her breath.

"Oh, you're there. Thank the Lord."

"Mum? Why are you calling at this hour?"

"I woke you, didn't I? I'm terribly sorry, darling." This was not the voice of a woman who had spent forty years drilling English history into teenage girls at a small private school. Nor was it the voice of a woman who had lost two babies to crib death, but scuppered fear and grief to see two more pregnancies to term. This was the voice of a woman who, the summer after her husband died, hid in a family heirloom.

The nearly forgotten image stirred: her mother crouched against grief in the Victorian wardrobe, refusing to come out for anyone but Tilly, the daughter who lived an ocean away.

"Wake me?" Tilly rubbed her eyes. "You know me, up with the larks. Bright and chirpy at—" she glanced at the clock again. *Six bloody a.m.?* "—six a.m."

"Darling, is something wrong?"

"Shouldn't I be asking that question?"

Tilly scooted across David's side of the bed and swung her legs to the hardwood floor. She used to dream of a rug in the bedroom, but David liked his floors smooth, bare and refinished every three years. Maybe this winter she would splurge, buy a rug. Or maybe not.

"Bit out of sorts," her mother said. "Fancied a chat."

Tilly gnawed off a hangnail. "Did something happen, Mum?"

Half a day away, her mother heaved out the biggest sigh Tilly had ever heard.

"Mum? You're scaring me." Tilly twisted the phone cord around her wrist, then untwisted it. Oh God, was her mother's voice muffled? Was she hiding in the wardrobe again? Tilly drummed her toes on the floor. Where were her flip-flops? Where?

"Now you're not to fuss. I'm absolutely fine. I've had a bit of a fall and broken my leg. Of all the ridiculous things. And I have five stitches in my left hand. Where Monty bit me."

"He *what*?" Tilly shot up. Her mother's springer spaniel, named after a British World War II general, was a wack job.

"Don't yell, darling. It was an accident. He was aiming for the hedgehog."

"Hedgehog?"

"It's all rather embarrassing."

"I'm coming home, right now." *As soon as I find my flip-flops.* Tilly dived under the bed. Well, lookie here—the overdue library books and the breast health pamphlet she'd been searching for. And wow, how about all those dust bunnies?

"Don't be ridiculous. You are *not* coming home." Thank God, her mother was using her teacher's voice, the one that had enforced zero tolerance in the classroom long before American educators adopted the phrase. "I'm perfectly fine. Feeling a tad foolish is all. I called to commiserate, not cause worry. It's perfect gardening weather, and I'm confined to the drawing room with my feet up. My list for today included tying back the sweet peas."

Typical, her mother was upset by the disruption, not the accident. Apart from the summer of her breakdown, Mrs. Virginia Haddington lived a neat life, greeting each day with a list written in specially ordered blue fountain pen ink. *Oh God.* In the ten years since her father's death, Tilly had been the gatekeeper of her mother's mental health, making sure she was taking time to garden, to read, to enjoy a social life. But in all those years, Tilly had never once worried about her mother's physical well-being. Sure, she was only seventy, but her mother had never broken a bone before.

Mrs. Haddington gave a sniff. "It's that blasted muntjac's fault, the one that treats my vegetable garden as an all-night buffet. I'm at my wit's end, Tilly. My broad beans are gone. Simply gone. When I was up at the Hall the other day, trying to persuade Rowena to join the rota for the church flowers—"

Tilly snorted. Her mother had to be joking. Rowena could barely tell the difference between a stinging nettle and a rose. And she had no interest in learning otherwise.

Her mother ignored the interruption and kept going. "I bumped into the gamekeeper and asked if I could borrow his shotgun, but the blighter refused to lend it to me."

Tilly rolled her eyes. Her mother had known the gamekeeper for thirty years, but still refused to call him John. Of course, the only person in the village who used his real name was Rowena, his boss. The Roxtons, Rowena's family, had owned and managed the three thousand acres of woods and farmland surrounding the village for generations. But on Rowena's thirtieth birthday, Lord and Lady Roxton gifted the property to their only child and skipped off to a new life on Crete. A dumbfounded Rowena, left only with a vague reassurance that she wouldn't be clobbered with inheritance tax provided Lord Roxton outlived the gift by seven years, had quit a successful career in the London art world to save her ailing inheritance: the Bramwell Chase estate and Bramwell Hall. As the new lady of the manor, she had hired contract farmers, financed a roof for her crumbling historic mansion by renting it to a movie crew, and had just scraped past the seven-year marker. Considering she was mining a financial dinosaur, Ro was holding her own, but no thanks to her parents.

"Wait a minute," Tilly said. "You were planning to shoot Bambi?" She imagined a new version of the Daddy game. What would Grammy do about the copperhead? Easy-peasy. Bash in the snake's head with the hoe and then put the kettle on for tea. "You've never fired a gun."

"Nonsense. I was a dab hand with your uncle's air rifle. Deer are large rodents, Tilly, and one should treat them as such. When I have rats, I pay the rat catcher to kill them. Why is shooting a deer any different?"

Tilly chewed her lip, determined not to swallow the bait. Her mother and Rowena had collaborated many times to accuse anti-beagling, anti-fox-hunting, anti-pheasant-shooting Tilly of being a namby-pamby country dweller.

"I'm sorry, Mum. My head's spinning, and I'm barely awake." Although her heart, galloping every which way, suggested otherwise. "How did we get from hedgehogs to deer?"

"A hedgehog. Singular."

Tilly rolled her eyes and silently renewed her vow never to be a mother who grasped every teachable moment and strode forth with it.

"Well, since the *gamekeeper* wouldn't help, I came up with my own solution. Very creative, too. When I took Monty out for his bedtime turn around the garden, I brought along that giant water blaster Rowena gave Isaac. Thought I'd soak the muntjac if I saw him. Works with next door's Lab when he bursts through the hedge to attack poor Monty."

Poor was hardly an adjective to describe her mother's dog. Not since he'd mauled a baby rabbit to death and terrorized the window cleaner with the carcass.

"What a ridiculous gift that water gun was. If only Rowena would settle down with a nice man, start a family…."

"The deer, Mum?"

"The deer? Oh, right. The deer."

Anxiety returned in waves. When she and Isaac were home at Christmas, Tilly had noticed her mother developing a new habit of becoming lost in her speech, as if she couldn't retain her thoughts. Was this early-onset dementia, history about to repeat itself, or wet brain from decades of drinking gin?

"It's quite simple really. Instead of a deer, Monty found a hedgehog. I tripped over the blessed thing in the dark, and then everything degenerated into a *Dad's Army* sketch."

Tilly laughed, remembering her's father favorite television sitcom, but stopped when she heard only silence from her mother. "How long till the plaster comes off?"

"Eight weeks."

"Eight weeks! Who's going to help you bathe, get dressed, walk Monty?"

"I'll muddle through. The twins don't leave for Australia for two weeks, which is an absolute stroke of luck. And Marigold's rallied my support system. Bless her, she does have a tendency towards drama." That was an understatement. Marigold, her mother's bosom pal of forty years, could create drama out of a downed washing line. "Trust me, darling—" Mrs. Haddington lowered her voice and sounded so far away "—this is nothing like before."

"You've had another panic attack," Tilly said. "Haven't you?"

Her mother hesitated for a second too long. "It was nothing."

"Right, we'll arrive after the twins leave and stay until the plaster comes off. Can you spring for the tickets? I'm strapped for cash since the electrics went on my truck."

If the panic attacks had returned, what choice did Tilly have? She had safeguarded her mother's secrets once. If need be, she would do so again.

"Darling, don't be rash. What will happen to the nursery if you leave for six weeks during the peak season?"

"Sari'll happen. She can take over." Bummer, she couldn't fire Sari after all.

The night before, Tilly had found the phone message explaining Sari's impromptu beach getaway and how, in the excitement, she had misplaced James's number and been unable to cancel his appointment. Right, that made sense. Clearly, Sari had forgotten blabbing about her terror of oceans—despite her love of sleeping with a sound machine set to play waves. Tilly had ignored the confession as an attempt at girl bonding. Besides, once you understood someone's fears, you were trapped in her world.

Could she trust the daily grind of the nursery to a person who had lied so blatantly? An employee who couldn't sit still for ten minutes let alone direct nothing but a hose for five hours a day? But Tilly felt oddly disconnected, aware only of Woodend lit up ahead, waiting for her.

"Besides, how can I miss seeing you recline the summer away like Lady Muck?"

Tilly loved her mother's bawdy laugh, so unexpected for a petite woman who came down to cook breakfast every morning wearing red lipstick and Chanel No. 5 *eau de parfum*. But the laughter ended. "There's another reason you might not want to come home."

"The village cut off with foot and mouth again? More mad cow disease?"

"Rowena has a new tenant at Manor Farm." Her mother

took a deep breath. "Tilly, it's Sebastian. He's living in Bramwell Chase."

Tilly dropped the phone.

✑ Four ✑

James slid from Warrior I to Warrior II and deepened the stretch. *The warrior poses are about strength and endurance.* The muscles in his calf tightened as a warm current of energy flowed through his body and into the ground, rooting him, making him strong. Defective, but strong. His thoughts became clouds floating away, and he concentrated on the rhythm of his breathing, trying to ignore the feeling that picked at the back of his mind. A feeling he must not acknowledge. A distraction he could not afford. Not if he was going to kick-start his plan.

He found his focal point—the edge of his yoga mat—and shifted his balance forward, raising his right leg and his arms behind him. If he held the pose for six breaths, he would relax into Downward-Facing Dog and then treat himself to a headstand. When he was upside down, everything was in sync. His mind and body aligned.

One, two, three, four—he began to quaver—*five...*no, there it was again, that swell of desire. *Let it drift by, James.* He tried hard, so hard, to push it away but couldn't. And with a resigned sigh, he toppled.

Lying on his yoga mat, James stared up at the ceiling. Was that a stain in the corner? He sat up. A stain he hadn't noticed before? Mold? He stood. Anthrax?

Don't go psycho on me, James. A stain is often just a stain.

It was getting harder to find his own thoughts. The voice was gaining strength, feeding off his lack of sleep, feeding off the stress of the move, feeding off his attraction to Tilly.

Two days. It had been two days and she hadn't returned his call. What if her answering machine was broken? What if she wouldn't call unless he moved his coffee mug to the right of the phone? He always put his mug on the right. Always. And this morning he'd put it on the left, which proved he had messed with his routine, dallied on the wild side with those who put their coffee mugs wherever the hell they pleased. See what progress he was making?

Why hadn't she returned his call?

He was running out of time and options. Tomorrow she and Isaac flew to England, which he only knew because Isaac had told him when he'd called last week. Isaac said his mom was rushing around like a crazed squirrel and it was best not to disturb her. He'd promised to give her the message, but had he? What if he hadn't given her the message? What if her answering machine was broken? What if that stain really was anthrax?

Why hadn't she returned his call?

Only two things had slowed the swarming gnats of anxiety in the past two weeks: Tilly's garden and Tilly's smile. And he needed to see both.

James glanced at the fogged-up shower and tried not to think about previous tenants, about the dead skin cells they'd sloughed off, about the dirt they'd tracked in. He hadn't lived in rented accommodations since he was a student. And then he'd been too fucked-up to think about anything. He rubbed condensation from the mirror and tossed the damp bath sheet into the shower. The laundry would have to wait. He tried to hold on to that thought, but it slipped away and doubt crept back in, roaming his gut, searching for a hold, second-guessing the decision he had made ten minutes earlier.

Decision-making was exhausting, a haze of uncertainty entwining one consequence around another. And there would be consequences for what he was about to do, but it was a risk worth taking. Tilly could help him—he knew it. And if the thought of seeing her again gave him a hit of pure desire, that was an inconvenience he could overcome.

The psychologist in Chicago had told him obsessions and compulsions were like wild mushrooms popping up constantly. That he needed to stay vigilant, always mindful of situations that could trigger his OCD, which didn't help when he was attracted to a woman who lived her life in dirt. A woman who didn't seem to care that the flatbed of her truck resembled a bag lady's shopping cart. If Tilly agreed to work for him, would she let him clean out her truck?

James admired the small tattoo of a coiled, black snake on his right hip, his constant reminder that when it came to snakes, he was phobia-free. Possibly even brave. And he was lucky—*might as well monopolize on this good mood*—that his body had aged well. On the other hand, that wasn't so much luck as a freakish amount of exercise. Was fear behind that, too, a determination to control his body if not his mind?

James stretched and enjoyed the air caressing his skin. Naked, he was released from fabrics that itched and scratched. Labels were the worst offenders. But then again, none of his clothes had labels for long. He amputated every one.

If he didn't know better, he might say he was relaxed, which was not an adjective he ever used to describe himself. James didn't *do* relaxed. Volted-up was how Sam, his best friend of forty-two years, described James. He liked that analogy. Besides, nervous energy had its uses. No to-do list was a match for James.

He leaned forward, the edge of the vanity cutting into his stomach. Retirement was playing havoc with his grooming. His hair hadn't been this long since grad school and the beard still threw him. He barely recognized the face staring back. Or was that the point. If he changed the outside, would the inside follow?

Humming "Straight to Hell" by The Clash, James walked into the bedroom and slid open the closet door with his elbow. He reached into a rack of black, long-sleeved shirts and pulled his lucky Vivienne Westwood off its cedar hanger. Why not? He had nothing to lose except his pride, and that had never stopped him when a woman was concerned.

~~ Five ~~

You had to admire a middle-aged woman, even one as invasive as evening primrose, who accentuated her large breasts and rolls of stomach flesh with Lycra. No hiding behind plus-size smocks for Sari. Although her puce wedgies, adorned with large plastic flowers that flapped like dying lunar moths, pushed the limits of taste.

Bucking through a sneeze, Sari tripped over an exposed tree root. *"Gesundheit,"* she said.

What, she doesn't trust me to bless her? Tilly continued marching toward the greenhouse.

"Time to fix the driveway, hon." Sari trotted to keep up.

If you didn't barrel down my driveway five mornings a week, screeching a duet with Bruce Springsteen and kicking up gravel, it wouldn't need fixing. Tilly bit back the retort. Speedy-Sari-bumps, that's what Isaac called the craters Sari's tires had gouged into the driveway. Potholes and noise, Sari had brought both into Tilly's life.

"You still pissed about the James thing? Is that why you don't want a lift to the airport tomorrow?" Sari smiled, but the gesture was laced with menace. Her challenge might have worked three years earlier, before guilt became a constant companion. But now? Hey, good luck on that one.

"Sari, you'll be too busy here to drive us to the airport." Tilly's voice dragged in the heat. "And ignore James if he calls." *Just as I'm ignoring my memories of Sebastian.* But there he was again: her first love, taking up space in her mind.

"James is...loaded." Sari increased her pace with a pant. "I...looked him up on Google."

Sari rabbited on, sharing details of her Google search. James had invented an interactive web game that millions of people were addicted to, including Sari's two teenage boys. She dismissed the game as having to do with accumulating assets and dominating the world. As always, it was the bottom line that interested Sari: James had made enough money to sell his software company in Chicago and retire to North Carolina at forty-five.

Sari batted away a mosquito. "Tils, you need to step outside your comfort zone, discover the world of clients rich and ready for the taking."

Tils. A lazy word that slid from the side of Sari's mouth, an abbreviation of an already abbreviated name. Tilly shook back her hair, forgetting she'd lopped it off a few weeks earlier with the kitchen scissors. Something clicked and scrunched in her head. Her brain rusting up in the heat? She shook her head again. *Click, scrunch.* What depressing sounds to come from the center of your consciousness.

"You have zilch vision," Sari said.

"Yup. Visionless and proud of it." There was no point disagreeing. Tilly didn't want vision, she wanted survival—hers and Isaac's. The jury was still debating the survival of Piedmont Perennials, a business that had sprung out of the infertility of grief. Her secret fantasy niggled, the one in which the business folded and she and Isaac retreated to England. Of course, Issac would be devastated, which made her daydream his nightmare. No, Piedmont Perennials had to survive, and for that Tilly needed the woman she longed to fire.

"Come on, hon. Look around you." Sari circled her arms as if she were an overweight swimmer flailing in a rubber ring. "You've created five acres of landscaped heaven out of jungle. You know a thing or two about landscape design."

How had Sari sneaked into Tilly's life? Was it the tricolor cookies? She had already disarmed Tilly with a nasally slide of vowels and dropped *r*'s that screamed "Brooklyn!" before dumping the pièce de résistance: Sari grew up two blocks from David's childhood home in Sheepshead Bay and still bought tricolors, moist and rich with raspberry, almond and semisweet chocolate, from the bakery in David's old neighborhood. She even had a box in her freezer and had promised to share. The tricolors, when Sari finally brought them over, were stale.

The pileated woodpecker hammered into a tree then flapped away. He was the reason Tilly hadn't hacked down the decapitated pine that, as Sari loved to point out, leaned over the propane tank. See? Sari was clued in. All would be fine, just fine.

"Sari, you've been a godsend." *True, until the James debacle.* "If you didn't load up my truck and not return till every shrub was sold, I'd be donating plants to the Salvation Army." *True again.* "But you want to rush around corners and see what's next, and I want to poodle along. Wholesale customers are easy. They demand x, y, z on such a date and I, or rather you, deliver. But design clients?" Tilly shuddered. "They'd suck up all my make-nice happy juices."

Sari harrumphed, and they trudged on.

Be nice, Tilly. Or at least fake it. "Look. My business is thriving, so why gamble? You have to dig in, hold on, because in twenty-four hours your whole life can come crashing down. One afternoon you're plowing along I-40, late for school pickup, when your husband draws alongside in his MGB, laughs—" Tilly stumbled over her most precious memory "—blows you a kiss and speeds out of your life. Twelve hours later you're watching him die from hypertrophic cardiomyopathy, a hereditary heart condition no one in his family has heard of."

Not just watching him die, letting him die.

Tilly ground her fist into the pain spiking out across her forehead. Silence, rare in the forest, followed.

They had reached the greenhouse and next to it, the studio, David's office and hallowed lair. The thick, sweet scent of wild honeysuckle hit Tilly like a sugar rush, but it also brought the familiar letdown, the sinking in her stomach. This place should resonate with David's presence. Standing here, she wanted to believe some essence of him watched her, that if she swung around she could catch him as easily as Isaac caught fireflies. But despite the tommyrot she encouraged their son to believe, David was nowhere. Death led to nothing.

Through the trees, a pair of turkey vultures tugged at the guts of a groundhog splattered across Creeping Cedars Road. At least in nature death led to some great, cosmic recycling of life. Roadkill became a feast, fallen leaves nourished new growth and rotting logs became bug suburbia. Tilly stared up at the giant oak, now a mutant thanks to the limbs the tree surgeon had removed from one side. Despite his dire prediction that the tree was dying, it was still home to a spectacular trumpet vine; and she would never give permission to fell such a magnificent piece of living history. The oak was safe on her watch, because she was just as mulish as David had been.

Tilly smiled at her *Piss Off I'm Working* sign and swung open the greenhouse door. Usually once she stepped inside, the greenhouse worked its calming magic. With a membrane of opaque plastic that let in only light, it was as if nothing else existed. But today, Sari followed, filling Tilly's hidey-hole with the powdery odor of department store makeup halls.

Tilly grabbed the edge of the potting sink and breathed through her mouth.

"Jesus." Sari gagged. "If I were in charge, I'd rip off the plastic and put in glass. Open the place up. I feel like I'm simmering in a Crock-Pot."

Tilly carved out a dirt angel with her foot. *Please, God, protect my nursery from this woman.* Sari didn't have to like this part of the job, but she did have to come in here every day for the next six weeks. Tilly appraised her artwork and smiled.

"What?" Sari said. "You think it's funny this place freaks me out?"

"Of course not." Tilly looked up. "Although it's hard to imagine you scared of anything."

"You don't think everyone has fears?"

Tilly picked up a bundle of white plastic plant labels and put them back down. "Okay, then. What's the deal with you and oceans?"

"I nearly drowned as a kid. Would've, too, if some stranger hadn't jumped in while my dad stood on the beach yelling, 'Kick your legs.' And afterward all he said was, 'You need to listen.' Pretty rich since the bastard couldn't swim."

Bastard, never a word Tilly would use to describe her own father, who had taught her to swim in the freezing ocean off the Cornish Coast, his hands floating beneath her. Whole weeks went by and she didn't think of him, but there would always be a gap in her life where he had stood. And, inexplicably, she thought of James Nealy's comment about childhoods.

"I'm gonna get some quotes on a watering system while you're off playing happy families," Sari said. "I mean, c'mon. How cost effective can manual watering be?"

Tilly sighed; Sari had blown the moment.

"We've been over this, Sari. The electric bills would tear into my profits."

"Yeah? What about your time? Is it better to spend five hours a day watching a hose piss or five hours a day potting up saleable plants?"

"Watering systems fail, but the worst thing a hose does is leak. Besides, if I can feel the water flow, I know the job's being done."

"Jesus, Tils. Lighten up. You wanna spend your life worrying about what might happen?"

If they were friends, Tilly would point out how ludicrous that question was. After all, the thing she had dreaded most *had* happened. What did a person have left to worry about after that? The mister system whooshed on, spraying a film of water over the newly rooted cuttings. The paddles of the fan whirred into action, and a belt of hot air walloped Tilly across the face.

"This is why you have to check the greenhouse *every* day." Tilly pointed at the fan and then drew a diagonal line through the air with her finger. "See how the fan blows the mist away from this flat? These cuttings will die if you don't watch that."

"Understood. That it?"

"No. See this mister up here?" Tilly poked a spluttering nozzle, and tepid water drizzled down her arm. "It gets clogged. Then *these* cuttings will die."

"Yup. Cuttings die, excellent. I'm outta here. See ya up

at the house." Sari tugged the door open, and a pale vehicle, probably the FedEx van, flashed past. At least Sari could sign for a package without killing anything.

Sod it. Tilly gave the mister head another poke. She was tempting disaster, but if the nursery went belly-up, so be it. She and Isaac would have to stay in Bramwell Chase. Or maybe not, now that Sebastian had decided to nest there. Tilly pinched absentmindedly at her left breast. What was he up to? Bramwell Chase had never been his home. Sebastian was a Yorkshire lad, and according to his mother's last letter, happily ensconced in Hong Kong.

At fourteen, Sebastian was her life. By nineteen, he was her ex-lover, and even though they drifted through two reunions and a near miss before she met David, Sebastian remained part of her life. When her father was dying, Tilly flew home alone, insisting David fulfill his commitment to a well-paid lecture in Montreal. (If he had ever balanced the checkbook, he would have known how desperately they needed the money.) Tilly had swept in, determined to take care of everything, but the magnitude of family grief had nearly crushed her. Until Sebastian had stepped forward to handle the practical side of death, freeing Tilly to console her mother and sisters. After that, their friendship was sealed. Or so she thought.

Tilly made plenty of excuses for his lack of contact in the years that followed. He had a new wife, a new baby; they moved and had another baby. But then her world imploded. David died, grief eviscerated her, and Sebastian mailed a condolence card signed by his family like a corporate greeting. And for that—Tilly tugged open the greenhouse door—she would never forgive him.

A basketball pounded the concrete and a man laughed. *No, absolutely not.* Tilly curved around the giant red oak and groaned. Tucked between Sari's bumper-sticker-covered Passat and the tumble of logs that passed for the log pile, was a sparkling Alfa Romeo convertible. Oh, this was too much. She had a thousand things to do, half of which she couldn't remember, but would if she wasn't being harassed by a wealthy retiree who was giving her son advice on free-throws and encouraging her only employee to giggle like a sixteen-year-old on date night.

Tilly paused at the end of the driveway, hands on hips. She was, if no longer a Haddington in name, a Haddington in heart. *One never has an excuse for rudeness.* Although James Nealy was testing her on that particular philosophy.

Since the conversation with her mother two weeks earlier, Tilly had developed a strategy for handling James: ignore him. She figured by the time she left for England, he would have lost interest. No one could be *that* persistent. No one, it seemed, except James.

"How many times do I have to say, 'I can't help you'?" She kept her voice light, jovial even, but anger foamed inside.

"I like repetition." He grinned, flashing even, white teeth. So, James thought he could whittle her down, did he? Big mistake, because she could play a mighty fierce game of chicken.

"Well, gotta run." Sari headed to her car. "James? It's been real."

"Want to tell me why you're here?" Tilly said to James. She could take him, no problem.

"Want to tell me why you don't answer your messages?"

Tilly threaded her thumbs through her belt loops and gave her bring-it-on smile. But as the Passat squealed onto the driveway, she glanced at Isaac, and the fight drained out of her. Poor love, even the promise of hostility brought a flush of dread to Isaac's cheeks.

"Now I feel as if I'm the one who's always apologizing," Tilly said. And how unreasonable was that, since James was at fault? "But I'm sorry. As Isaac told you last week, I have a family emergency to handle in England. We leave tomorrow. That makes me kinda busy."

There was a difference between persistence, which Tilly applauded, and pestering, which she abhorred. When someone pushed too hard, her instinct was to hunker down. It was a Tilly thing. And if her resolve had wavered with James's admiration of her garden, it had hardened the moment her life had started circling the family drain and he'd begun leaving phone messages that started with "Maybe you didn't receive my previous message."

And why was he wearing a black long-sleeved shirt in ninety degrees? Maybe he preferred air-conditioning to nature. A person, in other words, who had nothing in common with Tilly.

James crossed and uncrossed his fingers in a silent jig. "I believe Maple View Farm's ice cream is nationally acclaimed. And since you live two minutes away, I was hoping, if I promised to deliver you back here in half an hour, that you and Isaac might accompany me to their country store?"

"Could we, Mom? Pretty please with Cool Whip and sprinkles on top?" Isaac's grin stretched until he resembled The Joker.

"I'm a little grubby for socializing." Tilly brushed a cobweb from her T-shirt.

"You look beautiful." James sounded as if he were stating a historical fact. Okay, so she warmed to him. Not because he had thrown her a compliment, although that was appreciated, but because she was certain James would have said, "Yes, you look like shit," if he had believed it. And honesty at all times was another Haddington trait, Tilly's favorite.

"Shall we take my car?" James asked Isaac, who punched the air with enough excitement to spontaneously combust.

The forest often closed in around her, but on the farm shop porch, Tilly could breathe. When the real estate agent had first driven her by the farm, thirteen years ago, Tilly's heart had skipped at the lowing of a cow, the stench of livestock and the sight of a fox ambling across a plowed field. How excited she'd been to discover this yawning landscape of green space that reminded her of the Bramwell Chase estate.

The view hadn't changed in thirteen years, which was perfect. Monotony was Tilly's life preserver. Maybe that was why gardening fed her soul. She loved the predictability of seasonal change, the certainty that redbuds heralded spring, that lantana was the belle of summer, that *Coreopsis integrifolia* lit up her garden every Halloween. And yet—she shifted and her cutoffs chafed against her sweaty thighs—gardening, like life, was about the unexpected.

She eyed the stranger sitting next to her, his waffle cone mummified in layers of paper napkins. Now that Isaac had run off to tumble over the hay bale, James had retreated into silence, licking his two scoops of black walnut into a smooth, dripless nub with a single-mindedness that she had come to associate with him after only two meetings. How did she get here, sitting on a rocking chair next to someone she was trying to avoid? A stranger who projected complete focus while eating ice cream but whose constantly moving fingers hinted at something out of control.

James rose, opened the garbage can flap with his elbow, and lobbed his untouched cone inside.

"Why spend so long deciding which cone to have if you weren't going to eat it?" Tilly nibbled through the end of her sugar cone and sucked out double chocolate chip ice cream.

"Life is in the details, Tilly."

When they were talking, she forgot they weren't friends. "You've got something against cones?"

"Ones that have been sitting out in the air all day, yes."

"Worried you might catch a deadly disease?"

"Possibly." His eyes were hidden behind mirrored sunglasses, but he appeared to stare at her. Silence pressed on her chest, the silence of strangers who had no understanding and no shared history. "I need to go inside and wash my hands," James said and vanished.

A mud dauber hummed under the porch roof, and a memory tumbled out, so vivid Tilly had to gasp. Swear to God, she could hear Sebastian's giggle, the giggle that fizzed like soda spilling from a shaken bottle. Her memories must be scrambled if she was confusing wasps, Sebastian and laughter. He was terrified of wasps. Always had been, always would be, because he refused to acknowledge it. She took a huge, gulping breath and nearly choked on a lungful of clotted, late-afternoon heat. Sebastian didn't deserve her thoughts. She wasn't allowing him to steal them.

She waved to Isaac, who was tumbling around with two smaller kids, making buddies with ease thanks to equal doses of his father's charisma and his grandfather's canny way with people. She had never been as open and trusting as a child. Of course, she had been painfully shy for most of her life. Amazing how widowhood had knocked that out of her.

The shop door jangled and James reappeared. He shook his hair from his face and smiled at her. She grinned back; it was impossible not to.

Her smile, her smile doused the swell of anxiety.

"This is very noble of you," James said as he resettled next to her. He tugged at a loose thread on the hem of his shirt. "Going to look after your mother."

"My mother doesn't need looking after." Tilly took a tiny, birdlike bite from her cone. "I'm merely helping out."

James stopped moving. He recognized self-talk when he heard it, the belief that positive words could lead to positive thoughts. How he wished that were true. In an instant, he wanted to know her hopes, her fears, her family story. The works.

"Do you have siblings?" he said.

"I have two sisters, twins. Eight years younger than me. They were preemies, so it was a case of join in the mothering or fall by the wayside. And then my father died and—" Tilly strained to keep Isaac in her sights. "Boring family stuff."

Of course, that explained the big-sister bullishness, the duty run back to England. Finally, he had context within which to place her. "You're the family glue."

"I guess so." Her approval gave him a kick of triumph, the pride of being a kid with his first gold star—hell, his first trophy! When was the last time he made someone feel good about herself, paid attention long enough to *want* to make someone feel good?

But her expression suggested sadness, and failure swamped him.

"We used to be closer." Tilly paused to chew a fingernail, and James suppressed his revulsion. "Truth is, I've distanced myself. Widowhood's streamlined me. What you see today is the leaner, meaner Tilly."

Shit, he didn't see that one coming. "I assumed you were divorced."

"I wish. God, no, I didn't mean that. You're not...are you?"

"No. Never married." Thankfully, one mistake he hadn't made. But Tilly, a widow? Had he become so self-absorbed that he no longer recognized the emotion he understood better than any other: grief?

"How long?" He tried to make eye contact, but she was focused on another fingernail. She wasn't going to chew that one, too, was she? Couldn't she see the speck of dirt down by her cuticle? Anxiety curdled inside him, waiting to contaminate his thoughts. James shifted and silently counted six cows in the field opposite.

"Three years."

"I'm sorry."

"Don't be. The bottom may have fallen out of my world, but I have two passions, motherhood and gardening, and I get to indulge in both." Her voice was overly bright. "Hey, who needs Prozac when you can get down and dirty in the soil?"

God Almighty, how could she say that? James shot up and jabbed his hands into his hair. The chain that anchored his rocker to all the other rocking chairs clanked, and Tilly stared at him. He should try and explain, but he couldn't. His mouth was dry, and words wouldn't form. All he could hear was his father's voice, slurred with Jack Daniel's and his Irish heritage: *You fucking eejit, James.* This, this was why he stayed away from women, why he'd expelled desire from his life. It was too hard, too fucking hard.

Isaac waved and James tried to walk toward him in a straight line, but the impulse was too strong. He had to step on every other dandelion, otherwise he'd die, die from the cancer breeding in the soil. Tilly was watching; he could feel her eyes on him. *Don't do it, she'll think you're crazy.* But he could smell disease and death waiting in the soil, ready to pounce. Fuck, he must look like a kid zigzagging through a game of don't-step-on-the-cracks.

The panic eased, shifted like a rusted-up gear moving again. James's pulse slowed to its normal beat, but nothing mattered beyond his failure. Once again, he had succumbed to the compulsion. And what of Tilly? He glanced over his shoulder. Was she embarrassed, shocked, or scared to be out in public with a freak?

Did she miss something? One minute they were talking, the next James shot up and began weaving toward the hitching post in the most bizarre manner, like a child playing a game of don't-step-on-the-cracks. But that wasn't nearly as weird as him glancing at her and then turning away before she had time to respond. Embarrassed. He was embarrassed, which made her want to run after him, arms wide-open for a big hug. And that might be a little kooky for both of them, so best not. It was sad, however, that he had such a low opinion of her. She may be strung out on her own needs, but the day she became judgmental, someone should bonk her on the head.

What had he said on the phone about "one of my more annoying habits"? Was this goofy walk another one? Some kind of tic, like his twitching hands? Maybe he had a muscular problem. Okay, so now she was flat-out intrigued.

Tilly pushed up from the rocking chair and followed James quietly.

"Hey, James." Isaac rushed toward him. "Why're you walking funny?"

Excellent question, Angel Bug. Wouldn't mind hearing the answer myself. Tilly stopped and made a big deal out of scratching a no-see-um bite.

"It's a habit I have, one I can't stop," James said. "Does that make sense?"

Bingo.

"Sure. My best friend says that when he gets into trouble at school."

"What habits does your friend have?"

"He jumps up and down. It helps with his sensory integration. If he bounces out his wiggles—" Isaac demonstrated, and Tilly smiled "—he feels less buzzy. Do you feel less buzzy when you walk funny?"

"For a moment. Then I feel worse. More buzzy."

Fascinating. Buzzy sounded more mental than muscular. So James had some psychological thingy, like sensory integration, that caused him to act a little doolally? Sweat trickled down her armpits, but she didn't dare move.

"If it makes you feel worse, why do it?" Isaac said to James.

The answer slammed into her: *he doesn't have a choice.* Man, she knew how that felt, to be stuck going through the motions, trapped in a life you were never supposed to live. Behaving as a widow, when every instinct screamed that you were still a wife.

James took two folded tissues from his pocket, arranged one and then the other over his hand and bent down to pick something. "I do it because I have to step on every other dandelion."

"Why?"

"My brain tells me I have to." James handed Isaac the flower.

"Can't you tell your brain you don't want to?" Isaac chewed on the inside of his cheek, the same way he did when working through an advanced math problem.

James tossed back his hair, twice, and laughed. Some women would likely find him attractive. Rowena would label him a sexy beast. The stunning eyes helped, the kilowatt grin, that deep, warm laugh. But it was also the way he spoke—carefully, as if he'd given life a great deal of thought. Or maybe, like Tilly, he'd seen too much of it.

"Do you ever get hiccups?" James asked Isaac.

Isaac rolled his eyes. "*Allllll* the time. Especially after eating little carrots. Yum."

"Yum indeed. Little carrots are my favorite snack. Fortunately they don't give me hiccups, which is good, because I get terrible hiccups. But mine are silent. No one can hear them except me." James paused, and Isaac nodded. James still hadn't hinted that he was aware of Tilly, but she sensed he was talking to her, too. "You see, I have a hiccup in my brain. My brain hiccups out the same thought, again and again. Let's say you get this idea, to step on a dandelion. You do it and then skip off to the hay bale. The original thought, to step on the dandelion, has gone. But if I have the same idea, my brain repeats the message—*step on the dandelion, step on the dandelion*," James said in a booming, theatrical voice, and Isaac giggled. "There's a technical name for my hiccups, but the easiest explanation is that my thoughts get stuck."

My thoughts get stuck. Tilly nodded slowly. *A phrase that makes sense.*

"You mean like getting stuck on the idea of my mom doing your garden?"

"Exactly."

Isaac sucked in his breath. "How do you get unstuck?"

Good question. Do I have an out clause if I end up working for this chap? Of course, going to England the next day made that whole scenario pretty unlikely. James seemed to be on a mission to start pronto and she couldn't commit to anything before the school year started.

"How do you get rid of your hiccups?" James asked.

"My mom drops an ice cube down my back." Isaac gave an exaggerated shiver. "Yuck."

"Well, if your mother can help me create a garden—" James tugged off his sunglasses and gazed at Tilly "—that will be my ice cube."

"Cool," Isaac said, and reached for James's hand.

James hesitated. "I'm not good at holding hands. Another bad habit."

"No biggie." Isaac slotted his arm through James's, and they smiled at each other.

Poor James. She couldn't imagine not being able to hold hands. She loved that feeling of being weighted to another person. Holding hands was the best of the best, and the one thing she missed most about her marriage. More than sex, more than kissing. David had been a hand holder. He couldn't even sit next to Tilly on the sofa without reaching for her.

Tilly flattened her hand over her heart...and shrieked. Her sugar cone had collapsed, and icy sludge oozed down her legs.

Six

James paced the apartment with his hands clasped behind his neck, and tried to ignore the irritating flopping noises his leather slides made on the wood floor. He could take a Clonazepam, that might help. But there was no specific anxiety to dull, no chemical that could alleviate the tumble of emotions racking his mind, half of which were contradictory. The silhouettes of furniture surrounding him were exactly where they had been the day before. Nothing in this room—including the stack of week-old *New York Times* in the corner and the four remotes lined up on the right side of the coffee table—had changed, so why did the world around him feel so different? Was it because Tilly had gone, or was it because the hope of her had gone?

He tugged open the balcony door and sat heavily on a hard, wrought-iron chair, one of a pair he'd picked up earlier in Chapel Hill. He should have tried them out for comfort, but he needed, he came, he saw, he bought. He had relocated with nothing but essentials and too few even of those.

A fat moon as luminous as an Illinois harvest moon lit up

the sky and unleashed a rush of adolescent memories. All of them involved sneaking out at night, but not to find pleasure. His ongoing mission had been to plant evidence. He had flung joint butts into the barn, abandoned Jim Beam bottles on farm machinery and placed ripped condom packets in the back of his dad's truck. God Almighty, it was a miracle that he and his father hadn't killed each other. Maybe that was the reason his dad had caved on the Kawasaki. Why else would a parent let his teenager buy a motorbike designed only for speed and danger? Although James had never taken risks with that bike, never gone near it when he was high or drunk, never let anyone else touch it. He still wheeled it out once a month to clean it and to reminisce, but he would never ride it again. He was many things but irresponsible was no longer one of them.

See, Dad? James raised his face to the moon. *I'm a fully functioning adult, despite your predictions.*

How many years since he and his father had exchanged words? James knew the exact time his garbage was picked up every Thursday, but he couldn't remember how long it had been since he had talked with his dad. And now, of course, it was irrelevant. His dad was dead. Both his parents were.

The Carolina night skies were spectacular. He'd never seen stars like this. Maybe he should get a telescope. Isaac would like that, wouldn't he? James groaned and buried his face in his hands.

Get real. Isaac isn't your kid.

Fatherhood—another relationship he'd screwed up. Yes, Daniel took his phone calls these days, but he still refused to call him Dad, which was fair enough. James had done little to earn the title. In fact, he lacked the whole happy-family gene. That wasn't self-pity; that was honesty.

James flipped his hand over and stared at his lifeline in

the moonlight. He rarely looked at it, since it splintered into three. Nothing good ever came from an odd number.

It was time to shake off his preoccupation with Isaac and Tilly. A widow and single mother had enough to deal with; she didn't need someone as demanding as him. And Isaac certainly didn't need him as a male role model.

Maybe he should treat thoughts of Tilly and Isaac as if they were obsessions, tackling them with the big three of cognitive-behavioral therapy—boss back the thought, use logic, use disassociation. Or maybe he should give up the fight. Roll over and play lovesick.

He glanced at his watch: 9:00 p.m. or 2:00 a.m. in England. How many times had he checked the American Airlines website? Tracking them was easy, since there was only one flight a day from Raleigh to London. They would land in five hours, then clear customs and immigration. How long before they arrived at Tilly's mother's house?

Let it go, James. Stick with the plan.

But he couldn't. Meeting Tilly and Isaac felt almost inevitable; he was incapable of resisting. For years, James had struggled with trust, a one-way street that led only to a dead end. But Isaac and Tilly had sneaked under his defenses, and he wasn't sure how.

Those not-so-subtle hints he'd given Tilly at Maple View Farm were the closest he'd ever come to revealing his secret: "Hi, my name is James and I'm obsessive-compulsive." Had he been testing them on some subconscious level? If so, they had both aced the quiz.

He glanced back up at the Milky Way. When light came and his day started, Tilly's would be half over.

Seven

Tilly breathed in recycled air, heavy on the antiseptic and burned coffee, and grinned. She loved night flights with the dimmed cabin lights, the stirring of passengers settling to movies or sleep and the constant thrum of engines. She and Isaac were submerged in airplane twilight, wrapped up in blankets in a row of two. Life didn't get any better.

"I like James." Isaac nestled into her, and Tilly fought the urge to tug him closer. "Do you like him, Mom?"

She mussed his hair with her nose. *Just For Kids mango splash shampoo. Best smell ever.* "I'm not good at meeting people, you know that." Not exactly an answer, but then she hadn't prepared for the question. She hadn't given James a second thought since the ice cream incident. Although she was still miffed that he had asked her to sit on a towel for the short ride home. Who kept a clean towel, in a ginormous Ziploc, in the trunk of his car?

"But do you *like* him?"

The people in front had left their blind up. Tilly peered

through their window, but there was nothing to see beyond the small, white light blinking on the tip of the wing.

"I guess." She sat back. "Although I have no idea why."

"Does that matter?"

"I suppose not. It's just normally when you make a new friend you find common ground, a shared passion. Like gardening."

Isaac scowled. "Ro hates gardening, and she's your best friend."

"That's different. We've been on the same life raft since we were four years old. I could pick up the phone and say *help,* and she would catch the first available flight." Just as Ro had done after David died, camping overnight at Heathrow to come standby via LaGuardia. Tilly remembered the cab speeding down the driveway, Rowena flinging open the door while the vehicle was still moving, her only words, *Where's Isaac?*

Tilly twirled a lock of Isaac's hair around her finger. "Besides, she spoils you rotten."

"So—" Isaac picked a piece of fluff from Bownba, the once-fluffy FAO Schwarz teddy that now resembled a squashed possum. "You like James, then?"

"Clearly not as much as you do." Should she worry that her eight-year-old still dragged his teddy bear to bed every night? Tilly attempted to squish her feet under the seat in front, but between the bottle of duty-free Bombay Sapphire, her canvas backpack and her floral Doc Martens boots, there was no room.

"Are we going to help him?"

Why was her son suddenly more tenacious than a Jack Russell terrier? Bugger it. She had been enjoying the growing distance between herself and James, herself and Sari, herself and the stings of everyday life. Thanks to Isaac, they rushed back, and all she wanted was a reprieve.

"You need to understand, Isaac—" Oh crap, now he looked crestfallen. "It's not that I don't want to help James, but he has that neat I-want-it-this-way thing that screams perfectionist." Or worse, a Virgo, like Sebastian, and the last thing she needed was another Virgo. Although, technically, she didn't have a Virgo in her life, not anymore.

"Cripes. Not like you and me, then."

"Exactly!" Tilly wagged a finger. "Think of the trail of possessions you and I can leave across two continents. A woman as scattered as me could drive a man as uptight as James seriously nuts. You do the math. It ain't gonna work." She would be barmy to get involved with someone that persnickety. Which didn't explain why she had agreed to talk with James in September.

"Well, I've been thinking about this," Isaac said with great solemnity. "I hate hiccups. They scare me because I want them to stop, but nothing I do works. I need you to help me. That's a horrid feeling, isn't it? That your body won't do what you want it to do."

"Sounds like middle age," Tilly mumbled.

"I bet it's a whole lot worse if it's your brain that won't cooperate." Isaac paused. "I think we should help James."

"Nicely expressed, Angel Bug. I'll consider your opinion, but right now you need sleep." *And I need peace and quiet.* Tilly patted fleecy travel blanket into the gaps around Isaac.

"Tell me the story of how you and Daddy met."

Tilly covered her mouth. At best, this story was happiness and despair tied up with a bow. At worst, it was a form of self-mutilation, a cut that bled with the life she had lost, or rather thrown away.

"Please?" Isaac looked up with huge Haddington eyes, as

pale as her father's had been. Thank God for genetics. Even a hint of them tethered you to the past.

Tilly smoothed down his bushy hair but it bounced free, sticking out every which way. "Our story begins one summer."

"Just like now, Mommy."

"Except this summer is a new chapter in the epic story of Isaac and Super Mom." Tilly struck her Popeye pose and Isaac snickered. Given the turmoil in her gut, however, Tilly felt less as if she were about to write an exciting new chapter in their lives, and more as if she were free-falling without a parachute, waiting for the big splat when Sari destroyed her business, and Sebastian…. Great, now she had Sebastian to worry about as well as James.

Isaac poked her. "Mom? Are you asleep?"

"Miles away. Sorry." She resumed stroking Isaac's hair. "It was a beautiful Saturday in June." Fourteen years ago last week, another notch on the totem pole of survival. Isaac wriggled into her, as if trying to crawl back into her womb. "I had run away from London and escaped to Bramwell Chase for the weekend. Grammy was off with the historical society, and Grandpa was due back from Northampton for lunch. We had the whole afternoon planned: work on the roses, then hike across the estate. I was propping open the gates for him when—" She didn't want to remember this, not tonight. Tonight she just wanted oblivion.

"When you heard this funny noise because Daddy didn't know how to drive a stick, and he'd borrowed some old banger." Isaac over-enunciated the last two words using a perfect English accent. Tilly swaddled him into her.

"This MG lurched up the High Street, gears crashing. Your father said that was the summer he discovered his two great loves: MGBs and me. Of course, that was before you were born and became more precious than anything." Isaac made a soft noise, like a kitten's mew. "Daddy bought his MGB after he got home. The 1972 Roadster that will be yours one day." *If it survives being shrouded under a tarpaulin in the garage.*

Her heart contracted at the memory of dark ringlets framing David's face and his chestnut eyes sparked with ambition. She'd wanted to lose herself in those eyes, and she had. Watching David, as he enchanted a lecture hall or entertained a room of friends, could leave her paralyzed with love. And yet however large his audience, however far away Tilly sat or stood, his eyes always found her. She pushed the heel of her hand into her heart, but the pain tightened. How had she navigated three years without him, without his adoration, without his need to share every joy and every disappointment with her?

She took a shallow breath. "The car stopped, and the most gorgeous man I had ever seen stuck his head out of the window and said, 'Hey there. Can you help me?' And I thought, I'll help you with anything you like."

Isaac's giggle dissolved into a yawn. "Daddy was on his way to a conference, but he got lost 'cos he didn't believe in reading maps."

"Only your father could take off across a foreign country and assume he'd end up where he wanted to be. When he explained he was looking for the Open University, I laughed so hard I couldn't tell him anything, and Daddy started laughing—"

"And Grandpa turned up. And he liked Daddy straight-away."

"Absolutely." How could anyone not? David always had the right words, the right smile, the right inclination of his head. Only Tilly saw the fragile ego that pecked away underneath.

"And Grandpa invited Daddy in to look at maps. And

he never made it to the conference 'cos he stayed with you instead." Isaac's voice was tinged with sleep. "And when Daddy left he asked you to marry him. And you said yes."

"I never could say no to your father. Although at the time, I thought he was joking. But when your father saw something he wanted, nothing stood in his way." Tilly shivered as her thoughts bounced back, briefly, to James.

Isaac was silent for a moment. "That's not always good, Mom. Is it?"

"No." She kissed the top of his head. "But it was that day."

Isaac gave a shadow of a smile and, as if someone had switched him off, conked out. He looked younger in sleep. She could trace the face of the baby with the rosebud mouth suckling at her breast, the toddler with his father's luscious lips, the little boy who whistled through the gap before his front teeth descended. David had never seen those front teeth, had never seen Isaac read a chapter book, had never seen him whiz through math homework declaring, "This is so easy!" If she had learned to say no to David, would things have been different? Would he be here with them now?

The engines droned as the plane flew closer to England and Tilly struggled to keep her mind from Sebastian. But Bramwell Chase was a village. She could bump into him walking down the High Street or cutting through Badger Way. Even an imaginary meeting left her giddy.

Should she slug him and say, "Naff off, asshole?" No, that smacked of amateur dramatics. She could give him a curt "Do I know you?" Nope, that was petty. If only she could snap out a Rowena-comment, a one-liner that shriveled up your desire to exist.

What was his wife's name? And the kids—a boy called Archie and a girl? Archie and Isaac were the same age. They could even become friends. Tilly clutched at her throat. What if Sebastian turned up on the doorstep all smiles and "Remember me?" Her breathing eased. No, that was one scenario she didn't need to prepare for. Sebastian was a successful personal banker for a reason. He never dabbled in spontaneity, never took risks, not even for her. When Tilly told him she was engaged, Sebastian had said, "I'll catch you the second time around," and walked away.

Would she recognize him after ten years? Would he recognize her? Since they last met she'd hacked off her hair and donated every piece of clothing that didn't fit the jeans and T-shirt category to the thrift store. And now Sebastian was turning forty. He'd probably sprouted a beer gut and tufty, falling-out hair. Yes, a balding banker grown slack on the high life. That was the image to work with, especially the balding part. Sebastian had always obsessed over his receding hairline, unlike David, who'd had enough hair for two. But as her eyelids fluttered, and her head drooped against the plastic wings of the headrest, it wasn't David who visited her dreams. She was cornered in sleep by the sixteen-year-old with the puckish grin, the boy she had once craved as if he were a drug.

Eight

Tilly spotted him the moment the electronic doors jolted open. At least she thought she did. It could also be a mirage, brought on by lack of sleep and cheap gin—the airline had cut the Bombay Sapphire. It couldn't be Sebastian—one foot resting on the pillar behind him, head rolled back, hands thrust deep into the pockets of his white jeans, suede jacket slung through one arm. Not at 8:00 a.m. in the arrivals area of Heathrow. Except that the redhead jumping up and down next to him screeching, "Haddy! Over here, you twit!" was Rowena.

With a *dang* and a thud, Tilly's luggage cart rear-ended a chrome bollard. *How did that happen?* One moment she was gripping the metal bar so tightly she thought she might cut off circulation to her fingers, the next all she could think about was escape. She turned, but the door to the customs hall had closed behind her.

"Haddy!" Rowena waved and the bangles and beads on her wrists chinked against each other like gypsy bells. "Haddy!"

Isaac ducked under the barricade and hurtled toward

Rowena. "Hey, Rosy-Posy," he giggled, then launched himself into her arms.

Sebastian lowered his head, but appeared to have no interest in locating his ex-lover. He looked more dazed than intrigued, his expression that of a person who had just woken from a nightmare and was struggling to cobble together his surroundings.

Tilly experienced a sudden plummeting in her gut. Still beautiful, then. Maybe more so. But she hadn't really expected him to be fat, bald and ruddy. She had always known he would gain substance with age.

"My little man," Rowena squealed as she twirled Isaac. "I've missed you so much! I forbid you from leaving me ever again."

Isaac disappeared into a kaleidoscope of laughter and color, wrapped in Rowena's ankle-length skirt and clasped to the turquoise sweater that nipped in at her tiny waist and stretched over her perfect breasts. The sleeves were forced above her elbows in an effort, no doubt, to hide the holes. Secondhand cashmere sweaters—*they're recycled, Haddy!*—were Ro's standard uniform and she was loyal to the last thread. Even on toasty summer days she complained of being *fucking freezing.* But then Rowena, a landowner infamous for serving marijuana with her shooting lunches, had always lived outside the lines. Being with Rowena was like jettisoning yourself through a bubble wand and not knowing when you would burst back into reality.

Being with Sebastian, however, was to stay firmly on the ground, to do one's duty. Tilly's stomach lurched as if she were still on the plane and riding out a patch of turbulence. He certainly had the air of someone who crafted his appearance with care. The cuffs of his pale blue shirt—linen, had to be, since it crumpled in all the right places—were folded back to reveal a heavy metal watch worn, as the battered Timex had been, with the face on the inside of his wrist so that he alone could read it.

"Haddy!" The familiarity of Rowena engulfed Tilly: the smell of satsuma soap, the softness of cashmere, the thick curtain of coarse hair. "It seems like only yesterday I was waving you off at Christmas and crying buckets." Rowena drew back. "But you look horribly pale. Are you eating properly? Sleeping? And why don't you answer my emails, you lazy old cow? I've been worried sick."

"Missed you, too," Tilly said. "Now tell me what he's doing here." She nodded backward.

"Be nice," Rowena whispered. "Sebastian's had a rough week."

"But—"

"Poppet! How you've grown since Christmas." Rowena ran a hand from the top of Isaac's head to below her collarbone. "You're only a head shorter than me now."

Tilly inhaled sharply and spun around, glaring at Sebastian. *You first.*

Gradually, his face transformed into his lopsided smile. He pushed off the pillar and sauntered over, hands still buried in his pockets.

An announcement drifted through the Tannoy system. Rowena teased Isaac as she foraged in her carpetbag, and Isaac spoke in his knock-knock joke voice. But Tilly couldn't decipher words. All she heard was noise, distorted by the thumping of her heart. *Thump.* Sebastian took another step— *thump*—and another step. *Thump.*

Finally, he stopped in front of her. Was his heart running a marathon, too? He hesitated—oh crap, was he thinking about a kiss?—and his grin spread. *Bugger, he knows what I look like naked.* A plastic bag rustled and Isaac shrieked with glee, but Tilly didn't turn. If hell were tailored to fit, she was roasting in it, cooked to a mush before the man she had never wanted to see again.

"Hello," Sebastian said.

"Hey," Tilly replied with a deep breath.

He smelled of privilege, of dinner parties with port, cognac and cigars. Did he used to wear aftershave? She couldn't remember. In ten years Sebastian had navigated a life she knew nothing of and returned a stranger. Did he like a cocktail before dinner? She had no clue. Could he still lose a Saturday to watching cricket on the television, curtains drawn against the sun? How would she know? A decade of silence lay between them, and in an instant he became blank.

"Awesome! The new Dr. X! Look, Mom. Look what Ro gave me!" Isaac tugged on her cardigan. "You can turn him upside down and all the green stuff in his tummy sloshes around. Thanks, Ro! You're the best! Now I can have a huge battle with Action Man and—" Isaac dropped his voice "—the evil Dr. X. We did pack Action Man, right, Mom?"

"Right." Tilly swallowed. "Isaac, I'd like you to meet someone. This is Sebastian, an old friend of mine." *Ex-friend.*

"How come I've never met you?" Isaac zoomed Dr. X through the air.

Way to go, Angel Bug. You tell him.

"Your mother and I lost touch a while ago." Sebastian's smile wavered. "My fault, I suspect."

Was he goading her? Tilly yanked down on her rumpled T-shirt.

"I see you're a fan of Action Man," Sebastian continued. "So's Archie, my son. I think he has the largest collection of Action Man in the world, including the museum pieces I used to play with. Would you like to come over one weekend and meet him?"

"Yes, please!" Isaac's face glowed with ecstasy. "Does he live in Bramwell Chase?"

"Sort of," Sebastian said. His eyes narrowed slightly, not so anyone would notice, but Tilly had always gauged his mood from his eyes. So not a stranger, which should put her at ease, right? Wrong. She felt like a lump of leftover pudding, unsure of where to put her hands, her eyes, and—*sod it*. Her stomach churned again.

Rowena locked her arm through Sebastian's and gave him a supportive nod, a *we're-in-this-together* gesture. Wait…when did they become friends? Tilly had always been the fulcrum of their threesome. It was fact, as undeniable as chrysanthemums blooming in fall. Rowena and Sebastian had tolerated each other through high school, vying for Tilly's attention until she coerced them into a truce, but that was it. And now Rowena was renting Manor Farm to Sebastian. Had they become buddies when Tilly wasn't looking? And if so, why hadn't her oldest, dearest, *best*-est friend told her?

"Archie's at boarding school," Rowena was talking to Isaac. "Where they lock you up and throw away the key." She affected an evil laugh. "But he has an exeat coming up. That means he gets to escape for the weekend. And we're not far off the summer hols now."

Isaac's eyes grew wide. "Sleep-away school? Jeez-um. He must be tons older than me."

Sebastian disentangled his arm from Rowena's. "I think you're the same age. Am I correct?" he asked no one in particular.

"Exactly the same age." Tilly arched her back. *Slam-dunk, tosspot.*

Sebastian plucked at the back of his gold signet ring. Yup, she could still push his buttons. More flip-flopping in her stomach. Why couldn't he have stayed a stranger?

"I've never seen your hair so short." Sebastian spoke to Tilly as if he were making an accusation. "I didn't recognize you at first."

Yes, but I recognized you. Tilly crossed her arms. *I'd recognize you anywhere.*

"It's fab, isn't it?" Rowena glanced from Tilly to Sebastian and back again. "You look like a cross between Joan of Arc and a woodland sprite." She clapped her hands together. "Oh, we have so much to catch up on. Just like old times. And Isaac, I'm depending on you to help out tons with the pheasant poults."

Tilly ignored Rowena and spoke to Sebastian. "My hair got in the way when I gardened. So I hacked it off with the kitchen scissors."

"Kitchen scissors?" His tone was light, but his face gave nothing away. "Makes you look younger." And how would he know? He hadn't seen her in ten years. He grasped the metal bar of the cart, pushed forward with his flat stomach, and walked off with her luggage. Ever the gentleman. Still, he could have asked first. Then she could have said no.

Rowena and Isaac skipped after Sebastian, swinging their clasped hands, gabbing away as if they hadn't seen each other in six years, not six months. Rowena stopped to smack a kiss on Isaac's cheek, and they both erupted into laughter.

Tilly watched her little band with a sigh. Who was she kidding? Hating was such hard work, and she didn't hate Sebastian. Well, maybe only a smidgen. And yes, she could fault his radio silence, but history stood in Sebastian's favor. He had loved her, protected her, desired her when she had believed no one could, and she had thrown the relationship away not once, but three times. Technically, two and a half. Seemed he had every right to deny her his friendship. But if he and Rowena had palled up, Tilly would have to let him back into her life. The question, though, was how much.

She watched the back of Sebastian's head as he walked away. His hair, darkened to dirty-blond, was cut close to his scalp and gelled into non-rebellious spikes. It was a banker's haircut: sculpted, immaculate, expensive. And, unfortunately, it suited him, too.

Tilly and Isaac were trapped in Rowena's Discovery on a seat spackled with dried mud and imbued with the stench of wet Labrador. Bob Marley blasted into the back of the car as they hurtled around the M25, a loop of a racetrack with few signs and no billboards. A highway that skirted a capital city yet advertised nothing; a highway that didn't distract you with the lure of shopping or the promise of a fun family getaway. A highway that aimed to get you from point A to point B at warp speed. At least, that seemed to be Rowena's interpretation.

If David had been in Sebastian's seat, he would have insisted Rowena pull over so they could swap. But Sebastian appeared as unruffled by Rowena's high-speed lane weaving as he was by his reunion with a girl he'd sweet-talked out of her virginity. When the speedometer passed ninety, he turned away and stared out of the window.

"For gawd's sake, what does the plonker think he's doing?" Rowena accelerated up to the bumper of a French truck and blasted the horn. "Get out of the fucking lane, wanker!"

"Ro—" Tilly jerked forward and kicked the back of the driver's seat.

"Fuck. Sorry," Rowena said. Tilly kicked the seat again.

"Mom, what does fuc—"

"It's an outlaw word," Tilly raised her voice. "You are never to use it. Understand?"

Isaac shriveled into the seat. *Tilly, you loathsome toad of a parent.* She never turned to Isaac in anger, never, and being trapped in this sweltering car with Sebastian, shackled in her own private hell, was no excuse for nipping at her son like a snapping turtle.

"It's a bad word, Angel Bug." Tilly grabbed Isaac's hand and squeezed. "Or rather a word people see as bad. Which means that most people find it offensive. Which is why you shouldn't use it. Right, Ro?"

"Absolutely, dear heart. Ab-so-lutely. Always listen to Mummy. Never bad, foul-mouthed Aunty Ro." Rowena gave her right hand a playful slap.

"But—" Isaac glanced at Sebastian, as if checking for his reaction. "What does it mean?"

"This I've got to hear," Rowena muttered, and turned down Bob Marley.

"It's an ugly word for sex." Tilly's cheeks flamed, which was ridiculous. She and Rowena had spent half of their childhoods scouring *National Geographic* for pictures of naked tribesmen, the other half searching Lady Roxton's romance novels for sex scenes. And Sebastian had known Tilly's teenage body better than she had. So why did she feel as if she were swirling down a whirlpool instead of bobbing along in the slipstream of her past?

Isaac curled up his lips. "Are we going to have another conversation about your sperm, Mom?"

Rowena brayed with laughter that sounded like whooping cough shot through the nose, and the Discovery swerved.

"Let's make this a private conversation," Tilly said.

Isaac grinned; he loved mother-son secrets.

Then Sebastian giggled. How could she hear that giggle and not let her attitude toward him thaw? She imagined the expression that accompanied the giggle: eyes sunk into creases of laughter, nose puckered up, lips stretched back to reveal the sexy gap between his front teeth. This was the Sebastian she'd fallen in love with—the boy who chased kites across the moors, or sat cross-legged on Tilly's window seat holding his cigarette out of her bedroom window and laughing at who knew what. But that was before his father left and Sebastian prepared for a life of responsibility, before he grew old with worry for his mother, for his grandmother, even for Tilly. And that was the beginning of the end, because the more Sebastian coddled her, the farther she ran.

Tilly gave a fake cough. "My mother tells me you're living in Bramwell Chase, Sebastian?"

Sebastian stopped giggling. "I'm renting Manor Farm."

"Yes," Tilly said slowly. "My mother told me that, too."

"I didn't tell you first?" Rowena stretched against the steering wheel. "Sure I had. But since you don't answer my emails, I have no idea what you know."

Tilly bit her lip. Challenging Rowena was not an exercise for the jet-lagged.

"Anyway. It's a brilliant story, so I'm happy to repeat it." Rowena tailgated a BMW and flashed her lights, while Tilly sank lower in her seat. "I was in town for a meeting at the bank. No offense, Sebastian, but ruddy bankers. It's always something. I walked in and there he was. Well, I about died." She smacked the steering wheel and the baubles around her wrist tinkled. "Can you imagine?"

Yes, Tilly could. Rowena would have shrieked and people would have gawked. Sebastian would have been embarrassed, but would have concealed it and kissed both her cheeks. He certainly wouldn't have stood and stared as he had done with Tilly. She yanked a tissue from her pocket and shredded it.

"I had absolutely no idea he was back from Hong Kong not that he's ever handled the Roxton account have you Sebastian but we went to dinner—" jeez, was she going to pause for breath? "—and Sebastian told me he needed somewhere to stay and I thought the Farm with all that fresh air for the children and here we are."

Tilly glared at Rowena's headrest. Rowena's recent emails had been full of chatter about finding her gamekeeper passed out with an empty bottle of whiskey, and about Sunday lunch at Woodend with roast lamb and the first new potatoes of the season. But no mention of Sebastian. And Rowena didn't keep secrets. She didn't know how.

Rowena twiddled with the heat controls, and Tilly breathed through a surge of nausea. Was no one else suffocating in this car? If she threw up that would be interesting: Sebastian was vomit-phobic.

Tilly shrugged off her cardigan. "Back for good, Sebastian?"

"Yes."

"I thought you were in Hong Kong for the long haul. What changed your mind?"

"Who, not what. Fiona."

Tilly sat up and watched the silver belly of an airliner soar above them. "She'd had enough of Hong Kong?" Was the plane full of holidaymakers, businessmen and women? People fleeing?

"She'd had enough of me." The front passenger seat groaned as Sebastian swung around. "Mind if I smoke? In front of Isaac?"

He never managed to quit, then. And yes, she did mind him exposing Isaac to secondhand smoke. But she hadn't studied Sebastian's face until now, hadn't looked beyond the grooming to notice the purple welts under his eyes. She shook her head and prayed she had misunderstood, because Sebastian single plus Tilly single equaled a complex math problem. And she hated all things math. Sebastian cracked open his window. Cellophane crinkled, a lighter flipped open and she heard him breathe.

Tilly rubbed at a crust of strawberry jam on her jeans. "Fiona left you?"

"Yes." Sebastian dragged on his cigarette.

"I'm sorry." So, she didn't plan to forgive him, and she didn't want to hate him. Could she settle on indifference with a soupçon of pity? She could feel that for a squished squirrel on Creeping Cedars, and squirrels were public enemy number one.

A counterpane of fields ripped past, retreating from the invasive ground cover of London. What a different view this was to the one from I-40, where wide banks disappeared into acres of forest. Her body tingled with something that felt strangely like longing. But before Tilly could muse further, a sense of unease prickled, and she turned from the window.

Sebastian had angled the rearview mirror toward himself and appeared to be rubbing his eye. But it was a ruse; he was watching her. His eyes delved deeper—with curiosity, lust, wistfulness? Or was it need? Did he need her the way she had needed him after David died? If she were closer, she could concentrate on Sebastian's eyes. Were they gray, the color stated on his passport, or murky green, the color of ocean reflecting storm clouds? Before she could decide, he looked away.

Terrific, she'd have to forgive him after all.

She wanted to stay asleep, but hushed voices intruded, waking her before she was ready. Where was she? Oh, right, still ensnared in the Discovery. Rowena whispered, "Want me to tell her?" and Sebastian replied, "No, I'll take care of it." And Tilly decided to play possum.

"Doing all right?" Rowena asked. "Sorry. Bloody stupid question."

"Yeah." A lighter flicked. "Bloody stupid question, darlin'."

Darlin'? Said in jest and the dropped *g* made all the difference, but a term of endearment passing between Ro and Sebastian? Tilly held her breath, hoping that for once Sebastian would spill his emotions, not conserve them. But he remained silent, curled in on his thoughts like a turtle marooned in the middle of the road. And Tilly had to move; her buttocks were numb.

"Aha," Rowena said. "Sleeping Beauty and my little prince stir. Did we nap well, my darlings?"

"Not especially." Tilly's neck cricked and she tugged on it.

"We're here, Mom! Look!" Isaac grabbed at her. "We're here!"

The road dipped under an arc of overhanging beech trees. Ivy-covered banks rose on either side of the car, and they were thrown into a leafy tunnel of silvery shade. Tilly wanted to scream her happiness, to rush from the car and kiss the ground. *Who gives a monkey's about anything!* She was home, back in the place where life waited for her, unchanged. She lowered her window and inhaled cool air and the smell of fresh-cut grass. No heat, no humidity, no cicada buzz, nothing but the bleating of sheep.

They emerged into brilliant sunshine as the bank slipped into a hedgerow of hawthorn, bindweed and elder knotted with blackberry brambles. A blue tit churred, and Tilly's heart answered with a symphony of joy. Isaac's first English summer! He was in for such a treat.

A woman clopped by on a piebald horse and touched her velvet helmet in greeting, but Rowena, ever the sun-slut, was oblivious. "The sun!" She pointed and bounced like a child tied up with excitement on Christmas morning. "Oh, the sun!"

Rowena continued to pay more attention to the sky than the road, but thankfully, drove below the speed limit. Not that she would ever speed through a village.

"Now, poppet. What shall we do for this trip's outing?" Rowena said. "Isaac and I always have a day out," she explained to Sebastian. "Of course, being here in the summer has so many more possibilities. Tilly and Isaac normally come back for Christmas. Well, not to celebrate Christmas, since they don't."

"You gave up on Christmas?" Sebastian held his cigarette to the window, but turned briefly.

"My husband was a practicing Jew." Tilly watched a streak of smoke leak out through the open window. "And since we have a liberal rabbi, Isaac's been raised in the Jewish faith. He thinks Jesus lives at the North Pole with twelve reindeer, don't you, Angel Bug?"

Isaac rolled his eyes. "Mom! I haven't believed that since I was young."

"I converted after David died. It made sense for Isaac." Which was true. A five-year-old could hardly go to synagogue alone. At the time she had told herself she was giving David a final gift, and maybe, back then, she'd believed it. But today she saw her conversion for what it was: an act of atonement. *No.* She shoved the thought aside, but there it was again, coiling in her gut: guilt, the universal motivator for every major decision she had made in the past three years.

They crawled around the curve of the church wall and passed the yew trees that marked the mass graves of medieval plague victims. Beyond, fields dotted with chestnut trees and grazing sheep tumbled over the horizon. Tilly held her breath and waited. Nothing must taint this happiness percolating in her heart, because any minute...*yes!* She exhaled as they emerged on a small rise. Waves of pink and red valerian poked out from the foundations of the ironstone cottages hugging the High Street, their thatched roofs spilling toward strips of garden stuffed with lupines, delphiniums, fading roses and gangly sweet peas. Tilly's eyes scooted over every plant. How she had missed the gardens of Bramwell Chase, with untamed perennials rambling into each other and lawns dotted with daisies and clover. These were real gardens, not the landscaped yards of Creeping Cedars with squares of chemically enhanced grass, rows of shrubs lined up like marines awaiting inspection, and the gag-inducing smell of hardwood mulch.

"Now, dear heart," Rowena said to Isaac. "Name your outing. But not Legoland again. That gift shop bankrupted me last time. What about the Tower of London? You can see where they chopped off heads. And the crown jewels are good for a quick look-see."

"How about Woburn Safari Park?" Sebastian gave a shrug. "Archie and Sophie—" aha, that was his daughter's name "—love it. Monkeys climb on your car, parrots take nectar from your hand." Isaac sat still, mouth open. "And the gift shops are terrific." Sebastian gave Rowena that smile, the one that was more of a twitch at the right corner of his mouth. Tilly twisted her legs around each other.

"Fab idea. I—" A mechanical rendition of "Rule Britannia" chimed from Rowena's lap. "Bugger. Phone." Rowena rootled around in the folds of her skirt. "Sebastian? Take the wheel."

Cigarette dangling from his mouth, Sebastian shook his head in disapproval, but reached across and grabbed the steering wheel while Rowena chattered into her cell phone. Sebastian had grown up fawned over by women— his grandmother who had lived with the family, his mother, his two older sisters—and yet he'd always been oblivious to sexual cues, incredulous when confronted by lust. His effortless movements, however, suggested that he was finally comfortable with his sexuality. Which was good for Sebastian—Tilly gulped—bad for her. Life was so much easier when she had thought of him as dead. God, she needed out of this car.

"Cool," Isaac said. "Rowena can drive without any hands."

"Not cool." Tilly raised her voice. "Dangerous and illegal."

"That was Daddy. Thanks, Sebastian." Rowena snapped her phone shut and reclaimed the steering wheel. "Sends oodles of love. He and Mother are scheming to open a rest home for aging ex-pats. Think we should invest, Haddy? You could wheel me around in my bath chair while I find us a couple of geriatric Adonises. So many men, so little time."

Flashes of Rowena's ex-lovers whizzed through Tilly's mind. Poor Ro, she could never find enough love, whereas Tilly had had more than her share.

"But Isaac's my main squeeze." Rowena fired off a string of air-kissses. "Aren't you, poppet?"

"Yes. I. Am." Isaac thrust out his chest with eight-year-old machismo.

Tilly stretched and yawned.

"Feeling icky?" Rowena asked.

"Bit tatty round the edges."

"Rats. So you won't want to join us for lunch. Well I did say—didn't I, Sebastian—that you'd be too tired. We've a table for two booked for noon at The Flying Duck. I could easily make it four. But I can see you're both pooped."

Isaac sprang up and down silently as if to contradict her.

Tilly rubbed her temples. *A table for two?*

"Nope, much better plan!" Rowena thumped the center of the steering wheel, and the horn sounded. Tilly and Isaac jumped. "Come to Sunday lunch at the Hall! Tilly, bring your mother. Sebastian, bring the children. Isaac? It's time Aunty Ro taught you croquet. Croquet? What am I saying? Ever played cricket?"

"No. But isn't it the same as baseball? I'm good at that."

Sebastian doubled over and appeared to be choking.

"Poppet, we need to educate you in the ways of cultural diversity. And it just so happens that this man sitting next to me, the one who's about ready to pop his clogs—" Rowena smacked Sebastian between the shoulder blades. "Which, by the way, is an excellent reason for never taking up smoking, filthy habit." Rowena grabbed Sebastian's cigarette and sucked on it. "This man was the youngest pupil in the history of Rugby School to make the first X1, which is V.I.S."

"Very Important Stuff!" Rowena and Isaac squealed in unison.

Tilly didn't join in the laughter. She was chewing on her thumbnail, wondering why she had forgotten about Sebastian and the first X1, and why Rowena had remembered.

Nine

Tilly watched the Discovery tear out of the driveway and tried not to feel like the duped heroine in an episode of *The Twilight Zone*. Ro and Sebastian were locked in some conspiracy, and her mother? They hugged, and Tilly's fingers touched bone. Her mother had lost more than weight since Christmas. She had shrunk in on herself; she had aged.

"You look washed out," her mother said.

"And you look tired. The life of leisure too much for you?"

"You know me. I rarely sit. Having this much time—" Her mother cleared her throat. "Makes me feel old and dependent."

The shrill cry of magpies accompanied by a throaty *cuckoo-cuckoo* sneaked up from the paddock. As a child, nothing delighted Tilly more than the first cuckoo of the season. And everything in Tilly's favorite garden was as it should be. The cherry tree was wrapped in stockings to keep birds from the fruit, the herbaceous border was a mass of pinks, blues and lavender, and clusters of white rambling rector blooms smothered the stone wall. Her father had planted that rose.

How he loved his roses! How her mother interfered when he tried to tend them. But today, Woodend was a flat canvas; it didn't soothe.

In Tilly's mind, her mother was always forty years old, plowing through the black waves off the coast of Cornwall with her neck rigid and her hair dry. This morning, however, Mrs. Haddington looked less like a woman defying the Atlantic Ocean and more like an old dear who hadn't noticed that the left side of her silk blouse hung over the waistband of her skirt.

"I was so bored yesterday, I attempted to knit a tea cozy for the church bazaar." Her mother tucked in her blouse, then puffed up her thick, white bob. "Which is utterly ridiculous, given this." She waved her bandaged hand. "How was it, seeing Sebastian again?"

"Mum." Tilly issued a warning.

Her mother nipped a leaf from the Lady Hillingdon rose that snaked around the back door. "Black spot." She tutted. "You'll have to spray. Marigold says it's a nasty separation. Between Sebastian and Fanny."

"Fiona." Tilly watched a pair of sparrows frolic in the stone birdbath. "And Marigold knows this how?"

"She heard it from Sylvia, who heard it from Beryl, who has the same woman-that-does as Sebastian—Mabel Dillington. There's more."

Tilly had always wanted eyes like her mother's. Eyes you couldn't ignore. Eyes that were the bright blue of a Carolina sky. Tilly's eyes were pale and translucent, the color of porcelain brushed with a robin's-egg wash. They made her look ethereal, when she yearned to be an Amazon.

"There's evidence of a relationship." Her mother had yet to blink.

Tilly scuffed her Doc Martens boot through round, evenly

sized pebbles in coordinating sand tones. Unlike Tilly's gravel, which was made up of lumps of quartz and splinters of gray rock, her mother's driveway was perfect. "I'd forgotten how rumors fly in this place. Shame on you for listening."

"Hardly rumor. And there's no need to be sanctimonious. Mabel saw the Discovery parked outside Manor Farm yesterday at 6:00 a.m. Now. Where did Isaac and Monty disappear to?" Her mother hobbled up the stone step and through the back door.

Tilly raised her face into the damp, morning air. The sun had vanished, replaced by a fine Scotch mist. *So they're having sex. Big whoop. I just need to figure out how to avoid them for six weeks.*

An empty truck rattled along the High Street. Empty trucks—when did she stop calling them lorries?—sounded different from heavily loaded ones. It had to do with the way they hit the dip on the corner. She gazed through the gateway, the place where she had met David. And then she stared back at the house, the place she had longed to run to after he died. After he died because of her. She'd grown used to the guilt, but it was always lurking. And when she was tired, as she was now, it thudded inside her skull like a migraine.

"Tilly! Phone!" her mother called from the kitchen. "A James Nealy?"

"Good flight?" James grabbed the rail on the treadmill, let go and repeated. Six times. Would she shriek? Accuse him of being a two-bit stalker? But despite what the voice had told him yesterday—over and over—he wasn't a stalker. Although he had memorized the state harassment laws just to make sure.

"Are you an insomniac?" Tilly said. "It can't be much later than 5:00 a.m. your time."

He had prepared for incredulity or hostility, nothing else. And yet she'd asked about his sleep habits. What did that mean?

The treadmill whirred beneath him. "I exercise every morning from four-thirty to six-thirty." That was probably more information than she needed.

"You get up at four-thirty? Are you crackers?"

What the hell did *crackers* mean? Who knew, but it didn't sound good. So yes, clearly he had given her too much information. She was probably freaking out at this very moment, dialing 911 on her cell phone to report him for infringing the state harassment law that included: *To telephone another repeatedly, whether or not conversation ensues, for the purpose of abusing, annoying, threatening, terrifying, harassing or embarrassing any person at the called number.* Was he annoying her?

"Have you made a decision?" He spoke quickly, a preemptive strike in case she was considering hanging up.

"James." Her voice dragged with exhaustion. He should've waited another hour at least, given her a chance to unpack. But it had taken all his restraint to not call her at 4:30 a.m. "I promised you an answer in September."

"Can't wait that long."

"You're worse than a child. Isaac was never this demanding, even at three."

His pulse slowed as her accent, soft and warm, soothed him. He actually thought about crawling into bed and going back to sleep. After he'd showered, of course. "Do you talk to all your clients this way, or just me?"

"I have wholesale customers, not clients, for this very reason. And no, I haven't given your project one iota of a thought. I just walked in the door after twelve hours of traveling, and all I care about is where I packed my toothbrush and whether there's a pair of clean knickers nearby."

"Is that so?" An image assaulted him, of Tilly wearing nothing but a scarlet thong and gardening gloves. He shook back his hair and upped the speed on the treadmill.

"How did you track me down?" Tilly asked.

Sari ratted you out. Once he discovered her sons were fans, he had all the leverage he needed.

"You can find anything," he said, "if you're determined." That wasn't a lie, even though the voice told him it was.

"I'm trying to be patient. Really. But I'm dangerously close to telling you to jump off a pier. Only with a few choice expletives thrown in." She paused. "How're the silent hiccups?"

"You really want to know?" His voice was almost a whisper.

"Sadly, yes. I do."

"Worse." The treadmill creaked an indignant rhythm as he upped the speed a second time. He'd never taken it this high.

"So you're going to keep calling me?"

"Yes."

"Okay. Time for a deal, Mr. Nealy. You get an answer in one week—if, and only if, you agree to abide by my decision. And no calling in the interim."

Was that a yes? Or a no? Or a nothing? He hated nothings. But it could turn into a yes, right? "Agreed."

"And—"

"Addendums?" He panted. "Already?"

"I'd like the adult explanation of your hiccups."

"Will it…affect your…decision?" He was running hard now. Racing against the voice, which was stuck doing a circuit of: *If you tell her, she'll think you're a fucking weirdo.* James tried to drown out the thought with the lyrics of "Psycho Killer," but he couldn't get past the line that basically said, leave me the hell alone because I'm a live wire.

"Labels are merely a way of lumping people together like plants on a stall," Tilly said. "I don't much care what yours is." She was smiling. He could hear it in the pitch of her voice. "Okay, gloves-off honesty. I'm curious."

"What's…your…label?" His sneakers pounded the treadmill belt.

"I thought we were talking about you."

"I'm not…all that…interesting." *Once you edit out the crazy bits.*

"Okay, fine. I'm game for a little transatlantic show-and-tell." She gave a huge sigh. "I'm a guilt-ridden widow. No, that's too strong. I'm not drowning in guilt. It's just there, in the background."

James blew out a couple of breaths and slowed down to a fast walk. "You have to be careful with guilt." So, Tilly understood the horror of a damaged mind, which couldn't be good either for her, or for Isaac. "Guilt can become an intrusive thought. And that's my world. Thoughts that drag you back and under. Thoughts that never let go. Obsessive thoughts that lead to compulsive actions. Look up OCD on Wikipedia and read about cognitive-behavioral therapy. It's a way of redirecting unwanted thoughts. You might find it helpful." He shut the treadmill. At 5:16 a.m. the day was already too long. "I'll call one week from today. Same time."

James hung up and crumpled across the front of the treadmill. He had told her! Told her he was crippled by an anxiety disorder that popular culture equated with people to ridicule or fear: a television detective incapable of navigating life without a wipes-carrying assistant; a monster driven to murder by odd numbers; a billionaire recluse who couldn't touch doorknobs and died in squalor. James banged the heels of his hands into his temples. *Bang, bang. Bang, bang. Bang, bang.*

He never told anyone he had OCD—not family, not lovers,

not close friends. His buddy Sam guessed years ago, but it was understood, not discussed, which was what James wanted. It was no one's business but his own, because to say those words out loud was to brand himself. Tilly was right—OCD was a label, and with labels came stigma, and weakness, and pity. Everything that James detested, everything that reminded him how it felt to be ten years old, standing by his mother's grave, scared of the future, terrified of the thoughts unraveling in his brain, and desperate not to be the object of people's stares. Desperate to blend in and disappear, to be the person you never quite remembered, when he was more likely to be the person you wished you could forget.

She hates you, she's scared of you, she thinks you're a kook.

No, no. James pressed down with his palms. He was done with doubt. It would not pull him under again. He would not revert to the person he had been before he had decided to sell the business, the apartment, the farm. Before he had decided to save himself.

Besides, Tilly? Scared of anyone? He didn't think so. And yes, he was weird. He was weird! So what? He should be able to shout to the world that he was obsessive-compulsive, to do so without dreading other people's reactions. Maybe opening up to Tilly was the first step, and no different from his dad attending an A.A. meeting just so he could announce, "I'm a drunk."

That was a good theory and one James desperately wanted to believe. Acknowledging weakness gave you strength, but he'd slipped up, released personal information without having intended to, and that was out of character. Other people said things they shouldn't; he didn't.

But when he'd hinted at the truth that day at the farm, hadn't a small part of him dared to trust, dared to believe that he had met someone, finally, who might understand? How would Tilly treat him now that she knew? Would she look at him and see the OCD, not James? Was it even possible to separate the two?

His psychologist always said, "It's the OCD, not you," but the lines weren't distinct for James. OCD may have twisted up his mind, but it had crafted him, made him James, pushed him to succeed and bequeathed the only gift that mattered: the ability to perceive pain in others. He didn't always act on that knowledge, didn't always want to, but he was drawn to people in dark corners, could empathize with them. So now he was being altruistic. *Truthfully, you enjoy living alongside people who are more fucked-up than you.* That wasn't true of most of his friends, but it had been his M.O. in love.

His thoughts circled him back to Tilly. She would take him on. She would. But once they started working together, once they had regular contact, he would have to be more careful. Because if she saw behind the label, if he revealed the biggest truth of all, she would never understand. The end. The end.

An airlock rattled through the radiator, and Tilly peered into the disemboweled duffel on the twin bed with the patchwork bedspread garish enough to stimulate a corker of a headache. She enjoyed the nostalgia of sleeping in her childhood bed but not the experience. The mattress sagged in the middle, and she had to relearn how to sleep in a huddle, not stretched across her queen-size bed. Tilly had always wanted a king, the biggest bed imaginable so she could cover it with down-filled pillows and cushions of every size and color. David had refused; he said he needed Tilly closer.

"What do you know about OCD?" Tilly asked her mother, who was settled in the old nursing chair with a cup of Lady Grey tea and the *Daily Telegraph* crossword.

"Isn't that what Howard Hughes suffered from? A fear

of germs, I think." Mrs. Haddington stirred her tea, then tapped the spoon on the lip of the china cup. "Does this have something to do with that James chap? He sounded rather nice." The spoon clattered onto the saucer. "And you can wipe that smirk off your face. I may be old, but I'm not dead. I can still recognize a sexy voice."

Her mother concentrated on positioning the cup on the bedside table while Tilly stared open-mouthed. Her mother, who had avoided the *s* word for decades, who had refused to answer thirteen-year-old Tilly's questions about the facts of life—answers she would later glean from Sebastian—had just described a man as sexy. Tilly tugged her cardigan around her. Now she thought about it, her mother had started saying *damn,* too. Once, she had spanked Tilly for using it. Was this an attempt to be more relevant, to buck values ingrained since childhood? Or was it some sort of personality crisis? The beginning of Alzheimer's?

"I take it he's interested in you, this James?"

"Why would you ask?"

"The way he spoke your name, as if he were handling a precious object. Besides, the teacher in me knows when someone's hiding something. A case of unrequited love, is it?"

"No! He wants me to design a garden." Love? Absolutely not. Her mother was right about one thing, though. James was definitely hiding something. Tilly gazed through the window to the lawn below. Isaac was playing soccer with the ball she had bought on their last trip. In less than five minutes, he had unearthed the stash of possessions she kept at Woodend, the part of their lives she always left behind. Isaac positioned the ball and kicked, but Monty intercepted. With a snap of his jaw, he chomped down.

"Garden design," her mother mused. "You are rather good at that."

"Please, Mum. Stay out of this." Tilly pulled a long-sleeved T-shirt from the duffel, stuffed it into the mahogany chest of drawers and closed the drawer with her bottom.

"A little more care, darling. That's a valuable piece of furniture." Her mother peered over her reading glasses, their lapis frames intensifying the blue of her eyes. "If you ask me—" *actually, I didn't* "—you need to stop cowering on the edge of life, afraid to jump in. Whatever your beliefs, you are not responsible for David's death."

Tilly swallowed, forcing back bile. "As good as. I invoked his living will, Mum."

"You respected your husband's final wishes, for which I commend you."

"But I believe in the sanctity of life. You know that. Well, unless it's slugs or Japanese beetles." Tilly exhaled. "And before you say anything else, yes, I agree it was his decision to make. I accepted that when he drew up the living will. But I still have to figure out how to deal with the consequences of *my* actions." If only it were that simple. "And when other people push—" Tilly looked her mother in the eye "—it doesn't help."

"Darling, I know grief follows its own pace, but you can't shut out people who love you."

"Not even if they force me to boogie on the dance floor when all I want is to shuffle along with a Zimmer frame?"

"You're too young for a Zimmer frame."

Tilly hooked down the sleeves of her cardigan and curled up her fists inside. She was exhausted from talking, from thinking, from being. "I should have listened to my instincts, Mum. I should have said no. I always gave in to David. Anything for a quiet life, you know?" *Stop, Tilly, that's close enough.*

"Rubbish." Her mother rustled the newspaper on her lap.

"You made compromises—that's marriage. Besides, few women could have handled David. You certainly could."

Tilly's eyes prickled from dryness. She wished she could cry, but what would that achieve? Self-pity was not part of her agenda. Bad enough that on sleepless nights she could still hear David's breath gurgling through the disconnected tube protruding from his throat like a weapon.

Mrs. Haddington removed her glasses and clicked the arms into place. "Guilt surrounds death, darling. The secret is to accept that and not end up in the tizz that I did." How many euphemisms could her mother use for her breakdown? "Your father wanted to die at home, but I was so silly. Convinced myself that only professionals could nurse a cancer patient through his final days, and that if he came home, I would make it worse." She shook her head. "The poor man was dying. How much worse could it have been? But I gnawed on that guilt. Don't do the same."

Her mother was well-meaning but clueless. Some actions were too heinous to be forgotten or forgiven. Tilly grabbed a balled-up denim shirt from the floor, shook it out with a *thwack* and tossed it toward the laundry basket. How had she managed to pack so many dirty clothes?

"What about a good clear-out, starting with David's studio? It's a car boot sale waiting to happen." Her mother's blue eyes sharpened. "Why not donate the books to the university and turn the space into a shop that sells gardening doodads?"

"I can't just open a shop, Mum. There're zoning laws about that kind of thing. Besides, the studio breathes David's DNA. It's the reason we bought the house—"

"Poppycock. You fell in love with the land and David caved because he spoiled you worse than your father did. Bless him, I do miss your father." Mrs. Haddington appraised her engagement ring, a huge sapphire surrounded by a burst of diamonds. "He believed you had found yourself in North Carolina."

"Really?" Tilly smiled at her mother; her mother smiled back.

Footsteps thundered up the stairs, accompanied by a salvo of "Mom! Mom!"

Isaac poked his head around the door. "Monty barfed up soccer ball all over the kitchen floor. Can we go to The Corner Stores and buy a new one after you've cleaned up the mess?"

"Actually, no. I have a better idea." Tilly opened the drawer of her old dressing table and rummaged around until she found the medallion with the inscription: 1st place, 200 meters breaststroke.

"Here." Tilly handed it to Isaac. "The badge of your new status as Monty helper."

"Sweet. What do I have to do?"

Tilly draped an arm over his shoulder. "First, you learn how to mop up dog sick."

Isaac screamed and ducked away. Laughing, Tilly chased him along the landing and down the stairs. She paused on the sixth step, the one that creaked. The drawing room door was open, and she glimpsed a cardboard box next to the carved wooden chest, a chest formerly covered in photographs of family milestones. Was her mother, another memory hoarder, packing up their past? And if so, why?

The question tasted bitter. Woodend was a time capsule of Haddington family life. Nothing had changed here in decades, not even the paint colors. And if Tilly had her way, nothing ever would.

Ten

Bramwell Hall, isolated in a pocket of peace behind the churchyard, breathed a different tune from any place Tilly had ever been. The cavernous rooms were filled with the silent chill of history, but it was still a home, albeit a crumbling one with pieces that regularly dropped off.

The clock on the old stable block chimed 3:00 p.m., sheep bleated across the park and a home movie played in Tilly's mind. She was chasing Rowena around the north wing in a game of tag; she was organizing pony rides by the south wing for the Queen's silver jubilee; she was snuggling up to Sebastian on the lawn as fireworks boomed and sparkled in honor of Prince Andrew's wedding. Tilly's eyes panned up to the Hall's mullioned second-floor windows and lingered on Rowena's bedroom. Bugger, there it was again—that animated image from the *Kama Sutra* starring Rowena and Sebastian.

Avoiding Sebastian all week had been easy. She had chalked up only one ex-boyfriend sighting and that had been of the taillights of the Jaguar as she'd hustled Monty along the estate road for his pre-bedtime jaunt. Staying below Rowena's radar had presented the real challenge. Like the wild onion that peppered Tilly's gardens every May, Rowena could pop up anytime, anywhere. Only a person on a kamikaze mission crossed Rowena without an exit strategy, and Tilly needed to shake off her jet lag before she could line up her thoughts. But really, it had been surprisingly easy to hide behind a few rushed conversations. Easy, but heartbreaking.

In thirty-three years, Tilly and Rowena had feuded only once, when they were fifteen and Tilly accidentally scratched Rowena's "Nights in White Satin" single. The great-falling-out had been hardest on Rowena. Without the Haddingtons, she had no family life. But she was as stubborn as swamp sunflower and equally impossible to tame. It was Tilly who negotiated the peace and promised that nothing would nick their friendship again. As the sun pushed through a cloud to illuminate the Hall's sandstone facade with a warm, golden hue, Tilly remembered Rowena coaxing the first postfuneral smile from Isaac and silently renewed the promise, a promise that would not be broken.

She glanced down at Rowena, stretched out on the tartan blanket with her two black Labradors, Tiddly and Winks. Another X-rated Rowena-Sebastian image flashed, and Tilly shivered. What had she read on the OCD website about picking up your thoughts and putting them elsewhere? A brain trick, it was called. An appealing idea, that you could shove aside unwanted thoughts as if you were moving furniture. And yet shifting your mind was bloody difficult. How did James find the emotional strength? Not that she wanted to think about him, and not that she had decided to take him on, but he had captured her interest with his mention of OCD. After all, even she had an inner Doubting Thomas that whispered at her to double-check the front door was locked. But second-guessing yourself, she had discovered through her late-night excursions on the web, was nothing compared to the relentless obsessions, ritualized compulsions and furtive behavior of OCD. If James lived in perpetual anxiety, battling fears no one else could see, how did he find peace? Or was that the reason he wanted a garden? Maybe he was searching for some corner of the universe to control. If so, he was looking in the wrong place. Gardening was never about control.

"For gawd's sake, sit down," Rowena said, without opening her eyes. "You're making me all twitchy, not to mention blocking out my sun."

"Sorry. Just thinking."

"About?"

"Being lucky enough to have a healthy mind."

"Fabulous." Rowena yawned. "You can look after me when I get Alzheimer's. Now sit and tell me how you're really doing."

"Oh, you know."

"No, I don't know, since you've been dodging me all week."

Bugger, she'd noticed. Underestimating Rowena was a trap Tilly fell into repeatedly. The only consolation was that others made the mistake more frequently. Take the teenage vandal Rowena had caught spray-painting a stone balustrade. Rather than prosecute, Rowena had co-opted him into six months of free labor on the estate. Three years later, he still called her ma'am.

Tilly flopped to the blanket, lulled by the crack of Isaac swatting a cricket ball. Sebastian and the children were playing cricket down by the horse pond, and the snores coming from the deck chairs under the two-hundred-year-old cedar tree signaled that her mother and the vicar would not be eavesdropping. Tilly and Rowena were alone.

"Found a man yet?" Rowena said.

"Have you?"

Rowena smiled, an open smile that hinted at years of intimacy yet told Tilly nothing. "How about setting up an alternative family unit?" Rowena stretched. "You, me and Isaac at the Hall. Ever consider coming home and making me deliriously happy?"

"In my dreams. Not sure Isaac would approve, though." Tilly laid back and the short skirt of her dress puddled around her. She tugged on her waistband. What a meal! Three courses and four choices of desserts, none of which Tilly had been able to resist since they had all included chocolate. Grass pricked through the scratchy blanket and Tilly shifted, but, between the hard ground and her bloated stomach, failed to find comfort.

A loud snort, definitely male, came from under the cedar tree.

"Think the vicar's got the hots for your mother?" Rowena asked. She was tracing shapes in the clouds as they had done a lifetime ago. "They looked pretty cozy, heads locked together over dessert."

"He was asking if she had indigestion pills in her handbag."

"Bummer. I so want your mother to fall in love."

"Me, too, but it's not going to happen. She told me once that she could never love anyone but my father." Tilly rolled onto her side and propped herself up with her elbow. She slid the other arm between her thighs, clasped her calves, and curled up. "Maybe after a certain point you don't need romantic love. I mean, my mother's happy. She has a full life with Marigold and her cronies. Why does she need a man?"

"Amen, sister. Give me a vibrator any day, far less messy.

Besides, spunky old spinsters rock. I just wish my mother were more like yours. If anything happened to Daddy she would disintegrate."

Tilly wanted to disagree, but despite her beauty, Lady Roxton blended into her husband's shadow. Which, Tilly had always supposed, was why Lord Roxton married her. He liked an audience, not competition. He doted on his daughter but in a distracted way that placed Rowena below his gun dogs in the hierarchy of his affection. He treated her as a valuable painting—prized and largely ignored. When she messed up? It showed spirit. He admired that in dogs and in his daughter. Unfortunately, his wife did not. She glided through life, showing passion only for Lord Roxton and his heritage. The spectacular splashes Rowena created to earn her parents' attention may have garnered laughter from her father, but they earned scorn from her mother.

"Your mother's spunky," Tilly said. "Sort of."

"Fibber. Mother looks like a jewel but she's an inadequate human being. Remember how we used to pretend that Woodend was my real home, that Mother and Daddy were wicked godparents who'd kidnapped me at birth?"

"We shouldn't have done that."

"No. We shouldn't have. But your house was filled with pets, baking smells, you practicing the trombone, your sisters arguing…. My house was filled with the bawdiness of adults who were so besotted with each other they didn't even notice when I hit puberty. Did you know, your mother gave me my first sanitary napkin?" Rowena grabbed the last bottle of champagne and refilled her glass. Sebastian had donated two bottles to the day and Rowena had drunk most of them. Tilly would have been gaga by now, but Rowena was stone-cold sober. "Ever wonder what kind of a parent I would've made?"

"An amazing one." Tilly's pulse quickened. Rowena had provided an opening.

Tilly reached over, her hand steepled, and waited for Rowena to complete their childhood gesture of solidarity. But the tips of Rowena's fingers were cold and slippery. The steeple wobbled and collapsed, and Tilly found herself touching nothing but air.

"Archie and Sophie like you. But please, Ro, tread carefully. Getting involved with a family man, even one who's separated, could end in heartbreak. Yours." There, she'd said it.

"Bloody hell." Rowena shot up, her alabaster chest flushed with red pinpricks. The dogs stood to attention. "Where did that come from?"

"Mabel Dillington. She saw the Discovery outside Manor Farm at 6:00 a.m."

The wind shifted and brought a whiff of freshly spread slurry down from the fields, a smell rank with rot and decay.

"Bah. Let the old biddies gossip. I couldn't care less."

"If you guys are worried about telling me, you needn't be. I'm a big girl." Tilly pinged her bra strap. "Well, not as big as I always wanted to be."

"Haddy, I'm not sleeping with Sebastian." Rowena slumped back to the blanket. So did Tiddly and Winks, although, unlike Rowena, they sat up, their bodies alert. She emptied her champagne flute in one gulp, then tossed the glass aside. "You really thought we were doing the dirty on you? Crikey, that explains the cold treatment."

"So why spend the night?" Tilly fingered the hem of her dress.

"Talk with Sebastian, Tilly. This is his secret, not mine."

Tilly? Rowena never called her Tilly—Haddy, Petal, you old cow, but never Tilly.

Tilly shook her head. "We've never kept secrets." Secrets, no, but Rowena's emotions were like a fallow field with no-trespassing signs posted around the edges. A survival technique learned during childhood and fermented through years of boarding school when Rowena was disciplined for rebellious behavior and scorned for academic failings. She excelled only at art, which her mother declared a useless subject. Twice, she ran away.

Rowena stared at Tilly, her green eyes clear and cold. "Sharing's not always good."

"Ro—" Tilly grabbed Rowena's clenched hand. "You're so deep in my past that I don't know where your life ends and mine begins. Nothing could change that."

"Nothing? How could you ever, *ever* think that I would sleep with Sebastian? To betray you, Haddy, to risk losing you—" Rowena snatched her hand free and swiped it under her nose. "Unthinkable."

"Hey, hey. Don't get maudlin on me. I love you, too."

Rowena sniffed loudly.

"How long have you been Sebastian's confidante?" Tilly tried to sound disinterested, but her body tightened. Unease tingled in her chest, in her throat, in her fingertips.

"Since your wedding. Truthfully? We both felt dumped. Amazing how love for the same person gives you common ground." Rowena paused for another sniff. "And then you broke Sebastian's heart again."

"Now you've lost me."

"After your father died Sebastian stayed here, at the Hall, to be near you. I was commuting into the city at that point so we sat up most nights talking. Well, he talked. I listened."

Tilly gazed up at the sky, more white than blue. What an insipid color. But then again, when you'd experienced sky so blue that it made your eyes ache and distorted your vision, nothing compared. A microlight floated over; a small private plane bounced near the horizon; and a jet streaked silently toward some distant location. The sky over Southern England was as crowded as the roadways. Where did people run to when they needed to be alone?

A bumblebee droned near Tilly's bare feet. "I never realized." She sat up and hugged her knees. "He just materialized every day and dealt with the bank, the lawyer, the funeral home, all that crap. And I never questioned it. God, how selfish can one person be?"

"You weren't being selfish, Haddy. You were grieving. And telling everyone you were fine, when you weren't. Sebastian wanted to help, so offering him B & B seemed the least I could do. You mopped up after your mother and sisters—Sebastian and I mopped up after you."

Down by the horse pond Isaac whacked a cricket ball and Sebastian cheered, his voice blending with the chorus of birds and sheep. Tilly watched his arm arc through the air as he bowled and sensed Rowena watching him, too.

"If you're planning on rekindling love lost," Rowena said, "I recommend acting in haste. Half the choir ladies fancy him rotten. Rumor has it he's quite the talk of the vestry. Can't see it myself, can you?"

"Nah. Don't see it at all." Tilly smirked. Sebastian was wearing those tight white jeans again with a slim-fitting T-shirt that revealed a perfectly toned torso. Biceps to die for, or, in a woman's case, lust over. He had filled out physically as well as emotionally. It was quite a combination.

"Why *did* Sebastian give up cricket?" Rowena said. "Were you responsible?"

"Me? Hardly. It was his passion. I tried to persuade him to stick with it."

"You were his passion."

A sparrow hawk sailed overhead, then twisted effortlessly to the right and swooped toward a finch, closing in on its prey.

"First love distorts reality, doesn't it?" Tilly said. "We thought we were planning for a future, but we were just kids playing in a Wendy house. I counted imaginary babies while Sebastian prepared for his role as provider, so he could be everything his philandering, scuzzy father wasn't."

"His father was in the papers the other day. Conservative MP and wife number three. She looks eighteen." Rowena plucked two daisies from the grass. She sliced her fingernail through the stem of one daisy and then threaded the other daisy through the wound. "Tell me. Do you ever regret ripping Sebastian's heart apart?"

"Whoa! That's not fair. We outgrew each other. Sad, but true." Tilly's life might be a quagmire of regret, but not when it came to her relationship with Sebastian. Their past, well, up until the bit where he stopped speaking to her, was bundled up and tucked away. Safe and sound. "When I ended it he didn't react at all, which proved he wanted the same thing. You know how he hates confrontations. I made it easy for him."

Rowena added another flower, then another to her daisy chain. Finally, she closed up the link. "Oh, Haddy. You're so wrong."

No, you're the one who's wrong.

Sebastian strolled toward the blanket, trailing whining children. "That's it!" he declared. "Too much for an old geezer like me."

"Good timing, Sophie." Rowena held out the daisy chain.

"For me?" Sophie skipped toward Rowena. "Thank you."

Isaac bounded up. "Wanna go make a hideout?" he asked Archie.

Archie shrugged, but there was an eagerness in his eyes that Tilly recognized.

Sophie could have been anyone's daughter, with her round face and bouncy blonde curls. And Tilly could look at Sophie and feel nothing but admiration for her flare of defiance at lunch, when Archie had attempted to bully his younger sister into giving up her chair. But looking at Archie, Tilly's breath caught in her throat. She saw Sebastian's expressions, his stance, his features. The only difference between father and son was eye color. Archie's eyes were the dark blue of her favorite salvia.

"Hey, Soph." Isaac beamed at Sophie. "Wanna join us?"

Sophie nodded vigorously.

"He's good with younger children." Sebastian watched the kids trundle off.

"The power of Montessori," Tilly said. "He's in a lower elementary class, with first, second and third grades mixed together."

Sebastian frowned slightly. Obviously, he had no idea what she meant, but what were the chances he would ask her to translate the American grade system? Zero, since he had deflected every remark she'd addressed to him at lunch with minimum words.

Rowena laughed. "I hate to break this to you, chaps, but I think your daughter, Sebastian, has a crush on your son, Tilly."

Oh God, Sophie was prancing along beside Isaac, her hand tucked into his. This—Tilly tugged on the edge of the blanket—was too weird.

"Rowena." Sebastian sighed. "Sophie's six. She adores any older child who notices her. Christ, that sun feels good." He rested back on his elbows and crossed his ankles. "No doubt you've forgotten how we suffer from sun deprivation on this side of the pond."

So, he had finally directed an entire sentence at her. And it was about the weather. Tilly preferred the notion of him sleeping with Rowena.

"Ro, can we make a hideout in here?" Isaac's voice came from behind a huge Jerusalem sage, three times the size of the one Tilly had planted five years ago. Gardener envy—finally, an emotion she could handle.

"Coming, dear heart!" Rowena called out. "Best go check on the little pests." She flipped over so that she was resting on all fours, then wagged a finger covered in thin silver rings. "You two play nice, you hear?"

Tilly had a clear view down Rowena's purple lace camisole into her cleavage. And, given Sebastian's strained cough, so did he. Rowena leaped up and twirled toward the children, the sun highlighting her long, russet hair.

"She's one of those women who becomes more beautiful with age, isn't she?" Tilly said, but Sebastian didn't reply. He was staring toward the kissing gate that led into The Chase, the ancient woodland dating back seven hundred years. Which ghosts was he invoking? Those of two teenagers who sought refuge and privacy in the ruined Dower House on the far side of the woods? Or was he remembering the fourteen- and the sixteen-year-old who met at the bus station on a damp November Sunday? A gang of local boys was teasing her when this beautiful guy intervened. Of course, it was nothing she couldn't handle, but Sebastian became her savior that day, her protector. And here he was, twenty-three years later, back in her life.

Dear God, he could have been a male model. An almost-forty urban professional who had stepped from the pages of a Boden catalog. His skin was smooth, blemish-free and golden-brown. Unlike Tilly, whose face turned pink and broke out in a rash of freckles at the hint of sunshine, Sebastian tanned easily and evenly. How did a blond manage that?

His eyebrows were still a shade darker than his hair and neither too thick nor too thin. If Tilly hadn't known him at sixteen, she might have assumed he hired salon help to achieve eyebrows so impeccably arched. And of course, he had that straight, sized-to-perfection nose, those cute lips, those eyes that changed color with his mood....

"We need to talk," Tilly said.

"You never used to be so blunt." Sebastian gave his lopsided smile, but it didn't stay in place. "What happened?"

"Widowhood." She reached for the bottle of champagne. "I have no intention of doing this sober. You might want to follow my example."

He picked up Rowena's empty glass and held it out. Champagne fizzed and gurgled into the glass flute as tiny bubbles exploded, releasing a delicate, floral aroma that tickled the back of Tilly's throat. But the sensation was out of place. What, if anything, did she and Sebastian have to celebrate? They were together but alone, abandoned by death or desertion. Goodness, and she'd accused Rowena of being maudlin. *Pick up your thoughts, Tilly, put them elsewhere.*

"Let's walk." Tilly stood and so did Sebastian, but not before he had ignored her outstretched hand.

Tilly paid no attention to where they were heading. Neither, it seemed, did Sebastian.

"I heard you and Ro whispering in the car. About something you need to tell me?" Still barefoot, Tilly kept her head down as she sidestepped clumps of clover filled with bumblebees.

They had reached the edge of the lawn where it dipped

into acres of parkland sprinkled with grazing sheep and guarded by majestic sentinels of oak and chestnut. This was the countryside of her childhood. And when it was wrapped in the halcyon light of the English summer sun, nothing could compare. A pheasant coughed, a yellowhammer sang *little-bit-of-bread-and-no-cheese,* and Tilly's heart flipped with pleasure.

A black-faced ewe waddled over to the rusted fence and bleated at them.

"*Baa* to you, too," Tilly replied.

"My wife's pregnant," Sebastian said, and walked away.

Jealousy, an irrational response, winded her. Tilly grabbed the wire in front of her and it shimmied frantically, startling the sheep. Why couldn't she find traction with Sebastian? Why was she hurtling down this helter-skelter of overblown emotions—first hatred, now jealousy? This wasn't Tilly. She wasn't mean, she wasn't possessive and she wasn't thoughtless. Was she? How had she become the person who forced a man to make peace with an adolescent romp when he was lost in the turmoil of his marriage? Of course the poor man still loved his wife! Any nutter could see that. Blimey, she so needed to get out from under herself.

Tilly ran after him. "Well, that's good, isn't it? For a reconciliation?"

"It's too late for that."

"Crap. You love her? Fight for her."

Tilly linked her arm through Sebastian's and they strolled on, drifting nowhere. She expected him to stiffen or shy away. After all, public affection horrified Sebastian. Once, when she tried to canoodle with him on a street corner, he accused her of exhibitionism. But today he appeared anesthetized to her touch.

They passed a latticework of clipped hedges and towering topiaries, sloping banks of lavender, and massive stone urns half-filled with gray soil, their decorations chipped away by decades of frost. Empty flowerpots in midsummer were the absolute worst seasonal anachronism. Would Ro let her plant some red, spiky cordylines or maybe a pair of lemon trees? Tilly felt a tingle at the back of her throat, the gardener's equivalent of a foodie salivating over a Jamie Oliver recipe. God, she so needed to garden.

She was shocked to realize that Sebastian was talking. After all, his silences could stretch across days. "I wanted more children. Fiona didn't," he said. "I had a vasectomy after Sophie was born."

"Shit."

"Exactly." He gave his crooked smile. "My wife has not, apparently, demanded a vasectomy of my former squash partner."

"That's good. Keep that righteous indignation. Then go tell her how you feel."

"I can't have a rational conversation with her, Tilly. Her hormones are raging."

"Who said it had to be rational? Scream at her. Make her understand how you feel!" What a ridiculous thing to say. Sebastian? Scream?

"Archie and Sophie have already heard too much." His voice was cold. "A clean break is best for them."

"And what's best for you?"

He removed her arm from his. "How is that relevant?"

They had reached the wrought-iron gate of the walled garden.

"Let's sit for a while," Tilly said. "Enjoy Lady Roxton's garden."

Tilly thrust her hip against the gate. It yielded with a groan, and Sebastian followed her inside, his hand still gripping the champagne flute he had yet to drink from. His boots crunched across the pea gravel as he threaded his way through the garden, but Tilly froze. Behind once-symmetrical borders—now a sprawling mishmash of anarchy—espalier-trained fruit trees reached out as if holding up their arms in defeat. And who could blame them? Roses and clematis strangled each other and clutched at heirloom perennials; self-seeded annuals jostled with marauding weeds; ground elder choked blobs of thyme, sage and rue.

Tilly bent down and tugged up a handful of groundsel. Rowena had retained one full-time gardener, a hedges-and-edges man who seemed to spend his life mowing, but still. How could Ro condone such neglect? Her mother would be devastated. Or was that the point? Really, it was heartbreaking that a mother and daughter had missed every signal of love to become family members who shared nothing but a name. Tilly measured her happiness by Isaac's. Most days she could hardly contain her love for him, physically ached for him when they were apart. She would never let hate or distrust come between them. She had failed him once by not fighting for his father's life. That single lesson, never to be repeated, had taught her everything she needed to know about mistakes and regret.

Sebastian stopped by the bench under Lady Roxton's beloved Peace rose and threw himself down with one swift movement. He landed with his legs crossed carelessly and an arm dangling over the back of the bench. Tilly ditched the groundsel and joined him.

"If you don't tell Fiona how you feel, you'll never forgive yourself," Tilly said. "Best-case scenario, she still loves you. Worst case? You move on. What have you got to lose?"

He dragged his arm forward to grip the champagne glass with both hands. "Christ. You've become philosophical, too?"

"I would give the world for one last conversation with

David. To ask him—" But why follow that thought? The dead couldn't forgive. "His last day—I didn't say goodbye. Trust me, closure matters."

Sebastian rolled his eyes. "How Americans love their therapy jargon."

"That was uncalled for and you know it. You're wallowing." And she wasn't? She used to be good at this—finding words to comfort. Even in middle school she was an emotional fixer, an average student who never made an awards shortlist or the naughty roll, but who had one talent: listening. She could sit next to a stranger on a bus and know her life story within fifteen minutes. When had that stopped? Maybe she should take on James Nealy, teach him the joy only a garden could give. Maybe it would be therapy for both of them.

"Wallowing gets you nowhere," she said. "I should know."

"Tilly, I'm done. I've agreed to talk with a solicitor. All I'm asking for is a guarantee that I can see my children whenever I want."

"You mean you won't put them through the tug-of-war your father inflicted on you?" Bugger, she'd said too much. It still upset her, though, the fact of a parent choosing one of his children over the others as if he were placing a take-out order from a restaurant. But that's exactly what Sebastian's father had done by fighting for custody of his son and not his daughters.

Sebastian's fingers tightened around the stem of his glass, and the bones of his knuckles gleamed through his skin. "I'd prefer you not mention my father. Especially not in front of the children." His mouth twitched slightly, an involuntary tic she remembered from his adolescence, a hint of anger he would never release.

"Sebastian, you have to let go."

"Why? Do you?"

"No, but I'm a widow, which means I can do whatever I please and someone, somewhere, will criticize. I grieve too much…I don't grieve enough. I moved on too fast…I'm not moving on at all. I've stopped listening. Although my mother thinks I've tuned myself out completely. I like to think that Isaac and I stumble along in our own little fug."

She laid her fingers on his forearm, just for a second, hoping to reach the old Sebastian with the carefree giggle. "I thought you and Rowena were having an affair."

"Christ. Why would you think that?" He glared at the place where her hand had been as if expecting his skin to blister. Was that how he saw her—as a disease he could catch and never be cured of?

"Rowena's car outside Manor Farm all night. Remember?"

"Oh." He glanced up warily. "That."

"That."

"She turned up with some of her sloe gin as a housewarming present. It's good, by the way, although I don't recommend drinking an entire bottle in one night, as I did. Fiona had just called with her news when Rowena bounded in like a stray puppy.

"I don't remember much after the third glass," Sebastian continued. "I woke up the next morning, fully clothed, tucked up in my duvet. When the room stopped spinning, I saw Rowena asleep in an armchair next to me, wrapped up in the old dog blanket from her car. Christ, that thing stinks. One whiff and I was puking for England. I'm not sure which was more impressive: that she'd hauled me upstairs by herself—although, given the bruises I think she dragged me— or that she held me over the lavatory for so long." He shivered. So, he was still frightened of throwing up, still remembered nearly choking on vomit as a child with whooping cough.

"She called in sick for me, which wasn't a lie since I had

the mother of all hangovers, and then insisted I take the following day off and come to the airport. It was like being put under a suicide watch." He paused. "She thought seeing you might help."

"It didn't, did it?"

"No." He handed Tilly his glass then fished a squashed packet of cigarettes from his back pocket and shook one loose.

"You never quit?" Tilly nodded at the cigarette.

"Actually, I did. But extreme circumstances demand extreme measures. It was either take up smoking again or get my ear pierced." He flipped open his lighter, lit his cigarette and then reclaimed his glass.

"That would be a good look for you. Dead sexy."

He almost smiled, and for a few seconds she continued to believe that he would. "My clients don't want sexy. Besides, an earring at my age smacks of something."

How did he get so old at thirty-nine? "Come on, Sebastian." She jostled him with her elbow, but he eased himself away from her and picked a fragment of ash from his lips. "Everyone's entitled to go wild on the eve of forty."

"You remembered?"

"Why so surprised?" Tilly said. "Sebastian Hugh Whitterton. Turns forty on September 12. I don't forget things about people who are important to me."

"*Were* important. You don't know me anymore. People change."

"I don't believe that they do."

He stared at his cigarette, caught between two fingers of his splayed hand, then raised it to his mouth and took a long, slow drag. "Tilly—" He blew smoke away from her. "We've become irrelevant to each other."

"That's a pretty cynical view."

"My world's become a cynical place."

"Hey, when it comes to woes, mine's bigger than yours."
She gave him a nudge. *C'mon, Sebastian, lighten up.* "You're
still in woe-kindergarten."

He reached for a rosebud that lay discarded between them.
Its petals, never opened, had begun to shrivel. He tugged
them off, one by one, tossing them to the ground.

"That's a Peace rose," Tilly said. "Or rather, it was."

He cracked a smile and suddenly looked so boyish and
vulnerable that Tilly felt a flush of anger at Fiona, a woman
she had never met.

"How do you survive?" he said.

"I spend too much time with memories. And as a strategy,
it's deeply flawed."

The air swirled with dust motes and smells she associated
with the cemetery—dead flowers and rotting rose blooms.

"What do you remember most about me?" His question was
so unexpected that Tilly's mind became clogged with answers:
the devilish look that said, *I'm horny?* Or the lingering stare
that meant, *Don't leave me?* Or the angry birthmark hidden
by hair at the nape of his neck?

"Everything," she said, because it was the truth. "What do
you remember about me?"

"You're a screamer." He grinned, and she saw the scrawny
sixteen-year-old in stained cricket whites. "When you come."

Tilly shook away the image of Sebastian's smooth, hairless
chest. "Why didn't you get in touch after David died?" Ugh,
she didn't mean to ask that. Not yet.

"Christ, Tilly." Sebastian swiveled around; his knees jabbed
hers. "Are you going to ease up for one minute?" He hesitated,
clearly making a decision between the cigarette and alcohol.
He settled on the cigarette.

"I'm sorry," she said. "That slipped out, but I would like
to know."

"Does it matter? Does it really fucking matter?"

Across the parkland, children squealed with laughter.

"I'm afraid it does. You and I are back in the same orbit, Sebastian." How could he have moved to the village and not thought this through? "Our children seem to have bonded… you've become bosom pals with my best friend. It's only a matter of time before my mother reels you in. Trust me, this matters. Because I need to forgive you and part of me can't."

"Fine." He stood and squared his shoulders. "I had no choice, Tilly."

"Bollocks. There's always a choice."

"No, there wasn't. Because I had made a pact with myself." He blew a smoke ring, then tipped his head back and watched it disintegrate. "To forget you."

She rose slowly, to hug him, but he stepped, equally slowly, away from her.

"I put my life on hold for you after your father died, even took a leave of absence from work." For a moment Tilly thought he might cry. But how would she know? She had never seen him cry. Wasn't that what she remembered most about life with Sebastian—the struggle to interpret his feelings without the guidance of words?

"I didn't ask you to do that."

"I know. But you sucked up the family grief and no one was there for you. Not even your husband." He spat out the last word.

How dare he criticize David? "The decision for David to stay home was mine, not his. Do you have any idea how much a last-minute transatlantic ticket costs? We certainly couldn't afford two." Surely, the banker in him understood.

"I was there for you, Tilly, up until the time you flew back to America. And before you say anything, I know you gave me no reason to hope…but still, I had this idiotic notion that you would come back to me. Once you'd gone, I told Rowena that I was done, that I would forget you. And know what?" He tossed the half-smoked cigarette onto the gravel and ground it out with his foot. "I did. I fell in love with Fiona, accepted the position in Hong Kong and Archie was born. Christ, I was the happiest I've ever been. Unfortunately, my wife was not. When David died I couldn't contact you. I couldn't risk that you would reel me back in. Fiona never shook off the doubt that I had loved you more, and I could never convince her otherwise. She wanted absolutes, and I failed to deliver. It destroyed my marriage."

"She destroyed your marriage. When she left you for another man."

He raised the champagne to his lips, then hesitated and dumped it out. "I have nothing left to give you, Tilly. Nothing."

"Suppose I don't want anything?"

"That terrifies me just as much." He sounded beaten, as if they had sparred physically as well as verbally, and he had lost. "Because then I have less than nothing."

"You could've said no." She gestured to the empty glass hanging from Sebastian's hand. "If you didn't want the champagne."

"I can't, Tilly. That's just it. I've never been able to say no to you."

God, she understood how that felt. "Funny." She drained her glass. "Normally champagne goes straight to my head. But I don't even feel woozy. Why is that?"

"There are some things one should do sober." Sebastian brushed his lips over hers. "And don't ask me why I did that." He headed for the rear gate. "Because I don't know."

They left the walled garden in silence, emerging on the edge of a thicket, a forgotten place with dark smells of peat and decomposing timber. Tentacles of dark green ivy carpeted the ground and slithered up the druid oaks at the edge of The Chase. There was no scratching, no twittering, no snapping of undergrowth, no hum of crickets. Even the wildlife had abandoned this corner of the estate. But hanging from a huge oak bough, its rope gray with age, was a marker from her past. Tilly brushed her hand over the smooth wooden seat. How could she have forgotten about this swing?

"Hop on." Sebastian took her glass and placed it on the ground next to his.

She sat, almost tipping off when Sebastian grabbed the swing from behind. The hairs of the rope bit into her palms as she clung on.

"How high do you want to go?" he asked.

She leaned her head back until it rested on his shoulder and remembered the feel of his caress, the feel of him moving gently inside her. He was always gentle, always concerned that he might hurt her. A surge of pleasure long forgotten stirred in her groin.

"I want to go as high as I can," she said.

Sebastian released her, and Tilly soared. She pumped her legs and swung higher and higher, until all she could feel was the air rushing at her. And below, Sebastian leaned against a beech tree, watching. He was still, like a mannequin, and like a mannequin, his posture and expression revealed nothing.

Eleven

With the afternoon sun blazing down on him, James killed the ignition. He climbed out of the Alfa and patted the door twice before easing it shut. Should he be concerned that his longest-standing relationship these days was with his car? Other than his friendship with Sam, of course. Man, they hadn't seen each other in eighteen months. Time to prod Sam into negotiating with his wife for another guys' weekend.

That was a good distraction to cling to. He needed the tonic of a well-worn friendship, even if Sam's advice never varied: *Get your shit together, buddy. Stop hustling the smart women and chase after the hot babes with big tits and no brains.* Breast size James didn't care about, IQ he did. Sam knew this, but now he was married with three kids, he liked to imagine the life of a bachelor was all firm breasts and lacy panties. But that had never been James's fantasy, even when he had, briefly, endured the bar scene. No, the one thing James dreamed of was the one thing he'd proved himself incapable of sustaining—a family life. But with two kids, obviously, not three.

James stared at the garden that blurred his anxiety better

than a tumbler of bourbon. He had come here to remind himself that his relationship with Tilly was about fighting fear. For that he needed absolute focus. But…he had driven down this very driveway and seen her for the first time. A tiny, barefoot woman with freckles and hacked hair who had looked him in the eye and said no. A woman whose love he wanted to earn, even though she deserved better, so much better.

Tilly's garden, baking in the Carolina heat, was a riot of yellow, purple, red and orange. He couldn't imagine Tilly doing anything in pastels. His mother had loved bright garden colors, too. Not that she had been a gardener of Tilly's caliber, but she'd definitely had the gift.

He glanced down at his black watch, his black T-shirt, his black pants, his black sneakers. How would it feel to live a life splashed with color, with spontaneity and laissez-faire? Maybe he should go to University Mall on his way back to the apartment and find a new watch. Splurge and buy something with color. A red watch. Tilly liked red, didn't she? *Fuck*. This was getting worse. He dragged his hands through his hair. Already, he was making assumptions about her taste. Already, he was acting as if he were her lover. James shivered at the possibility.

The day after tomorrow he could call her. He had lasted five days without talking to her, without hearing her beautiful English accent bastardized by the occasional American phrase. He missed her voice so much that he had developed a new habit—as if he, obsessive-compulsive James, needed one—of listening to the BBC World Service every morning. But it wasn't enough. Nothing was enough.

Not checking with her had been exhausting, but they had made a deal, and he had forced himself to stick with it. Fear of cheating could be convenient, even though the OCD twisted it, tried to con him into believing he had lied when he hadn't. As it was doing right now, telling him Tilly wouldn't speak with him tomorrow since he had lied to her. But he hadn't, had he? When had he lied to her about anything?

Boss back the thought, James, boss it back.

He had used the last week wisely, creating a virtual tour of his property to share with her after she agreed to take him on. Unfortunately, that had placed him at his unfinished house more than usual. He was pushing the contractor to the edge, driving him too hard on every detail. Poor bastard was close to quitting, and who could blame him? Tomorrow James would give the guy a break and stay away.

A hawk screeched, and James spotted the huge bird with the rust-colored belly sitting guard in the ancient oak, the tree that made his insides itch with its lack of symmetry. Were hawks territorial? Was this the same bird he had seen the first time he came here? The hawk screeched again, and its cry resonated in his gut.

James yanked off his sunglasses. "I know, my friend. I miss her, too."

Twelve

A strange westerly wind had picked up that morning, heralding the new workweek with a rumbling in the treetops. It had battered the garden since dawn, covering the lawn in rose petals and forcing the hollyhocks to the ground. The rusted weathervane creaked as another gust roared through, and Tilly tucked her hands into her armpits. At Creeping Cedars a summer wind this strong swept in with a red flag warning and the threat of forest fires.

The pony in the field behind whinnied its distress. Poor creature had been racing around all morning, trying to outrun itself. If only she could do the same. Why did she feel so jittery? Was it the recent phone conversation in which Sari had casually mentioned her five-year business plan? Or was it the omnipresent specter of Sebastian?

A burst of magpie cackle fired, and Tilly jumped. How ridiculous to let a stiff breeze and a bossy bird startle her. Monty whimpered as he shoved his snout through the bars of the garden gate, but Tilly ignored him. Isaac was down in the paddock, practicing his bowling—with a tennis ball—

away from windows and away from the dog. Sebastian had promised more cricket at the weekend, and Isaac was thrilled. Tilly jammed her hands deeper into her armpits. Should she discourage this? Was Sebastian merely seeking a substitute for his childless weekends? Suppose he did reunite with Fiona? Unlikely, given the pregnancy, but then he had returned without question each time Tilly had invited him back into her life. If he reconciled with his wife, would he dump Isaac the way he'd dumped Tilly after David died?

Sebastian. For the past twenty-four hours Tilly had reminded herself that he was single only in living arrangements. But there he was again, prowling around her thoughts, looking gorgeous in a dark, well-cut suit. What was he doing right now? Excelling at efficiency while directing a loyal assistant from behind an uncluttered desk? Mahogany, of course, with a watercolor centered on the wall opposite, a landscape of an inhospitable stretch of Yorkshire coastline, a view Sebastian could escape to.

Tilly scratched under her arms. Damn chigger bites had yet to heal. When she moved to North Carolina, people warned her about the obvious threats—stepping on a copperhead, flipping up the lid of the composter and exposing a black widow spider, grabbing poison ivy with a handful of weeds. But the things she had come to dread most were almost invisible: disease-carrying ticks and minuscule red chiggers whose bites stung like burns. Tilly scratched harder.

And stopped when her fingers rested on a small, smooth lump moving deep beneath her skin.

The next morning Tilly sat in the driveway, unable to do more than listen to the car engine idle and the turn signal blink. She must have sounded desperate for Dr. Fulton to squeeze her in before his first appointment. Or, with his knowledge of the cancer that had claimed both her father and her grandmother, was he more concerned than she was? Except—she held her right hand level and watched it shake— she wasn't *concerned*. She was tear-at-her-skin, scream-at-the-world, grab-at-her-son-and-never-let-go terrified. If only David were here to hold her and say, "It's okay, babe. We'll handle this together."

"And where are you?" she yelled at the sky. "Dead, which is *so* not helping."

In ten years of marriage, she had never raised her voice to her husband and never criticized him, although she did argue with him once, over the behemoth of a stereo he wanted to blow a month's salary on—she won. And there were a few times she'd locked herself in the bathroom and mouthed "asshole" at the door. But now that he was less than air, she was gunning for a fight. Empirical evidence that, in the past twenty-four hours, she had become a fruitloop.

Her mother's Matchbox car chugged, the vibrations keeping time with the tremors of her heart. *Get a grip, Tilly. Women have lumps in their breasts all the time, most of them benign. Think about that, not the genetic soup sloshing through your veins, heading for your lymph nodes.*

Before her father was diagnosed with advanced kidney cancer, he had taught Tilly to be wary of monsters masquerading as men. But what if the monster wasn't nameless and faceless? What if the monster existed within you?

Tilly flopped onto the steering wheel and stayed there. Life tripped her up every day. Sort of like fiddling with a Rubik's Cube, which she'd never had the patience for. You struggled to line up all those silly little colored boxes and with one click, they tumbled out of whack. Of course, with a Rubik's Cube you could always reshuffle and start over. Defeat didn't have to be an option. Tilly raised her head. She was a gardener;

she didn't know how to quit, let alone wave a white flag. And while gardening gave her staying power, widowhood showed her, every day, the futility of melodrama.

With a flourish, Tilly canceled the indicator. Who the hell could see her signal, anyway? Time to pull onto the road and slam into her future. She chopped at the air with her right hand. Aha! A woman in control of her destiny. Then she sighed: *As if.*

Okay, break this down into manageable chunks. First things first, turn left. But into which lane, on which side of the road? Tilly hated driving in England. She approached roundabouts she had zipped over as a teenager like a terrified tourist, her American driver intuition telling her to treat them as four-way stop signs. Which, of course, ticked off every car stacked up behind her. And as for the narrow country lanes she had whizzed along at eighteen, how could anyone drive that fast on roads designed for single file?

Tilly edged out of the driveway, and the wipers scraped across the windscreen. So much for the sun. The English summer had reverted to form, the sky filled with lumpy clouds the color of Isaac's white sports socks after she washed them with his jeans. Actually, the sky had the consistency of two-week-old white bread, which suited her mood; she felt pretty moldy herself.

"Driver must be in the middle," she muttered. "Stay in the middle of the road, Tilly. Stay in the middle of the road."

A supermarket run had provided the perfect cover, especially since Isaac was happy to stay at Woodend perfecting his bowling technique. Guilt poked at her, prodded her with a big, sharp stick. She had stood in her mother's kitchen ten minutes earlier and spouted a juicy, fat lie, which, like Pinocchio's nose, had continued to grow. Tilly was a pitiful liar; Isaac was bound to see through her. But wasn't it easier to bury the truth in words, to keep heaping them on until even the speaker was lost in their meaning? After all, one simple sentence—*Daddy is dead,* or *Mommy has cancer*—could rip out a child's heart.

Isaac mustn't suspect anything, not until she could bounce up to him with a game plan, not until his summer had stretched out marked only by the thrill of learning cricket. Rowena was right: some truths weren't for sharing.

But some things demanded a map. And dammit, she'd forgotten to dig out a street map of Northampton. She always went astray in the town's one-way system, which seemed to mutate every year during her absence. If she got lost in North Carolina, she opened her mouth, let her English accent pour out, and garnered more help than she needed. Maybe she'd just drive around until she recognized a landmark or two from her teenage playground. Anyway, it hadn't been that long since she'd visited the tall, thin doctor's office, squished like an afterthought between a hair salon and a podiatrist. Was it as a college student with mono? No, Dr. Fulton had come to her that time. House calls—her American friends would never believe it.

Of course, the Dr. Fulton who had nursed her through mono and measles had retired years ago. She hoped the younger Dr. Fulton, junior if he were an American, had warm hands. She hated male doctors probing her.

Armfuls of yellow hawkweed flowers and pink rosebay willow swayed as the car brushed past, and a yellowhammer flitted from the old-man's-beard in the hedgerow. Her summer memories of Bramwell Chase were chock-full with birds, and yet she had seen so few since coming home. Except for pigeons, which evidently outbred rabbits these days. What had happened to the turquoise-breasted kingfisher, the chaffinches and goldfinches, the trotty wagtail? Even the dawn chorus of her childhood had dwindled to a lone thrush. That was the problem with memories: you could protect them like fragile knickknacks on a shelf, but they still gathered dust and irrelevance.

Tilly's thoughts slipped to the array of birds that lit up her woods every day with color and music. She missed the cardinals on the birdfeeder and the hawk that seemed to watch her when she gardened. And she missed her gynecologist, the person who had shared every moment of Tilly's twenty-two hours of trench-labor—David had been stranded in St. Petersburg and he'd missed the whole thing. But she didn't need a pain partner this time. Other people might confuse her, distract her from following her gut. No, it was simple, like turning onto a road. She must find her position and stay there.

If the lump were malignant, the breast had to go. But that might not be enough. If the doctors found cancer, she would opt for a double mastectomy, whip them both off! She slapped the dashboard. What did she need breasts for anyway? Her nursing days were over and her boobs had never been her best feature. They were miserable little nodes and now lumpy, too. Wasn't that the kicker? She'd always wanted voluptuous breasts like Rowena's perfect 36C. Breasts that strained against lace and gauze and cupped into tantalizing cleavage. Instead she was stuck with the figure of a thirteen-year-old boy. But what the hell. According to her husband, she was damn sexy. So why did she need breasts? She'd had enough regrets in her life. For Isaac's sake there would be no more. Goodbye, breasts! And if the cancer stood its ground—what then? What would be best for Isaac? A clean break from the past or a husk of it to cling to? Should she consider a living will?

Nope. Not going there.

The car revved under her, and Tilly squeezed the gas pedal. She was going to fly down those country lanes just like she used to. And hope she remembered the location of the speed cameras as she got closer to town.

James slammed down the phone and before he could consider the action, punched a hole through the drywall. *Fuck!* He shook his throbbing knuckle. *Fuck!* Physical pain didn't bother him, but Tilly not waiting for his prearranged call felt like emotional disembowelment. How could she not be there? She knew how important this was to him; she knew.

He stared at the powdered debris on the polished wood floor, at the mess he had created. After he'd cleaned up, he would have to get someone out to fix the hole, and then call his landlord and explain what had happened. He raked his hands into his hair and found his breath. *Inhale—one, two, three, four, hold to the count of two, exhale—one, two, three, four.*

He never released anger, not anymore. He had spent thousands on therapy so this kind of shit didn't happen ever again. What was wrong with him? And what was wrong with Tilly? Why had she instructed her mother to pawn him off with a feeble excuse? Tilly wasn't intimidated by him, would have no qualms about saying no. The day they met, she turned him down with nothing more than a smile. Curiosity was the only reason she hadn't enforced that rejection. What had happened? Was she injured, sick, in the middle of a family crisis? Did she need help?

His mind buzzed, trying to decide where to settle—on worry for Tilly, or on this non-answer, this unexpected delay. His heart raced and fear pounced, too strong to resist. Delays; he couldn't handle delays.

James paced in circles. Faster, tighter. Round and round, round and round, round and round. He rubbed his arms, up and down, up and down, up and down. A fog of panic closed in. Thicker, darker panic dragged him into the abyss. He couldn't resist, couldn't stop this.

Helpless, he spiraled.

Tilly rustled two half-filled shopping bags, hoping a few sound effects might lend plausibility to a three-hour supermarket trip that had yielded three four-packs of Cadbury's chocolate mousses, a packet of chocolate-covered HobNobs, a box of Roses chocolates and ten bars of Cadbury's Fruit and Nut. And one bruised Granny Smith apple. It was reassuring to know she hadn't given up on her health, although slightly disturbing to realize that she had no memory of buying the apple. Or the chocolate.

Thanks to the heat thrown out by the Aga, the kitchen was unbelievably stuffy. Cramped, too. Woodend used to seem vast, but now the rooms felt pokey after her open-plan house on Creeping Cedars. Damn, it was hot. Tilly tugged at the neck of her T-shirt.

"Darling?" her mother called from the drawing room.

Tilly didn't reply. Why bother? If Mrs. Haddington wanted an answer, she got one.

Dr. Fulton, who did, indeed, have cold hands, had confirmed the obvious. Definitely a lump, he had said. Nine out of ten lumps are benign, he had said. It could just be a fibroadenoma, he had said, but since she didn't check her breasts regularly—he had paused at that point to emphasize her failure—there was no way of knowing. Then he railed on the National Health Service while slashing his blotter with a shiny, silver letter opener. And asked what the job opportunities were for a GP in North Carolina. Finally, he referred her to Northampton General.

Tilly had assumed, wrongly as it turned out, that she would get an appointment the next day. After all, if a time bomb were ticking in your armpit, didn't every second count? But the breast clinic took a minimum of two weeks to notify patients about appointments. Two weeks! In two weeks she might just gnaw off every finger. She needed to take charge of this horror, to be halfway through chemo, bald and sporting a natty Joan Collins turban.

"That nice James telephoned." Her mother's voice boomed along the hall. It was her classroom voice, intended to carry to the farthest desk. "He seemed a little miffed that you weren't here. Said he'd ring back later."

Tilly unwrapped a bar of Fruit and Nut, snapped it in two and shoved the biggest piece in her mouth. *Bugger, bugger, bugger.* Priority number one: ditch the guy with more issues than the crazed, cancer-riddled single mother. And where was Isaac? She ached to hold him, and yet the thought of seeing him unhinged her completely.

Monty's toenails scrabbled on the parquet hall floor, followed by the clunk of her mother's cast and the squeak of the rubber-tipped crutch.

"Can't talk to him, Mum." Tilly sensed her mother in the doorway but didn't look up. "Not today." *Yum.* She crunched a hazelnut.

"Tilly? Is that…all you bought?"

"Selective memory loss." Tilly unwrapped the second bar and bit off another chunk of chocolate. Raisins squished between her teeth. *Delicious.*

"Does this have something to do with Sari's telephone call?"

"Hmm." Tilly munched slowly. Some days it didn't matter how much chocolate you stuffed into your mouth, it was never enough. Just as some days stretched into a never-ending lie. Of course, the latter was a new experience, but surprisingly easy to master as new experiences went. Go figure.

"I thought so." Her mother sighed. "You haven't been yourself since that conversation."

Tilly reached for the rest of the half-eaten bar of chocolate. *Myself. When was the last time I felt like myself?*

"When James phones back," her mother said, "shall I tell him you'll call in a few days?"

Tilly winced as a jagged nugget of chocolate lodged in her throat. She swallowed hard. "He's not going to like it. I have a feeling Vesuvius could erupt and cause less damage. Sure you can handle that?"

Her mother's sapphire eyes sparked with mischief. *Yeah, silly question.*

"Leave him to me," her mother said.

Gratitude blasted Tilly's fortifications, tempted her with the lure of an emotional dump: *Hey, Mum. I have a lump in my breast.* Confession might bring relief, but at what cost to a woman who had buried two daughters and watched her husband die of cancer?

No, Tilly must keep this to herself until she had answers. Why scare her mother needlessly? Two weeks extracted from a lifetime meant nothing. *And, what d'ya know?* She had enough chocolate supplies to guide her through.

James slammed down the phone again, but this time he was prepared. He knew the rejection was coming. Although it wasn't a rejection. Tilly was playing for time, and he wanted to know why. He stared at his MacBook Pro with its oddly relaxing mandala screensaver. He needed to slow down the world so he could push aside the voice, figure out if this was just another case of serotonin deficiency sounding a false alarm.

His psychologist always asked him to identify the fear lurking behind the toxic thought, behind the worry. But this wasn't OCD fear, this was real. This was James: *Something's wrong, I can feel it.* Why was Tilly using her mother as a shield? None of it made sense, contradicted everything he knew about Tilly. God Almighty. How could he presume to know a woman he had met only twice? But he did know her; he did. And he could help her; he could protect her. But protect her from what? Herself?

James picked up the bottle of Maker's Mark and his tumbler and headed onto the balcony, back into the heat. Heat kept him on the edge, and he needed that to bar the OCD. Worry for people he loved could pervert his reasoning and force him to see tragedy where there was none.

He poured bourbon into his glass and held the glass up to the sunlight to check the level. Not too little, not too much. Perfect. He took two sips and relished the warmth at the back of his throat. Now he could think.

If something were wrong with Tilly, then Isaac was at risk, too. Shit. Wasn't it bad enough to feel the way he did for Tilly? After twenty-seven years he had to develop paternal instincts, but for someone else's kid?

He emptied the glass in one gulp, refilled it and repeated. By the time the bottle was a quarter empty, he knew what his next move would be. A boneheaded stunt? You betcha. Financially reckless and potentially embarrassing? That, too. Did he care? Not a fuck. He sat still, which he rarely managed. How could he not do this? He wasn't fatalistic, but meeting Tilly and Isaac felt like predestination. Great, now he was a recovering Catholic who spouted Calvinist doctrine. Wasn't he messed up enough without adding religion back into the mix? But if Tilly and Isaac were in trouble, he had to be there for them. It was that simple.

Tilly sank back onto her heels and rubbed black cobwebs from her jeans. She was half-buried in the cupboard under the stairs, along with her father's Victorian safe, a tangle of Christmas tree lights and a mountain of cleaning supplies. The cupboard smelled dank and ancient. Who knew what nasties lurked in the corners, nasties that once upon a time would have terrified her? Still, living with the threat of cancer had emboldened her. To test that theory, Tilly shoved her hand into the darkness. And yanked it back quickly.

Why did Saturdays throw a different light on troubles? Was it the change of pace that allowed contemplation to worry away at emotional scabs and then cause you to do something as insane as reorganize your mother's cleaning supplies? Or was sleep deprivation eliciting a wee bit of mania? The last three days she had been up at four o'clock, listening for the squeak of the letterbox and the plop of mail on the hessian doormat.

"There you are! Gracious." Her mother peered down. "What on earth are you doing?"

"You do realize you have four partially used tins of Brasso in here?" Tilly heaved a box from the lower shelf and nearly gagged on the stench of polish. Now that she thought about it, a sudden eagerness for domestic chores was akin to yelling, "Look at me, I'm a Looney Tune!" After all, Tilly's housework aversion was the stuff of family lore.

Her mother gave a low *ahem* before speaking. "Since Isaac's checking on the pheasant poults with Rowena, I thought we should snip some roses and take them to the cemetery. I haven't put fresh flowers on your father's grave since you arrived."

"Excellent!" Tilly sprang into action, showering the hall floor with dusters and rags. "Give me five minutes to grab a fresh tee and detangle my hair. Oh, and I haven't brushed my teeth today."

"Darling, we're visiting the dead. They hardly care about personal hygiene."

"Silly me. Roses it is, then," Tilly said, and dashed outside before her mother could ask what was wrong.

"Hey, you." Tilly stroked the smooth marble of her father's headstone and conjured up his belly laugh. Other memories may have dulled, but not the sound of her father's happiness.

Her mother's secateurs snipped rhythmically and sunshine tickled the nape of her neck. Sheep bleated across the estate, and on the school playground beyond the lime trees, children hollered and cheered through their end-of-year sports day.

Tilly stretched, enjoying a rare sensation of serenity. Even as a child, she had felt the village cemetery was a place to celebrate life, not dwell on death. She caught the intoxicating sweetness of wild honeysuckle, her sensory marker of survival, and smiled. But the smile wavered as she watched her mother yank dead roses from the container sunk into her father's grave. The stitches had been removed, but should her mother be using her injured hand? What about the risk of tears or infection? Her mother had grown careless with her safety, reaching at awkward angles, hobbling about without crutches, carrying cups of scalding tea as Monty wove between her legs.

When Isaac was learning to walk, Tilly had hankered after a future of me-time. Amazing, that she had been so naive. Her son needed her more, not less, as he grew—more ferrying around, more guidance in a world of hidden traps. And so, she realized with rising dread, did her mother.

"It's going to be a beautiful afternoon. Simply glorious." Her mother snipped leaves off a fresh rose stalk. "After you've dropped Monty off at the groomer's, why don't you stretch out on the lawn with a book and a nice glass of chilled elderflower cordial? I have a fancy to take Isaac down to the church and teach him the art of brass rubbing, and you could put some color back in those cheeks."

Yuck, a tan to draw attention to a body conspiring with an unseen enemy.

"Yes. A quiet afternoon might be just the ticket." Her mother reached into the trug and handed Tilly the shears. "Do me a favor, darling, and hack around the headstone. That young lad cuts the grass and thinks he's done. Never touches the edges. I keep telling the parish council to hire someone else. I've made a decision, by the way." Her mother dumped out fetid water from the flower container and refilled it with fresh rainwater.

"A decision about what?" Tilly tore at the long grass around her father's headstone, the blunt shears squeaking with each abortive cut. "Supper?"

Her mother straightened up and rubbed the small of her back. "Goodness, so stiff these days. No, I'm selling Woodend."

"You're—" Laughter sneaked out. "What?"

"Selling Woodend. I'm putting it on the market next week."

The shears clattered onto the marble base of the headstone. Tilly's legs wobbled and then crumpled. She collapsed to the grass, unable to move despite the damp that seared through her jeans and pressed wet denim against her skin like cold steel. The rain had petered out two days before, but the dew had been heavy that morning. An invisible mass of high pressure now hovered over Southern England and gleeful weather forecasters popped up everywhere predicting fine weather for weeks to come. Some even talked of a real summer. Amazing, how people desperate for sunshine could latch on to the smallest ray of hope.

Her mother wasn't serious. She couldn't be. She couldn't punch a hole in the frayed bottom of Tilly's world, because then Tilly might fall through. "This is a joke, right?"

"I'm sorry, darling. I've been trying to find the right moment to tell you. Then I realized there was no such thing. Go ahead, ask your questions."

Tilly looked up into her mother's eyes and read resolve. Her mother had found her own position in the middle of the road. She had dissected the whole aging-woman-alone-in-a-big-house problem and had settled on a solution without consulting her family. And why shouldn't she? Virginia Haddington was a seventy-year-old widow entering a new phase of life, one no longer steered by the demands of motherhood.

Tilly asked the only question that mattered: "Why?"

Her mother continued arranging flowers. "The accident was quite an eye-opener, you know."

"Oh God. You have osteoporosis, don't you?"

"Lord, no. Why would you think that?"

Tilly grabbed the cardigan that was tied around her waist and struggled to put it on. But the sleeves were inside out; everything was twisted.

"My life is changing, Tilly, and I can no longer ignore the inevitable. I'm not saying that I'm a decrepit relic, Lord forbid. But I lay on that sodden grass for over an hour. Cold and alone, calling out in the dark. A weekender from one of the barn conversions heard me. Do you have any idea how humiliating it was, to be found by a stranger?"

A tsunami of failure swamped her. Her mother had needed her, and Tilly hadn't even been in the same time zone.

"The ambulance men addressed him as if he were responsible for me." Her mother clutched at her pearl necklace. "They called me Virginia, for goodness' sake."

"I hate to point out the obvious, but you are Virginia, Mum."

"They should have called me Mrs. Haddington. It was

disrespectful. Lying there, remembering that summer nine years ago, I can't be that person again. Not if it means depending on strangers who call me Virginia."

"But Woodend has been your home for over forty years. You can't sell it."

"It's too big, Tilly."

"Hire help."

"I have help."

"Hire more." Tilly's anger rose with her voice. Selling Woodend wasn't a solution. It was a ridiculous act of sacrifice, a misplaced desire not to be a burden.

"It will solve nothing," her mother said. "Woodend is a house for children, not memories. Marigold and I have been talking about one of those nice cottages along Badger Way."

"What if Isaac and I come live with you?" Maybe life was offering her an opportunity, the *get out of jail free* card Isaac would need if the lump were cancerous. With Rowena, her mother, and her sisters around, he would be immersed in love and protection. And besides, if she had to stare down death, wouldn't she rather do it at home? Tilly leaped up. "It's so perfect I can't believe I've never thought of it. I've always wanted to return to Bramwell Chase. Why not now? I could start a new gardening business. Here."

"Why, in heaven's name, would you want to come back here? Your life is in North Carolina."

So, not a good idea. But she had sprung it on her mother, and her mother hated surprises. Tilly needed to examine the financial implications, talk to a banker—talk to Sebastian. That would impress her mother. Her mother always listened to Sebastian. Tilly jiggled from foot to foot, eager to get home and call him.

"My life *was* in North Carolina, but now it's a place of ticks and snakes and hurricanes that play havoc with my homeowner's insurance. But Woodend—" Tilly swallowed, aware that her voice was running ahead of her thoughts. "You're right, Mum. Woodend needs a family. And you shouldn't be alone. None of us should be."

"I won't be alone. That's the beauty of my plan. You and your sisters have your lives, which is as it should be, and I'll have mine with Marigold." Her mother ran a hand down her throat, then let it rest across her chest. "Now, no more talk of you returning to Woodend."

"You say that like it's a bad thing. But I'd do anything to save Woodend."

"It's not the house that needs saving." Her mother spoke with quiet precision, and her eyes bore into Tilly's. That was it, then. Her mother was hauling up anchor and pushing out to sea, leaving Tilly adrift in the shallows.

She gazed at the dandelions springing up over her father's remains and tried not to feel like a spectator as her life atrophied. Her mother gave a small "Well," an empty word, a last-minute substitute for an entire sentence: *I'm so glad we had this discussion*. Then Mrs. Haddington began picking up gardening tools and clearing away cut grass and dead flowers. Making sure everything was all neat and tidy before heading back through the lych-gate.

Tilly stood still, surrounded by dead people. If only her father were here to squish her into one of his bear hugs that smelled of cigar and sandalwood shaving soap. Or if David could reach for her and say, "What's wrong, babe?" then throw out his sexy grin that obliterated every worry. But there was no one to cushion her. No one.

Inside Woodend, Monty barked a welcome, and the gravel under the car's wheels made popping noises that echoed Tilly's mood. *Pop, there goes a breast. Pop, there goes Woodend.* Could things get any worse? Yes, clearly they could.

Sebastian sat on the back doorstep lobbing gravel into an upturned flowerpot like a disaffected teenager. Fabulous. Her brain was more crowded than a city parking lot flashing the full sign, and now she had to find space to park a problem that brought a flood of adolescent passion. How could she have forgotten Sebastian was due for lunch and a ruddy cricket lesson? No wonder sleep deprivation was the preferred torture of dictators worldwide.

Sebastian rose and gave her that look—head tilted, gray eyes stretched wide—a precursor to sympathy, to handling Tilly as if she were a cracked egg. Suddenly, she was eighteen again, with Sebastian so much older at twenty. They were sitting in her father's Rover, the hood buried in a ditch. Sebastian's voice droned around her: *What were you thinking, Tilly, swerving to avoid a badger? Suppose you've jarred your spine?* Then he left her alone in the night and ran to the nearest farm for help. She had pleaded with him to stay, to hold her until she stopped shaking. But Sebastian's pattern was always to suffocate her with the practical, while she longed for the comfort of the physical.

"Tilly?" Sebastian's voice was as low and concerned in the present as it had been in the memory. She shoved the car door open and looked at the arch of crimson shower rose, its partially open buds glowing against the paint-water sky. Her father had transplanted that rose from her grandmother's garden. A rose with Haddington history, history her mother was prepared to walk away from.

She should help her mother climb out of the car; she should answer Sebastian; she should…run. Tilly wriggled past him and raced through the kitchen, through the hall, and into the cloakroom. She slammed the door, turned the brass key in the lock and slid to the prickly brown carpet tile. Thirty-seven and hiding from her family in a bathroom. Life hadn't evolved much, had it?

The cloakroom—or powder room as Isaac called it—was cool and silent as a bunker. Thick walls provided natural heating in winter, natural air-conditioning in summer and year-round soundproofing against the outside world. The pipes behind the cistern rattled, signaling that someone was using the kitchen tap. Sebastian, no doubt, as he filled the kettle and prepared to brew a pot of tea, the English cure-all. No! He would tiptoe around her laden with solicitude. Isaac was too perceptive, would realize his mother was in trouble. Mind you, didn't he suspect already? Wasn't that why he'd begun trailing her around the house, Bownba in tow? In the past three years she had worked relentlessly to shield her son from the ugly side of life, but what if she let it all hang out in one sniveling, tearstained admission? What if he realized that his mother was as vulnerable as his father?

Panic ripped through her chest. No, no. Tilly pushed down on nothing. Isaac believed her to be Super Mom, the big boss momma who kept him safe. And that's what she would be, as soon as she concocted a few sure-fire tactics to keep her defenses in place. She rubbed her palms down her thighs and contemplated the cloakroom walls. "Oldest walls in Bramwell Chase." So said the village builder who used to sneak her illicit toffees. These walls were constructed of wattle and daub. Mind-blowing, that medieval mud and reeds could blend, unseen, into the modern world. Tilly jumped up. That was it—a way to weave back into everyday life so Isaac would suspect nothing. Everyone knew how she felt about Woodend and would anticipate a smattering of gloom-and-doom on her part. She would use that to her advantage until she got to grips with the whole lump thingy. See? Sometimes all you needed was to rearrange the facts, to click the Rubik's Cube in a different direction.

"Mom!" Isaac pounded on the door. "We're back and Rowena wants to know if you have the squits. Grammy says you've been in there for ages."

Tilly flushed the lavatory—who knew why, but the action steeled her—and called out in a cheerleader chirp, "Coming, Angel Bug! I want to hear all about your morning."

Right, time to face Isaac. Tilly tugged up her jeans, but they slipped down immediately. How had she managed, yet again, to buy the wrong size? Had it been to prove Sari wrong, after she had cheerfully pointed out, "You need them skintight, hon. That way they'll still fit once they're broken in." Skintight wasn't Tilly and never would be, but no matter how often she fried these jeans in the dryer, they would never fit. And life was too short for jeans that didn't fit. Next time, she would get it right.

Thirteen

High above, swallows circled, scouring for insects. Tilly didn't believe in omens, but she did believe in reading the behavior of birds. And swallows that high? Definitely a portent. Good weather was here to stay.

Sprawled across the old lounger, facedown, she listened to a wren belt out its melody. What an impossibly deep, rich sound for such a tiny bird. This was a moment to savor, a memory-in-a-bottle moment, with life at a full stop and her only company the birds and the garden of Woodend.

Her mother had dragged Isaac and Sebastian to The Flying Duck for a ploughman's lunch—*best in the county*—and Rowena had taken Monty to the groomers. Tilly had said three words to Rowena, "I need space," and Ro had shepherded everyone out. Was that the secret of a good relationship, space to be alone without needing to explain why?

Two pigeons cooed in the lilac tree, and Tilly hoisted up her forelegs and swung them back and forth. She closed her eyes and, for some totally unknown reason, hummed the *Sesame Street* theme song.

The pigeons shot toward the paddock, flapping furiously, clearly startled. *Now what?* Tilly dragged herself up. If Sebastian had sneaked back, he would be sorry. Very sorry. She snorted out a breath and turned, prepared for battle.

"Absolutely not." She rubbed her eyes. "Either I'm dreaming or you're insane."

"I'm obsessive-compulsive, not insane." James stepped closer, throwing his shadow over her. "I was expecting an answer from you. I didn't get one."

"You flew all this way to find out if you'd hired a landscaper? You've got to be joking."

James shook his thatch of hair from his forehead; within seconds it tumbled back. "I just spent $8,000 on a plane ticket. I hardly call that a joke."

No, but it did strike her as funny that in the past six hours two people had sprung monumental surprises on her and she hadn't seen either coming. Blimey, she'd forgotten about James. She had delegated him to her mother and not given him a second thought. Or a first thought, for that matter. Tilly pursed her lips. What on earth had her mother told him?

"Would you mind if we sat?" He nodded to the bench beneath the cherry tree. "I'm exhausted."

Tilly led the way in silence, her mind trying to unscramble the fact of James's presence on the lawn at Woodend. Was he, indeed, a nutjob? After all, who jumped on a plane for such a capricious reason? David. David had tried to do the same thing after her father died. Would've succeeded, too, if Tilly hadn't restrained him with a serious money talk.

She sat down, scooted to the far end of the bench and waited for James to settle with a respectable distance between them. But he sat butted up against her, his rucksack clasped to his chest. He glanced at the seat as if inspecting it, leaning into her as he did so. His thigh muscles tightened under his black jeans, and Tilly suppressed the impulse to fan heat from her face.

"I'm still in motion," James said. "It's been a long day. A long day. There wasn't a single seat on the direct flight, not even in first class. I had to change at JFK." He glowered at Tilly. "I never change planes."

She would have pulled away, if she'd had anywhere to pull to.

James rubbed at a blemish on his forearm. "What's your decision?"

"That's it? Straight to business, no foreplay?"

"I don't do small talk, Tilly."

"Of course not. You're driven by your need." Tilly flexed her fingers. "I'm sorry, but I can't help you. You're free to hire someone else."

"This is a heavenly spot." James's voice softened. "Quite heavenly."

"Thank you. I think so."

"May I ask why you're turning me down? I felt as if we had connected."

In the paddock, a woodpecker laughed.

"I can't give you the attention you need." A hopelessly inadequate response, but what else could she say?

"In that case I gambled and lost. I'm not in the habit of doing either. I shouldn't have told you about my OCD. I realize that now. Normally, I wouldn't. Life has taught me the value of concealing my quirks. But then, I'm usually an accurate judge of character."

"This isn't about you, James. It's about me. I don't care if you're purple with large green ears and a tail. I can't pander to any client right now. I have a truckload of my own problems to deal with. No room at the inn, I'm afraid."

He gave a sigh, but it was a sigh of acceptance, not surprise.

He glanced at the bench again and then heaved his backpack onto it. "Let me help."

Was he for real? No wonder James was so successful in business. He probably never saw obstacles, just kept on trucking toward his goal. "Thank you, but I don't think so. I'm sorry for the deception, by the way. My mother was spinning a yarn for my benefit, although you seem to have that sussed. She knows I'm out of sorts…she just doesn't know why. And no offense, but if I haven't confided in my mother, I'm hardly likely to turn to a stranger."

"You're not a stranger, Tilly. You're someone I recognize."

In the four weeks since they'd met, James's beard had filled out and been trimmed. It now had shape and style. His hair, however, was shaggier, wilder, and he had more earrings than she remembered: two stainless steel studs in each ear. He looked like no one she had ever met before. But when he forced his hair behind his right ear and turned into her gaze, she sensed empathy, a tangible feeling she remembered from her young widows' support group. Why had she quit? Had the oppression of other people's grief driven her away, or had it been the horror of examining her own?

"And Isaac's remarkable. Remarkable." James continued to watch Tilly as she continued to watch him. "My mother died when I wasn't much older than Isaac, but I never handled myself as well as he does. The most complimentary adjective anyone used about me was *weird*." James gave a smile, but the edges turned down. "I understand the tenuous balance between an only kid and a grieving parent. How easily it can be tipped. How you might need someone to fall on other than Isaac."

"No offense, but this isn't A.A. You're not the buddy I call when I slip off the grief wagon. My life's taken a bit of a

U-turn, which is fine. I can deal. But I need to close ranks, sort it by myself."

"You told me gardening was your Prozac," he said. "Are you gardening?"

Tilly drew up her legs, wrapped her arms around her knees and huddled into the arm of the bench. "Look. I appreciate the concern, but I'm trying to have a personal crisis here. Emphasis on personal. As in no audience allowed. As in go away. As in none of your business that I have some ocean-fearing megalomaniac running my nursery, that my childhood sweetheart materialized out of nowhere with two children and no wife, that he's been spilling his guts to my best friend who forgot to tell me he'd taken up residence in a farmhouse *she* owns, that my mother wants to sell my childhood home, that I have a— Bugger." A tear leaked onto her cheek. She rubbed upward, trying to force it back.

He reached into his rucksack and removed a small Ziploc of folded tissues. Without a word, she accepted the tissue he offered her and blotted her eyes.

"I want to be clear—I'm not crying. Crying is for wimps." She sniffed.

"Crying is good for the soul. Everyone needs to cry, Tilly."

"Do you?"

"I bawl over the slightest jab, physical or emotional. I'm so terrified of needles that I have to sedate myself before having dental work done, and I blubber through happily-ever-after movie endings, death scenes in literature…" He paused. "And coffee commercials."

She raised her head. "That sappy one when the son pulls up in a taxi on Christmas morning, sneaks into the house, makes coffee, and the mother comes down in her dressing gown and says, 'Oh, you're home'?"

James's loose smile said, *Guilty as charged.*

Tilly blew her nose, not that she needed to, but it gave her an excuse to look away. "How come you have pierced ears if you're scared of needles?"

"You think suffering for vanity is a female prerogative?" James hooked his thumb inside his waistband and, lowering the edge of his jeans, revealed a small tattoo above his hipbone. Tilly shivered, but whether from the inked, coiled snake or from the glimpse of black underwear, she wasn't sure. "I was drunk." He gave the smallest of shrugs.

A pierced, tattooed pirate—the new best friend she didn't want. Isaac would love this.

"Been a bad few days. Probably some hormonal crap. Womanhood's a bitch, you know. But I'm fine now, really." Her bottom lip betrayed her with a wobble. "Chip, chip, chipper."

Her vision blurred; he handed her a fresh tissue.

"Don't be nice to me." She honked into the tissue. "It won't help. And it certainly won't make me change my mind about your garden."

He laid his arm across her shoulder, the weight of it so unexpected. Without pushing her down or tugging her close, his arm was just there. And yes, she could dismiss what she was about to say as the math of timing: Good listener + need to talk = Tilly blurts out all. But it was more than that. He was a fellow survivor, a companion plant sharing the same pot, feeding off the same balance of sun and shade. He understood pain, not the kind that came with blood or broken bones but the kind that tore through your being, tunneled into your soul and exploded in some unseen place you hadn't known existed.

"I have a lump," she said, and all the pieces of butt-kicking optimism she had struggled to keep in place toppled. Tilly was shocked to realize that the gulping cries were her own. What an awful sound, like that of a hungry baby ripped from his mother's breast. And throughout James sat still, his body framing hers.

"Breast?" he said, after she lapsed into dry sobs.

She nodded.

"I can help." He squeezed her shoulder lightly. "I can help. I'm a walking encyclopedia on breast cancer. It's an old obsession, my original obsession."

Tilly gave him a sideways look. "Girlfriend?"

"Mother. Everything goes back to the same starting point for me."

So, he, too, had lost the person he loved most. Tilly sucked in a breath that seemed to bruise her internally. She had forgotten that breast cancer killed people with faces, people with names, mothers with young sons. She caught the corner of her lips with her teeth and bit down. A warm, rusty taste filled her mouth. She swiped her finger across her lip and inspected it. Blood, she was staring at fresh blood.

"How old were you?" Her voice sounded thick and phlegmy.

"Ten. The same age that I lost my life to OCD."

"There's a correlation?" She sniffed. "Between OCD and grief?"

"My family tree is a map of addiction, mental illness, hypochondria…enough red flags to suggest my OCD is genetic. But, yes. There is a link between grief and the onset of OCD."

"Oh, dear God." Tilly drilled her fingers into her temples. "Isaac."

"Your son doesn't have an obsessive-compulsive gene in him. If he did, I would have noticed. He's fine, Tilly. He's fine."

"But if something were to happen to me?" She wanted to clutch at James, snatch his reassurance. "Couldn't that push him over the edge? I mean, it's a double whammy for a child who's already lost one parent."

"Now you're awfulizing. You have to stop the thought right there."

Pressure built between her eyes. "Awfulizing? Is that even a word?"

"If you have obsessive-compulsive disorder, yes."

"You guys have your own language?"

"The fringe benefits are myriad."

He smiled at her and Tilly felt some small measure of release. Her head drooped onto his arm, still draped over her shoulder, but she tensed immediately. Would he misinterpret her need for physical comfort, do something as inappropriate as attempt a kiss? If he did, that would be a shame, because then she would have to slug him. But his arm didn't move, and she relaxed into the knowledge that James was someone she could trust.

"You do realize that nine out of ten lumps are benign?" he said.

"So the professionals tell me. But the waiting is chewing me up. I need answers so I can figure out where to go from here. I can walk around the supermarket without a list, but I can't deal with a crisis without a game plan. I must have one for Isaac's sake. And it could be another ten days before I get an appointment. How do I distract myself for ten days?"

"By gardening."

It was the right answer; in fact, the only answer. But was it just a lucky guess? Or was he, once again, motivated by his own need?

"I realize you can't design a garden long-distance," James continued, "but I've loaded a virtual tour of my property onto my laptop. I was hoping we could explore some ideas together."

'Course you were. Tilly rolled her cheek along his arm so she could stare down his smugness, maybe guilt him into wiping the victory smirk off his face. But his expression offered only understanding. Once again, she thought of her support group, and an idea began to form.

"Did you bring any luggage?" she asked.

"I left it at some quaint place called The Flying Duck," James said, with a scowl. "A temporary measure until I find a real hotel. I had no idea that travelers in this day and age were expected to share *a* bathroom."

"How long are you staying?"

"Two weeks. I had to pick a return date and two is a favored number for obsessive-compulsives. We like pairs." He stretched out his long legs and crossed his ankles, but his arm stayed in place. "Two is a perfect number. Perfect."

They sat quietly, losing time, and Tilly's eyelids grew heavy. If she could just rest her eyes for five minutes…but the church clock chimed three. Where had the afternoon gone?

"If you're staying, you can help me run an errand." She yawned and stood. "How do you feel about mentally challenged springer spaniels?"

An impenetrable barrier of dog rose, seeded stinging nettles and six-foot-high hedgerow shielded the car on either side from fields strewn with black plastic bales of silage. Once, Tilly counted the species of shrub along this stretch of road and came up with eleven, which, at the rate of one species per century, dated the hedgerow back to Anglo-Saxon times, before the Norman Conquest. Hadn't James mentioned that he was a farm boy? He might be interested in some English country knowledge, such as how to determine the age of a hedge. Or maybe not. He had remained silent since they'd collected Monty, crammed into the passenger seat with his head grazing the car roof, his knees pulled up and his arms pinned to his chest. Monty sneezed from the back and a stench, as pungent as skunk, wafted into the car.

"Fox." Tilly tucked the car farther into the stinging nettles as the switchback road narrowed to one lane. "You might want to close the window."

But James scratched at his black T-shirt, his fingers fluttering like a dazed bird that had crashed into her deck door.

"These roads close in on you a bit, don't they?" Tilly said.

He didn't answer.

"Omigod. You're claustrophobic. How did you manage on the airplane?"

They reached a passing place carved into the side of the bank, and James blew out a shallow breath. "Yoga breathing and self-medication. Bourbon," he added with a glance at his watch, a plastic object of clashing colors and sharp-angled design. "It's 4:02. We're going to be late to pick up your mother and Isaac. I've noticed you don't wear a watch. Why?"

Tilly turned her attention back to the road, swerving to avoid a ragged line of pheasants staggering like Friday-night drunks. "Life is stressful enough. Why set a timer to it?"

"Because without one—" he inhaled loudly and then exhaled slowly "—how can you arrive where you're meant to be when you're meant to be there?"

Wasn't the answer obvious? "You wing it."

"Wing it," he said, as if repeating a phrase in an unknown language.

"Don't worry. Work with me long enough and you'll figure it out. So, what else do I have to contend with, other than claustrophobia and severe punctuality? I thought you just had OCD."

"No one has just OCD, Tilly. OCD likes to come with

a buddy—bipolar disorder, ADHD. I told you, it's all about pairs."

The car whooshed past a gap in the hedgerow flanked by two massive oak trees, their trunks bandaged in ivy.

"Terrific. What's your OCD partnered with?"

"Generalized anxiety disorder. More of the same. Does this mean you're taking me on, as a client?"

They approached the cluster of two-up, two-down cottages that denoted the edge of Bramwell Chase.

"Nope. Better idea." Tilly braked and they crawled under the fluorescent speed camera. "I'm going to teach you how to do it yourself."

"I'm sorry," James said. "I don't understand."

"I'm going to give you a crash course in gardening 101. By the time you fly home, the gardening bug will have bitten hard and you won't need to hire anyone. What better way to spend early retirement? You can sniff around local gardens, see what thrives and—" she grinned "—wing it. Oh, and start a compost pile."

"Compost?" His voice rose sharply. "As in rotting food?"

"Absolutely. With broken-down horse manure mixed in. We have crap soil in our area of the Piedmont. You want to garden? You compost. Of course, some people will tell you to bring in truckloads of topsoil, but that merely masks the problem. Eventually the roots break through into what's beneath. Gardening's like life, you have to work with what nature gave you. Hey, don't look so worried. I'm good at this. And I happen to know a garden that's screaming out for help. I'm going to teach you how to get dirt under your fingernails, James Nealy. And once I do, you'll wonder how you ever managed without it."

Tilly flashed James a smile, but he shot forward and grabbed the dashboard. Apprehension wormed through her stomach.

Oh crap, was it too late to renege? Why was he gripping the car like that? And what was he doing now? Dear God, he couldn't be serious. She reached across and grabbed his wrist, preventing him from releasing the door lever.

Okey-dokey, this guy wasn't a sandwich short of a picnic; he was missing the whole ruddy picnic basket. But he wasn't a crank, and she wouldn't treat him as one. His spurts of energy weren't firecrackers of anger. It was fear that kept him fiddling, twisting, tapping; fear that isolated him in a private cell. What was the description she had read of OCD, the one that had stayed with her? A crippling allergy to life. Although that was a pretty accurate description of grief.

"Bad idea," she said, "leaping out of a moving vehicle. Land in those stinging nettles and I'll have to rub calamine lotion into all your nooks and crannies. I might enjoy the experience, but I doubt you will."

James slumped back and combed his fingers into his hair. "Thank you."

"For what?"

"For this," he said, and laughed.

~ Fourteen ~

Always barefoot, Tilly moved with a grace James found calming and sexual at the same time. Had she trained as a classical dancer? Back ramrod straight, knees bent, she balanced on the balls of her feet as she retrieved an oven mitt from the floor.

He could watch her for hours.

Tilly straightened up and smiled over her shoulder. James smiled back, the silence between them a balm for his exhausted mind, which, even as it accepted the completion of the trip without catastrophe, spat out darts of anxiety about the plane ride home.

The plane's going to crash; you're going to die.

James tried to shake the thoughts loose, but they kept recycling. Over and over. The never-ending repetition of OCD. And he was so friggin' tired.

At least Tilly wasn't a chatterer. He couldn't deal with other people's voices right now. Women who yakked nonstop grated on his patience, not that he had much to begin with, but every word Tilly spoke mattered. She was an extraordinary woman, but God Almighty—she slapped the salmon on the broiler pan, no olive oil, no chives—she couldn't cook.

James picked up the magazines scattered across the kitchen table and sorted them into a pile. A pile that created order, that gave his hands purpose and stopped him from interfering. Please, God, she wasn't going to boil the carrots into baby food, was she? He turned over a Mini Boden catalog, so much smaller than the other catalogs, and placed it, front cover up, on top of the pile. He nudged it to the right, back a bit, no, a little more to the right. Perfect.

Muttering something about the heat, Tilly stripped off her denim shirt and tossed it toward the nearest chair. James told himself not to stare, but the red bra strap peeking out from under the skimpy tank top was a lure no man could possibly resist. And yet why did her right shoulder blade stick out more than the left one?

Instinctively, he stepped toward her and traced her S-shaped spine.

Tilly turned, her eyes, the color of frosted sea glass, watching for his next move. "No one's ever noticed my scoliosis before," she said quietly. "How did you know?"

"Your right shoulder blade juts out." His eyes moved down. "And your waist's lopsided." How had he not noticed that her torso was asymmetrical? Asymmetrical! The daydream from the plane, in which he'd imagined making love to this perfectly imperfect woman, warped into a waking nightmare. He grabbed at his hair and began twisting.

"Unbelievable," Tilly said. "I think of my curved spine as a private deformity."

"You didn't have surgery as a kid?" His voice sounded flat and strangely normal. That was something, huh, to feel one way and act another. The legacy of a lifetime of practice. He yanked his hand from his hair and buried it in his pocket. Just-a-guy gesture. A regular, non-fucked-up guy gesture.

Tilly gave a sad smile. "Surgery wasn't an option. My

mother freaked at the idea of me going under the knife, so I wore a spinal brace until I turned eighteen. Big mistake now I'm a manual laborer."

Of course, the spinal brace explained the posture. "Was it painful?"

"Mostly just annoying." She arched her back. "Although in the summer the leather corset rubbed my hips raw."

This time the urge to touch her was stronger and undeniably carnal. James retreated to behind the table and clenched and unclenched his fists.

The plane's going to crash; you're going die. You deserve to die. You're a letch.

"I hated the attention the brace brought." Tilly stretched. "It's hard to be anonymous when you bend like a robot, but Sebastian protected me well. That's how we met—the local oiks were teasing me and Sebastian leaped in. He has this thing about social injustice. Then he and Rowena built a pyre on my eighteenth birthday, doused the brace with gasoline and pouff." She threw up her hands. "Burn, baby, burn. The best present a girl could wish for."

And it came from Sebastian. Fuck, how could he, James, compete with the guy who had loved her at her most vulnerable? He didn't want to act like a jerk when he met this Sebastian tomorrow, but even his name made James want to scratch off his own skin. And Tilly used it constantly. What kind of a name was Sebastian anyway? It sounded like a character from a Gothic novel.

"I guess we were both damaged teenagers," he said.

"I guess so."

"Here." He reached for her gin and tonic. "Go sit with your mother. I'm taking over the cooking as payment for the—" he gulped "—the gardening lessons."

Tilly hesitated and then took the glass. "I would argue with you, but there's little point, given that I loathe cooking. You sure about this?"

"I can cook—you can't." Shit. Was that too honest?

"Amen, brother." She toasted him and left the kitchen.

Don't look at her waist, James, don't look at her waist. But he did anyway.

James grabbed the edge of the table. Wasn't this what he'd wanted—to meet his fear head-on? But now the lines were fuzzy, blurred by desire and jealousy. And Tilly's asymmetrical waist. Images attacked him. First, he saw Tilly ripping off her tank top to reveal a red satin bra, while a faceless man called Sebastian reached for her breasts. Then he saw her lopsided back.

James pushed away from the table and smacked his hands on either side of his skull. He needed to tear through the open back door, into the golden light that reminded him of the Mediterranean evenings from the only vacation he'd ever taken—twenty years ago. He had started the trip with a lover, but after she grew tired of his excuses for avoiding the beach, he had finished it alone.

He could leave now and Tilly would never know the whole ugly truth about him. But he was falling, fast and hard, and even if he wanted to, he couldn't stop.

"Are you bonkers?" Rowena yelled over Monty. "You want to unleash a stranger who doesn't know a pair of secateurs from a chain saw on Mother's walled garden?"

"Pretty much," Tilly yelled back.

"Quiet." Rowena slapped her hands on her knees and glared at Monty. "Or I'll send you to the knacker's yard."

Monty stopped barking and cowered behind Tilly.

"If there's one thing that pisses me off," Rowena said, "it's a badly trained dog." She patted Tiddly on the head, then

Winks—or was it Winks, then Tiddly? They had been sitting like onyx statues for the past five minutes, ignoring Monty as he'd ricocheted from chipped terra-cotta urn to chipped terra-cotta urn, spraying pee and barking. "Your mother spoils that animal. I keep telling her, 'Give me two weeks, Mrs. H, and I can lick him into shape.'"

Two weeks. Tilly tottered as she craned to look up into the clear, pale sky—a one-dimensional mural hanging so low it could, surely, fall and crush her. At Creeping Cedars she could see only snatches of the sky through the trees, but it felt vast and distant, like an ancient wonder. The sky over Bramwell Hall was, to quote her mother's new favorite adjective, nice, an uncharacteristically bland word for her mother to lean on. After all, her mother had taught Tilly words had power. But gazing up at the sky, Tilly understood. *Nice* was a word you used without investment, a word that allowed you to hurry through, a word like *fine*. Tilly had used *fine* to deflect every postfuneral how-are-you-doing question. After all, most people didn't want to be bogged down in truth. They wanted to express sympathy and move on. Although she wasn't sure that applied to James. His questions were heat-seeking missiles, targeted to strike and explode.

Her mother, however, was sticking with *nice*. And humming "Onward Christian Soldiers" as she hobbled around the house, recycling her possessions with color-coded labels that meant "keep," "give to the girls," or "donate to the village jumble sale." At the rate she was working, her mother would have packed up forty years of her life in the next two weeks. And Tilly, what would she be dealing with?

"Amazing what you can do in two weeks," Tilly said. Monty shoved his snout into the back of her knee. "Save a dog, save a garden."

"My answer is no. *N-O.*"

Tilly longed to retaliate with, *God, you sound as imperious as your mother,* which would be a stupid, self-defeating thing to do.

A flurry of birdsong erupted in The Chase and died. The air hung leaden and still, the day already a scorcher, which was nothing to smile about. Heat in England meant non-air-conditioned misery as everything, including tempers, became dry and brittle. Worse, her mother would draw the curtains to banish the sun, and Woodend would be sealed in stale darkness.

The church bells pealed out their Sunday morning tune, and Tilly sighed. Her mother would be waiting for a lift to Matins, cardigan buttoned, reading glasses in one pocket, a pound coin for the collection in the other. But rushing Rowena was like snuggling up to a copperhead and saying, "Give us a kiss." Tilly remained quiet, silence the only weapon she had left.

When Rowena spoke, her voice was low and steady. "Clearly you have forgotten the tantrum Mother threw when I forgot to shut the gate, and bunnies chomped on every… fucking…plant. What you're proposing makes Peter Rabbit look like a founding member of the gardening club. You let a novice within sixty feet of the walled garden, and Mother will take me off speed dial faster than you can say, 'Boycott French cheeses.'"

"Rowena, love—" Tilly maintained eye contact, despite the thunder flies swarming over her chest. Minute invaders that didn't bite or sting, thunder flies could tickle you into madness, as they were threatening to do to Tilly at that very moment. "Your mother's pride and joy is more wasteland than garden these days. But if I could restore it, well—" Tilly gave up and scratched manically "—she doesn't have to know it was me, does she?"

The quick movements of Rowena's green eyes betrayed her: She was thinking. Time for Tilly's ace. "She might even call on your actual birthday this year."

"Okay, Ms. Clever Clogs. And suppose your protégé kills the David Austin roses?"

"I'll call your mother and fess up. Either way, you win."

Rowena's eyes grew wide and sparkly, like a child at a pantomime. She fanned out her long-tiered skirt and released it; crinkled silk swished around her psychedelic Wellington boots. Wellies, in this heat? "You mean I swipe your role as Ms. Goody Two-Shoes, and you become the slutty, cannabis-growing, non-grandchild-producing daughter." Rowena tugged a flaccid elastic band from her wrist, grabbed her hair and bunged it into a fat ponytail. "I might even be forgiven, twenty years late, for flying out of my bedroom window after sniffing glue and flattening Mother's favorite rhododendron. Brilliant. I absolutely adore this plan. Go." She waved Tilly off. "Destroy the walled garden with my blessings."

"Thanks," Tilly said. "You're a doll. Pimm's at one, by the way, and lunch at two, cooked by your soon-to-be sous-gardener."

"A new man in the village." Rowena twirled the end of her ponytail. "And one who likes to cook. Is he sexy?"

Tilly shrugged. "He has ni— His eyes. There's something about his eyes."

Rowena tossed her ponytail over her shoulder. "You're telling me he has *nice* eyes? Hardly a hunk endorsement."

James, a hunk? Not exactly, but he was sexy. Sort of. Tilly concentrated on untangling the dog lead from around her legs, relieved, for once, that Monty had tied her in knots.

★ ★ ★

"You do know your stealth bomber's rubbish." Tilly yanked the paper plane from the box hedge and handed it back to Sebastian.

"At least it made a landing. Which is more than can be said for your alien astro blaster." Sebastian nodded at the remnants of paper plane dribbling from Monty's jaw.

"Enemy interception," Tilly said. "How can a girl predict that?"

A warm thrill flickered in her gut, then disappeared—tucked away but waiting. Tomorrow morning she and James would attack the walled garden, and nothing could darken her mood. Not a diseased breast, not a brooding ex-lover, not a dog that was moving on from eating paper planes to crunching on a stinky rabbit carcass. James had been right about one thing: She needed to garden. Actually, he'd been right about many things, such as how crappy she was at cooking. Although she did feel bad that he was stuck in the kitchen preparing Sunday lunch for a gaggle of people he didn't know. But, as he had explained over and over—and over—why should she trawl through hell with a task he could complete effortlessly?

"I win!" Isaac bounced with more energy than any person had a right to exhibit on a hot day. "My Saturn V went the farthest. I win!"

Archie continued to pound a flattened daisy with the toe of his sneaker. Tilly had yet to find his Spitfire, which had nose-dived into the spirea on its maiden voyage. She suspected Archie had intended this to happen. After all, she had watched him bowl; he had his father's targeted aim.

Archie should have been in school, but his housemaster had proposed "special dispensation" in the form of a weekend with his dad. Evidently, Fiona and Sebastian had told the children about the pregnancy the previous Sunday night, and Archie had fallen into the deepest funk, dragging his misery around school like leg irons.

Sebastian screwed up the stealth bomber and thrust it into the pocket of his cargo shorts. He had circled his son all morning, trying too hard, creating fancy paper planes when he might have done better with a stack of two-folds-and-off-you-go paper darts. He had lost Archie's attention hours ago. A rare day together and father and son were communicating through glares and grunts, dealing with a crisis by steaming in opposite directions.

Tilly chewed on her thumbnail and replayed the conversation that she and Isaac had danced around the night before, when she'd explained she would be incredibly busy for the next two weeks, saving the walled garden with James's help. Isaac, who only weeks earlier had urged her to take James on, had accepted the news with a silent stoicism, which, in anyone else, Tilly would have interpreted as jealousy. Or maybe he'd read her explanation for what it was—a feeble cover-up.

Sebastian squeezed Isaac's shoulder. "Well done," he said.

Archie stopped pounding the daisy, scooted around and turned his back on them, but not before flashing what Tilly used to call Sebastian's granite face. Cold and set like a statue, it was the closest teenage Sebastian ever came to a pout.

"Right," Sebastian said. "Time for you boys to go and ask Mr. Nealy—"

"James," Tilly corrected him.

Sebastian ignored her. "If you can help in the kitchen."

Archie and Isaac groaned in camaraderie.

"Don't bother, chaps." Rowena pushed through the French doors that led from the drawing room onto the patio. Her hair was looped on top of her head and secured with a kitchen baggie clip, and she was balancing two cans of Coke on a tray of salmon-and-asparagus rolls. "I have everything under control. I am Ms. Kitchen-Skivvy, sidekick to the infamous— but *oooh* he has such a sexy *arrrrrse*—" Archie stifled a giggle with his hand. "Mr. Fussy-Wussy! Who insists on washing up every bloody utensil as he goes." Rowena put the tray down on the wrought-iron table next to Mrs. Haddington, who awoke with a jerk.

"Goodness." Mrs. Haddington rubbed her eyes. "How embarrassing. Nodding off like a doddery old has-been."

"Rubbish, Mrs. H," Rowena yelled. "You're resting from the demands of state."

Joke about it, but since when do you nap, Mum? Her mother could make a thousand excuses, but she was slowing down. Tilly hadn't watched her father age. His decline had been swift, but his family—*my harem,* he called them—had stayed close, nursing him like a tag team. But what if the next time around, Tilly was the one who needed nursing? She shook her head. *Not these thoughts, not today.*

Rowena snapped open a Coke can and handed it to Archie. "Consolation prize, sweetie."

Archie giggled. "Dad doesn't let me drink Coke."

"Good thing I'm not your father then." Rowena handed the other can to Isaac. "Grub's up in fifteen minutes, so shoo, the pair of you. Go do whatever vile things boys do."

A look sparked between the kids. "Let's go climb that big oak tree," Isaac said, and he and Archie ran, shrieking, toward the paddock.

"Rowena!" Sebastian might well have been shooting for parental outrage, but he missed his target by yards. "Did you just give my child Coca-Cola?"

"I most certainly did. Got a problem with that?"

"Not if you share your last fag with me." Sebastian's

lopsided smile stretched across his face, but his eyes, the color of stirred-up river silt, followed James as he came through the French doors.

"Can I offer you a refill, Virginia?" James asked her mother. He held a cut-glass pitcher of Pimm's in one hand, and a goblet of red wine in the other. He had been skeptical about the Pimm's, commenting that he preferred his alcohol undiluted and without a floating garnish. At this point in his life, he had said, he knew what he liked.

"Wonderful, thank you." Mrs. Haddington held up her glass. "I must say, in less than twenty-four hours you have certainly perfected the art of making Pimm's. Are you sure you don't have English genes?"

"Pure Irish-American mongrel," James replied.

Sebastian leaned into Tilly. *No aftershave today. Thank God.* "How long is he staying?"

"Two weeks." Tilly dunked a bobbing piece of strawberry in her glass and tried to ignore Sebastian. His tone had suggested petulance. The same tone, in fact, that he had used on the night she had refused to relinquish her virginity in a musty old sleeping bag. *Sod it.* Why did every conversation with Sebastian trigger a mental reel of adolescent sex highlighted by fumbles to rebutton blouses and tissue-up spills before someone—human or pet—crashed open the door? No wonder they'd run to the Dower House for privacy. The ghosts of a ruin had disturbed them less than life at Woodend.

A fighter jet roared over the patio, and Tilly hunched her shoulders. Military aircraft had zoomed over the village since she was a child, but every sighting, every crack that split the sky, still unnerved her.

"Why're you so interested in James's plans?" she said. "You jealous?"

Sebastian spluttered into his drink. "Christ, Tilly. Keep your voice down."

"It's just if you're not jealous, you should stop staring at James. You'll give him the wrong idea. And don't snap...no one heard me over the jet."

"I did not snap." Sebastian's voice was crisp, a voice that closed deals and signaled his intention they should stay closed.

See? This was why she didn't want a man in her life. Who had the energy to deal with hand-me-down emotions, to second-guess a partner, especially one whose life was guided by propriety? *Thou shalt not reveal thy emotions.* Had she ever seen Sebastian break down, either from rage or ecstasy? He was a sweet drunk and a silent lover. He could probably step on a copperhead and not whimper.

His competence at life had appealed to Tilly-the-teenager as she'd struggled to curb a constant bubbling urge to scream at the world. Even when faced with her temper, his devotion had been quiet and solid, expressed not verbally but through the way he handled the minutiae of her life. But would she settle for that now?

Tilly blew an imaginary bubble from her lips. Thank God she worked with plants, not humans. Take those leggy pinks in her mother's herbaceous border. One swift round of deadheading and they would bounce back with fatter, healthier blooms. Sebastian on the other hand...had grown rigid. He was glaring at a wasp perched on the rim of his glass.

Best say nothing. After all, Sebastian would prefer it that way.

If she grabbed Sebastian by the shoulders and gave him a good rattle, would any emotions fall out? Was it so awful to admit that you loved a person who had abandoned you or that wasps terrified you? As Sari had commented, everyone was frightened of something. Except for Rowena, who was more likely to skip toward danger, arms open, shouting, "Yippee!"

Sebastian cleared his throat, signaling that the wasp had gone. "Are you free next Saturday night?" he said. "For dinner at The Flying Duck?"

Symmetrical cubes of fruit—*that takes talent, James*—floated on the surface of her drink, refusing to sink. She looked up. "A date?" Might as well establish the ground rules.

"No, Tilly. Not a date." Sebastian picked at the back of his signet ring. "I'd like to talk to you in private."

Good thing she got that sorted, then. Tilly flicked imaginary lint from her sundress. Still, his timing was spot-on. She could ask for advice about buying Woodend. Her mother might be shut down to the idea, but if Tilly could get Sebastian on her side....

James appeared in front of them, silhouetted by brilliant sunshine.

He looked different today and strangely exotic in the setting of Woodend, like a black swan that had flown off course and found sanctuary in an alien habitat. Maybe it was his black silk shirt or the chunky swirls of earrings that reminded Tilly of the @ sign on a computer keyboard. Maybe it was the mere fact of his height, which meant he had to duck under every interior doorway of the house. Tilly was still trying to place him in her world, and then he smiled. His smile suggested he was drawing her into a conspiracy, which, technically he was. But even if you hadn't deciphered his code, it would be impossible to resist such an intimate gesture. He had that rare gift, the ability to give you his attention without distraction or restraint.

Tilly shifted her focus to her glass. "Cooking for the whole crew is above and beyond, James. Thank you."

"It's the least I can do," James said. "Since you've found me a room with a shower."

"Really?" Sebastian sounded bored. "Where?"

"With me!" Rowena released the baggie clip and swung her hair free. "Think I should warn him that my bathrooms are circa World War I, and the shower is a rubber contraption one has to shove up the taps?" She made a lewd gesture and laughed. "Makes sense, though," she explained to Sebastian, "since he and Tilly are going to be noses-deep in my soil every day."

James blinked several times, paused and blinked again. It seemed oddly ritualistic. Was this a compulsion, an outward sign of OCD? If he were standing closer, Tilly would put her arm around him, or stroke his back. Instead, she jiggled her head to catch his gaze, hoping he could read her intention. But before she could clock his reaction, she jumped.

Sebastian's arm had curled around her waist. His other arm claimed Rowena. And then he tightened his grip.

Fifteen

James threw his right leg on top of his left, and let his ankle rest on his knee. Good casual posture, just your average crazy waiting for his first gardening lesson. Despite being perched on the edge of the bench to avoid a small stain. He jiggled both legs like a psycho on an amphetamine high and fretted with the lace of his red Converse high-tops. *Red. The universal color of danger, of warning, of stop. Of stay away, Tilly, for your own sake.*

But she entered the walled garden with a wave. He wanted to wave back, honest to God he did. Instead, he jumped up and began wringing his hands as if washing them with air. What a stellar impersonation of Lady fucking Macbeth. Now what would Tilly think?

He couldn't do this. On no level could he do this.

The gate clanked shut behind her, and Tilly dumped the basket she called a trug on top of a mutant dandelion. Biggest fucking dandelion he'd ever seen. Dandelions. There had been dandelions at Maple View Farm that day everything had changed. The day Tilly had let him in. That was a sign, a good sign. Right?

"I don't suppose there's any point explaining that gardening is therapy for the soul?" Tilly said. "You look as if you're waiting to be hung, drawn and quartered. And I'm pretty sure that hasn't happened in Northamptonshire since the Tudors were knocking around."

His fingers flew to his hair and he scraped it back from his scalp in two fistfuls. Then he emitted a noise that was halfway between a choke and a laugh. Feral. He sounded feral.

"An apt analogy, but it could be worse, far worse." His speech raced. *Pull back, James, pull back.* "My fear thermometer hasn't hit a ten." His hands juggled imaginary weights. "It helps to grade fears. Ten being the worst. I'm at an eight." He pushed his hands into the pockets of his jeans and clutched at his legs. "Eight and rising."

"Peachy. Should I hide all the sharp implements?" Tilly nudged the trug with her foot.

James exploded into laughter laced with mania.

What must she think? Why was he putting her through this?

She was explaining something. He should listen. It could be the distraction he needed. As if. He was too far gone for distraction, the anxiety too high. He needed to crash and burn. Hit a ten and let it all out, but that wasn't an option. Never done a ten in public before. Ten was private hell. Private all the way.

You're panting. Stop panting. Slow it all down.

Breathe, concentrate on your breath.

Words. Tilly talking. Something about amending soil. Was she serious? Him? Pick up a fistful of soil and *shake it all about?* He gave two laughs, two hyena barks, as he pictured a conga line of people singing the Hokey Pokey.

Tilly gave him a quizzical look. "Is this a ten?"

"Nine and a half, nine and a half." He grappled with his T-shirt. He wanted to gouge through his clothes, through his skin.

Inside he screamed: *It's too strong. I can't control it.*

Tears stabbed behind his eyeballs and an image flashed, an awful image, one he couldn't ignore: Tilly—gray, wasted, ravaged by cancer, dying. *No, not Tilly, not Tilly.*

Fear ambushed him from all sides, telling him to knot his hands around themselves. If he did this six times Tilly wouldn't die; the soil she'd just shaken off that *Day of the Triffids* weed wouldn't contaminate her. She would not die.

"James." Tilly sat back on her haunches and peeled off her gardening gloves. "You haven't told me everything, have you?"

She had no idea, no fucking idea. What kind of a bastard was he to inflict this on her? He twisted his hands for the sixth and final time and then backed away. He hit something solid—the wall?—and sank to his heels.

"I'm sorry, I'm sorry." *I'm sorry, I'm sorry.* "I can't do this, Tilly. I thought I was ready. But I'm not. Get me out of here, please."

She walked over to him and held out her hand. All he wanted was to take it. To take her hand, to hold her goddamn hand. But he couldn't. She had a smear of dirt on her knuckle.

Tilly shrugged and smiled the most beautiful smile he had ever seen. "How about a stroll through The Chase?" she said. "I can guarantee it's unlike any place you've ever been."

He blinked his agreement, too exhausted for words.

The gnarled trees of The Chase created a wall of green so dark that your eyes saw black. Most newcomers dithered when they reached the kissing gate at the entrance to the wood, but

James entered without hesitation. His head grazed the tangle of dog rose and elder that arched over the gate, and a dusting of white blossoms fell to his black T-shirt like snowflakes.

Tilly took a deep breath and followed him in.

Immediately, the light changed from harsh morning sunshine to a soft, luminous yellow. Tilly loved the light in The Chase—like a dusky sky glowing with the charge of a million fireflies. The gardener in her called this bright shade, but the romantic in her preferred fairy light. She glanced down at the grass tickling her ankles. It was fluorescent, an unnatural tone that suggested magic lurked under every blade.

The cool shade thrown down from twisted, sagging boughs was refreshing after the dry heat. There was no shade in the walled garden, no relief from the day's brutal sunlight.

James stopped and Tilly took the lead. Arms above her head, she wove through the bracken where it reached over the path. Leaves wobbled a few feet from her, betraying the antics of wildlife. Squirrels or rabbits, she hoped, not adders. One poisonous snake this summer was one too many.

They joined the public bridle path, a trail worn bare by generations of ramblers and riders, and James pulled alongside her. She tripped several times over the hard, lumpy ruts of compacted earth. James, however, didn't even stumble. He seemed to have a sixth sense for the hazards ahead.

They moved deeper into The Chase, sidestepping tree stumps filled with new plant life and hoofprints sculpted out of caked earth. Echoes of traffic on the far side of The Chase disappeared, and the melodies of bullfinches, chaffinches and goldfinches—the bird songs Tilly had been listening for since arriving in Bramwell Chase—played all around them.

A brace of pheasants shot across the path, and Tilly felt a familiar jab of trepidation. She glanced over her shoulder, half expecting to catch history replaying itself. Walking here, usually alone, was the only time she believed in ghosts. She inhaled the intoxicating scent fermented over centuries: the musk of trampled earth, the odor of fox, the old-fashioned floral perfume that she could never quite identify. Once, not long after her father died, she could have sworn she'd smelled his cigars in this very spot.

"You love this place," James said. "Don't you?"

Tilly peered into a mass of red campion flowers. "Time stands still in The Chase, which I find reassuring. Rowena and I used to climb that tree." She pointed at a sprawling oak, its trunk bulging with knots. "And have picnics in that glade." She indicated a mass of dead bluebell heads skirting a grassy clearing.

"How old is The Chase?" James asked.

"Ancient. Used to be a royal hunting forest in the Middle Ages, but I'm sure it goes back way, way further. Can't you imagine druids racing through—"

"The beat of a horse's feet, and the swish of a skirt in the dew."

"Rudyard Kipling, 'The Way Through The Woods.'" She turned to examine the long, angular face with the large, almond-shaped eyes. "My favorite poem."

"Mine, too. I slept badly as a kid, so I read poetry in the middle of the night. Mainly about ghosts and ghouls. I think my subconscious was searching for answers, even then." He interlaced his fingers as if in prayer and held them under his chin.

They watched each other in silence.

"You're smiling," he said at last. "You had me cast as a techno-geek, didn't you?"

"Anyone less geeky I can't imagine. Although the ghost stories make sense. You're a little scary to a short woman, you know—I'm guessing over six foot?"

"Six feet two and a half inches."

"And that beard—"

"You don't like the beard?" He sounded like Isaac, hurt but eager to please.

"Nothing personal. I'm not a beard-moustache-goatee type of gal. Had it long?"

A buzzard circled high above them.

"No," he said. "It was an experiment. A failed one."

"Let's sit." She gestured to a downed bough lying beneath the multifingered limbs of a sweet chestnut tree. On the other side of the trunk there was a small heart engraved with the initials S.W. and T.H. followed by the word forever. Had Tilly honestly believed, at fifteen, that forever was real?

"Do you have chiggers here?" James cast his glance in every direction.

"No."

"Fire ants?"

"No."

"Poison ivy?"

"Nope. Just nettles. But keep your hands away from the undergrowth. Hogweed and bracken can bring you out in a nasty rash."

He swiveled around. "Bad?"

"James." The buzzard gave its plaintive mewing call. "Just sit."

He did, but writhed and squirmed as he positioned his legs. Finally, he dragged them up and rested his elbows on his knees. He kept his hands open, then began grinding his palms together, filling the air with the sound of flesh rubbing against flesh.

She preferred sitting when they talked; it diminished the space between them. Although, once again, he sat too close, his knee resting against hers so she could feel his warmth.

Tilly leaned forward, using the movement to wiggle space between them, and stole a glance at James.

He was pinching his skin randomly, covering his arm in angry pockmarks. She considered stopping him, as she had done when he'd attempted to fling himself from the car, but decided against it. Wherever he was, there wasn't room for two.

"So what's the story on the beard?" Tilly said.

"I wanted to be someone else."

"And why, exactly, would you want to be someone else?" She understood the New Year's pledge for self-improvement, the desire to become someone who didn't chew her nails or lose library books. But you couldn't erase the essence of you, and why would you want to try? Tilly picked up a small branch and traced patterns with it on the forest floor.

"If I were someone else," James said, "I could sit on a log without thinking of the consequences. Or pick up a stick as you just did. And some days?" He kicked aside a twig. Leaves rustled as it disappeared into a clump of stinging nettles. "I just need a break from being me. The guilt that you mentioned on the phone, is it survivors' guilt?"

She moved her head from side to side, trying to decipher the pattern she'd created in the dirt, but all she saw was a squiggle of circular lines that led back on itself. Should she talk about this? Probably not, since it was best to lock these things away and never examine them. To drag this out, to confront the memory, would only sharpen the pain. But since finding the lump, hadn't the memory begun to fester and ooze? She tossed the branch away and scooted farther back onto the log, wincing as bark scraped her skin.

A fox appeared ten feet ahead of them, froze and then padded away—one more living thing passing through her life. And Tilly remembered a nurse. Amazing, that she could recall new shards of fact from such a blank time, as if the memory were returning thread by thread. Yes, there had been a nurse with her in the doctors' lounge, the place where they had taken Tilly—isolated her—to give her the news. A nurse with warm hands who had brought comfort and a disgusting cup of tepid tea. And Tilly had lacked the heart to tell her she was a Brit who didn't drink tea. This nurse, this stranger, had been someone Tilly had held on to for a while. As she wanted to do now, with James.

"My guilt," she said, "is the guilt of failing my family."

A nuthatch hopped up a tree, with the simple goal of finding food. How easy life would be if you could live only in the moment, if you could erase the past and the future.

"I was doing pretty well in the big scheme of guilt." She tried to smile but it could have escaped as a grimace. "Then I found this lump, and here I am, stuck like a player in Monopoly with the *do not pass go, do not collect $200* card, wondering, yet again, if my husband died because of me."

Tilly rubbed her hands back and forth along her upper legs. The rocking motion felt good. Was that why James moved so much? Did an active body ease pain in the mind? "My husband had a living will. I don't. It was the one area of our marriage in which we agreed to disagree. He argued it would allow the three of us to move on quickly if something catastrophic happened. Whereas I pointed my moral compass north and refused to budge." She tugged on the back of her neck, her fingertips worrying at a tension knot. "I always thought there was time. To talk him round. Who knew time was the one thing we didn't have."

She refused to imagine what could have happened if David had woken up. "My husband was a brilliant man who had a horror of being trapped in an unresponsive body." She paused. "Like the sun in the walled garden, he was relentless in his need to shine. He had to maintain control, even in death, which is why I told the doctor about the living will. I thought that was what he wanted. And therein lies my mistake. Because—" she stared at the ground until it blurred "—I think he changed his mind."

A creature scratched on the forest floor. A woodcock? No, woodcocks were far too rare. There was a time she could identify every sound in The Chase. Not anymore.

Tilly sucked in her breath then forced it out. "He held on, for five days. They unhooked him, pulled the plug, and he held on. I remember being grateful—isn't that appalling?— that I could touch his skin and feel life. Some days I even convinced myself he was asleep. So he held on, and I watched him die. And did nothing. Afterward, I started thinking, questioning. Had he hung on for a reason? Had he, in the end, chosen life, expecting me to do the same?" Tilly wrapped her hand around her mouth and pinched her lips between her thumb and forefinger, squeezing as hard as she could. "Did you ever see *Groundhog Day?*"

"At least six times." James grinned. "I like repetition, remember?"

"I feel as if I'm the hero in that movie, constantly reliving the moment I said—" Tilly shuddered. She was back in the room where her life had stopped—listening to David slowly die.

"Your mind is stuck, like mine," James said, his voice hushed, the sort of voice you used in the middle of the night when everything around you was quiet.

"No one can share what goes on in here." He tapped his temple: two fingers, two taps. "But if you're lucky, you can find someone to help ease the pain."

With a deep sigh, he stood and stretched, his T-shirt rising up to reveal the tattoo she'd glimpsed a few days earlier. A man who was scared of everything had marked his body with a decorative, coiled snake. Why? Tilly tried to draw her eyes away, but she was captivated by the white skin on his abdomen, translucent against the black ink of the tattoo and much paler than the skin on his arms and his face. She tried to picture James sunbathing on a beach, listening to palm fronds clack in the breeze, but even in her imagination, he couldn't stay still.

"Tell me your story," she said. "I need to know."

He had tried to deflect the conversation from himself, but she'd outsmarted him. How much should he tell her? What could he risk exposing? How could he find words that didn't scare her? James often imagined himself trapped in a burning building where no one could hear him scream. But Tilly was offering to reach in. Could he accept her hand? She had trusted him; could he trust her? He picked at a small scab on the back of his wrist, and then snapped his fingers away when he released a trickle of blood.

"You're not turning bashful on me, are you, James?"

"I'm not good at editing my thoughts. I might say too much." And that was a terrifying truth.

"And bore me to death? Look around you…we're alone in a forest and I have nothing to do but listen. I told my mother and Isaac to forage for lunch, that I'd promised the day to you."

She'd promised the day to him. He didn't dare look at her. Didn't want to see pity or horror. What he did want to see, he had no right to hope for.

"It's hard when you're invested in the outcome," James said.

"But you've already made your impression, become a friend. The rest is merely frosting."

"Frosting?" He laughed, but kept his eyes lowered. If he looked up, he might kiss her.

"Yeah. Sometimes it's too sweet and you want to spit it out. Sometimes it's just sweet enough. Besides. I just told you something I've never told anyone. It's your turn to share."

"I wish this *were* just frosting. OCD is more like the basic ingredient of my life."

"Would it be easier for you if we walked? We can go forward." She signaled with her arm, waving as if directing a jumbo jet on the tarmac. "Or back. Even sideways. The choice is yours."

What had he done to deserve friendship from this woman? She was a karmic gift; she understood. He started walking, quickly, because the alternative was worse than a kiss. His body was burning with need for her. Right here. Right now. He couldn't allow himself to slow down, or worse, turn and face her.

A pheasant coughed and James strode ahead, his mind settling into a rhythm that matched his gait. The shade grew deeper, the brightness disappeared and the birdsong became less frequent. He drew strength from Tilly's presence, knew that with her behind him, he could speak words he had never uttered outside a psychologist's office. Still, it was, at best guess, ten minutes before he talked.

"OCD creates fear in the absence of real threat. It bombards you with unwanted thoughts and marshals your body to ward off danger no one else can perceive. The cause may be an illusion, but the terror is genuine."

That was pretty much his thesis statement, but where did his story go from there? Should he start with his mother or with his father? And then his memory stuck on the camping trip he and his dad took six months after his mother's death.

It was supposed to be a beginning, and in many ways it had been: the beginning of the end.

"A kid trips over a rotting log, says, 'Is it poisonous, am I going to die?' His dad laughs and says, 'Don't be ridiculous, that isn't poisonous.' The kid grabs at the reassurance and craves more, becomes locked in a cycle of escalating fear, a belief that he *is* about to die. But his dad sees only a rotting log. He loses patience, tells his self-absorbed son to snap out of it. When that doesn't work the father threatens, and delivers, punishment. How long before this boy internalizes his fears and transforms himself into a ticking bomb?"

"You were the boy," she said softly.

James twisted around, using his torso to pin back a branch, but he trained his eyes on the ground. When Tilly had passed, he resumed the lead.

"Ten years old, split open by grief, yet nothing terrified me more than my own thoughts, the uncertainty of what they'd tell me to do next." He sighed. "I masked my symptoms at school, but they exploded when I got home. Dinnertime became a fiasco because I couldn't stop washing my hands, and every morning I missed the school bus because of my rituals." Goodness, he could summarize all that horror in one sentence? "I'm not sure Dad recovered from either loss— Mom's life or my sanity."

"Dear God," Tilly said. "How did you both cope?"

"He shouted, rescinded my privileges and retreated in Jack Daniel's, where he stayed. And I slammed into anything that gave release—the speed of motorbikes, drugs, sex. I was casual with life, but for some reason I survived."

"Why do you twist your hair?" she asked. "I've been dying to ask, but I was worried it was too personal. Sorry, I'm just curious."

"Why apologize? Since we're baring our souls here, I think

all bets on intimacy are off." With every sentence he relaxed more. "It's a compulsion. The OCD tells me terrible things will happen if I don't twist my hair."

"What things?"

"Irrational things."

"Such as?"

"Catch cancer from you and die. Which sounds crazy, right?"

"No." Her voice sounded like a spoken shrug. "So a compulsion is a quick fix, right?"

"One as addictive as heroin." *Keep going, James. Keep going.* "Rituals start out small but become more complex as the fear mutates. If you make a mistake, any mistake, you must start over. Imagine how that translates for a kid struggling with homework. How can he complete the assignment when he's always checking, always erasing, always moving backward?"

"How did you?"

"I was a straight-A student who never slept." Shit, he didn't mean to turn and face her. Really, really didn't mean to do that. But when she smiled, he was pathetically glad he had.

Tilly put her hands on her hips and looked around. "I think we're lost."

"No, I know where we are." He wove his fingers together across his neck and stretched. Nothing he had said—so far—had shocked her. "It's good to talk, Tilly. Thank you."

A bird sang and her stomach gave a single, loud growl. God Almighty, how could he be so thoughtless? It was way past lunchtime; she must be starving.

"I'm sorry," James said. "Once my brain starts tumbling I forget everyone else isn't on the same carnival ride. Let's head back." He began walking again.

"Good plan. I'd hate to turn native and start eating nettles."

"You're good at using humor," he called over his shoulder.

"Laughter is a vital tool for diffusing anxiety. After all, the two are hardly compatible, unless people are making fun of you. No one jokes about a broken wrist, but you hear sniggers when you pick a dandelion with a handkerchief."

"We didn't laugh," she said. "That day at Maple View Farm."

"No." He slowed, allowing her to catch up. "You didn't."

Tilly had a fleeting sensation, one long forgotten, of relying on someone else to make decisions. Only minutes earlier she'd been staving off the panic of being lost, but James had wheeled around with purpose, and she had followed. She visualized him as a child, but shook away the mental picture of a young boy alone with his grief. Unbelievable, she had just done something James could never do: brush aside an unwanted thought. He was like a person without facial muscles, a person marked by a difference few could comprehend.

Despite the shade, the midday heat was building. She was eager to hear the heart of his story and get back to the garden. What was driving her impatience—hunger? Or was it the knowledge that her project with James was a hiatus from life, a distraction, a conversation she had struck up with a fellow traveler while stranded midjourney. It was a good conversation, but the kind that never survived beyond baggage claim. After all, when you cared about someone, you couldn't rush the learning. It took ten years of watching David with books to notice, in the last week of his life, that his lips moved when he read.

James strode ahead, his shoulder-length hair licking the neck of his figure-hugging T-shirt.

Tilly swallowed. "OCD must be hell on relationships."

He hesitated. "By the way, you should warn Rowena that I've reorganized her toolshed."

Well, that wasn't the answer she'd expected. In fact, it wasn't an answer at all. "She doesn't have a toolshed."

"She does now."

Tilly laughed. "So you're really a Virgo with a bit of extra umph."

"You're a Virgo?"

"God, no. I'm organizationally impaired. Surely you've guessed that by now. No, Sebastian's the Virgo. Anal as they come. Even in school his study had to be just so. If you picked up a Biro and didn't return it to the exact same spot?" She slashed a finger across her throat and made a gargling noise.

James trailed his fingers behind as if reaching for her, and Tilly almost skipped with joy. But when she leaned forward, he slipped his hand into his pocket. *Oh.* Poor man was probably just stretching again, or maybe she was hallucinating, thanks to hunger and heat. Anyway, he didn't hold hands. Tilly sighed. How she missed the everyday touches of a life shared.

James spun around, and Tilly jerked back. "Is Sebastian ancient history?" he said.

Why did James do that, ask questions that cornered her?

"I don't know." Tilly looked away, a flotilla of tiny black thunder flies the only witness to a blush that rose up her neck and wrapped itself around her cheeks.

"What about women?" She turned with a burst of brightness.

"What about women?" He smirked.

"Oh, you know." Tilly put on her ditzy voice, the one that was so useful when she wanted to hide. "Partners, lovers. Women—or men, if that's your fancy."

"No men, sorry to disappoint. I'm boringly heterosexual. But there have been a great many women in my life. Too many." The laughter in his eyes vanished. They began walking again, abreast this time. "Starting relationships was never my problem. Keeping them was the challenge, and not because of my compulsive behavior. My problem was the one my dad accused me of as a kid. Being self-absorbed."

"As a workaholic? Building your internet empire?"

"No, that came easily. I'm a stereotypical overachiever. Enough is never enough for me. But once you start running, leaving others behind, it's hard to stop." He flashed her a look. Was he talking about himself or issuing a warning? "I'm determined to change that. With a garden."

"But how?" Tilly heard restraint in her voice. She felt as if she were sneaking up on a rare creature, one easily startled.

"I've been reading about exposure therapy, when you expose yourself to your fears, starting with the smallest. Unfortunately, I don't function that way. I have to aim for the top." He hesitated. "Gardening is the main trigger for my obsessions. It's the key to everything."

"I mean no disrespect, but gardening is pretty benign." Tilly ran her fingers up the velvety flowers of a solitary foxglove, standing rigid amongst the bracken. How she loved wildflowers. The ninth circle of hell was, in Tilly's mind, reserved for wildflower pickers. What was it her father had said, that cut flowers smiled, but flowers in the ground laughed?

"How can anyone be frightened of gardening?"

"There's no logic to OCD, Tilly." James's voice was flat, his patience worn. "You conquer one fear…another detonates in your face. There's a viscous lump of anxiety inside me waiting to stick to anything I pass. I see mold on a tree—it's anthrax. I hear an alarm—it's warning of nuclear war. I look at a garden—I see cancer." A twig snapped under his foot. "I see my mother digging frantically, turning the soil with her handheld fork while my father explains to me that she's dying. And as she becomes sicker, and her garden withers, I feel cancer breeding in the soil, destroying her life and ours. Dirt, Tilly, is my greatest fear. I'm forty-five and terrified of dirt."

He gave an uncertain smile. *He's gauging my reaction,* she thought, *like Isaac does when he's desperate for my approval.*

"I'm a gardener who's terrified of worms. How ludicrous is that?"

He sighed, she assumed from relief, and continued talking. "I thought I had broken the cycle of anxiety. I distanced myself from my father, stumbled into yoga and threw myself into work, never allowing time for my thoughts to catch up."

"But something happened," she said, "to upset the balance. Am I right?" Oh crap, where were they going with all this?

He nodded. "Eighteen months ago my father died. We were estranged, but his death brought back a rush of issues, issues I need to face. Once again, my mind is under siege, haunted by images of dirt beneath my mother's fingernails, dirt she scrubbed off potatoes, dirt she trekked into the house, dirt—the conductor of disease and death." He stared at his hands as if they had betrayed him. Then he reached up and tugged on his hair. "Cognitive-behavioral therapy has helped, but it moves too slowly for me."

"What about medication?"

"There's no cure for OCD, Tilly. SSRIs, antidepressants, can take the edge off, but not if you have a low tolerance for them."

"Care to explain?"

"I became hyper," he snapped, and sped up.

A slither of bright light peeked through the overgrown opening ahead. They had reached the kissing gate.

"So how does all this end up on my nursery doorstep?" she said.

"They're instituting clinical trials at Duke University in exposure therapy. I sold the business, my apartment in Chicago, the farm, and moved south to be part of those trials. Unfortunately, they've been postponed until the spring, and I'm not a patient man. So I created a plan, one that involved you. Although my original idea was to watch you garden, then ease myself in when no one was around. But you've altered everything." He smiled. "And given me an opportunity. Do you believe in fate, Matilda Rose?"

The past brushed across the nape of her neck, and for a moment she considered bolting for the kissing gate, leaving James and his probing questions behind. No one ever called her Matilda Rose, except for her father.

"How do you know my full name?" Was he a stalker after all?

"Baptismal roll. I took a nocturnal walk yesterday and found the church open. I was quite surprised—I expected it to be locked."

"It should have been." She marched toward the kissing gate, but James reached it before she did. He held the gate steady, preventing her from swinging it around and squeezing through.

"You didn't answer my question," he said. "Do you believe in fate?"

He had done it again—jabbed at her weakness. Yes, she used to believe in fate, the same way she used to believe in forever. After all, without fate, how could she explain the random act of meeting David? But to talk about fate shifted the balance between her and James. Fate was a word with serious connotations. It was like glimpsing the tail of a black snake on the garden—a harmless snake, but still a snake—and knowing that she was in its territory, destined to spend the rest of the summer gardening with one eye casting around for its presence.

"I want to believe that people who need each other find each other." She stared up into eyes that had grown tawny in the light of The Chase, speckled with gold like a stone flecked with mica. "And I want to believe that you can move through another person's life and make a difference, feel richer for the experience." And if not, what did she have to lose? A fortnight, a fleeting period of time. Little more than a hiccup.

"Tell me what I need to know," she said, "if you hit a ten."

James grinned. When he smiled, really smiled, it transformed him, smoothed out the sharp edges. And suddenly, she yearned to touch his face.

"Did Isaac have night terrors," James said, "when he was younger?"

She nodded. "Some."

"How did you handle them?"

"Guided him back to bed and then lay on the floor until he slept peacefully."

"Then you know what to do. Once I start spiraling it's a question of waiting out the storm. I'm sorry. You don't need this right now, do you?"

"I was widowed at thirty-four. I can weather the odd storm."

James stepped back and Tilly entered the confined space created by the swinging gate. She was neither in The Chase, nor in Bramwell Hall's park. She was in no-man's-land.

"There is a positive side," James said, "to hitting a ten. Your body can't sustain a level of anxiety that high for long."

"Lovely. Remind me of that when we're both in hell. What if we forget digging and start with pruning, the favored chore of gardening neat freaks? Some gardeners will tell you to prune in the spring, some in the fall, but it's codswallop. You prune when your secateurs are sharp. Are you game to try?"

"Terrified, but it won't stop me." He held out his hand and they both watched it vibrate. "And now that I've scoured myself raw, you're still here, Matilda Rose. Why is that?"

Tilly stared at the barbed wire fence that penned the sheep in the park. A cobweb of wool, snagged on the wire, shivered in a snatch of breeze. "I used to prattle endlessly to Isaac about plants. 'Shall we pot up those salvias? Have an adventure and sell them at the farmers' market?' My hobby became our lifeline and then my business. Gardening saved my sanity."

"But it destroyed mine." James followed her through the kissing gate.

"Exactly. And that's the most heartbreaking thing you've told me today."

Sixteen

"I've found nirvana," Tilly groaned.

James dragged his hands up her back, elbowed her straw hat into her lap and slowly stretched her spine. If not for his hands keeping her upright, she would dissolve into a puddle of bliss all over Lady Roxton's bench. His fingers crawled up into her hairline and kneaded her scalp in lazy, circular strokes that tingled through every nerve ending.

"Where did you learn massage?" she wheezed.

"I pay attention to what feels good." James leaned over the back of the bench and she caught the sour odor of sweat. After two hours of hauling debris to the bonfire in fierce afternoon heat, she felt pretty ripe herself, not that it seemed to bother James. He leaned closer still. "Your nirvana is called the will-you-marry-me stroke."

"And the answer would have to be yes," she said and tensed. *Bugger.* Was she flirting? Worse, would he *think* she was flirting? She was so out of practice with men, and trying to make sense of where she was heading with James was harder than driving on a country road at night in a doozy of a thunderstorm—with a flat tire and no headlights.

He collapsed beside her, legs flung open, arms flung out. How could someone who waged a constant war against his mind be so assured in his body? Every time he stretched she got goose bumps, honest to God. Were his fluid movements payoffs from all that yoga? Amazing, that he could stand on his head every morning—chest bare, eyes closed—and not even wobble. Headstands balanced his mind, he'd explained. And revealed his abs, Rowena had commented.

James rumbled through a slow, deep moan. And Tilly had the same weird feeling she experienced when a thunderstorm brought the smell of ozone to the forest—that palpable awareness of unharnessed energy surrounding her.

"Didn't I warn you gardening was a serious workout?" Tilly tried to move, but the muscles in her lower back had locked. "Think of the fortune you'll save on gym fees."

"Right," James said.

High above, jackdaws mocked.

Tilly winced as her right shoulder blade throbbed with sickening persistence. She had overdone it, again, and would have to relinquish a chunk of her evening to lying supine on the floor, legs stuck up in the air with a hot water bottle jammed under her spine. Still, it was worth it. Those perennials in the white border finally had room to breathe. The bed was too neat, like an overclipped show dog, but as the season wore on the plants would settle; the garden would find its character. *A job bloody well done.* Sari might have been right, about expanding into garden design. Although Tilly's talent appeared not to be creating, but rescuing. Garden rescue, now that was an idea to ponder.

After James flew home at the end of next week, she would finish what they had started. Sadness nudged at her. In six days, she and James had established routines. She would miss them, and she would miss James. Although probably not his endless need to check the bonfire every few minutes. No, she would miss that, too. And the way he pruned: legs split, breathing even, bottom lip caught between his teeth. He pruned only from the path—refusing to step on the garden—but even so, his spirea was the first symmetrical spirea she'd ever seen. Too symmetrical; Tilly preferred her plants unkempt.

Slowly, so as not to aggravate her back, Tilly reached down and snapped off a piece of creeping thyme. "Monday morning we move on to deadheading perennials. For the sake of the shrubs." She crushed the thyme between her fingers and inhaled the citrus scent. "Here, smell this."

James cupped his hands under hers, raising her palm as if to drink from it. His hands were steady and his breath warm, but he twisted a fraction, as if to rest the weight of his head in her hand, and the bristles of his beard grated across her skin. Tilly couldn't help it—she flinched. And James pulled back.

"Smells like thyme," he said, as if nothing had happened. Maybe it hadn't.

Tilly sighed. "Exactly. I think you should start with a herb garden, when you get home."

"Good idea." He blinked slowly. His eyelashes, the color of a sable paintbrush, were too long, too beautiful for a man. "But I won't be returning home for a while."

Now what was he up to? And why did she have a niggling feeling it included her?

"I've changed my flight to an open ticket." He tossed back his hair. "You won't learn anything at the appointment, so I'm staying until you have the results. What have you told your mother and Isaac, about next Friday?"

The gardening spell broke; the day was ruined. After the

letter had arrived that morning, Tilly had told James about the appointment, then pushed it from her mind. But he couldn't leave things alone, could he? He had to pick at the details.

Tilly considered the foul-smelling dipping pond. Behind it, the now-silent cherub fountain held open its arms as if to say: "This is all I have left to offer, a putrid spill of algae slime and mosquito larvae."

"I've told them another lie." She kicked at the gravel, and the letter from the breast clinic crinkled in her back pocket. "That we're visiting a specialist nursery. And I'm rancid with guilt."

"Rancid with guilt?" James gave a small smile.

"Isaac accused me of being mean, for not allowing him to join us. It's the first time he's said anything hurtful to me."

"Wait until he's sixteen and vows to hate you for the rest of his life." James stood, clasped his hands behind his back and bent slowly at the waist. Tilly looked away.

"I'll make it up to Isaac," James continued. "But you'll have to deflect questions about the outing. I'm not wired for lying."

"An OCD thing?" Tilly turned back to watch him, her interest piqued.

"Obsessive truth telling." James ran his hands up and down the small of his back.

"Really?" What fabulous information. Too fabulous to ignore. "How's your sex life?"

The world around them was as still and as quiet as her forest during a snowfall.

Omigod, how could I ask that? Tilly grabbed her wide-brimmed straw hat and shoved it back on, hoping to conceal her flaming cheeks. "That was totally out of line. I can't begin to apologize for being so, so…it's just there's a level of comfort when we're…you know…I feel I can say anything, well, obviously not anything." She shook her head. "You can help me out here, you know. Jump in, anytime."

"I'll take it as a compliment that you asked." He raised his eyebrows. "Although I have no intention of answering your question."

"See? This is why I don't want clients. I get too friendly and then ask completely inappropriate personal questions." Why did she feel so ridiculous? Most men she knew would leap into any conversation about sex, but never divulge one thing about their emotional lives. With James, who could fathom the ground rules? It was as if he did everything backward. There were moments when she knew him intimately, followed by moments—this being one—when she didn't know him at all.

"Let me redeem myself by asking something totally bland," she said. "What do you do for fun?"

He raised his eyebrows again.

"Other than cooking," she said with deliberation.

"I go rollerblading."

She gawked at him, open-mouthed. Was he joking? The guy who was terrified of everything had a lethal hobby? You couldn't pay her to strap on a pair of Rollerblades!

"I'm attracted to speed." James shrugged. "You're not a fan?"

"I'm fearful of wobbly things with wheels. No sense of balance, you see. And besides, I took a nasty header over some handlebars when I was Isaac's age." She paused, remembering chewing with a swollen face, rolling onto bruises at night, and stiffness that lingered in her joints for weeks. "I have a long memory for pain."

"I gathered that. However, it is heartening to know you're fearful of more than worms." He bent down and began retying the lace on his right sneaker, even though it was tied in a flawless double bow. "What's your greatest fear?" he said. "Dying?"

"No. Dying and leaving my child alone." She banged her palm against her head. "Sod it. I really don't want to think about this, James. Please don't make me."

His hair, which had flopped forward to shield his face, was almost long enough now for a ponytail. Underneath it was mahogany-colored, untouched by gray. He must have been a heartbreaker when he was younger. Although probably not as sexy as he was at forty-five.

She gouged out some dirt from under her fingernail.

"Distraction will ease you through the week ahead, lower your anxiety." His voice sparked with mischief. Whatever he was planning, she didn't want to know. "Which brings me back to Rollerblades."

"No, it doesn't. I need less stress in my life, not more. And I was perfectly distracted until you brought up the subject, thank you."

"You're welcome. Think of it as your exposure."

"That's a cheap shot."

"How about a pact?" James straightened up. "If I can restore Rowena's herb garden by myself, you come skating with me. The old road behind the Hall is perfect for Rollerblades. Perfect."

"It's full of potholes. Very, very, *very* not perfect."

A scenario popped into her mind: James fighting with a lover, slamming a door, then rushing back into the room to apologize and throw himself into earth-shattering makeup sex. Fabulous, now she was a voyeur. Or was that a pervert?

"The potholes are at the far end." One corner of his lips puckered in a quivering smile.

Crap, he looked far too smug. "And you know this how?"

"I've been skating there every morning." He pulled his

sunglasses from the V of his T-shirt and put them on. "I never leave home without my blades." His smile grew. She was stumped, and he knew it.

She rose and was instantly eclipsed by his height. "You travel with Rollerblades? In your suitcase? You're weird, you do know that. I mean, I like weird...weird is good, outstanding really, but— What's wrong?"

James was transfixed by a pile of rubble on the other side of the Tibetan rhubarb. Silently, he pushed Tilly behind him and held her there. "Hey, what the—"

"Yes!" he whispered. "I thought it was—a female adder."

"What?" Tilly poked her head around his arm and spied a flash of something that resembled the pattern on a copperhead's skin. She gulped.

"Snakes were my childhood obsession. A good obsession for once. I love snakes."

"Bully for you, because they terrify me shitless. Why do you think I hate worms?" The tattoo was about a boyish fantasy? Snakes and Rollerblades. Unbelievable. She kept searching for some common denominator, but really, there was nothing to bind them beyond grief.

"Is Isaac still reading his comic book on the lawn?" James gave her a gentle push. "Go, fetch him. I'll keep an eye on the adder."

"I am not bringing my child near a venomous snake."

"Tilly, I know what I'm doing. Trust me." His head moved from side to side as he appraised the snake. "Aren't you beautiful," he said.

He made it sound so simple: *Trust me.* But trust was a quagmire. Take one step too far and you sank. And so could your child. To relinquish control of Isaac's safety to James was to hurl herself into the unknown, and possibly place her child in danger. And that was not a risk she was willing to take, which didn't explain why she was halfway to the gate.

"You told me England didn't have poisonous snakes, Mom. Right after we found the copperhead. You said that if we lived in England we wouldn't have to worry about poisonous anything." Isaac glared at her, hands on his hips. Where had this new contrariness come from? Was he mimicking Archie, or was he resentful of James?

"Did I say that? I'm sorry." See? She should know better than to lie to her child. If she wasn't careful he would excavate her biggest lie of all and discover that she and James were visiting a breast clinic the following Friday, not a nursery in the Chilterns.

"Is it dead?" Isaac inched toward the snake, but James held out an arm, like a protective bar, to halt him.

"Sluggish in the heat." James squatted down to Isaac's eye level. "Would you like to help relocate her?"

"Absolutely not!" Tilly yelled. "This isn't a Boy Scouts' cookout."

"Can I, Mom? Please?" Big Haddington eyes melted Tilly's resistance.

"I know what I'm doing," James said to her. "As a teenager I spent summers working for a wildlife expert, rescuing snakes from yards and playgrounds. He trained me well. Very well. I've dealt with water moccasins."

"Cottonmouths?" Isaac gave a whoop of admiration. "Are they *totally* aggressive?"

"Not without severe provocation." James smiled. "They're sorely misunderstood. As are many of us. But before we do anything, Isaac, I want to make sure you understand one thing." He placed his hands on Isaac's shoulders. "You must never, ever try this. If you find a snake, any snake, you leave it alone. You with me, buddy?"

Isaac nodded as if he were pledging allegiance.

"Good. Even a nonvenomous snake can give a nasty bite if threatened."

"Why don't we leave this one alone?" Isaac asked in a reverential tone.

"Trapped in a walled garden with two noisy humans scaring away her food supply is far from ideal. And with that rabbit wire under the gate, I doubt she can escape without getting snared. Besides, your mom looks petrified. If we don't move this snake, that'll be the end of my gardening lessons." James stood. "He'll be fine, Tilly. I've done this many, many times."

"You have. He hasn't."

"No, I mean I've done this with a kid. Well, not in a while. My son's twenty-seven now and a successful environmentalist. Although he kept the promise he made at sixteen—to hate me. Nealys are stubborn to the core."

Words scrambled around her mind, but sentences didn't form. "Bloody hell," she said.

"Mom!" Isaac giggled.

"Bloody and hell," James agreed. "Both accurately describe fatherhood at eighteen."

Eighteen. If she'd been a mother at eighteen, Sebastian would be her child's father, a child who wouldn't be Isaac. She and Sebastian would have stayed together. She might never have gone to college. She certainly wouldn't have spent five years in London working as a publicist for a textile company. And she would never have met David. Or would they have met anyhow, and it would have been too late? So much of life was chance, wasn't it? Stopping to ask directions and falling in love, picking a landscaper out of a phone book and finding someone to share your pain. But parenthood at eighteen? No wonder James had retired at forty-five. He must have burned out on life.

"I thought you said no spouses?" she croaked.

"I did. Marriage isn't for me; I'm a serial monogamist. My son's mother was my first great love, but she moved on to the captain of the football team with some haste."

"Mom, what does mon-ogy-amist mean?"

"That you're loyal and faithful to the woman you love," James replied without missing a beat. Tilly shivered, a deep head-to-toe shiver. "Isaac," James continued. "Rowena has some potato sacks in her shed. Go find one. We're going to bag us a snake."

"Aye, aye, Captain!"

"Tilly? See if Rowena has anything I can use as a snake hook. A long-handled grabber would be ideal. A yard broom will do if you can't find anything else. An adder!" James cracked his knuckles and moved forward. Transfixed, Tilly watched, seeing the child inside the man. Had this boy, who was so thrilled by nature, been as carefree as Isaac until grief and fear had capsized his world?

"James," Tilly said slowly. "You might want to look at where you're standing."

"Shit. I'm on the garden. I'm on the garden!" His hands shot to his hair. "Tilly?"

"Yes?"

"Help?"

James loomed out of the heat haze with an empty hessian sack slung over his shoulder like a slimmed-down, out-of-season Santa Claus. Isaac skipped to catch up, every step a bounce of joy. Their chatter filtered through the chirps and tweets coming from The Chase, but neither James nor Isaac acknowledged her; they were lost in boy pleasure.

Could it have been any more obvious that James was a father? How had she failed to notice? How had he failed to mention it? Once again, he had blindsided her with revelation. Or was that betrayal? If he could keep his fatherhood from her, what else was he hiding? He had confessed so much, yet held back more. What kind of a man revealed his secret fears, but never once bragged about his son? Was James cavalier with his parenthood, which was reason enough to dislike him, or did he not trust her enough?

Hate, James had used the word *hate* in the context of his relationship with his son, and yet Isaac lit up around James. How could that be?

Tilly walked toward them, trying not to run. Should she be worried? Had James committed some heinous act against his son? Or was he incapable of sustaining a close relationship? And why did that last thought hurt so much more than the others?

Her shoulder blade started to throb again. Truth was, she didn't know what to think. She nipped at a stalk of seeded grass and pulled upward, catching the seeds in her palm. Then she tossed them toward the white-hot sky and followed their progress as they twirled back down. James had told her fighting OCD meant one step forward, ten back. But that was how she felt right now, about their friendship. Although this was more than a few steps backward. This was a ruddy huge leap in the opposite direction.

"Did you have lots of copperheads on the farm?" Isaac asked James.

"Yeah." James gave a laugh and tried to push away the riot of memories. He shook back his hair but couldn't dislodge the swarming images of his father cussing him. "I used to organize copperhead hunts to freak out my dad."

"Whoa. Excellent. Would've freaked out my dad, too. He hated snakes and bugs and pretty much the whole outdoors."

"That doesn't seem to be a problem for you."

"Nah. I get my love of nature from Mom," Isaac said.

James had forgotten how he loved kid-conversation. Why had he walked away from fatherhood? Laziness, he supposed. Or possibly guilt over whether his unreasonable demands for perfection had contributed to his son's adolescent breakdown. Whatever the cause, nothing could alter the truth that he had failed Daniel as a parent. He had never intended to mention the disastrous fact of his fatherhood to Tilly. Ever. Must have been the excitement of finding the adder. What a beauty, and interpreted by his warped brain—that sought meaning in everything—as a good omen, one that had lowered his guard.

James had never believed in sharing. Sharing was not good; sharing just tore you apart. The shock on Tilly's face had pretty much confirmed why he kept his personal life private. Now she knew the whole truth: that he had no family left to call his own. How long before she figured out he was to blame? And how would such a devoted mother, daughter and wife respond to that?

James sighed. "And what do you get from your dad?"

"Love of math."

"He was a math professor?"

"Nope. Economics. He wrote a book about *globalll-izzz-ation* that was *so* famous it was on the *New York Times* bestseller list. We still get money from it, money Mom uses for my education." Isaac gave a proud nod. "She says Daddy would have liked that."

Isaac skipped on ahead but James stopped. Silverberg. *David* Silverberg?

"I don't suppose your father was David Silverberg?" James said.

"Yup." Isaac looked around like a startled jackrabbit. "You've heard of him?"

What were the chances, eh? What were the fucking chances. "I've read his book." Not only read it, but bought twelve copies for Christmas gifts. He felt he owed David some royalties.

"You and every other businessperson in North America," Tilly said, striding toward them, looking pissed as hell.

Daniel, David... Panic tightened across his chest. Thank God he didn't believe in tarot, because if he did, he'd be holding a deck of death cards. That was it. The end of any hope he'd ever, ever had with Tilly. Talk about cruel cosmic jokes. Wasn't it bad enough that he had to deal with the pretty-boy ex-lover who represented everything James wasn't: dad-of-the-year and a man so stable other people trusted him with their money? Now James had to contend with ghosts, too?

"Where's the adder?" Tilly said.

"We relocated it." Isaac swaggered up to her. "Down near the stream. We thought that was best, didn't we, James?" Tilly wrapped her arms around her child—a little too tightly, given Isaac's resistance. The glance she threw at James was definitely a warning to back off. See? Sharing was bad. No way would he tell her about David.

"Hey, James." Isaac bobbed free. "Rowena's taking me badger watching tomorrow while Mom and Sebastian have their hot night out. I get to stay up really late. Wanna come?"

"Hot night?" Tilly said. "What are you talking about?"

"Ro says you and Sebastian have always had the hots for each other. She says you like each other so much you might have a sleepover."

"Isaac!" Tilly blushed. "Sebastian and I aren't... We don't—"

"Thank you, Isaac," James said. *Slow down, James, slow down everything, then walk away.* "I'd love to come badger watching. But if you'll both excuse me—" he turned toward the Hall "—I have a migraine coming."

Seventeen

"KBO, keep buggering on." Rowena sat cross-legged on the floor, wearing a blue camisole that barely covered her breasts and what had to be the ugliest pajama pants James had ever seen. They were covered in tartan Scottie dogs. A bottle of single malt and two cut glass tumblers sat next to her on the threadbare Oriental rug. So much for sneaking out into the night.

James leaned against the archway at the entrance of the great hall. "Keep buggering on—is that English for 'suck it up'?"

"More like British war mentality. Sir Winston Churchill used to say it. He also said, 'If you're going through hell, keep going.' Wise man, for a politician."

With its leaded window three stories high, empty stone fireplace the size of a carport, and oil still lifes of dead game birds, the room that had once hosted Queen Elizabeth I was definitely a suit of armor short of a Scooby-Doo soundstage. And yet each time James stepped down into the great hall, as he did now, the room reached out and welcomed him, despite the plethora of lamps. The artificial light was overly cheerful, but the squishy floral sofas and sagging armchairs said, "Come sink in us," and the sound system, ten years out of date but still impressive, begged to be switched on and cranked to full volume. There was a hint of raucous parties and sedate social gatherings long gone, but no personal detail beyond two photographs—one of a smiling baby Isaac, the other of Tilly as a radiant bride. James swallowed shame and glanced away. How could he look at that picture now and not see the man whose absence filled the silver frame? How could he not have realized Tilly's husband, a brilliant man with the last name Silverberg, was *the* David Silverberg? But why had she never referred to his first name? And why didn't Virginia have at least one photograph of her son-in-law in the house? What a sick comedy of errors.

"You could venture forth on another nocturnal walkabout and brood over tomorrow night's date—" Rowena patted the floor next to her "—or get shit-faced with me. It's good to have options, isn't it?"

James hesitated. He desperately, pathetically, wanted approval from Tilly's oldest friend, but Rowena made him wary. She was charming and eccentric, but her flamboyant surface concealed ice and steel. She was a werewolf in a Wonderbra. Although clearly she wasn't wearing one tonight.

He scanned the worn carpet for dog hairs and dirt but it looked surprisingly clean. Old but well cared for. Finally, he sat and eased his legs into the Lotus position.

"How's the headache?" she said.

"Be a lot worse tomorrow if I drink tonight." He reached for the bottle.

"Did you know—" Rowena moistened her lips "—that Sebastian and Tilly were about to reconcile when she met David?"

"Clearly not from Tilly's point of view."

"Actually, yes. Tilly always bounces back to Sebastian. He's her foundation, her rock."

God Almighty, when those green eyes locked on you, you felt like prey.

"She'd invited him for the weekend," Rowena continued, "but he had to cancel at the last minute—some crisis at work. A decision that haunts him still, I suspect."

Outside, an owl hooted. James downed his whiskey in one gulp and winced as it burned his esophagus. "Is there a point to this?"

"James, I like you. I see you as a kindred spirit, another reformed wild child. Or not so reformed?" She flashed a smile that made him shiver. "Tilly barely knows where she belongs these days. She needs space, she needs time, she needs to sort through her feelings for Sebastian. She doesn't need—no offense—you."

He couldn't fault her on that one. "Are you in love with her?" James said. The question shocked him; he had no idea why he'd asked it.

"I owe Tilly my life." Her green eyes hardened. "Never underestimate what I will do to protect her and Isaac."

James refilled his glass and raised it in a toast. "In that case, you and I have more in common than you realized."

Perfection—unless you were a Virgo—was vastly overrated. Sebastian was clucking over some hairline scratch on the passenger door when Tilly swung around to unfasten her seat belt and froze midwhimper. Her back ached so much she wanted to laugh. She should listen to her body more, read the symptoms that shouted, "Stop!" But quitting had never been one of her talents. If it had been, she wouldn't have spent years drifting across Sebastian's wake, dragging him through the mess of on-again, off-again. And here they were once more, on the brink of something that felt precarious even before it had begun.

"Is your back bothering you?" With one hand resting on the roof of his Jaguar, Sebastian reached in to help. Tilly nodded, unease squirming in her stomach. He was too close, his aftershave too thick, and oh cripes, his head was parallel with her boobs. Ugh, she had forgotten these tussles of sexual attraction, the thrill of sensing your body spark pitted against the terror of feeling you were attempting to stand in a dinghy that was pitching in a monstrous swell.

"My back hasn't been this bad since I was pregnant." *Bugger it*. Was her speech filter completely defunct? "God, Sebastian, I'm sorry. My brain, my mouth, there's a missing link."

"Don't worry about it. I don't intend to." He unclicked her seat belt and paused to touch her arm. "How did you get those scratches?"

"Pruning. Well, James prunes. I haul away debris." She gave her we're-one-big-happy-family smile and tried to pull herself from the car. Sebastian gave a *huh,* which could have been a sigh or a laugh—who knew—and, slipping his arm around her waist, heaved her out like a sack of spuds.

"I thought James was the pupil." Sebastian released her. "Did you skip the lesson on indentured servitude?"

"Ha. Ha." She fumbled with the rayon of her short, flippy dress, desperately searching for pockets, or rather, a way to keep her hands busy. Were they shaking?

Sebastian aimed his key ring at the Jaguar, and the car flashed and beeped. Once, she would have teased him for locking a car in Bramwell Chase, but that was before a national gang of thieves stole lead from the church roof and the butcher was robbed at gunpoint. Tilly wanted to believe that Bramwell Chase had remained the dozing hamlet of her childhood, where the most salacious news was that a dog had worried the sheep, but since she was currently facing a cookie-cutter housing development on what had once been her favorite pasture, Tilly knew that was no longer true.

"James is a little phobic about soil, so he chops and I pick up," she said. Was that a betrayal of James?

"He's phobic? About soil?"

"We've got it under control." She strode toward the pub, and Sebastian followed.

A car whooshed past and Sebastian stepped around her so that they could walk as they had always done, with Tilly tucked safely on his inside.

"Tilly." This time there was no mistaking Sebastian's sigh. "You're alone with a strange man all day and Rowena's alone with him at night. How much do you really know about James?"

Tilly shrugged. *Plenty…enough…nothing.*

She stepped down into the cool stillness of the pub, and a memory blasted. The last time she came here with Sebastian was to drop the news that she planned to marry another man. Well, that was an auspicious beginning to Sebastian-and-Tilly Act Two-and-three-quarters. Except this wasn't a date. Sebastian had made that clear.

She grabbed at an older, happier memory—Sebastian reeking of Brut cologne and giggling as they huddled behind the inglenook where no one could see them grope. Bugger. That just reminded her that they were picking at the carcass of a teenage relationship.

She walked carefully across the uneven sixteenth-century flagstones. This was a floor to pay attention to, a floor that had tripped up many a drunk, including Sebastian the night he had learned about David. Shit. Was she becoming obsessive?

Could you contract OCD through osmosis? Tilly shook the thought away.

Yuck, the pub stank of manufactured floral scent. And was that classical music playing, oh, so softly in the background? What had happened to the cigarette smog and the yeasty smell of spilt beer, the thrum of darts spearing their target, the jukebox stuck in the sounds of the eighties? The jukebox had been ripped out and the dartboard replaced by a garish print of a fox that could have been a pro- or an anti-hunting statement. More disturbing still, the toweling beer mats reeked of fabric softener.

"Bit different since the brewery chain took over, isn't it?" she said.

Sebastian signaled the barmaid with a discreet nod. "It's ruined," he replied, and then ordered two gin and tonics without consulting her.

Tilly nodded at a handful of villagers whose genealogy she could trace by reading gravestones in the cemetery. They had remained loyal to the pub, despite grousing to Rowena about the changes, but they would never accept Sebastian. To them, he would always be a weekender, an outsider. She should warn him that if he intended to rebuild his life, Bramwell Chase might not be the place to start.

Thankfully, Sebastian agreed to sit in the garden. Tilly loved the long hours of English twilight living, when blackbirds trilled and the evening air became heavy with the perfume of nicotiana. In North Carolina summer darkness fell instantaneously at eight-thirty. And noisily, thanks to the tree frogs.

A gaggle of children giggled as they raced between the tables and trestle benches, and Tilly listened for her child. It was an instinct she couldn't outgrow. And with it came the sad acceptance that she would never have another child.

Despite David's reticence, she had dreamed of a large family. But that dream lay buried along with her husband. And now she was back before any of it existed, in the place where she and Sebastian had pledged their love with more engraved initials. Goodness, they had certainly stamped everything as theirs. Had they been that confident in their future?

"Too bad," Sebastian said. "The old tables are gone. Would've been fun to find one with our initials on."

They used to do that the whole time—pick up fragments of each other's thoughts. How did you move on from that closeness, that bond you had believed could never be broken, and yet, somehow, you'd managed to discard like an old report card from middle school?

Tilly sat at the first vacant table, scooting along the bench so Sebastian could sit next to her. He didn't. He settled opposite, then picked up a cardboard beer mat and dismembered it layer by layer.

"Want to tell me why you look like a kid who smashed a cricket ball through the kitchen window?" Tilly sniffed the posy of sweet peas in the middle of the table.

Sebastian grinned. "I didn't want to admit this, Tilly, but I've missed you."

"There's another *but* coming."

"Yes, there is. First, though, an apology for being such a git last weekend." Sebastian tugged on his signet ring. "I don't handle emotion well."

That was an understatement. "Does anyone?"

He pushed aside the scraps of beer mat. "I never meant to hurt you after David died, and I certainly don't intend to hurt you now." He took a deep breath. "I want to stay in Bramwell Chase, put down roots." Had Sebastian ever said "I want" before? "I need," "I'd like," but "I want"? "I want to buy here. A house that lends itself to children."

"No," she whispered. No. That was her line. "Please, anything but that."

"Tilly, someone has to buy Woodend. Why not me?"

Because I want to buy it, even though I can't afford to, and my mother doesn't want me to, and my child will be devastated, and my nursery will go belly-up and.... "Because. Because you might marry again and not let me in the door. Because you might rip out the herbaceous border and put in a swimming pool." *Because I love Woodend, and I always will. Because returning home is my dream, the only one I have left. Don't steal it from me.*

"A pool? That's not a bad idea." He offered up his crooked smile as reconciliation: Sebastian at his most irresistible.

"Don't, Sebastian. This isn't funny. If you must know, it stinks." And that was putting it mildly.

"What if I promised you'd always be welcome?" He reached for her hand, but she wrenched it free.

Was perpetual hurt their new cycle? "Yuck. That's something you say to a vicar—'Do drop by for tea'—not the women you had sex with in every venue from a historic ruin to the backseat of your mother's Mini."

"Shh. Tilly. Not so loud."

"Don't shush me. You can't do this, Sebastian. You can't take my home."

"Your mother's home, which she intends to sell." He took her hand again but this time flipped it over.

"Nitpicker." She clung to her fury even as it faded. No way would she give in and make nice, no matter how softly his thumb traced a never-ending circle on her palm.

"Yilly, Yilly, quite contrilly."

His thumb stopped moving and they stared at each other.

"Christ, I'd forgotten I used to call you that."

"So had I," mumbled Tilly.

★ ★ ★

Being with Sebastian was like ambling around a friend's garden and pausing to enjoy the expected. They laughed over Tilly's screams of pleasure that had fueled the gamekeeper's insistence of ghostly goings-on at the Dower House, and Sebastian relived the moment of their meeting. He told Tilly that she had been the most beautiful, fragile-looking creature he'd ever seen, and how appalled he had been when she'd started swearing at the gang of boys teasing her. "The mouth on you," he said, shaking his head.

But then he asked permission to approach her mother about Woodend, and Tilly plummeted back into confusion. She wanted to scream at Sebastian, tell him he couldn't buy Woodend, but what was the point? He would shoot her down with reality, would force her to think in black-and-white, and she liked every shade in between.

Tilly watched a daddy longlegs hover over the table then whirl away with small, jerky movements. "My father believed houses are emotional tape recorders," she said, "that they record the past and hit Replay when you trigger a memory. Woodend is my tape recorder. You'll never shake the ghosts."

"Woodend was my refuge, too, and it could be one for my children. They're living in a rented flat, for Christ's sake, trying to adapt to life in England, the separation, their mother's pregnancy, a man they hardly know...." He shrugged off his jacket, slung it over the bench next to him and rolled up his shirtsleeves. More linen. How did he have the patience for all that ironing? His metal watch strap clacked against the edge of the table. "Tilly, please. My children need this."

Even if her heart exploded into a gazillion pieces, how could she argue with that?

"Do you remember what we used to say?" Tilly drew a line through the condensation sliding down her glass. "If

Woodend was ours, we'd build an aviary and fill it with budgies?"

"And a pair of lovebirds," he added.

"I don't think I can watch you do this."

"But you won't have to. You'll be back in North Carolina." His voice grew hesitant. "Won't you?"

"I have two plane tickets that say I leave England on August 7, but I've been thinking about my mother growing old alone, about where I belong…. Truth is, part of me has never left Bramwell Chase, and that part has been reeling me back in. And you just complicated everything." *And he didn't know the half of it.*

"You mean you might—stay?" Was the hitch in his voice criticism or shock?

"I swear I don't know," she said. And she didn't. Woodend had always been her anchor. And giving up and walking away? She had never been able to do either.

They sat in silence, surrounded by the conversations of others and the occasional fizz of the fluorescent mosquito lure zapping an insect. The white fairy lights draped through the apple trees clicked on as dusk fled, and a smattering of stars jostled through the blackness. Tilly ruffled her hair, which was long overdue for a chop, and failed to think of anything to say.

"Christ, you look sexy when you do that." Sebastian rubbed at his mouth.

Tilly stretched across the table and kissed his cheek, her pulse scampering in one direction, her mind in the other. To hurt Sebastian again was unthinkable, and she would never allow anything to develop unless she was confident of the outcome. But for a moment she had wanted him, and she sensed the desire had been mutual.

"That spring, before you met David," he said, "we came close, didn't we, to reuniting?"

Tilly was about to answer when she realized it wasn't a question. Sebastian was drifting on his own memory trip, and she turned away. But as she fought to breathe through the sudden constriction in her chest, she forgot about Woodend, about Sebastian, about everything. Two figures were coming toward them, one waving, one scowling. And she realized that true sexual attraction, the kind that slammed into you when you were cruising along, oblivious, was a great deal more treacherous than facing a rogue wave in a dinky boat. True sexual attraction blacked out the world and then splashed it with the fiery colors of her favorite tropical plants.

She grabbed a flint of ice from her glass. And as the cold bit into her fingers, she prayed that Sebastian wasn't tuned into her wavelength, sharing the thought that on the eve of another reconciliation, history was set to repeat itself.

The blush that covered her freckled face and her neck and the chest he dreamed of kissing punched away his jealousy. Her hair, which had become shaggy and unruly since they'd met, was shoved behind her ears to reveal huge, silver hoops that grazed her neck. God Almighty, she was beautiful, sitting with her bare legs entwined around each other, some floaty shawl thing draped through her arms and a floral dress slipping off her shoulders. No red bra strap tonight. In fact— James swallowed—no bra.

"Yoo-hoo!" Rowena called as they walked across the grass.

People raised their hands in greeting to Rowena, and a guy who looked about ninety wobbled up to standing and doffed his cap. Rowena acknowledged him with a wag of her head. And Tilly stared at James.

She was annoyed, wasn't she? He had tried to talk Rowena

out of this, but she was bullish in her focus. What had seemed funny at 2:00 a.m. when they were both smashed, and mildly inappropriate half an hour ago, blew up in his face—a practical joke turned cruel. And James had no tolerance for cruelty. He tried to leave, but Rowena clamped herself to his arm like a pit bull with lockjaw.

"You have a face," Tilly said. Was that approval or disapproval?

"Indeed." James smiled at her, which was pointless since Tilly was busy picking at a stain on the table and no longer watching him.

"Isn't he dishy without that appalling beard?" Rowena said. "Whoever knew he was hiding that sexy cleft in his chin!"

Sebastian drained his glass in one long, noisy gulp.

"Why did you shave it off?" Tilly asked, but didn't look up.

"I met someone who reminded me to be myself," James said. True, but wasn't his timing a childish attempt at one-upmanship, a pathetic desire to distract her from Sebastian?

"We decided a nightcap was just the ticket," Rowena said. "We're not interrupting, are we?"

"No," Tilly and Sebastian replied in unison.

Rowena detached herself from James and he stood alone, exposed, his nerves jangling. Should he go? Should he stay? Fear he was used to, lack of confidence he was not. If only Tilly would give him a sign that she wasn't angry. She'd never judged him before, but had he overstepped her threshold of tolerance? Why, why had he let Rowena talk him into coming here?

"Budge up, sweetie." Rowena grabbed Sebastian's jacket, draped it around her shoulders and squeezed in next to him. He, James, should go; he should definitely go. But if he stayed, he could sit next to Tilly. He might even brush against her naked shoulders. Fuck, he was acting like a fourteen-year-old wrung out with lust. But he had to touch her. Even if it meant he would crash and burn. *You're going to hell, James, straight to hell.*

Rowena's bangles chimed as she sipped her Guinness. "Didn't see one blessed badger," she said. "Heard some snuffling but that was about it. Still, my beloved godson is pooped. Fell asleep in the car, poor poppet. James carried him upstairs to bed in quite the Christopher Robin moment. Oh! Nearly forgot. I have a little pressie for you, Sebastian." She fumbled in her bag while Sebastian balled his right hand into a fist. And who could blame him? What kind of a jackass blundered into another man's date?

Finally, Tilly raised her head. "Ro, is that your fifth form satchel? It is! I can see the scuff mark where your mother scratched off the 'Anarchy in the UK' sticker." She laughed and James lost track of his thoughts.

He folded his body into the shrinking space beside her and counted to six. Six was a smooth, round number, the perfect number, as perfect as Tilly's laugh.

"Eureka, found it!" Rowena shook out a crumpled flyer and handed it to Sebastian. "Welcome to village life, where we abuse you something rotten. The vicar needs a volunteer to organize the kiddies' cricket match at the village fete, and he practically wee'd in his cassock when I told him about you."

"Thanks." Sebastian's hand relaxed. "Archie and I could do this together."

"Exactly," Rowena said, and began discussing the village fete with him.

Tilly remained tense and silent.

She hates you, James. She hates you.

James angled his head toward her. "I'm sorry, I'm sorry," he said, and had to fight the impulse to keep apologizing. *I'm not a bad person. I've apologized twice and twice is enough.* "I tried to talk her out of it." *You have to keep apologizing, if you don't she'll hate you forever.* "I'm sorry, I'm sorry. I'm—"

Tilly pressed against him, her hand on his shoulder. "I thought you were going to work on the whole apology thing," she said. "One sorry is fine."

But it wasn't fine. It was far from fine. An image had ambushed him, an image of broken glass and blood. An image that echoed fact, that stole a memory and perverted it. In his mind, he had picked up Sebastian's beer glass, smashed it against the table and ground the jagged edge into Sebastian's face. James let out a sharp breath, overwhelmed by the horror of a violent act he could never commit even though the OCD told him otherwise, told him that he had been a monster once before and would be so again. *Showed* him that he was a monster.

Tilly's hand slipped down his back in a steady, firm stroke. She understood. He'd said nothing, and yet she understood. Wasn't that all anyone ever needed—someone to understand? And why, since he was ten, had he worked so hard to deny anyone that chance? But not anymore, not anymore. For the first time, a person he loved understood. Even if she was David's widow, even if her childhood sweetheart was the better man, the better father, James would not be noble. He would not step aside; he would not deny these feelings.

"It's not real," she whispered.

"No," he said, not caring who heard, "but this is."

Eighteen

If only sexual attraction were as easy to remove as a parasitic plant. Tilly stared at the sticky Willy she had wrenched, roots and all, from a wild forget-me-not. Its hairs pricked her arm searching for purchase, but she brushed it to the ground. And stomped on it.

How had she arrived at this place—psychological and physical? What exactly *was* she doing sitting on a wooden stile at the edge of a wheat field? To find James attractive was beyond inconvenient. It threatened something that suddenly felt as necessary as breathing. Watching him force aside fear every day reminded her of the elasticity of the human spirit, of how she had survived after David's funeral, when she had been stretched so tight that she could have snapped at any moment. But she hadn't, and neither had Isaac, thanks to the garden.

It had started with the salvia coccinea, a scarlet annual that tossed its seed around like a soused soccer fan celebrating an FA Cup win. After the service, Tilly had embarked on a cleaning frenzy that included her plants. But there were too many salvias to give away, so she and Isaac started selling them at the farmers' market, a place they came to love for its bright babble. The following year, cheered on by Isaac, she created Piedmont Perennials and began channeling despondency into the life force of gardening. And wasn't that what she'd been doing up at Bramwell Hall every day, thanks to James and his persistence?

Think of the devil and there he was, stalking toward her as if he had a soul to claim. The flat of his hand smacked a violent rhythm against his thigh, and the flecks of shade in his eyes had spread, turning his irises black. Oh crap.

"I waited for thirty minutes, spent fifteen minutes walking from Bramwell Hall to Woodend, twenty minutes having coffee with your mother and another—" James consulted his bright plastic watch "—twenty-five minutes making my way up here. You've been AWOL for ninety minutes. Would you care to explain?"

"I hate Tuesdays?" Tilly swung her legs like a recalcitrant child.

"Funny. Except that I'm not laughing."

"I noticed. No one ever kept you waiting before?"

He tapped his watch twice. "Not for ninety minutes."

Blimey, he was grumpy today. She sighed, a long sigh that leaked out and took the urge to fight with it. "I started walking and just kept going." She jumped to the ground, stumbling as she landed on a sunbaked rut. "How did you find me?"

"I did the same." He gave her a measured look and Tilly turned away. Without the beard there was less to distract her from those huge eyes. "Is it my imagination," he said, "or does the dog reek of rotten eggs?"

"He went swimming in the cesspit formally known as the duck pond." Normally, she put Monty on the lead when they entered this field to prevent him from dashing for the stinky sludge behind the rushes. But this morning she was two strides from the pond before she realized where she was.

"And this was how long ago?" James said.

Tilly glanced down at the dog asleep in the clover. His pink tongue lolled between his teeth and his legs twitched as he chased through a dream; dried pond slime was matted into his fur. "A while."

"And you've been here ever since?"

Why did he make it sound like a bad thing? "Pretty much."

James stepped under the shade of the beech tree at the edge of The Chase, its branches laden with beechnuts the color of toffee apples. One limb dipped so low that she and Isaac had turned it into a swing at Christmas. What a different visit that had been. How could so much change in six months? Exhaustion overwhelmed her, a sudden need to stall out from life.

"I can't do this anymore," Tilly said. "Hide with you in the walled garden. I need to run, but I don't know where to go. I want to yell, but I don't know what to say. Tell me how to fight fear, tell me more about this cognitive-behavioral therapy."

"Tilly, there's no point."

She glared at him. He didn't accept defeat; why should she?

"There's no point—" James softened his voice "—because your fear is real."

She squinted into the sunlight. What had she been thinking, sitting out here without a hat? She sighed and joined James to stand in the shade. "Fear is still fear. Tell me anyway."

James stretched out a foot and rubbed at the only patch of Monty's flank not encrusted with muck. "If you're fighting a compulsion, you change the structure of it, reverse it, or better still, delay it. If you can postpone a ritual for ten minutes, the

impulse passes. At least that's the theory. If it's a nasty image—
embrace it, don't deny it. Doctor it, try and make it ridiculous,
or focus on it until your mind becomes bored and wanders.
As for fighting obsessions, you have three choices. Counter
with logic—*what are the chances*. Cultivate detachment—*I'm
going to let that thought float away*. Or boss it back—*fuck-off-
you-fucker*. And if you're desperate, all of the above. That's
cognitive-behavioral therapy, the précis."

His smile hinted at years of failure. She wanted to hug him,
but didn't dare. If she put her arms around him, how would
she know where to stop?

"Harder than it sounds?" Tilly batted away a horsefly.

"Like pausing mid-drown to teach yourself to swim."
He combed his fingers through his hair. "What were you
frightened of, as a child?"

"Snakes and exams. I still get exam nightmares."

"How did the fear manifest itself—before an exam?"

She squeezed out the memory. "My adrenaline pumped,
my pulse raced, and just as I thought I would throw up my
Marmite toast breakfast, I hit this plateau of calm. I remember
the feeling as wide-awake sleepwalking. Very surreal."

"In other words, you confronted the fear, which means the
panic crested and subsided. I'm not an expert on psychology.
But you're out here, alone, for a reason." He grabbed her
wrist and held on so tightly that the tips of her fingers tingled
with constricted blood. "Look at your fingers—chewed
raw." He let go. "Yesterday I deadheaded every knautia
plant, and you didn't notice. The day before your T-shirt
was inside out. Have you considered allowing yourself to
crumble and fall?"

A dandelion clock blew between them and twirled up
into the sky.

Tilly flexed her fingers. "So you're telling me to throw up my hands and say, 'Take me now, fear'? That's not an option."

"Why not? I don't understand."

A group of ramblers processed toward The Chase, and two children on ponies clopped along the estate road that led to Manor Farm.

Tilly's eyes followed the children, rising and falling to the trot. "Because I'm a mother."

"This isn't about Isaac, Tilly. This is about you."

"I don't handle parenting advice well. You might want to back off."

A kestrel hovered above them. How wonderful, to be able to drift on air currents, to float over everything and hear nothing below.

"I read this book once about kids and grief—" incredible, did he not understand the core of social interaction, the follow-the-lead-of-your-audience approach? "—the essence of which was this—secure your own oxygen mask before attempting to help your kid put on his. That's a philosophy to live by, don't you agree? How can you help others if you can't help yourself?"

"Sounds like you're telling me to be selfish."

"Then you're choosing to misinterpret me."

She glared at him, but he merely cocked an eyebrow.

"Maybe," James said, "you should ask, 'What's the worst that can happen?'"

"I die, which is kinda sucky."

"I know it's not death that terrifies you."

"Then you don't need to ask the question, do you?" Why did he have to bring this up again? She'd warned him off once; once should be enough.

"Kids survive. My son is evidence of that." Monty gave a sneeze and jerked awake. "The best thing you can do is prepare for the worst-case scenario. For example, what provisions have you made for legal guardianship?"

"That if anything happens to me, Isaac lives with my mother." *In Woodend. So much for mapping out the future.* "Now that she's downsizing, I suppose I'll ask Rowena."

"What about David's family?"

"My in-laws adore Isaac, but they live in a retirement community in Florida. And his sister skipped the maternal gene." Tilly squatted down and began easing sticky Willy seeds from Monty's fur. "Besides, she lives in Manhattan, and skyscrapers terrify Isaac. He thinks they're going to fall on him."

"Smart kid. I have the same fear." James rubbed his chin and looked momentarily surprised, as if he'd forgotten how it felt to be clean-shaven. "What about a living will?"

"Whoa, time out." She stood and put her hands on her hips. Now he'd gone too far.

"This is what it means, Tilly, to fight fear. You can't withhold the punches."

"You don't know how to quit, do you?"

"Unless I'm having an out-of-body experience, you asked for my advice. I'm giving it the only way I know how—as an obsessive-compulsive, not as Mister Rogers." He flashed a smile, but his eyes darkened again. Tilly stood and inched toward the edge of the shade. Sebastian was right. She didn't know enough about this man. "My tribe isn't exactly filled with people who look on the bright side of life, Tilly."

What the hell was she doing, baring her soul to someone she'd known for what, a little over a month? "How long have we known each other?"

"Six weeks, but I don't see the relevance. You and Isaac became part of my life the moment we met."

Was he really that naive?

"Come on, boy," James said. Monty shot up, wagging his tail. "Time to go home."

"That's it? You're taking the dog and buggering off, leaving me in a field?"

"You chose the setting." James walked away but stopped and turned. "I suggest you scream and cry. Works for me. And while you do that, Isaac and I are going to design a tree house for the magnificent oak in the paddock."

"You know how to build a tree house?"

James tossed back his hair and grinned. He was wearing two silver hoops and two small diamond earrings today. The stud in his left ear sparkled in the sun, dazzling Tilly. "You'd be amazed what a farm boy can do with a pile of boards and planks."

Monty and James started down the hill, heading for Woodend. "Put on your oxygen mask," he called over his shoulder. "And don't scare the wildlife."

Even as she watched him walk away, Tilly screamed a silent *Come back!* How could you miss a person you could still see?

She stared at a flattened skeleton of a hare, half-hidden in the long grass at the edge of the path. This whole exploit was pointless. Being out here with Monty she could pretend they were resting midwalk. Without a dog she felt silly, and too damn hot. Heat in England was awkward—holiday weather that belonged in another country. Although it didn't appear to bother the birds in The Chase, who were as noisy as the birds at Creeping Cedars. She should buy a tape of birdsong when they returned to the States, learn to identify more of the natives back home.

Tilly jerked up, disturbed by the thought that had dropped, unbidden, into her mind. Unbelievable, while she was distracted by something as banal as the weather, her mind had coshed her with a hard little fact: The sounds of home came not from finches and blackbirds, but from the cries of hawks and the chitters of hummingbirds. What else did she miss? The fireflies, definitely! Her gardens? Omigod, yes!

Did that mean that her heart could belong to two places, despite her determination to force it into an either-or choice?

As she clambered back onto the stile, her mind flitted to James stepping on every other dandelion at Maple View Farm and to the view she loved just as much as the one laid out before her. This scene hadn't changed in thirty years and would still be here in another thirty years, whether she was part of it or not. Whether she lived or died. James was right—Isaac's guardianship should be her priority. Isaac should be with someone who had shared her past and could carry those memories into his future. Rowena was the obvious choice.

And suppose…just suppose she were dying. What about a living will? *Damn you, James, for planting the seed.* If she knew that Isaac would be the center of someone else's universe, should she plan for the swiftest death possible? Would that be less painful for him? Eight years ago, when she had refused to discuss the issue with David, her world had been spinning in a different direction. Eight years ago, she could afford ideals. But hadn't grief revealed that one-size-fits-all was a lousy doctrine?

James had talked about falling apart so you could put yourself back together. Could that simple philosophy save Isaac if she died? When he was a rambunctious three-year-old, she encouraged him to bend his knees if he fell: *don't hit the ground rigid, or you'll shatter like Humpty Dumpty. Rigid,* that was a good adjective to describe Tilly. But how else could you cling on, stop yourself from tipping into blackness? Or, sometimes, did you have to let go?

She closed her eyes against the vista, against the birdsong, and remembered the hidden hours after David's death, when she had allowed herself to mourn. Allowed herself to *crumble and fall.*

Nineteen

For the first time in twenty-two hours and thirty-eight minutes, he was alone with her. The agony of caring this much was crushing him. Every hour, every minute, every second, James thought of Tilly. He could no longer separate her pain from his, her needs from his. And he knew what she expected of him, but he couldn't deliver. Why did his OCD have to flare up this morning when he was trying so hard to be the person Tilly could depend on, not screwed-up James with the misfiring brain?

They had to leave now or they'd be late. Late was never an option, but he couldn't do what she was asking of him. He couldn't. Ominous clouds loitered behind the Hall and humidity stacked up in his lungs. A storm was rolling in.

"I'm sorry, Tilly. I'm sorry." They faced each other across the hood of the Yaris. "I can't drive. I can't."

"But you're the one who offered to take me, remember?"

He'd rankled her. He could hear it in her tone.

Rowena had said Tilly craved space. In the past two days, James had done everything he could to provide it, coercing

Isaac, Virginia, even the psycho dog, into helping with the tree house, leaving Tilly wide-open to shut out the world, which she'd done, packing away family memorabilia to a borrowed soundtrack. *His* borrowed soundtrack, from *his* new iPod classic. For once, the scorpion pit of sharing had been worth the anguish. Watching her sashay around humming the Gipsy Kings had affected him in his heart, in his gut and in his groin. And pelted him with images of Sebastian. Sebastian, who had held her and made love to her.

She doesn't love you, she loves Sebastian.

Which rival haunted him more—the dead husband or the very much alive ex-lover, the stand-up guy who was in London all week to be with his kids for their end-of-school festivities? How could you hate someone that decent?

Tilly doesn't need you, she needs Sebastian.

James let the thoughts tumble, too tired to resist. He hadn't slept in two nights. Rowena was away at the Great Yorkshire Agricultural Show, and he'd fallen into a new ritual of checking every door and every window every night. The Hall freaked him out. What choice did he have?

She doesn't love you, she loves Sebastian.

"Tilly, when I said I would take you, I meant accompany you to the clinic. I cannot, cannot, drive on the left-hand side of this arcane road system with signs bearing down on us that read *Warning—kill your speed, Warning—police radar, Warning—red route, thirty-eight fatalities in three years.* If I drive, we won't make it to the breast clinic alive." He closed his eyes and tried to concentrate on the doves flapping and cooing in the dovecote. It didn't work. "I have images—" he opened his eyes "—of you and me trapped under a semi. In flames."

"Fine. I'll drive the death trap," Tilly said, and slammed the door. Then waited for him to squash into the passenger seat before they sped off, tires grinding through the gravel.

★ ★ ★

They passed the second memorial of plastic flowers marking the death of someone's husband or wife, father or mother, son or daughter, on a road too narrow and twisty for modern traffic, and still, she didn't speak. Since she was pissed at him, he might as was tell her about David, get it over with. A week ago he had decided she must never know, but that was before his childish alter ego jumped into the arena. Before he felt abandoned. In the past two days Tilly had withdrawn—at his suggestion, but then he'd never operated on the same field of logic as everyone else—and now he burned with the need to haul her back into his confidence, to make her understand that fate had brought them together. At least he hoped she would believe it was fate and not really shitty karma.

God Almighty, he felt ridiculous jammed into this toy car with his legs jutting up. Whether he was inside or out, England was a cramped, Lilliputian world. Even parking spaces were smaller.

He practiced two yoga breaths, then two more.

"When are you going to say, 'Told you so' about the road?" Tilly said.

"I'm not. But since you are talking to me again, I would like to ask you a question." He snapped open the strap of his Alessi watch, the watch he always wore for good luck. Then he snapped it shut. Open, shut. Open—Tilly reached across and stopped him.

"If you want to drive," she said, "the answer's yes."

James scratched through his hair. "I can assure you I would rather take my own life."

She glanced at him. "You could do that, take your own life?"

"It was a joke."

But she didn't laugh. "You could, couldn't you? I believe that of you."

"Tilly, I won't lie to you. I've visited some dark places. But the past is the past." Please God, she believed *that* sentence. "I did want to ask, though——"

"You tried to kill yourself?"

Was it his imagination, or did she jerk away from him? *Keep going, James. Keep going.*

"There have been moments in my life——" *one related to your husband* "——when I've understood the hopelessness that drags you down to the point where life seems worthless. And I believe that each person has the right to choose his threshold for pain, whether of the body or of the mind."

"I can't imagine," she said quietly, "deciding that life is not worth living."

"And yet thousands of people do. I'm lucky; I've always come back from dark places, because I'm a survivor. As are you." The acrid taste of bile hit the back of his throat. Enough preamble. "Did David have a scar on his right cheek?"

"How do you know about his scar?"

He squeezed sideways to face her and almost lost resolve. In profile she looked so girlish, so vulnerable. Everything about her was delicate: her pale skin, her button nose, her blond eyebrows. He wanted to draw her close and protect her, which was crazy. She was tougher than he was. Just how tough, he was about to find out.

James placed a finger over his lips and considered his answer. But really, what else could he say? "I gave it to him."

An empty supermarket bag tumbled along the sidewalk, whipped up in their backdraft. It joined a flattened McDonald's Happy Meal box and a ripped packet of condoms under the spindly hedge by the edge of the road. Tilly slammed on the brake. James jerked forward, the seat belt whipping across his torso. *Ouff,* that wasn't so bad, even if the car had stopped in the middle of a divided highway, ten feet from a roundabout.

"You were the crazy grad student with the bar stool?" Her voice was unnaturally high.

"That would be me."

"You were at the University of Chicago with my husband?"

So far, so good. She hadn't thrown him out of the car, not yet. "David was new to the Ph.D. program, and I dropped out shortly after the incident. It was the only time we met."

"You left grad school because of my husband?"

"No." He felt strangely calm. Who would have imagined full disclosure could be so cathartic? "I left graduate school because I have no patience. Academia moves too slowly for me. I didn't mind the work, just the time it takes to reach the top. Although I assume David made a meteoric rise. I enjoyed his book, by the way."

A car honked and James swiveled around. "I hate to be a backseat driver, but there's a line behind us. You might want to pull forward."

"And why, exactly, did you attack my husband with a bar stool?" She fed the steering wheel through her hands as they curved onto the roundabout, then hit the gas pedal and they shot across two lanes of traffic.

James clutched at his door. Shit. Was she going to kill him after all?

A white van tore past, honking, and the driver flicked two fingers at Tilly.

"Sorry," she mouthed and slowed down.

James relaxed his arm but kept both eyes on the wheel. "Your husband slept with the woman I loved. Although, had I paused to think, I would have realized that he was blameless. She was a repeat offender, you see, but I loved her beyond reason. And yes, before you ask, that was the time

I considered suicide." He paused, waiting for a reaction she didn't give. "I had to see the affair through to its bitter end. Fortunately, that turned out to be David, since it was the run-in with your husband that led me to therapy, not the struggles with ritualized behaviors and obsessive thoughts. I realized I was spinning too fast, responding to everything with anger." James fiddled with one of his diamond stud earrings. "I had a temper like a twister in those days."

"You and my husband fought over the same woman?" Tilly sounded cautious, but not angry. Would this be okay? Would she forgive him as her husband had done?

"David was blameless, Tilly. I stormed into the bar, picked up the stool and charged him. He stumbled, backing away from me. A logical response. Perfectly logical. Unfortunately, he took the table with him and landed on a broken glass." James dug his hands deep into his hair and thrust back his head. Suddenly, the memory was fresh. He had dragged David up to pummel every last breath from his body and seen so much blood. "The blood jolted me back to reality. Although—" he paused, waiting for what? Reassurance? "—I was more shocked by it than he was. I took him to the hospital, paid his bill and drove him home. We had, of course, made peace before then. He had no idea that Isha was involved with another guy. And he was extremely gracious. He could have pressed charges, but he didn't. If anything, he understood. I've always been grateful for that." *Now what?* He waited.

She exhaled. "Thank you."

Of all the responses, he would never have anticipated that one. "For what?"

"A gift from the grave." Tilly glanced up in the rearview mirror, then clicked on her turn signal. "I always felt there was a piece of his story missing. Now I understand why. He was ashamed that he'd slept with another man's girlfriend. David's ego might have filled the East Coast, but honor was a merit badge for him." They rolled toward a red traffic light. "And yes, he would've understood. He was drawn to people in crisis, people who needed him. I think it made him less insecure."

The light turned to amber, then to green. James liked that about English traffic lights, that they gave you more time. In America you had to go from stop to start with nothing in between, but James could never have enough transition time.

She flashed a smile at him. Thank God. He'd been right to tell her.

What a blessing truth could be! How it lent perspective! Now she knew, one hundred and one percent, that she could never fall for James. His revelation had leveled the space between them, put their relationship on a plane she understood—finally. After all, no way could she fall for the man who'd disfigured her dead husband.

I mean, come on, how much guilt can one person carry?

"If David were drawn to underdogs," James said, "I fail to see how you fit in."

"I kept his life uncluttered so he could produce brilliance. I was the subservient partner."

"Your theory's off."

He'd lost her, totally. "Excuse me?"

"If David relied on you to shore up his life, then you were the power behind the throne, not the handmaid. Don't sell yourself short, Tilly. You're a strong, capable woman who created a successful business out of tragedy."

Interesting, she'd never looked at it that way, but that didn't mean James was right. She appreciated his "Go, Tilly" speech, but really, he had no clue. "It wasn't deliberate, James. I was clinging to the life David and I had created, keeping our world the same for Isaac's sake. Since my business allowed me to do that, it was a means to an end. Enjoying the work was a bonus."

Tilly braked and they crawled into another traffic jam. She felt a pang of longing for swaths of empty roadways that cut through Carolina forest, for dodging turkey vultures picking at roadkill, for stopping to rescue turtles. She glanced at a tiny roadside garden spilling over with pastel colors and longed to see her sun border vibrating with hot tones.

They started moving again, and as they turned left toward the hospital carpark, a memory jarred from four months before David died. They were camped out in the basement following an ice storm, with no power and no running water. She could hear David's retort to her suggestion that they invest in a generator: "Forget it, babe. We won't be here long enough to make a generator cost-effective." And to prove his point, once phone service was restored, he floated the word that he was for hire. After five days of struggling to burn frozen logs and melt ice to flush the lavatory, David announced he was done with country living. And once David made decrees, he didn't back down. But Tilly had her garden, her friends, a world of her making she couldn't relinquish. Wasn't that why she'd used the leftover life insurance money to put in the generator David deemed so pointless?

Had guilt enabled her to edit the past, erase the bits she didn't like? Yes, she always knew North Carolina was little more than a career pit stop for David, that he was using it as a rung on his career ladder. But the ice storm had sped up his desire to head back to civilization—his words, not hers. And that—Tilly pulled into the hospital parking lot—would have led them into a head-on collision.

The car spluttered into silence, and Tilly reached into the

back for her rucksack. Okay, then. Time to meet her future. But the future was only safe when you knew where you were heading. And a triple assessment at the breast clinic was an unmarked detour. And so, a hidden voice hinted, was the man sitting next to her. The one she could never fall for. Tilly flung open the car door, and her stomach did some weird hula dance.

"James, we have a problem. My legs won't work."

He frowned, then clambered out and walked around to the driver's side. As he leaned forward and placed his hands on her seat, his black shirt flapped open, allowing a glimpse of black chest hair and the dark shadow of a nipple. Lust socked her, good and hard. How did James Nealy kiss? Slow and tantalizing, or fast and passionate? She shook her head.

"When you asked about fears the other day, I didn't mention one." Her eyes scanned the parking lot frantically for a distraction and settled on a license plate. "I should have, when I said I couldn't drive, but I didn't want to sound silly, didn't want you to think…I mean, no, that's not what I mean." Great, she was babbling. James crouched beside her and said nothing. "I watched Daddy die in this hospital. And then David, watching David for five days—" Pinpricks of heat stabbed her chest. Was this a hot flash? Wasn't she too young for this premenopausal crap? "Hospitals," she forced out the word. "Can't deal with them."

Heat shot through her body as the parking lot shrank. Actually, it didn't shrink so much as break into pieces and tumble like fragments at the end of a kaleidoscope. And her legs were tingly and heavy. Wow, this was freaky, like being fall-down-drunk without the alcohol. Except that her hands were trembling. And her chest was tightening, as if an imaginary vise were squeezing her into nothing. Terror swamped her.

"No—air," she gasped. "Can't—breathe." Oh God, she was having a heart attack.

James clamped his hands on either side of her head. "Watch my lips, breathe with me. In and out. Good. Use my lips as a focal point and keep breathing. In and out. Think of this as a yoga exercise."

She was dying, and he wanted to teach her yoga? "N-no!" Her heart thumped against her ribs, struggling to break free. *So not a good idea to watch those lips: Could lust kill?* "Get. A. Doctor."

"Listen to me." He increased the pressure of his hands. *Such elegant hands for a man; such long, thin fingers; such clean, neatly trimmed nails.*

"You're experiencing a panic attack," James said. "Something doctors call the fight-or-flight response. Your body is merely reacting to information from your brain, preparing to fend off a perceived threat, trying to decide whether to fight or flee."

"Make it—stop." Talking was as painful as breathing.

"Okay, okay. Concentrate on my words. Do you like the ocean?"

She nodded.

"Are you frightened of waves?" he said.

She felt the roughness of his palms, calloused from the shears. "No— You?"

"Now there's a short question with a long answer." He grinned and her body began to slow. "I'm terrified of being dragged out to sea by tsunamis or the undertow. Of being stung by a Portuguese man-of-war or dismembered by a great white shark. See how much better it is to have a common fear of hospitals?"

She smiled and discovered it hurt less than breathing.

"But this is your dream," James said. "Which means that

we're on a deserted beach with a sparkling sea, clear to the sandy floor." He tilted toward her. "Close those beautiful eyes and listen to the water lap the shore. Now walk toward the ocean. Can you smell it?"

She nodded, but all she could smell was the cool scent of wintergreen on James's breath.

"Good. Now head for the wooden rowboat drifting offshore, the one with scented purple and pink flowers trailing over the side, those sweet peas that you love. But pause to enjoy the sensations—the sea caressing your ankles, your toes sinking into waterlogged sand, the sun stroking your back."

She loved James's voice, his soft middle-America burr with the slight lilt that she assumed was a legacy from his Irish father. Tilly was conscious of the solid warmth of his hands holding her still, his touch as soothing as his cadence.

Don't let go, please. "Will you come into the water with me?" she whispered.

"No, because I'm not as brave as you. I'm cowering on a beach towel doing a ritual that makes me look like an escaped mental patient."

She managed a smile.

"But you glide through the water, feeling it swirl around your knees, your thighs…." James fell silent for a moment. "You reach the boat and tip in your thoughts, then push it toward the horizon. The boat floats away, taking your thoughts with it."

"All my thoughts?"

"Only the ones you want to dump. The rest you can keep."

She opened her eyes to find James watching her. Often his gaze unsettled her, stripped her bare, and other times she drew strength from it. But today it overwhelmed her. Her mouth was dry and her voice silent.

He tweaked her nose and then stood. "Ready to go inside?"

She dragged herself out of the car. "You're wrong about one thing. I'm not braver than you. You're the bravest person I know."

James didn't reply.

Plastic chairs in a hospital waiting room were the pits. Unyielding, uncomfortable, un— Her mind failed her, just as it had done half an hour earlier, when James insisted they play Geography to keep her preoccupied. She was crap at Geography, so Tilly had taught him The Minister's Cat, her mother's favorite word game. They had reached *d* and it was Tilly's turn, but the only adjective her brain spat out was *dead*. *The minister's cat is a dead cat.*

Her stomach flipped through another loop-the-loop.

"Mrs. Silverberg?" A blonde nurse strode into the room with the air of a buxom prison guard. She crossed her arms over her clipboard, and her diamond tennis bracelet chinked against it. Was she trying to hide her boobs from a roomful of women clutching mastectomy pamphlets? In fact, should a woman with a Dolly Parton shelf be working in a breast clinic? Come on, that was perverse.

The nurse zeroed in on her, and Tilly's mind pitched into chaos. Another angel of death was searching a hospital lounge for Mrs. Silverberg. Time to bolt. Tilly shot up, but James grabbed her hand and moored her to his side. She swung around, looking down on him for once. Since when did he start holding hands? Although this felt more like a death grip. His eyelids flickered, and then he shook his head slowly.

"Your husband can join you," the nurse said. "If you'd like him to."

James seeing her half-naked, splayed on an examination table while members of the medical profession prodded her boobs. Wouldn't that just top off the day.

"Honey?" James glanced up through his eyelashes. "Should I join you?"

Tilly burst into giggles. She could kiss him; she really could. "No." She stopped laughing, aware of a roomful of cold stares. "Just promise to wait for me."

"Always," he said, but he didn't release her hand.

She'd never seen him sit so still. He looked almost tranquil. And whatever he was about to say, she didn't want to hear.

She yanked her hand free and left the room ahead of the nurse. OCD she could out-rationalize, but his real thoughts terrified her as much as that one word: *always*.

James watched a pair of swans glide along the River Nene. They hadn't spoken since she told him she would get the results in six days. Six, that was a good sign. The best. So why was the car filled with silence? Was she mad at him because he'd hinted at his feelings? Although he hadn't actually hinted. Hadn't said anything aloud. But the static in his head repeated over and over, *You scared her off. You blew it, you troll.*

A rumble of thunder tumbled toward them, and the sky crackled with anticipation.

"Want to get drunk tonight?" Tilly said. "I think I've earned the right after having my breasts pummeled, flattened between two icy sheets of metal and stuck with a needle."

He scratched at his thighs six times, six so Tilly wouldn't get cancer and die.

Tilly sighed. "I need to apologize."

James stopped moving. Apologize for what? He was the one who'd been a jerk.

"I've been selfish," Tilly said.

Tilly, selfish? She wasn't wired for selfish.

"Dragging you to a breast clinic, forcing you to think about your mother and—"

"My mother wasn't occupying my thoughts." James stared at his watch, his lucky watch. "You were."

"Okay." She hesitated, which proved how smart she was. "Do I want to ask why?"

No, you don't. "My OCD was telling me, was telling me...."

"That I'm going to die, right?"

"Yes." James slammed back into his headrest.

"Hey, I have no plans to die. So you can tell that bastard OCD to bog off."

"Bog off? I like that." He tried to find his breath. "But if anything happened to you—"

"Wow. Stop right there. That's the OCD talking. You don't need to listen."

"And if it isn't?" James sat up. "What if this is me? What if I were to ask you, right now, how you feel about me?"

"That's a little forthright. Even by my standards." Her voice was hushed, her face pale. She braced her arms against the steering wheel and stared straight ahead.

Now would be a good time to back off, to leave her be, but he couldn't. Being obsessive-compulsive meant never being able to quit. It meant sticking with the same lousy thought, the same emotion, the same project over and over. It meant being at the top of his class. Every. Single. Time. "That's not an anwer."

"Because some things defy description, James. They just—are. Like an eclectic planting with a handful of plants I grabbed on instinct and bunged in a pot. It shouldn't work, but it does. Don't make me examine what's sparking between us." She sounded angry. She was definitely pissed, and he was an idiot. "Because my hospital phobia is nothing compared to my fear of boy-meets-girl. The last time I went on a date was with my husband of ten years. And afterward—" Tilly paused for effect "—we had the kind of sex that you never forget."

Wow. That was unnecessary. It would have been less painful if she'd kicked him in the teeth. He almost wished she had. James tapped the right side of his seat, six times. Six times so Tilly wouldn't get cancer and die. And six more times so she wouldn't hate him.

"Don't box me in," she added. "You won't like the fallout."

He had blown it, pushed too hard despite Rowena's warning. Why had he asked the question when he'd known the answer would terrify him? Couldn't he be happy, just once, in the murkiness of uncertainty? No, he couldn't. Not when the stakes were this high. He was trying to change a lifetime of habits in one sitting. Failure—the word ground into his gut—should be expected. But not when it came to love, never when it came to love.

He should speak, reassure her that he wasn't some petty louse who nursed grudges.

"What's that yellow flower by the roadside?" His voice sounded reedy. A fake voice used to snare Tilly's goodwill with fake interest in a plant. See? The OCD was right. He was a creep, a lowlife who had taken advantage of her.

"Ragwort. Deadly to horses, but pretty, isn't it? Thrives on neglect. Definitely my kind of plant." She smiled, but her smile was as false as his words had been. "What I said—"

"The fault is mine." He didn't mean to snap, but it was either spit out a short sentence or keep apologizing. And Tilly knew him too well, would classify his apology as checking, the telltale sign of an obsessive thought, which, of course, it was.

"I saw a sign a few miles back for Green Thumbs Nursery. Can we take a detour?" He reached for his wallet. "If we've been at a nursery all day, I've bought gifts for Rowena." He forced out a smile. "Although you'll have to plant them. And

Twenty

Despite the humidity, the crack that greeted Tilly as she stepped from the car was not thunder. It was leather on willow, the sound of cricket. With a fortifying glance at Woodend, she walked across the gravel. A bead of sweat slithered down her temple, and she sensed James tracking her.

She passed under the rose arch and took an imaginary step backward to quiet the hammering in her head. The beautiful man playing cricket with her son was Sebastian, the boy with the angelic smile who had loved and desired her when she'd felt more cyborg than human. His shirttail spilled from his suit pants, his loosened tie flapped against his chest and his arm cartwheeled through the air. The debt might be long paid off, but she had owed Sebastian so much. He was a good soul—kind, supportive, loyal. And there were no surprises with Sebastian, nothing left to discover. He was safe, familiar and predictable. The opposite of James.

Tilly swallowed and tasted bitterness. Or was that guilt? She wove her fingers together and held her arms rigid in front of her, trying to fend off the sensation of having been

I'm pretty sure I've bought a spectacular rose to add to your mother's collection. She can take it with her when she moves."

But the magic of distraction sputtered and died. He was so tired of playing games, of hiding his OCD. He didn't want to have secrets from Tilly. For the first time in his life, he wanted another person to know every distorted twist of his history. Maybe she did already.

"I push too hard," he confessed. "I always push too hard."

"I know," she said, and returned to silence.

And James watched the broken white lines in the middle of the road disappear under the car, marking off the remnants of their day together.

caught out. Hardly a legitimate reaction, but her body seemed to think otherwise. Heat rose in her cheeks and her pulse picked up speed. Was this the fight-or-flight response James had mentioned earlier?

Isaac whacked the ball with a banshee wail of delight and Monty tore after it, accompanied by hoots of *no* from Isaac and Sebastian. They hadn't noticed her; she still had time to tiptoe away.

Uh-oh, Monty had spotted her. With a yip of delight, he skidded around and tore across the herbaceous border, flattening the sweet peas. Tilly's leg shot out to restrain him, but the reflex came too late. He crashed into her like a runaway bulldozer, and she collapsed under the brunt of him.

"Hey, Monty," she wheezed. "Miss me, did you?" His reply was a drool-drench that stank of rotting carcass. "Yuck. Stop!"

As she tried to wriggle free, she glimpsed James's black sneakers, the hem of his black jeans and the long fingers that picked up a partially masticated tennis ball and lobbed it into the hedge. Monty yelped, rocketed into the air and hurtled after it.

James had done that? Despite his fear of dirt, he'd picked up a revolting object that she wouldn't touch? Goodness, he really was the bravest person she knew.

"Thank you," Tilly said, but James didn't respond. He was scrubbing his palm against his thigh and watching Sebastian saunter toward them. Tilly tugged down the hem of her sundress, hoping she hadn't flashed anyone in her fall.

"Mom!" Isaac ran forward and burrowed into her. "How was the gardening place?"

Baby sparrows tweeted from their nest in the guttering, demanding food, and reality crushed her. She hadn't rehearsed an answer, hadn't spun a plan. What kind of mother didn't protect her child with a plan? Her mind was empty, closed for business. A shut-up shop without a single thought, not one—

"Your mother has practically bankrupted me," James said, inspecting his palm and then scrubbing it some more.

Sod everything; she would have to hug him. But Isaac beat her to it.

James stopped wiping his hand. "Sebastian."

Sebastian paused to shove his shirttails into his pants. "James."

"Never go plant shopping with this woman."

"I don't intend to," Sebastian replied.

In three years Tilly hadn't looked at a man. Not one. And here she was sprawled on her mother's lawn watching two men square off, secretly thrilled at being the cause. Or rather, the possible cause. Worse, she was trying not to picture herself having sex, although her partner's identity was fuzzy. Was this some midlife deviancy, the result of three years of celibacy, or was she so worried about losing her sexuality along with her breasts that she had transformed into a pubescent schoolboy mainlining testosterone? *Sex wanted, partner unknown.*

Sebastian gave a sigh. Faint but not disguised, it was the kind of sigh David used to terminate a conversation. Then he held out his hand. James hesitated and Tilly tensed. Sebastian would be insulted if James didn't shake hands, when really, it was incredible that James was still standing there, that he hadn't run inside to find the nearest bottle of hand sanitizer.

"I don't think you want to touch my hand." James stared at his palm, his lips curled back in revulsion. Oh crap. Had he ever looked sexier?

"Can we work on the tree house now?" Isaac clung to James. "Pretty please, before it rains? Grammy says it's going to storm, for sure."

Sebastian hauled Tilly to her feet and kissed her on the

mouth—a firm, dry kiss that felt like a brand of ownership and bequeathed a stale aftertaste of tea.

"What are you doing here?" Tilly asked him.

"London's a sauna today." Sebastian moved his hand down to the small of Tilly's back and kept it there. He smelled of overheated train carriage and diesel fumes. "I decided to skive off work and come talk to your mother. I was hoping I could surprise the children with the news this weekend."

So, unlike Tilly, Sebastian had a plan. Unlike Tilly, he'd been organizing, lining up his assets, turning her daydream into his reality. And what had she been doing? Surviving.

"Tilly! Is that you?" Her mother bellowed from an upstairs window. "Sari's on the phone! Something about a broken mister head in the greenhouse?"

"Brilliant! Be right there!" Tilly backed toward the house while Sebastian and James glared at her. Well, Sebastian didn't glare, but she was pretty sure he was as ticked off as James, who was practically steaming with repressed anger. And making no attempt to hide it. "Just be a sec. Make yourselves at home. I'll rustle up a pot of tea, shall I?" She tottered over a tub of geraniums. "Silly me. Tea? Much too late for tea. Drinks anyone?"

Then she ran inside before either man could answer.

Sebastian held up both hands as he squeezed past her in the kitchen. *Anything to avoid touching me.* What had happened to the old Sebastian Tilly had glimpsed the weekend before, the man with the seductive glint in his gray eyes? If not for Rowena and James, last Saturday night would, undoubtedly, have ended in a bedroom at Manor Farm, not in a flurry of cheek-pecks in the pub carpark after Tilly had refused a lift from Sebastian or Rowena and, despite James's disapproval, had walked home alone to clear her head. But tonight Sebastian was skittish, the intimacy from that evening lost.

"Shall we try another night out?" Sebastian hacked up a cucumber on the kitchen table. If he made the pieces any smaller, they'd be drinking gazpacho, not Pimm's. "How about next Friday?"

"Sure. I'd like that."

Sebastian chopped furiously. "Any idea when he's leaving?"

"I assume you mean James. And no, I haven't a clue." Tilly put her hands on her hips. Enough of this schoolboy jealousy crap. If Sebastian had feelings for her he should come out and say so, as James had done. Or not as James had done. Bugger. She was utterly lost in this man-woman malarkey. Was it time to tug her widow weeds back on and be done with it?

The knife clattered to the table and Tilly jumped.

"Christ, I'm being a complete prat," Sebastian mumbled.

Silently, she agreed. But beauty and contrition were quite the combination. How could a girl resist? She walked over and eased him into her arms.

Tilly wasn't sure how long they stood together—Sebastian slumped against her, hands dangling by his sides, head bowed like a penitent sinner. Pulling away was unthinkable; holding him felt too much like a homecoming. But when the hair at the nape of her neck bristled, she lowered her arms and turned toward the doorway. It was empty, but his echo remained. Isaac had seen them, she was sure of it.

Was that the moment the evening went horribly wrong? Or was it when her mother toasted Sebastian and Woodend to the accompaniment of a thunderclap, and Tilly's mind screamed no? Or was it when James asked, "Is he buying you, along with the house?" and she slapped him. She'd never slapped anyone before, which proved she should stop flip-flopping and decide that she was not in lust with James Nealy. Or was it her child's announcement that he was too tired for reading, so could she please shut the light and let him go to sleep, thank you very much?

Isaac's rejection eclipsed everything. When she and Isaac were lost in the pages of a book, Tilly was content. And as she lay alone on her childhood mattress, the worn sheet under her so wrinkled it felt like a pincushion, she craved that reminder of life at its richest.

She considered creeping into Isaac's room and sneaking out with their current read, *Arthur: The Seeing Stone,* a historical novel with language so lyrical it made Tilly want to weep. She loved the substance of words. Words stayed with you, no matter what happened. But where was the joy in discovering the story without Isaac?

An owl hooted outside and a car chugged up the High Street. Pretending sleep would come was pointless. Tilly kicked the duvet aside and crawled to the window. There was no glimmer of moonlight over the garden, no neon glow, nothing but blackness and a silence that felt solid. Cool, damp air squirmed under the open sash. She gathered her sloppy T-shirt around her body and shivered. In three weeks she and Isaac would be at Creeping Cedars, surrounded by the symphony of nature that croaked, screeched and buzzed every night until Thanksgiving. And her mother, Rowena and Sebastian would be eavesdropping on silence.

Tilly's forehead flopped against the windowpane, her mind a mess of rotting thoughts: Should she forget about Piedmont Perennials and fight for Woodend, even though she couldn't afford it? Was this where her heart lay, in Bramwell Chase? Was she ready for love the third time around? If so, with whom? Could she afford to make another mistake, or was she all out of redemption cards? If only she could hear David say,

"This is what you should do, babe." But he had been quiet for so long, and it was time she listened for her own voice.

She closed her eyes and concentrated, the shock of the cold glass on her skin refreshing. Only one question mattered: What did she want at this point in her life? And the answer was obvious: to live, so that she could whoop and holler at her son's college graduation and cry an embarrassing amount at his wedding.

The landing floorboards groaned and feet paddled up the steps to her room. The door creaked open and light from the dim bulb at the top of the stairwell stole across her bed.

"Mommy?" Isaac's face, muffled with Bownba, appeared around the door. "I can't sleep."

"Me neither, Angel Bug." She patted the mattress. "Want to try a story?"

"No, thank you." He leaped into her bed and circled like a dog trying to nest. "I have a question."

"Then I'll try to have an answer."

She snuggled in beside him and wrestled the duvet over them.

Isaac curled his legs up into her chest, as if trying to steal back inside her womb; Tilly wrapped her legs under his as if aiding him in the journey. They had been lying this way since Isaac was a toddler. If only she could lie here forever—forget that the future would deprive her of these moments. But then Isaac spoke, and she knew a fissure had opened between them already.

"Are you going to marry Sebastian?" Isaac said in a stiff, oddly grown-up voice. "Because if you do and he buys Woodend—" He tugged on Bownba's ear. "Woodend's your place of memories, but it isn't mine. I want to go home, Mommy." He rubbed his eye with his fist. "I want to go home."

Tilly chewed a flake of dead skin from her lip. "I'm not marrying anyone, my love. The truth is, I still feel married to your father."

"Mom?" Isaac wriggled against her. "Do you miss anything about home?"

"Tons." And it was true. "I miss our garden so much it hurts."

"I miss the fireflies." Isaac sniffed.

"Me, too!" Could she let go of Woodend? Could she force herself to say yet another goodbye? She looked at her child, his face puckered with uncertainty as he stared up at her. Yes, for Isaac's sake, she could. "We are going home, my love. I promise."

"Will Sebastian be mad if we leave?"

"Sebastian? He doesn't do mad. It's not in his genes."

"Is he your boyfriend?" Isaac pouted. She'd never seen him pout before.

"No. He used to be, a long time ago. But that was before I met Daddy."

"I saw you hugging." Isaac's bottom lip quavered. "And it made me feel funny inside. Don't you love Daddy anymore?"

"Always and forever." There it was again, the word James had tossed at her: *always.* She stroked Isaac's back using the firm, downward strokes that had soothed him as a baby. Was she capable of loving someone the way she'd loved David? No, but that didn't mean she couldn't love someone else in a different way. When people asked if she had a favorite flower bed, she always replied that each one was unique. And wasn't that the same with relationships?

"I will always love your father. But I also believe that the human heart is like a pie."

"Can it be pumpkin?" Isaac shimmied closer. "With Cool Whip on top?"

"It can be anything you want. Mine's blackberry and apple. With English double cream."

Isaac yawned. "What do we do with our pies?"

"Slice them up and share the pieces. You can never reclaim a piece, but there's always more to give. I gave you and Daddy the biggest slices, and one day I might give away more, but right now, there are only two things I know with certainty." She brushed back his tousled hair and kissed his forehead. "I love you to Pluto and back, and our life with Daddy will always be precious. Nothing, and no one, will ever change those two facts."

"Will you give James a slice of your pie?"

"Why would you ask that?" She feigned surprise even though she knew the answer to her own question. She knew even before Isaac explained.

"When you walk away, James watches you go. And then he watches for you to come back. He watches you a lot. Haven't you noticed?"

And Tilly shook her head. Each truth she hid from her son was easier to conceal than the one that preceded it. She needed to tread carefully because if she didn't, this whole business of lying could become her personal pandemic.

Twenty-One

"Don't speak." James slammed his thumb knuckle into his forehead. Rain drummed on his shoulders but he ignored it. He needed to get Tilly inside the Hall, out of this downpour, but first, he must explain. He must make amends.

He grabbed the hood of her slicker and yanked it up. Why didn't she look after herself better? The rain had flattened her normally wayward hair giving her the appearance of a waif—small and skinny but with huge, beautiful eyes. Trusting eyes. Eyes that had seen him at his worst. How could he have sunk so low the night before? He had provoked her out of jealousy, an emotion he had struggled to chain all these years. What was happening to him? Since meeting Tilly he was unraveling. He was losing control. That was not good, not good.

"Last night I was out of line." He shivered. His clothes were soaked and his body numb, and yet inside he blazed with humiliation and regret. "Forgive me, please? I was unforgivably rude, unforgivably rude. I had no right to say that, no right."

"For the record, I slapped you. I'm the one who should apologize."

He stared at the gravel. "I was so rude, so rude."

"Hey, handsome. Look at me."

Handsome, she'd called him handsome. That had to mean something, right? He dragged up his head, hoping for what? Anything but the sight of Tilly sticking out her tongue. So, she was going for a gag line, a joke, nothing more. The knowledge stung.

"There," she said. "Now I've been ruder. Shall we call it quits? Then we can get you into some dry clothes. No one ever told you raincoats are a fabulous invention?"

"I could say the same thing about hoods."

"Touché."

James shook back his sopping hair, releasing a fine spray. "Can I say one more time how sorry—"

"Nuh-uh." Tilly held up a finger. "Apologies are *soooo* last season. How high's the fear thermometer?"

The OCD was all-powerful when it latched onto Tilly and Isaac, and yet with that one sentence, she'd thrown him a lifeline. She had remembered about fear thermometers, had known instinctively to use a command code from the war against obsessive-compulsive behavior. How could he walk away from this woman? How could he not? Sebastian could give her Woodend and a ready-made family. All James had to offer was a lifetime of anxiety. For her sake, he needed to accept failure and walk away. For her sake, he needed to become a quitter.

"Down to a seven. I'm down to a seven. But the OCD is telling me hateful things will happen to you if I don't keep apologizing."

"Big fat whoop. Yesterday it told you I would die. And yet

here I am—slightly damaged, but very much alive. Blahdy, blahdy, blah. Same old, same old, if you ask me."

Every time she found the right words. And yet, it wasn't enough. It never would be. He was greedy; he wanted more than she could give. But God Almighty, she was incredible, and she needed to realize that. It might be the only gift he could ever give her.

He took a breath. "Will you follow me?"

Say always, say always.

"Of course," she said with a smile.

A polite, noncommittal answer, the response he didn't want but the voice told him he deserved. If only he could reset time, return to the previous day and their talk of tropical beaches. He hated the beach, couldn't deal with sand. Particles of grit that wormed between his fingers and toes, grains of disintegrated rock that leeched onto his skin with unseen pollutants. But in the hospital parking lot, when they had talked about the ocean, he'd read happiness on Tilly's face. If he could scoop her up right now and take her to the best beach in the world, he would. For Tilly, he might even forgo the beach towel and sit in the sand.

They slogged across Rowena's lawn, following one of the perfect lines mowed the day before by an ancient-looking worker with a graveyard cough, which was, hopefully, nothing contagious. Sheep bleated mournfully across the park as James's sneakers squelched through the spongy grass. The hems of his jeans were weighted down by moisture.

When they reached the gate to the walled garden, he cupped a hand under Tilly's elbow and released a slow breath. Touching her hand in the hospital, a hand that was buried in dirt every day, had been impossibly hard, and yet touching any other part of her body was a powerful sedative for his battered psyche. "Close your eyes," he said. "And promise not to look."

"Gardener's honor," she replied, and let him guide her inside.

Why did she trust him? She really did deserve so much better. He couldn't fault the voice on that train of thought.

James took his hand away but stayed close so he could still feel her spirit, her fire. "You can stop now."

Tilly was smiling before she opened her eyes. "I can smell rue," she said.

"It's only a beginning." His eyes flitted across her face. "But what do you think?

Tilly turned toward the rows of thyme. Two perfect rows he had created for her. "You're amazing, James! How did you manage it?"

No, she was amazing. He was only able to do this because of her. "Rubber gloves and two trash bags per arm secured with duct tape. I couldn't bring myself to dig, but I pulled up the weeds."

Tilly glanced at his pile of tossed plants and frowned.

Oh. They weren't all weeds.

"I'm screwed on our little bet, aren't I?" she said, offering him a smile he hadn't earned. But he would.

James tapped his leg twice. "I should warn you that I'm fastidious when it comes to finishing a project. I never miss a deadline. How about Wednesday afternoon for your skating lesson? Rowena's offered to drive me into Northampton to buy Rollerblades. I gather you're the same shoe size?"

"Aha! Therein lies the flaw in your otherwise brilliant plan. You can't garden in this deluge. And tomorrow's the family outing to Woburn Safari Park. I wouldn't be so confident about winning, Mr. Master Gardener."

"I'm not coming tomorrow," James said.

"Oh, pish posh—don't be so competitive."

She elbowed him playfully and he almost caved. But he had spent all night agonizing over this decision, and he was sticking with it. It was the only way he knew how to protect her from the greatest horror of all: him.

"Look, James. I'll skate with you even if you don't finish. You deserve a reward for that alone." She nodded at the thyme. "See? You don't have to stay here and garden."

"I don't intend to garden. I have personal matters to take care of."

"But we've been planning this all week. Driving through the animal enclosures in the morning, junk food at lunchtime, then feeding nectar to the lorikeets followed by pedallos on Swan Lake. How can you miss out on that much fun?"

She was whining, and Tilly wasn't a whiner. This was what he had done to her. He had been right to come up with a new plan. A plan he would put in motion tomorrow while he was alone and no one could talk him out of it.

He kept his face blank, his mind closed to her. "Thank you, but no."

Twenty-Two

"How about a pair of peacocks?" Sebastian said as the electronic gates of the monkey enclosure slid open. The safari drive was at an end, and Tilly had fingers and toes crossed that the children wouldn't demand a repeat circuit. Yes, it had been fun, but no matter how much she shifted, the ache in her shoulder blade left her nauseated. Worse, it was a constant reminder of her work with James and the feeling that she had been careless with something she should have treasured. Once again, he had pulled her close only to shut her out. Mind you, she had left a red welt across his cheek. Was he the type of person who held a grudge? His sudden coldness suggested he was, but who knew. Being around James was worse than risking the roads after an ice storm. You could put the car in low gear and pump the brake pedal until your foot dropped off, but if you were on an incline, you were merely along for the ride.

Sophie, who was sitting between Sebastian and Tilly on the backseat of Rowena's Discovery, bounced with indignation.

"Peacocks? Don't be naughty, Daddy. You promised me a white pony. And you told Archie he could have a puppy."

"I don't know, chaps," Rowena said from the front. "I'm in the market for that male lion in the Kingdom of the Carnivores. Did you see the size of his...pride? I bet his lionesses are happy." She winked at Mrs. Haddington, who chortled.

Rowena drove forward slowly. "Which animal would you adopt, Haddy?"

"A giraffe."

"Interesting," Rowena said. "Would that, by any chance, be because giraffes are tall with big brown eyes and eyelashes any woman would kill for?"

"No, Rowena." Tilly stretched back her arms until her elbows dug into the seat. If she could just get comfortable.... "It's because they're a contradiction. Their legs look so brittle, and yet they move with grace and power."

The car rocked as Archie and Isaac shrieked from the fold-down seats in the rear. A patas monkey had landed on the hood of the car, its cheeks puffed out with food. It stopped chewing to stare at Rowena, then turned and mooned her.

"Struth," Rowena said. "Not sure anything quite so small and hairy has ever shown me his privates before."

Archie's laughter ricocheted around the car, and then everyone else joined in. Everyone except Sophie, who tutted dramatically. Tilly sat back, watching. The group dynamic was lighter without James. He was the cuckoo in the nest, the interloper who didn't belong.

Personal matters, my ass. James had stayed behind because he realized it was easier this way: without him.

Tilly hunkered into her hoodie and shoved her hands deeper into her pockets, fending off the chill that had swept in with the storm the night before. Her fingernails raked up lint from the seams: detritus she'd brought from North Carolina without even knowing.

"I'm off for a wee," Rowena announced. Her green eyes were bright and her normally pale cheeks were flushed from the cold. She waved at Sebastian and Sophie, who were pedaling a huge fiberglass swan across the lake. Isaac and Archie steamed away in another swan, giggling and clearly plotting. Mrs. Haddington was presiding from a bench, looking every inch the proud matriarch despite the slightly grubby cast.

Tilly turned to her mother. "Ro's in a good place these days, isn't she? D'you think it's because Isaac's become Tweedledum to her Tweedledee?" She hoped so; it lessened the guilt of what she wanted to say.

"Oh, I'm sure that's part of it," her mother replied. "He calms her down...she pushes him to be less pliable. But no, I think Rowena has finally found her niche. Sit with me." Mrs. Haddington began buttoning her cashmere cardigan, working from the bottom up, and Tilly felt the conversation slip away from her before it had begun.

"Such a shame James didn't join us." Tilly felt her mother's gaze. "He's extraordinarily intuitive for a man—giving you and Sebastian space."

"I hate to burst your bubble, but there's nothing going on between me and either man." Tilly held up her right hand. "Scout's honor."

"You were never a Girl Scout. Or a Brownie. You refused to wear the uniform, as I recall, and made some precocious comments about conformity." Mrs. Haddington examined her engagement ring, moving her finger to let the stones catch the sunlight. "Did you know that I used to watch you sleep in your cot? Your father assumed it was out of concern that you, too, would be taken from me, but he was wrong." Her mother pursed her lips. She never talked about Henrietta and Clemie, who had died in their cribs before Tilly was born. "I knew you'd survive. Such a strong, healthy baby. But I sensed that happiness would come at a terrible price for you. Sadly, I was right." She gave Isaac a small wave and then returned her hand to her lap. "I thought if I watched over you I could keep you safe. Protecting one's child is an instinct one never loses. And it begs the question—is Sebastian the easy way out? After all, he is your Achilles' heel."

"To be honest, I think he's *your* Achilles' heel." *Especially now you're happily selling him our family home.* Even if she could accept the loss of Woodend, she didn't have to celebrate Sebastian buying it.

"Do you? How interesting." Her mother gave a hearty sneeze and removed a lace handkerchief from her cardigan pocket.

"When we messed up, your anger was directed solely at me. Why was that?" Tilly tried not to remember the weeks of punishment after her mother caught her and Sebastian in bed.

"Well, apart from the fact that you set the tone and Sebastian followed, he was far too frail for chastisement." Mrs. Haddington used her isn't-it-obvious voice. "Gracious, I didn't dare look at him sideways after his father left. The dear boy puts on a brave front, but one doesn't have to look hard to see the cracks. Your father and I were very fond of Sebastian, but we always knew you'd outgrow him."

"And now?"

Her mother wiped her nose, then repocketed the hanky. "Oh, I think the future's a little more complicated, don't you?"

The sounds of summer squealed around them despite the

cold and the mud. "Are you really okay with this, Mum? Doesn't it hurt like hell watching him claim Woodend?"

"Second-guessing one's decisions is an utter waste of energy, darling. Besides, pain is part of the process of moving on."

Amazing what you learn from hiding in a wardrobe. "Talking of decisions—" *spit it out, Tilly* "—I've asked Rowena to become Isaac's legal guardian."

"Excellent," her mother said. "She's agreed?"

Tilly blew out the breath she'd been bottling up. "You're not upset?"

"Darling, I would move heaven and earth for Isaac, but God forbid, if he needed to live with a guardian, wouldn't you rather he was at the Hall than bunged in a cottage with two gin-swilling biddies who spend the winter reading seed catalogs? I'm only surprised you didn't ask Rowena sooner. What changed your mind?"

"I'm having a rethink, on the map of life."

Her mother bent down, grunting as she used both hands to shift her plastered leg away from the wet grass. "If something were wrong, you would tell me?"

"Uh-huh." Tilly inhaled sharply. The air was heavy with the musk of damp earth, a smell she normally loved. But this afternoon it dragged her down, along with her thoughts.

Her mother looked up. "Goodness, I think they're going to crash."

Isaac and Archie wore matching grins as they pedaled frantically toward Sebastian and Sophie. Sebastian had pulled forward, his body language saying, *You're on.* The air was filled with chatter, laughter and the plash of pedals slicing through water, but the sounds melted away until Tilly heard only Sebastian's giggle.

Twenty-Three

Tilly breathed in the orangey perfume of Lady Roxton's philadelphus and enjoyed a rare moment of nothingness. Except that James's gardening notebook lay temptingly close on the bench next to her, his Montblanc rollerball marking his last entry. One peek wouldn't hurt, would it? She would never commit the sin of privacy invasion, but scribblings about plants could hardly reveal intimacies. Beside, James didn't have the brain circuitry for mixed content. On the other hand, he might go nuclear if she messed with his possessions. Everything in James's world had its place.

A tractor rumbled in the distance and Tilly swallowed. Her throat was sore from hours of prattling. Lecturing, while James hung back and scribbled in his little book. Black, of course, since everything about James was black today, from his earrings to his mood. He had expressed no interest in the Woburn jaunt and had ignored her probes about his day alone. Not that she needed to ask how he'd spent his time, since mounds of rosemary now circled evenly spaced rows of thyme, sage and rue. Clearly, he'd fobbed her off with that crap about *personal matters.* Tilly gnawed on a hangnail. Frustrated didn't begin to explain how she felt. But then again, all things James had become wrapped in barbed wire since his bombshell about David. Maybe gardening was all they had left to share.

James had certainly been an eager pupil that morning, sparking with energy. "Elaborate," he kept saying, his fingers jiggling as if he were speed learning. When she explained that gardening was plagued by the unexpected but offered so many comeback lines that defeat was never an option, he wrote it down and underlined it twice. The trick, she told him, was to adapt to every curveball that nature threw at you. If a plant had outgrown its space, you cut it back. If a plant wasn't thriving, you moved it.

Tilly glanced at the notebook again. How long had James been gone? Five minutes? She had explained elevenses—English snack—during their first day in the walled garden, and every morning, when the clock on the stable block chimed eleven, James disappeared and returned with treats. She never put in a request; she didn't need to. He kept a Tupperware of her favorite chocolate in the Hall fridge. Tilly's stash, Rowena called it. What would James bring her this morning? Easy-peasy, a Cadbury flake. Perfect for a sunny, sixty-degree day. He had studied her well. By the time he flew home, James would have learned more about her than about gardening. And what would she have learned about him?

She set the pen aside and pried open the nappa-covered notebook. For a moment Tilly stared at James's writing without seeing words. Then she stroked the small, compact letters, so different from her large, loopy style. He took notes in complete sentences, each line of text a grammatically correct, self-contained thought with no abbreviations. She flipped through, stopping when she reached an angry doodle that spread like a bloodstain over an entire page. Every line was sharpened to a point, the pen strokes carved with such force that they had broken through the paper in several places. James hadn't drawn a single curve.

"Find anything interesting?" he said.

Tilly shrieked and dropped the notebook. How could she not have heard him approach?

He positioned one of the two mugs he was carrying on the armrest next to Tilly and then fished out a Cadbury flake from his jean pocket.

Tilly thanked him and tried not to think about the reason for the flake's slight warmth.

She retrieved the notebook from the ground, dusted it off on her T-shirt and flicked through to find the right page to mark with his pen. "Why're you taking notes today?" she said.

He pushed up his sunglasses, scraping his hair back to expose his high, pale forehead. At some point in his life he must have worn his hair short. Is this how he would have looked? His thick, dark eyebrows were now his most prominent feature, and his cheekbones were more pronounced. Only the eyes remained the same.

"I don't want to forget anything you've taught me—" he watched her "—after I leave on Friday."

"What!" She shot forward and spat out a mouthful of coffee. "But I thought you were staying until I have my results?"

"I am." He sat next to her. "Which is why I booked a Friday flight."

"But what if it's malignant?"

"Then a stranger won't be much help."

"Crap." She thumped her cup down on the ground, spilling coffee over her Wellington boot. "This is crap, and you know it. Been there, done that, had the conversation. You're not a stranger. And if this is some lame excuse to get me to confess...."

He pulled his sunglasses off his head and shook his hair free. "Confess to what?" He sounded so indifferent she expected him to yawn.

Tilly gave a snort and stared at the puddle of coffee glistening on her boot. She wasn't claiming feelings she didn't own, or suspected she didn't own. "The garden—" She pointed at the rose bed with its pruned canes, excavated edge and compost-rich soil. "We're not done with the garden."

"I think we are, Tilly."

"But the tree house."

"I'll finish on Thursday, while we wait for the surgeon's call."

"Why, James? Why are you leaving?" She swallowed the word *me,* worried it would sound petulant.

"I butted into your world, forced you to take me on." James gave a rueful smile. "We both know it's time I reconnected with my own life. I need to check on the house, and then I'll drive to Chicago to visit friends, leave the Alfa there and fly to Seattle for an extended trip." He raised his mug, with both hands, to his lips. "I haven't seen Daniel in twelve months."

"Who's Daniel?"

"My son. He lives in Seattle."

The breeze brought the faint, but discernible, scent of wild honeysuckle from The Chase, and the echo of a pheasant's cough. Tilly could almost hear the morning ticking away as she sat in Rowena's walled garden exchanging words with a stranger.

She prodded a stray rose petal with her foot. "If you're leaving at the end of the week, it's time I showed you how to plant."

★ ★ ★

"Promise one last time that I can't catch cancer from the soil." His words spilled out as he crouched on the thyme-covered walk.

"I've promised five times already," Tilly said. "That's enough."

But she hadn't made it to six. "Please?"

"No. That's your OCD asking, not you."

A mob of starlings flew over the walled garden cackling and James imagined shooting them. He hadn't fired his dad's rifle in three decades, but today he felt primal, like a Neanderthal hunter waiting to kill. And it disgusted him. Vile images hijacked his mind. He saw himself with his fingers clasped around a bird's neck, wringing the life out of it, which was bogus. He knew in his soul he could never kill a bird. He'd felt bad enough about flattening that moth in his bedroom the other night, and moths creeped him out.

James took off his sunglasses and pinched the bridge of his nose. A headache was drilling through his skull. His bangs, now long enough to tuck behind his ears, flopped forward. Pinpricks of anger jabbed at him. Why did he ever think he had the patience to grow his hair? He wanted to jerk it out by the roots.

"Come on, James. What are the chances of catching cancer from soil?"

He looked up. "Less than zero?"

"Exactly." Tilly smiled, but he couldn't imagine why. Quite possibly she was relieved this would be their last gardening lesson. "Ready to try again?" she asked.

No. He didn't want to disappoint her, but his focus was broken. He needed to distance himself—from this garden, from Tilly. In his mind he had left already.

"No. I'm done," he said, and used his wrist to force the

web of hair from his face. He eyed the discarded gardening gloves, ripped off and abandoned after his abortive attempt to dig up a daylily. An excellent plant, Tilly had told him, for a first lesson on subdividing. Even Isaac couldn't kill a daylily. No, but James could.

"Listen," she said. "Hear that song? *Tsee-tsee-tsu-hu-hu-hu.* It's a blue tit."

And doubt about leaving returned. But doubt was part of his DNA, and he had to find the strength to ignore it. That had been his goal before he'd met Tilly, before he had allowed jealousy and desire to distract him.

The agony of leaving her had begun, but heartbreak, like anxiety, faded. And even if he couldn't tackle the ultimate exposure, did it matter? Thanks to Tilly, he had made incredible progress. He would never forget the hope that she had given him by caring, by reminding him to laugh. But the fantasy was over. He knew it; so did she.

"I'm going to miss sharing my private hell." James stared at a topiary of ivy that had long since broken free of its shape.

"Me, too," Tilly sighed. "Me, too."

Twenty-Four

She…was going…to die. How insane was it to strap toy-size wheels to your feet with the sole purpose of tearing along like a bullet train? She was a single parent desperate to survive to her next birthday, not a bachelor happily risking life for asinine thrills. Leg muscles Tilly had never been aware of ached, and her feet were as heavy as blocks of concrete.

"I'm done." She plopped, bottom first, onto the verge and picked at the weld of knots James had tied on her right boot.

Ignoring her whinges of protest, he bent down and hoisted her back up.

He smelled of satsumas today, which was hardly surprising. Glass jars of satsuma soap sat by every washbasin in Bramwell Hall, as if Rowena were terrified that she could run out. Tilly loved the scent of satsumas, too, although maybe not today, when it distracted her with Christmas memories—the crackle of the drawing room fire, the aroma of mince pies baking, choral descants on the radio. The first time she and David toured the house at Creeping Cedars, Tilly bounded into the great room and announced, "That's the spot for a

Christmas tree." But David overruled her. Once they had kids, he explained, a Christmas tree would overshadow Hanukkah. Why had she abandoned her cherished family traditions without a fight? And why had she conceded on the in-line skating? Was she, yet again, contorting herself to fit someone else's expectations?

"You've mastered the basics," James said. "Now it's time for some speed."

Great, just what she needed—a little speed to ensure she embraced death at full tilt.

"No, no and no." Tilly tried to shrug him off, but wobbled like a marionette with broken strings. She grabbed at the solid warmth of his forearms.

Her stomach lurched and her pulse danced to some hot-blooded Latin beat. This was such a bad idea on so many levels.

"If I fall," she said, "the tarmac will tear me to pieces." And that would be the least of her problems. If she pulled him down on top of her they could end up entwined heart-to-heart, groin-to-groin. *Oh, bugger.*

His muscles tensed under her grip. "Do you think I could let you fall?" There was a sharp edge to his voice, but his face spoke only of hurt. Devastating hurt, as if she had betrayed him.

"James, I would trust you with my life." Wasn't she, in fact? "But you and I get our jollies differently. I'm a coward at heart, and this is way outside my comfort zone."

A smile tugged at the right corner of his mouth. He was too close, but she couldn't let go. Without him, she wouldn't survive this ridiculous ordeal.

"We're going to roll forward, just a little momentum, okay?"

"Not okay, far from okay." Tilly scrabbled at him, her heart now pumping terror, not lust.

"Remember—ankles strong. Don't let them sink inward. Left foot forward a little, then push. Right foot forward a little, then push. As if you're marching. And brake gradually."

"Ankles strong, got it. Left foot, push. Right foot... bugger." She collapsed around her waist, twisting his skin as she clasped his arm. "I have *so* not got it."

"Relax." He was gliding backward, dragging her with him. "Let me do what I do best—worry enough for both of us."

Okay, she would focus on his mouth, on that seductive smile unwrapping like a slow stretch at the end of a day. Of all the ways he could decompress, he chose this?

As he offered his face to the sky, the cleft in his chin became an inky hollow. She had called him handsome a few days earlier as a joke, but she wasn't laughing now. David was flat-out stunning with his dark ringlets and uncanny resemblance to Botticelli's Mars. And Sebastian's refined features made his face close to perfection. But James? He was breath-stealingly gorgeous, and, quite possibly, the sexiest man she had ever met.

They whizzed past the crinkle-crankle yew hedge. Wait! How had they picked up speed so quickly? They were going too fast too soon. His hair whipped across his face, obscuring his mouth, and Tilly tried to speak but couldn't force out *stop,* let alone add *please.* Drowning, she was drowning in air. But then James caressed the inside of her elbow, and the restriction in her throat vanished. She laughed; she actually laughed. He was leading her somewhere she could never have imagined she wanted to go. And it was kinda fun.

She threw back her head and shrieked into the cloud-covered sky. James answered with a rich, sultry laugh that was even more precious than one of his smiles. The terror, the sore muscles, the imminent heart failure, all were worthwhile for that laugh. Which was just as well, since it was, quite possibly, the last thing she would ever hear.

Time stretched to accommodate multiple sounds and thoughts: tires whooshing on the tarmac; the honk of a horn; panic racking her body—*how do I brake;* her breath escaping with an *ouff* as she flew into James; her heart crashing against her ribs—a wrecking ball smashing apart every preconception about how it would feel to hold James.

Many times—more than she wanted to admit but when death hurtled toward you in a muddy Discovery, self-honesty was the least of your problems—she had wondered how their bodies would fit together. *Awkwardly* was the adverb she'd settled on, given the disparity in their heights, her wonky torso and his lean frame of hard muscle. How wrong she had been. His body cushioned hers and his arms secured her like a custom-designed harness. A perfect fit.

She followed the tempo of his pulse, heard him breathe and imbibed the feeling of James. Gradually, she stopped shaking and screamed a silent *yes.*

"Having fun, are we?" Rowena leaned out of the driver's window.

"Hi, Mom! Hi, James!" Isaac called from inside the car. "Can I join in?"

Tilly snapped back, her cheeks on fire. She pushed free of James, shimmied, and flopped over the hood of the Discovery.

"No," she said to both questions and instantly regretted her answer.

Twenty-Five

Monty barked, then stopped. Some poor sod had dared to walk past on the High Street, no doubt. Tilly turned back to admire the herbaceous border, where there was nothing left to deadhead, tie back or dig up. At her mother's request, Tilly had stopped working in the garden so the gardener could feel useful. Interesting concept, feeling useful. Was that why James had hung around? Yesterday, she had spooked both of them with nothing more than a failed flicker of desire, and tomorrow he flew home. But what of today? She balled up her hands in the sleeves of her fleece and shivered. It was another cool, gray day—an appropriate end to her time with James, because really, today was an end. Whatever the outcome of her tests, James would leave and that would be that. But what if she wanted him to stay?

Monty trotted around the side of the house, tail wagging.

"Scare them off, did you, mutt?"

Too late she realized he was not alone. James appeared, his black leather backpack slung over one shoulder, the black cord from his iPod earbuds snaking down his chest into his jeans pocket.

She watched, anticipating each movement before he made it. The man had a method for everything, even unplugging his iPod. He would wrap the earbud cord around two fingers to create a neat bundle, secure it with a black twisty tie, then slip it into the small, aluminum container he kept in the outside pocket of his backpack.

Tilly smiled, but it was an empty gesture. She knew his every quirk and still she couldn't slot him into her life, much less keep him there. What had been troubling her since dawn was not whether James would appear, since she knew he would, but how he would react if the surgeon gave her the all clear. Would James stay to celebrate, or would he dash off to pack, convinced that she no longer needed him?

Tilly repuffed the cushions on her mother's lounger and tried not to remember the feel of the man who had scarred her husband, the man she didn't dare love.

He strode onto the patio. "Any news?"

"No. And don't stare." Tilly nibbled a fingernail. "My mother already told me I look consumptive."

"Consumptive, really? I was going to say you look like shit."

"You were?" She gave a hollow laugh. "In that case you can stay."

A pigeon flapped in the birdbath and a car backfired on the High Street. Neither of them moved.

"I should work on the tree house," James said, his voice lacking conviction.

"No." Tilly grabbed his hand. "Stay with me. But I can't guarantee conversation. I didn't sleep last night."

He sighed. "Me neither."

"Wired yet?" James handed her a fourth cup of coffee and smiled. He had the widest smile she had ever seen. It lit up his face and gave her the sensation of sinking into a deep bubble bath when outside the world was ice and snow.

"I'm completely out of whack." She stared at her leg, jerking against the patio table. "I just want this day done with, but when it's over…you leave." *And I can't convince myself that's a good thing.*

James scraped his wrought-iron chair across the concrete and sat, as always, too close. He pried one hand from her mug, crushing her fingers into his. Were the two of them slipping into love while neither of them paid attention? And if so, why did it hurt so much? Was it because of David or because of Sebastian? Or was love irrelevant? Was this nothing more than need, the same quick fix as one of James's compulsions?

Sheep bleated across the fields. She always heard sheep, never cows. What had happened to the cranky Charolais, the scourge of her childhood? Was it the result of mad cow disease, the foot-and-mouth culling, or had time robbed the landscape of the life she had known?

After all, the village school had been gutted and turned into a home by faceless Londoners; the High Street was now scarred by a pedestrian crossing no one used; the village green no longer buzzed with the Friday night chaos of the fish and chip van; and rumor had it the post office would close within the year. Bramwell Chase had become a commuter community, a place people passed through, a place Tilly no longer belonged. Everything around her felt unfamiliar, except for the stranger sitting beside her, squeezing her hand too tightly. The man she couldn't fathom.

"Tilly, darling. Are you down there?" Mrs. Haddington's voice boomed from her bedroom window. "Someone called Beth is on the phone. Oh, and Isaac says to tell you he just put up a hotel on Bond Street. Little rascal's going to beat me!"

Beth was the buxom breast clinic nurse who had blatantly ogled James.

Isaac giggled in the distance, and Monty barked for attention. Tilly ground her teeth and wished, with everything she had, that she could transport herself to another time and place. Upstairs playing Monopoly with her mother and son would be good. Anywhere but stranded in one of those solitary moments in which the world kept turning, and you handled despair alone.

This time, however, she wasn't alone.

"I'll take it in the study. Thanks!" Tilly called back.

James shot up, shoving his chair aside. "Should I wait here?" His fingers wove through a sign language only he understood.

"No." She reclaimed his hand. "Come with me."

They walked through the French doors into the drawing room, but when they reached her father's study, James let go, and she entered alone.

She stumbled over a hole singed into the carpet, and a memory flashed: her father seated in the leather desk chair when she blurted out, "David wants to marry me," and the shock on his face as he dropped his cigar onto the Oriental carpet her mother adored. It was the only time she heard her father swear.

The study smelled, as it had that day, of overheated vacuum and musty law books, of cigars and lavender—her father loved lavender. Or was she imagining the cigars? She walked to her father's desk and picked up the phone.

"Tilly?" Beth's voice was brusque, ready for business. *Good news, bad news, what?*

"Can you wait a minute, please?" The crackling on the open line kept pace with the thumping in Tilly's chest. "You can hang up now, Mum!" she yelled.

Fumbling came through the extension, as if someone—
Isaac no doubt—had dropped the phone and was struggling
to pick it up.

James closed the study door and hesitated, his hand gripping
the crystal doorknob. As a child, Tilly had marveled at how
the sun streamed through the window behind her and hit the
doorknob, transforming it into a prism of color. But today
there was no sun and no rainbow. The doorknob was buried
in James's hand; it revealed nothing.

The extension clicked into place on the cradle and James
turned but stayed rooted by the door. *No.* Tilly shook her
head. *I need you closer.* She reached for him across the blotter
stained with ink from her father's fountain pen, and James
replied with a nod of understanding. When he was in place
behind her, she clamped both hands on the phone and leaned
into his chest.

His hands grazed her arms, then fell to his sides.

"Sorry," Tilly said into the phone. "I'm ready now." Her
head moved to the beat of James's shallow, quick breaths.

"It's a C2, great news, Tilly." Even though Beth spoke with
quick efficiency, her timbre suggested a smile.

Tilly swiveled round to look up at James. His eyes were
still, his gaze penetrating hers as if he would never lose sight
of her. "It's benign?" Tilly said.

"Yes. Seems your mother's GP was right after all. A
fibroadenoma. More common in younger women, but then
again—" Beth gave a girly laugh "—you look about sixteen.
What's your secret?"

"Gin and gardening." But Tilly was hardly listening, even
to herself. She was watching James's lips move as if he were
reciting a silent prayer.

She relaxed against him. "What now? Leave it be?"

"In younger women we say watch and wait. Not do

anything unless it becomes painful or larger. But since you're over thirty-five, Dr. Parker recommends excisional biopsy."

"In idiot terms?"

Beth gave another laugh, and Tilly felt as if they were friends with decades of shared experiences. She could even forgive Beth for eyeing James. "Have it surgically removed," Beth said. "But it's up to you."

"Can I wait two weeks, until I can see my gynecologist back home?"

"Of course. But if it changes in size or becomes painful, contact us immediately. I'll post you the paperwork." The efficient voice had returned; Beth was ready to move on to her next patient. "Should I use the Bramwell Chase address?"

"Yes." Tilly swallowed. "And thank you. Omigod-thankyou."

"You're welcome. Safe journey home." Beth paused. "And regards to your gorgeous bloke."

Safe journey to where? Into a blank future that was hers to write, one that might contain the gorgeous bloke she was going to kiss right here in her father's study, consequences be damned?

The dial tone buzzed and Tilly slotted the receiver back into place, relishing this new certainty. She turned, surprised to discover James had inched away from her.

"Don't." She grabbed a fistful of his shirt. "Just don't."

Stretching up on tiptoe she yanked down, not caring if his shirt ripped. His forehead sank to hers, and she breathed in the scent of him—cedar and honey and a mystery element she could define only as James. Her mouth skimmed his cheek, pausing when his breath warmed her skin.

"Tell me now if you don't want to do this—" her lips slid over his "—because in a moment's time…I won't be able to stop."

★ ★ ★

"Is this what you want, Tilly?" James removed her hand from his shirt. Not that he cared if she shredded it, but he couldn't think, couldn't breathe when she touched him. And if they were to be together, he needed to confront the fear that she loved someone else.

"A kiss?" She raised her eyebrows and looked so confused, so vulnerable, he had to force himself not to kiss her. "Yes. I want to kiss you, live in the moment. Is that so wrong?"

He touched his bottom lip, moist with her saliva, and sadness gored him. He had hoped for, had wanted, so much more. Not a kiss, but a commitment.

"For me? Yes, it is." He pinned her hand to his chest. "I can't play at love, Tilly. I do all or nothing. I *want* all or nothing." Was he facing his fear or reverting to the subtleties of obsession by seeking reassurance where there was none?

"Is that what you think of me? That I'm toying with you?" She tried to pry her hand free, but he held on.

"No, Tilly. I think you're confused about what—and whom—you want. I'd like to tell you it's me. But I can't do that." He paused. "Can I?" There was still a chance, still a chance, but even as she started to speak, he knew he'd botched it. Again.

You're an eejit, James, a fucking eejit. Why didn't you take what she offered you?

"James, my life has yo-yoed all over the place this summer, and I've been hanging on, nothing more. But the ride has included you. And I know this is horribly selfish, but I want you to stay. I can't give you reassurance—" she'd rumbled him, but he wouldn't expect any less from her "—I can't even explain it. I just don't want you to leave. Please don't go."

She gave the saddest smile, and he wanted to kiss her. It would be so easy to kiss her. Why couldn't he kiss her? Why couldn't he take one non-premeditated risk? Because he was a guy who couldn't think outside his obsessive-compulsive box.

James gave a deep sigh. "I see you with Sebastian. There's still love between you."

"If you know that, then you know more than I do." Tilly's huge opal eyes gazed at him.

He released her hand, but she flattened both her palms against his chest. Was she trying to push him away or keep him close?

"Not love then," he said. "But a connection I can't compete with."

"So it's better to walk away?"

"I have no interest in runner-up badges, Tilly." How he loved the feel of her name on his tongue. *Tilly*—such a soft, beautiful name. The most beautiful name he had ever spoken. "I want to win, every time. I could offer to wait while you figure out which one of us you want, but I'm not capable of delayed gratification." He stroked her cheek, then slid his fingers into her hair. "You were right to tell me not to hem you in. Cornering people with ultimatums is one of my talents. I can grind love down until it's nothing but hate. I've done it before, but I won't do it again, not with you. Never with you."

He twisted the hair at the nape of her neck—tighter and tighter. She grimaced, and he let go. See? He could offer nothing but pain, and she should be showered with joy.

"If I stay, I won't like the person I'll become and neither will you. I have to walk away because I can't, I won't, take the risk that you'll wake up one morning hating me." As his father had done when he'd thrown James out. As Daniel had done after he'd been diagnosed with depression and James had been unable to offer more than a deal-with-it mentality.

But neither of them had hated James more than he had hated himself.

"Can't we be—"

"Please don't say *friends*. I didn't force myself to sit on a plane for eight hours battling images of fireballs in the sky, of plummeting into the Atlantic Ocean, of overshooting the runway and crashing into the control tower…I didn't face my fears because I wanted a new friend." He backed away from her and headed toward the door.

"No, you came because you wanted a garden."

"The garden was the excuse, not the reason."

A ray of sunlight burst across the room and the crystal doorknob became a kaleidoscope of refracted light.

"No?" Tilly said. "Then why did you come?"

His hand hovered above the doorknob, and the kid in him, the kid who had died with his mother, said, *Touch the rainbow.* He did, but merely snuffed it out.

"You." James stared at his hand. "It was always you. You're the reason I came, and you're the reason I must leave." He opened the door and a blast of noise rushed in, a scraping and a thudding from above.

"You're in danger, Matilda Rose, of becoming my greatest obsession."

Twenty-Six

"Mommmyyyyy!" Isaac's wail tore through her body. *Where was he?* Tilly ran to the study door and shoved James aside.

Crutches clunked on the floorboards above and paws scrabbled down the stairs, chased by the thunder of distraught child. That had to be good, right, had to mean Isaac wasn't hurt? Tilly stumbled and grabbed the newel post as Monty shot between her legs and tore across the drawing room.

Isaac reached the bottom step and whispered, "Mommy," but his gaze was fixed on the open French door; Tilly might have been a ghost. But she *was* there, her child needed her and she *was* there. She hadn't prayed in years. Truth was, she had held on to her belief in God by her fingernails and had done so only for her child. But Tilly was light-headed with gratitude. Her child needed her and she was alive. *Thank you, God. Thank you.*

"I'm here, my love." Tilly swung around onto the stairs. "I'm here."

"Mommy?" Isaac hiccuped a sob and threw himself at Tilly. James moved swiftly and silently into position behind

Isaac, helping her create a protective bumper, a parental bumper, around her child. Tilly shivered, and imagined James humming as he soothed a screaming baby, as he took that incredible focus of his and applied it to fatherhood. Instinctively, she began to rock Isaac, while James stroked his hair.

"Tell your mother what happened," James said, his voice low. "So we can help."

We. James had claimed her trauma and relabeled it *ours.* Once again, she had underestimated him. His words, spoken minutes earlier, returned: *You're the reason I came.* But he hadn't confessed the whole truth. Clearly, Isaac was part of that reason, too.

"Monty—" Isaac gulped. "He jumped on the bed while we were playing Monopoly and, and—" He jerked in his breath, then released a tsunami of tears. "He ran off with Bownba. I hate Monty. I hate him."

When Isaac was little, Bownba was the fourth member of the family. An imaginary friend in teddy bear form with his own place setting at the dinner table. To lose Bownba, or worse, see him mauled to shreds, was unthinkable.

Tilly pulled back to hold Isaac's face, her thumbs wiping his damp cheeks. "Have I ever let you down, Angel Bug?" Isaac shook his head. "Then I need you to stay with James while I rescue Bownba." She raised her chin with a sniff of bravado. "James, can you look after Isaac and help my mother downstairs?"

"Oh for goodness' sake, Tilly." Mrs. Haddington lowered herself onto the top stair. "I'm not an invalid. I can manage perfectly well by myself." She hurled her crutches down the stairs, muttering, "Oopsy-daisy," when they clattered into her grandmother's spindle-legged table. "Go after the dog."

She waved Tilly off and then bumped down to the next step on her bottom. "Go!"

Isaac spun around and flung himself at James. And it took all Tilly's self-control to not tug Isaac free. Four words stabbed at her: *It should be me.* But she couldn't always be Isaac's first line of defense, couldn't always be the person to comfort him. She had tried to shut out others—fewer people, fewer chances for heartache—but she had simply been running away, dragging Isaac with her. Until James had blocked their path.

And now he was stepping into her role like a well-rehearsed understudy. James tucked the sobbing Isaac into his chest and resumed Tilly's rocking. This was a keeper moment, one she wanted to squirrel away with the scene of Isaac and Sebastian playing cricket. But that had been a snapshot of happiness, an image she would have captured on film had she not stopped using her camera except to record Isaac's birthdays. This, however, was a private tableau.

She kneaded her forehead. *Think, woman, think.* She used to be good at this. Handling crises had been her talent within the Haddington family.

Tilly jumped back, her mind blissfully clear. She ran into the kitchen, levered off her clogs—surely an Amazon faced battle barefooted—and turned the tap to cold. Water spluttered out, splashing slowly into the washing-up bowl. Tilly cursed and jabbed the tap with her elbow. Where was efficient American plumbing when you needed it?

At least that bastard dog couldn't go far. The paddock gate was latched and the outer gates shut. Monty was trapped, his only bolt hole the place under the hedge where he dragged all his kills. And if she had to worm in after him like a tunnel rat, she would.

The tap squeaked and juddered as she screwed it shut.

Then, muttering every obscenity she could muster, Tilly hoisted the bowl from the sink and lurched out of the back door with her load. Monty was tearing around the lawn in circles, delighted with his new game. Keeping her eyes on his, she edged onto the lawn and crouched down. Icy water slopped onto her jeans, but she didn't flinch. Balancing on the balls of her feet, Tilly anchored her toes in the cold grass.

"Monty." She dropped her voice and rammed the ground with one finger. "Come. Here." Then she reestablished her grip on the sides of the bowl.

Monty wagged his tail and spread his front legs, poised to spring.

Tilly narrowed her eyes. *Do it, dirtbag.*

As Monty bolted toward her, she knew he'd veer to the right. Damn, but he was predictable. She sprang up and threw the contents of the bowl at him. Monty skidded to a halt and dropped Bownba.

"Do that again—" Tilly reached out and drew Bownba toward her "—and I'll give you to Rowena. Got it?"

Monty gave a whine and flopped onto his stomach.

"Bownba's safe!" Tilly called out, and then collapsed onto her haunches. She was the victorious, all-conquering mom-heroine. *I am mother, hear me roar.*

Isaac catapulted into her. "You saved him, Mom! You saved Bownba!"

"Super Mom to the rescue." Tilly hoisted the damp, slimy bear over her head and waited for James to claim it.

"That's a nasty wound," James said. "But I have no doubt Super Mom can fix it."

Mrs. Haddington, who had hobbled onto the patio, bellowed with laughter.

"Mom doesn't sew," Isaac explained.

Tilly glanced up at James, but he was eyeing the teddy

dangling from his pincer grip, disgust etched on his face. He really was the sexiest man she'd ever met, even though he wouldn't kiss her.

"Don't sew, don't dust, don't bake." Tilly gave a ragged laugh. "I'm a lousy cook and I lose socks in the wash." Was she trying to prove that she was worthy of him, or that she wasn't? "I'm the anti–fifties housewife."

"As every woman should be." James dug a folded white tissue from his pocket—one of those super-large super-strength kind—and swaddled Bownba like a mummy. "Luckily, Isaac, I have everything we need to mend Bownba. Would you fetch my backpack from the hall?"

"Sure!" Isaac bounced off.

"I see the two of you have the situation under control," Mrs. Haddington said. "I think I'll go and settle myself in the kitchen. It's almost time for *The Archers*. Monty, come with me, you bad dog." Monty snuffled her leg. "And no, it's no good trying to make nice. That was a despicable thing to do. No pizzles for you, in fact I...." Her voice trailed off as she hopped over the step into the drawing room.

Silence, thick as Carolina humidity, settled on the patio, broken only when the sounds of a radio soap opera drifted through the kitchen window. Tilly smiled nervously, tempted to say: *Now, where were we?* But it was James who spoke first.

"Pizzles?" He placed Bownba on the patio table.

"You don't want to know...." She tried to add something witty, but her humor failed her. And without it she felt exposed. Talking to James had always been easy, but Tilly's stomach prickled and burned as if she had poison ivy on the inside.

"Is there anything you don't carry in that backpack of yours?" she blurted out. *Terrific. Nothing like an inane comment, Tilly.* Why couldn't he have kissed her? One little kiss. No biggie. Or maybe it was a huge, effin' biggie. The first guy she'd attempted to kiss in three years, and he'd rejected her.

"Since I don't do spontaneity, I need to be prepared for every eventuality." James unfurled the tissue, then used it to cover his fingers as he splayed Bownba's limbs. "But you know me well enough to have figured that out."

Yeah, right. She'd figured him out so well that she'd tried to kiss him, which seemed to be the last thing he wanted. "Isn't flying home tomorrow spontaneous?"

"Hardly." He smiled and lifted his head, and once again she saw the child in the man, a passionate child, quick to find enthusiasm or anger. "If I stay I'll end up brawling with Sebastian. And contrary to what you might believe, I like the guy. Well, I respect him."

She hugged her stomach. "Being here without you is going to feel so strange. You've become part of the scenery." Ugh. That's not what she meant. Not even close.

James stared at a clump of dead aubrietia trapped between two paving slabs.

No. This was not ending in a failed kiss. "We need to talk, James, about what you said."

"Not now." James gave a nod toward the house.

Isaac staggered out, James's bag clutched to his chest. "Jeez-um. That's heavy." He dumped the bag next to Bownba.

"For good reason," James said. "Isaac, would you care to assist with surgery?"

Isaac's eyes grew wide with delight. It was so easy to help a child bounce back. Simply hold out warm arms and wait for the scraped knee to be forgotten, the tears to become a smile. Love and kindness, the cure-all for kids.

And yet Tilly, who was surrounded by boatloads of love, was still sinking in quicksand. Thoughts scrambled through her mind, jostling for prominence. This quicksand, this sadness that sucked her down every day, was it the final remnant of grief? Or was it the tug of stolen dreams—the children never conceived, the old age she should have lived with David? Dreams she had lost but couldn't abandon. And how daft was that?

She sank to a cold, wrought-iron chair and watched James's long, thin fingers thread a needle on his first attempt. He would be a gracious lover, a skilled lover, a gentle lover. And no making love in the dark. He would want his lover exposed—she shivered—he would want to see.

Maybe her mother was right. Maybe she was holding back from life. If so, what was she so scared of? That she couldn't love again, or that she could?

Tilly bundled a sopping Bownba into a pillowcase, knotted it, then placed it in the drum of the dryer. The tree house was finished and supper cleared up. James had run out of reasons to stay, and Tilly had run out of excuses to create more. He leaned against the fridge in the scullery, arms crossed, as if waiting for her to speak.

"How about a coffee?" She was grasping at air—James didn't drink coffee in the evening, but panic bred desperation.

"No, I need to go pack. My taxi's coming at six."

"I wish you'd let me drive you to the airport."

"I know, but I'd prefer not."

"Then give me a minute, and I'll walk you back to the Hall."

"No, Tilly." James straightened up and extended his hand.

He had *got* to be joking. After all they'd shared, or not shared, he wanted to shake hands? She slammed the dryer door. "Dammit. You're not walking out on me, not without an explanation."

"I gave you one." He slid his hands into his pockets.

"Rubbish. You threw some garbled speech at me. It meant nothing."

"It meant a great deal to me."

She felt color bursting on her checks, and it wouldn't be attractive. A blush this strong would manifest itself in scarlet blobs that resembled an alien strain of measles. Great, the final memory he'd carry home would be of Tilly the Martian.

James, however, was drained of color. Pale and unnaturally still, he seemed taller than ever. The expression on his face had tightened, as if he had locked down his features, preventing them from betraying emotion. Although one muscle rebelled, twitching in his neck.

"Get your shoes on." His voice was flat. "I'm saying goodbye to your mother and Isaac, and then I'm leaving."

And after he stalked out, his anger remained.

James strode through the paddock and across the wooden slatted bridge over the stream where she and Rowena used to collect jam jars of tadpoles. He ducked under the brambles dotted with hard, green blackberries, threw open the gate to the field, and left Woodend without a backward glance.

Evidently, he was taking the scenic route to the Hall—via The Chase.

The stream gurgled beneath her as Tilly clomped over the bridge, desperate to keep James in her sights. Man, he could walk fast. She paused to heave the gate shut, since James had wedged it into the hedgerow, then huffed out a breath and gave chase. But every step was like trudging through a snowdrift. Tilly's feet slid around her mother's Wellington boots making a strange *thwup* sound. Not one of her better decisions, and she'd have huge blisters the next day to prove it. But when she'd grabbed the nearest footwear, her only thought had been to guard the exits so that James couldn't sneak out. And he hadn't. He had stormed out of the back door and challenged her, with a thunderous expression, to follow.

"Could you slow down, please?" *Before I trip and break my neck.* "Better still, stop." Tilly jumped over a clump of bracken and drew level with James.

"I'm curious." He ground down on a thistle with his right foot. "Do you honestly believe that I'm here because of gardening lessons?"

The air was laden with moisture; Tilly could smell rain coming.

"No," she said. "I think you'll find that was my idea."

"I suggested using humor to help deal with the truth. Not hide from it."

Hide? What did he mean? "What am I hiding from?"

"The real reason I came here. The fact that I'm impulsive when it comes to love."

Déjà vu. She'd had this conversation before, or a similar one, in this very spot. She stared at the mutilated thistle by his foot. "If you're not spontaneous, how can you be impulsive?"

"Another sadistic twist of OCD. I want something? I can't see beyond that need. Once again my mind is stuck, seeking instant gratification. Of course, there is another explanation." He smiled, but it hit Tilly like a slap. "That when it comes to love, all bets are off."

Yup, same conversation.

The Shetland pony at the far end of the field swished its tail. Tilly and her sisters had dreamed of keeping a pony in this field. They'd even corralled their father into approaching Lord Roxton. But their mother had put her foot down at one mongrel, four budgies and two incestuous guinea pigs.

Beyond the pony, two elders daubed with white florets framed the gate to Woodend. This view had been a tonic for so much of her life, and yet how many times had she stood here and talked about love: courtly love with Rowena, teenage love with Sebastian, the passion of a lifetime with David? The pony snorted, and Tilly imagined herself toppling into a black hole as it collapsed from the inside out. She could almost feel herself fall, the world around her spinning out of focus.

"So this was never about the garden?" she said.

"You can't avoid every truth." He extended his hand. "Goodbye, Tilly. And thank you."

What was it with him and handshakes today? "No." She refused his hand. "You can't dump talk of love on me and bugger off to parts unknown. We need to talk about this."

"Talk about what? Talk about how you captured my heart the moment you walked toward me, gin in hand? Talk about the second when the image of your face burned itself into my mind and became the one image I've never wanted to erase?" His voice was sluggish, dragged down with sadness that seemed to have blasted away his anger. They had both followed their emotions, and look where it had led them. Tilly sighed, echoing the despondency she sensed in James. Why was she forcing his hand, when she didn't know where she wanted the conversation to go?

"That first day," he said, "the day we met, you stood up to me. I can steamroller people, Tilly, but with you, I never stood a chance. You sneaked in and peeled away every defense and I let you. I held up my hands in surrender and let you see me lose control. I've never done that before with anyone. I felt safe with you, because you saw the real me. And it didn't scare you."

He tucked a strand of hair behind her ears. "Three years ago I was in love with a woman I hoped might be the one. And yet I never let her in. I never wanted to. And when she left, I vowed I was done with love. But I met you and I knew, I just knew...." He closed his eyes. "I smell your hair—pears and vanilla—in the middle of the night when I can't sleep from wanting you."

He wanted her, but he wouldn't kiss her?

"Your voice never leaves me, and your eyes? I see your eyes every time I close my own."

He pinched the bridge of his nose, a gesture Tilly recognized. A headache was sneaking up on him. She reached for a spot above her right eye, the epicenter of every one of her migraines. Migraines, something else they shared that involved only pain.

"Do you know what happens when I fall in love?" James said. "The OCD latches on and tortures me with my passion. You talk about solitude as if it's the Holy Grail. But it's not a choice for me—it's survival. Every day I wake to the dread that something terrible will happen to you. And then?" He opened his eyes and gave a bitter laugh. "The OCD moves on to my jealousy, distorting my feelings into self-loathing. I'm on fire, consumed by images of you with Sebastian, you with David—" His hands tore through his hair. "I see David—" his voice turned hard "—before he fell in the bar, his face full of shock and disgust. I see his ghost watching us, repeating over and over, *Anyone but him.* I see Sebastian, his face full of your history, saying, *I know more about her than you ever will.* If I asked you to walk away from Sebastian, never see him again—would you?"

A thought picked at the back of her mind. Suppose this quicksand she'd imagined earlier was of her own making. Did that mean she had the power to tug herself free?

"No," Tilly said. "Because it's not your decision to make. It's mine." And for the first time in days, she felt calm. No, it was more than that. She was flooded with relief—relief that she hadn't kissed James; relief that she hadn't started down another life path that wasn't hers.

"I never wanted to lose Sebastian's friendship, and now I have a second chance. I don't know where it will lead, but I want to find out, as much as I want you to stay. Does that make me fickle? Possibly. But I'm not a gambler, James. I want to bumble along, take time, not risks. You were right. I don't know what I want, but I need the freedom to find out."

And I'm so not ready to talk about all-consuming love and passion. Been there, done that. And it ended in death.

"I gave up my name, my home, my career for David. I lived my life through him, through his achievements and his ambitions. I stopped wearing red. Red's my favorite color, but he liked me in brown. And guess what?" She tugged on her red long-sleeved T-shirt with the sparkly swirl over her chest. "No brown these days."

She patted her noncancerous breast and felt strong in health and purpose. "This lump has tied me into knots of regret, of second-guessing myself, of thinking my life forward and backward and inside out. Self-flagellation's great for the soul, isn't it?" This should be an evening to celebrate, not the time for another farewell. "But it's also smashed my world to pieces, and Sebastian is one of those pieces. If I'm going to put everything back together, I need to figure out where he fits in."

A surge of anger came from nowhere, like an invisible fist punching her in the gut. She wanted to scream at David and pummel his chest. She wanted to hate him for abandoning her, hate him for leaving her to face the threat of cancer alone. More than that, she wanted to hate him for dying, so that, once again, she was standing in the spot where he had proposed, facing the knowledge that she could circle through love and loss a second time. And who had the willpower for that? Three years ago, James had cut love from his life. Three years ago, the same thing had happened to her, but not by choice. Today she had choices, and she was going to take them.

She blew out her breath. "Your determination, your single-mindedness, remind me so much of David. And that terrifies me. I worry not that I can't love you, but that I can. You're a man I could fall hopelessly, helplessly in love with. And lose myself in the process. That's a trade-off I won't make. I can't follow someone else's blueprint for my life again. I just can't."

She thought of Sebastian—dependable, reliable, predictable. Like Monty, he would always veer to one side. And she knew, in that instant, that James would leave and she would let him go. Hadn't it been inevitable from the beginning, when he'd wanted to hire her? She should have agreed, should have signed a contract, done the work, then walked away. But then again, she'd never been neat, not even in relationships.

"I want the easy way out," she said, "because some things are too painful to be repeated. And you must agree, otherwise why leave?"

"No, I disagree. I believe that pain of the heart, like pain of the mind, should be met head-on—demystified." James tossed back his hair. "And I would stay and battle every monster in my head and beyond if I thought it would bring you to me willingly, certain only that you loved me." He paused. "What I don't believe in is allowing myself hope where there is none. I may be many things, but I'm not a fool." James's eyes followed a horse and rider along the horizon, galloping over the ridge. "I don't understand why you're so hard on yourself. Where you see weakness, I see strength. I see an incredible woman who could never cower before a man, even one as demanding as me."

He took two steps toward the wooden stile that led into

The Chase and then paused without turning. "But I can't love you, Tilly. It's destroying me."

The druid oaks threw a blanket of quivering shadow over him and he vanished, swallowed by the blackness of The Chase.

James thumped his fist into his palm. Of all the stupid, self-destructive— What the hell was he doing? Why was he leaving the arena? She'd admitted she could love him. He should stay and fight for that honor. He could easily beat the crap out of Sebastian. The guy was a Wall Street suit and a slight one at that. He didn't even have a regular workout routine—playing a game from England's imperial glory days didn't count. James could snap every bone in Sebastian's puny English body and not break a sweat.

And what did he, James, mean—that he couldn't love Tilly? He couldn't stop loving her. Hadn't he tried? Hadn't he used every piece of logic in his arsenal, and it had changed zip, nada, nil, nought, zero, nothing?

He had loved her the day they met, he would love her tomorrow when he got on the plane, and he would love her every week, every month, every year after that. He wanted to touch her; he wanted to take her, claim her as his. *Mine.*

She was meant to be with him, not with Sebastian.

Jealousy and rage, contaminated feelings he couldn't contain, seeped out of him. He folded his arms over his head and longed to disappear. How could he be such a fuckup? None of this would have happened if he'd kissed her. All she had wanted from him was a kiss. He should have kissed her and made it count, made it matter. Forty-five years of age and he couldn't kiss the woman he loved. Any progress he'd made fighting fear this summer was lost.

He couldn't make sense of what he'd done; he couldn't

make sense of what he was doing now. OCD and his temper had always been powerful allies. When they aligned, he was pretty much screwed. Which was the real reason he had to leave.

Bravo, James. Once again, self-preservation trumps all.

The bird of prey, the buzzard, cried overhead and James watched it circle.

And then he did the only thing he could do: he ran.

Twenty-Seven

The day was killing her by minutes, time moving as slowly as it had on Isaac's first morning at preschool. Tilly had been watching the clock since 6:00 a.m., marking James's progression from her life: *He'll be getting in the taxi; he'll be boarding the plane; he'll be gone.* Every part of her ached, exhausted from the weight of her thoughts.

She wanted to huddle up and ignore the world, but she had promised her afternoon to Isaac, her evening to her mother and her lunchtime to Rowena—if Ro ever hung up the phone.

"Countryside Steward Scheme Payment Rates," Tilly read from the pamphlet abandoned on Rowena's desk. And tried not to listen as Rowena, who was seated opposite with her feet up and the phone cradled into her neck, berated her banker.

Tiddly and Winks snored on their tartan beanbags, the large, black clock on the wall ticked a funereal knell and rain tapped against the estate office skylights with the even sound of persistence. At home, days like this were precious. Summer rain in North Carolina fell only in torrents that flattened plants and swept away soil before disappearing back up into the sky. Pretty much like James.

A bluebottle buzzed through the dust on the windowsill, and Tilly stretched. Yuck, there was that scrunching noise behind her ears again. Was this how middle age sounded— could you hear your body failing as everything drooped and sagged? Well, at least she didn't have to worry about that with her boobs. See? There was always a positive side. Just as tomorrow she would wake up, post-date with Sebastian, and know that James's departure had been a blessing. Right?

Wasting time was strangely unsettling, like walking into one of those fancy salons David loved sending her to for some exotic-sounding beauty treatment when really, he could have said "I love you" by ordering Hawaiian pizza once in a while. (According to David, the only acceptable pizza topping was pepperoni.)

She stared at the bamboo flooring, an unexpected choice that certainly made a statement. Lord Roxton's estate office had been a hole of a place lined with dark paneling and cluttered with tack and shotguns. Tilly shuddered, remembering the dried mud ground into the floor, the odor of damp and the scuttling noises that kept her hovering by the door.

The current estate office, with its whitewashed walls and track lighting, had the atmosphere of a studio. Unlike the dumping ground that was Rowena's bedroom, her office was neat and ordered, except for the scrunched-up balls of paper that had failed to reach the trash can. The huge plot map flanked by insurance certificates, the neat piles of receipt books, the clumps of paper layered symmetrically and the shelves of binders labeled income and invoices, spoke of efficient business practices. The only personal items were a peg of dog towels that reeked of wet Labrador and a multicolored photo frame. Tilly picked it up and smiled at Isaac.

"Bloody bankers." Rowena slammed down the phone.

Tilly replaced the frame, angling it toward Rowena.

"So, James is gone." Rowena squeezed her tea bag against the side of her chipped mug. "Did you know that he reorganized that mound of wellies in the butler's pantry? Paired them all up. And cooked me a fab breakfast at eight every morning. I'm going to miss that Yank." Rowena blew across her tea, sending a ribbon of steam toward Tilly. "This is when you say, 'Yeah, but I'll miss him more.'"

"I'm not sure that I will, though." Tilly paused. "Miss him."

"Give it up, Petal. If you're going to start lying, take lessons from me. I'm guessing James confessed undying love?"

Tilly nearly said yes. But was it a confession of love or words of obsession?

Rowena kept her eyes trained on Tilly. "That's a yes?"

"He rabbited on about pain and then left. It was hardly a Hallmark movie moment."

"Hallmark movie?" Rowena frowned. "Is that a cultural thing?"

"Smushy saga with tears." Although there had been tears after James left, and Tilly had cried until her head throbbed. But the tears had been for David.

"Ah." Rowena thumbed through a stack of papers on her desk. "That explains why I didn't hear the two of you bonking out your goodbyes last night. Multiple orgasms seemed inevitable after I saw you skating along my private road looking all lovey-dovey." Her green eyes flashed with glee. "I hope he at least gave a decent farewell snog? Or a toe-curling grope? Strikes me a man that sensual would know what to do with his hands."

"Don't be crass."

"Don't be a prude."

Tilly picked up the Countryside Steward Scheme pamphlet and placed it on top of the stuffed in-tray. "It's always about sex with you, isn't it?"

Rowena shrugged and then jerked when her ancient desk chair wobbled. "Romantic relationships are sex, Haddy. Otherwise, what's the point? I mean, who spouts this twaddle about marrying your best friend? I have a best friend—you. Shouldn't the whole partner thing be on a different level? And doesn't sex, the most intimate thing you can share with another human being, take you to that level? What else is there?"

"Love."

Rowena gave her the how-stupid-do-you-think-I-am look.

"Come on, Ro. You're the one who believed in white knights. What went wrong?"

"Brilliant tactic." Rowena clapped slowly. "Deflect the conversation from yourself."

"It's not a tactic. I don't want to talk about some guy who floated through my life and then vanished. You, on the other hand, are here to stay. Best bud till death do us part. And I'm curious…. How *did* you morph from the poster child for Elvis Costello's 'I Wanna be Loved' to spokesperson for Spinsters R Us? You're not going to devolve into Miss Havisham, are you?"

"Ha, bloody, ha. I also used to believe in Father Christmas, but you don't rail on me for not hanging up my stocking every Christmas Eve." Rowena threw one leg on top of the other, so that her right ankle rested on her left knee. Her gypsy skirt cascaded between her thighs while she picked at a hole in her fuchsia sock, making it larger.

"Let's just say that I grew up and realized my happy ending

didn't feature a man. The love of my life is, evidently, three thousand acres of land so beautiful that I get choked up every time I look at it." Rowena's chair creaked as she turned around. "Although maybe not today."

The landscape behind her was shrouded in gray light that was more suited to a November afternoon.

Rowena swung back. "You know how hard I fought against this, how determined I was not to spend forty years of my life without a decent holiday. Not that we would have been capable of doing the family bucket and spade thing even if Daddy had been able to get away...but the world took on a rosy glow when I discovered conservancy. Corny as it sounds, I'm making a difference. For the first time in my life, it's not about me. And when I die, the estate goes to The National Trust, so the land can't be gobbled up for more naff housing developments. Keeping Bramwell Chase a village will be my legacy, not perpetuating the Roxton name." Rowena tugged around her ponytail and braided then unbraided it. "Besides, mice have eaten the Roxton christening gown. Definitely a sign that there isn't meant to be a future generation of Roxtons tripping off into the great blue Christendom yonder. Does that bother me? Not a jolt. I have a grand life. Why ruin it with a man?"

When Rowena was on a tear, there was little to do but listen. Tilly sighed and gave up all hope that they'd make it to The Flying Duck in time for lunch, not that she was hungry. In fact, the thought of food made her feel sick.

"Men are like combine harvesters," Rowena said. "Big and loud and programmed to churn up your life with ridiculous provisos like watching rubbish telly before going to bed at nine o'clock every night. Sod that. Sometimes I sit up all night watching films because I can."

Tilly thought of David's 10:00 p.m. lights-out and the

nights she had waited for his breathing to fall into a rhythm so she could tiptoe back into the great room and read.

"It's bad enough having male worker bees buzzing around me." Rowena opened and closed her desk drawer. What the hell was going on with her today? She was more fidgety than James. "Every day I have to contend with inadequate men—an alcoholic gamekeeper, two farmworkers no one else would employ, and let's not forget the ancient gardener whose sole talents are mowing in a straight line and maintaining a picture-perfect crinkle-crankle hedge. Why I promised Daddy I wouldn't fire them is a mystery to me."

Promise, my ass. Your heart has a gooey center.

"Thank God I'm down to one tenanted farm," Rowena continued. "Otherwise I would have even more useless specimens of manhood in my life. Of course, that excludes my darling Isaac, who is male perfection personified. And Archie has potential, and James is pleasingly lacking in testosterone."

Tilly opened her mouth to ask about Sebastian, but Rowena started talking again.

"Men are good for little more than a quick poke, Haddy. And for the record, I've given that up. Eight months celibate and counting."

Tilly's jaw went slack. Rowena hadn't been celibate since she was sixteen.

"Yes, my gyny bits are rusting away as we speak." Rowena peered down her sweater.

"Okay, so forget the sex, but what about companionship? Don't you get lonely, Rowena, patron saint of the countryside, rattling around in a house we used to call The Museum?"

Rowena flip-flopped her head. "Nope. The estate's given me purpose, and the Hall is history incarnate. How can you beat that? They define me, announce to the world: this is Rowena Roxton. What defines you, MRH?"

"Motherhood."

Rowena grabbed a piece of paper from her desk, screwed it up and hurled it at the trash can. And missed. "I said *you*, Matilda Rose Haddington."

Tilly flushed with anger. "I can't claim motherhood?"

"Scrape away motherhood, widowhood, wife-hood. Tell me what defines *you*."

Tilly stared through the huge picture window into the soggy, monotone countryside, and saw her woods filled with bright shadows and the cries of hawks. "My business."

Rowena began riffling through all the papers on her desk. "Convince me."

Tilly sat on her retort, the one that said *shan't*. Wasn't she a teensy bit proud of Piedmont Perennials, a business she had built on word of mouth, not an advertising budget? Why not read that fat business plan Sari had mailed her, the one Tilly had shoved, unopened, into her knickers' drawer? Besides, wasn't that part of the reason she'd pushed James away—so she could figure out what *defined* her?

"I might expand into a retail nursery." *And why not?* Tilly felt herself thawing inside.

"Damn, but we did good, didn't we, Haddy? Found happiness in the rubble of our lives. I wish we could say the same for Sebastian, poor pet." Rowena jangled her car keys. "Aha! Found them. Think he'll stay…in the village?"

"Woodend is his, if he wants it."

Rowena grew still. "Now why don't you sound as happy about that as you should?"

Tilly shrugged; it was easier than attempting to explain.

"James has really wee'd in your bathwater, hasn't he?"

"Yuck, Ro! What a horrid image." Although apt, since James had certainly muddied the waters, not that they were clear to begin with. "James is irrelevant here." What a heartless thing to say, but she had to stop this thread. James was gone, and that was that. "I've been offered a second chance with someone who was wound through my life like ivy. How many people get that?"

Rowena held up an unopened envelope and crinkled the window in an attempt to peek inside. "Isn't this a third or fourth chance, or have we stopped counting?"

Tilly watched the day die and waited for her sense of disconnection to do the same. She squinted through one eye, then the other, but there wasn't much to look at beyond mildew-colored clouds lumbering across the sky. And an empty gin glass. Everything swayed, even her emotions, although hopefully not too much, otherwise who knew what she might say if probed about James. She would acknowledge this once and not think on it again: she missed him, and it hurt like hell, the tear-me-apart-and-trample-on-the-bits-that-show-signs-of-life hell. Either that or she was blottoed.

"Where's Isaac?" Sebastian, who had been closeted in the study with her mother, stepped onto the patio.

"Tree house." Tilly closed her eyes, but the world continued to rock.

"James get off okay?"

Clearly, James's departure was the hot topic of the day. Everyone had asked her about it. First Isaac—*Can James come over to hunt for black snakes when we get home?*—then Rowena, then her mother—*I'm going to miss James, and what about you, darling?*—and now Sebastian.

Tilly rubbed her eyes before opening them, but the scene in the sky hadn't improved. "Yup. James is gone, vamoosed." She waved an arm in a dramatic swoop. It hung in the air for a moment before dropping to her lap, where it lay as inert as a bag of potting soil. Definitely blottoed, then. "Left on a jet plane never to return. Happy?" Would her legs buckle if she tried to stand?

"Extremely." An impish grin flickered on Sebastian's lips.

Tilly smiled, a Pavlovian response to his beauty, but inside she cried. Sebastian might be happy, but she wasn't. Far from it. She leaned forward, waiting for him to drag his chair up to hers, then slumped back, shocked to realize she had anticipated the movement James would have made. As if to ram home the point, Sebastian positioned his chair a good eighteen inches away and sat heavily. He crossed his legs and his arms and said nothing. Which was a blessing that gave her less to focus on.

The church bells clashed through the first peal of Friday night bell ringing practice. Jeez, they were loud, but not loud enough to drown out the babble of thoughts, all variations on a theme: Where was James? Was he over the graveyard of the *Titanic* or halfway down the Eastern seaboard? This was *sooooo* not good. Unwanted thoughts, very unwanted thoughts. What would James tell her to do? *Let them drift away, like clouds floating across the sky.* She looked up again. *Same old clouds hanging around, looking nine months pregnant.*

The blackbird tuned up for his evening serenade, swallows dipped and circled overhead and soil shot from under the hedge as Monty excavated another carcass. The garden was fresh with the smell of rain and Tilly inhaled deeply, desperate to harvest the memory. But the buzz of happiness sputtered and died, crushed by the cold realization that Woodend would never be a Haddington stronghold again. The garden, the furniture, the decor, all would be unrecognizable. Oh God, she and Sebastian could end up having sex in her parents' bedroom one day.

"Isaac likes nature, doesn't he?" Sebastian bent down and picked up a dead peacock butterfly, which he placed on the table between them. "I think I'll frame this for him. I've just emptied a ton of photo frames."

"Throwing away pics of Fiona?" Tilly lacked the mental wherewithal for marriage guidance, but she raised her eyebrows in what she hoped was an encouraging gesture. Now and again you had to be a passenger in the conversation, especially if you were the drunk girl.

"All but one that I've kept for the children's sake." Sebastian sighed. "I couldn't decide who James was after—you or Rowena."

"He came here to hire me, Sebastian. End of story." If she repeated it enough, she might believe it. And she needed to believe it so that Sebastian would. James had been banging on about truth, but truth was overrated. Why torture Sebastian with it? One of them was in alcohol-induced purgatory; that was enough. She really shouldn't have had that second gin. Or the third one that tasted like paint stripper because she couldn't leave a dribble in the bottom of the bottle.

Sebastian uncrossed and recrossed his legs. "I realize you're a talented gardener, but if you're moving back to England, shouldn't you consider returning to publicity? After all, your earning potential would be far greater."

This was what happened when she let Sebastian steer the conversation. They jumped from dead butterflies to ex-wives to James to free financial advice. The guy was firing conversational blanks. What did he really want to say? Goddess divine, come back to me?

"Return to PR? I'd rather eat the contents of my compost bin. It's a career for—" she hiccuped. God, she was plastered "—second fiddles." Tilly drained her glass, even though it was empty, and slammed it onto the table. She liked the sound, so she did it again. "Anyway, I'm expanding my *highly* successful wholesale business into a retail nursery."

Wow. That wasn't a throwaway statement intended to goad. She felt none of the hesitancy she had earlier when she'd made the same declaration to Ro. Double wow.

Sebastian glanced over his shoulder as if seeking re-inforcements. Or was he considering a runner? Who knew with him?

"I thought you wanted to move back here?" he said.

Oopsy. She should have told him she'd shelved the England dream. But then again, she hadn't been entirely sure until that moment. She grappled for his hand and folded it into her own.

"Nope, not staying." Once again, she had boxed them in. But they weren't teenagers anymore, desperate for a quick grope. They'd worn down the treads of their lives. They could take things slow. "If I leave, that doesn't have to mean anything for, you know, us." *Us?* There was no *us*. Damn, she was worse at this than he was. "Why don't we just stay connected and see what happens?" Now that didn't sound too scary.

"Forget the whole sex thing you mean?" Sebastian grinned at her.

"You look relieved." And what did she feel? Nothing. One huge nothing.

"James brought out the tomcat in me. Made me mark territory. I was worried I had become my father's son, thinking with my dick. And now the pressure's off? Yes. I am relieved."

"'Cos you're in love with another woman?" The question sat on her chest, heavy and solid. No one had mentioned Fiona in weeks, and Sebastian had grown lighter, as if he'd wiggled free of his worries. Or maybe he had simply followed the standard Sebastian operating manual and buried his feelings deeper. He might be ripping up photos but he still loved his wife. He'd told Tilly as much that day they'd had lunch at the Hall.

"You still love your wife, don't you?"

Sebastian eased his hand away and shuffled his chair closer. "The answers to your questions are yes and no. Tilly, can we kiss?"

She hadn't kissed a man in three years, hadn't kissed anyone but David in thirteen, and wasn't sure her failed attempt with James meant anything. The equivalent of a victory dance, surely. But this was Sebastian, the first boy she'd ever kissed. And even if her brain panicked and said, "How do I do this?" her body would remember.

He flung his arm over the back of her chair. "Please?"

"Sure." How could she refuse when he asked so politely? "Kiss me." She threw her arms around his neck, falling into a dance she hadn't practiced in years, but knew with clarity. Their lips fit together like the last two pieces of a jigsaw, but her pulse didn't race. It slowed. So, that was why he'd asked for permission. Suddenly, she felt sober.

"There's no passion. Is there?" she said, before he could.

"I'm sorry, Tilly." Sebastian's eyes were clear blue today. "I had to be sure."

They remained tethered by her arms, surrounded by silence laden with history: The first time she saw him, so beautiful she couldn't breathe; their first kiss during the school bop, with Paul Weller singing "You're the Best Thing" and everything tingling from her toes up; the first time they made love—the latex smell of the condom, the act itself clumsy and painful; his face when she said, "I've met the man I'm going to marry."

His face seconds earlier, before he kissed her for the last time.

"I guess I succeeded," Sebastian said, "when I vowed to cut

you from my life." He hadn't moved, hadn't pulled away from her. They were suspended in time, delaying the moment that she had been deprived of with David—a final goodbye. She ran her fingers up into Sebastian's hair, desperate to remember the softness. But his hair was matted with gel and her fingers retreated. It felt nothing like the memory.

"It would have been so easy," Sebastian said, "to slip back into what was. Please believe me when I tell you part of me wanted that."

"Just because something's easy, doesn't make it right." After all, her favorite hiking trail behind Creeping Cedars wound through a forest of poison ivy and prime copperhead habitat. The other trails were less hazardous but lacked the spectacular vista. Amazing, what she'd risk for a view that stole her breath.

"I'm sorry, Tilly. I can't love you again. It's just…not there."

Men who couldn't love her seemed to be a new theme in her life.

Something snapped in her mind. She almost heard it ping.

"You know, I'm not ready for this merry-go-round of love. With anyone." A smile sneaked out. She had fantasized about two men, neither of them David, and the sky hadn't fallen. That was enough for now—a start, a hope for some unimagined future where love would come easily. And thanks to James and Sebastian, she had a parachute. "Will you at least send the odd email this time, so we can take a stab at friendship?"

But instead of answering, Sebastian jumped up and knocked a small, potted fuchsia from the patio table. Tilly made a dive to catch it but missed. The ceramic pot smashed onto the concrete, and Sebastian dropped to his knees, his face scarlet.

"Christ," he mumbled, scooping up potting soil and pieces of pottery. "Sorry."

Tilly wanted to reassure him, but he looked so pathetic that words failed her. Instead, she grabbed the fuchsia and shoved it into her glass. "Here." She held it out. "Pack in that handful of soil." But Sebastian stood, dirt tumbling down his leg.

"That must have been quite some kiss," Rowena called from under the rose arch. She strode across the lawn, swinging a large wicker basket shrouded with a tea towel. "Didn't mean to spoil the party. I assumed you'd be up at the Farm." She lifted the edge of the tea towel and a delicious warm smell sank into Tilly's stomach. "Got bored and did some cooking, but you know me—over the top as usual. Made three of them before I'd realized what I was doing."

"Hmm. Pheasant lasagna," Tilly said. Damn, she was famished. "You doll."

"Thought I'd offload this one on Mrs. H. But here, you chaps have it." Rowena put the basket on the table and backed up with exaggerated steps, like a cartoon character preparing to run away. "Snog on without me."

"Wait!" Tilly reached across the table. "Why don't the three of us have supper here? Like old times."

"No." Sebastian was frantically brushing dirt from his chinos. "You stay, Rowena. I'll leave."

"What's going on?" Rowena scowled at Tilly. Then she turned to Sebastian. "Sebastian?" But he hooded his face with his hands and didn't reply.

Rowena whirled around, her arms tensed as if grabbing an imaginary bar. "Aren't you tired of this game yet, Tilly—spin Sebastian around and break his heart? Well, it's not on."

"Wow. Time out. Why're you angry?" Tilly considered saying something along the lines of *It's his fault, he did it*. But instead she opened her arms in surrender. "It's not what you think. Sebastian's not in love with me. He's still in love with Fiona." She made soothing downward motions with her palms. "Nothing bad happened here. No massacre of anyone's heart. Sebastian's fine, I'm fine. One big happy family, right John Boy?"

Sebastian raised his head. "I have to leave."

"Did I say something wrong?"

"Drop it, Tilly."

"Okay, so I forgot you used to hate *The Waltons,* but you don't have to dash off all embarrassed. I don't care that you still love your wife and neither does Rowena. No, that came out wrong. Of course we care. We care deeply, don't we, Ro?"

"Stop." Sebastian's shout jolted Tilly into silence. She and Rowena exchanged glances. When had he ever raised his voice? "I'm not in love with my wife. Happy?"

"So why did you tell me—" Tilly stood.

"I didn't. You made that assumption and I let you. Christ, Tilly." He rubbed his jaw, leaving a smudge of soil under his mouth. "Why do you always force me to examine my feelings? Do you know how painful that is? I shut down, follow assumptions people make, because it's the only way I know how to protect myself. I'm not like you and I never will be. I can't talk about love. I'm a coward—" he held up his hands "—one who believed, up until this moment, that anything was easier than facing the truth. And its repercussions." His glare shifted to Rowena, but the frown fell away, his face transformed by the saddest smile Tilly had ever seen. And this time he didn't have to test his feelings with a kiss.

Expletives formed in Tilly's mind. She opened her mouth and yet nothing came out, not even a squeak. Not that Sebastian or Rowena would have heard her. They were staring at each other, Rowena so washed out even her lips were colorless.

"I love you," Sebastian said, his eyes dancing over Rowena's face as if he were committing her features to memory. "And I understand if you want me out of the Farm. I can pack up this weekend." He sucked in his chest. "If you don't want to see me again, tell me now. I'll have to talk with Mrs. Haddington, explain that I can't buy Woodend."

"No!" Rowena screamed. Inside the house Monty howled a macabre duet, and Mrs. Haddington ordered him into silence.

Rowena grappled for the back of a chair, the one Sebastian had been sitting on minutes earlier. "How dare you say that after twenty-three years of being my best friend's boyfriend, my best friend's ex-boyfriend, my best friend's? Twenty-three years, Sebastian. Doesn't that count for anything?" She shoved the chair away; it crashed into the table. "If this is some petty attempt to get back at Tilly for James, to make her jealous, I'll rip out your gizzards. Tilly and Isaac are my family, and if you want to hurt them, you have to get through me first. Go back to the Farm and pack up your possessions before I have you evicted." She pointed at random, waving her arm toward a revolving horizon, her bangles clanging against each other. "Get out!"

You tell him, sister. Tilly put her hands on her hips.

"No. I've changed my mind. I'm not leaving." Sebastian spoke slowly, in sharp contrast to Rowena's staccatos of fury. Tilly stared agog. He was going to get such a mouthful. "I want to make a declaration of love for the woman who has stood by me always, even though I've been too stupid to realize." He stepped toward Rowena. "And I'm going to admit to the fact that I'm buying a house to be near the woman I love." Tilly gasped. Sebastian talked over her as if she were air. "When we went out for dinner and you offered me the Farm, it was as if we were meeting for the first time. And you looked—" He gave a soft smile. "Christ, you looked like an angel come to save me. I felt as if I were returning from the dead. And then you told me Tilly was coming home, and I allowed myself to listen to uncertainty. I thought I was too messed up to know my own heart. But when James was alone with you every night, I—I wanted to kill him."

Was Sebastian having a spiritual awakening or a breakdown? Or maybe it was Tilly who, as Rowena would say, had lost the plot. Tilly felt as if she'd rushed out of a movie for a popcorn refill and wandered back into the wrong theatre. Only it wasn't just a different movie, it was a different genre. In Japanese. Without subtitles.

"I love you. Christ, I love you." There was a definite touch of madness in his voice. Rowena would deck him for sure. "And I have no intention of leaving. I'm staying and I'm buying this house. Because I think that you love me, too."

"You arrogant bastard," Rowena whispered.

"Do you love me?" He lurched forward and grabbed her shoulders.

Rowena sagged, as if someone had suctioned out her bones. "Don't," she cried. "I'm begging you, Sebastian. Don't ask that."

"Why not? I love you!" He laughed.

Yup, crazy as a loon. Although Rowena was acting strange, too.

"Please, leave me alone. I love Tilly. I love Isaac. I—I've made my peace. Please, just leave me alone." Then Rowena gave a feeble wail, as if the last thread of her voice had ripped.

Tilly fumbled for the edge of the table, a thousand blips from the past bombarding her, making sense for the first time: Rowena's diatribe after Tilly confided her loss of virginity; Rowena's alcohol poisoning the night after Tilly and Sebastian reunited the first time; Rowena so distracted that she cooked three pheasant lasagnas.

Rowena hung limply. She would have collapsed onto the

concrete if not for Sebastian holding her up. She looked like one of the matching rag dolls Tilly's mother had made for their eighth birthdays. Tilly knew where hers was, but what had happened to Rowena's? Had she been as careless with Holly Hobbie as she'd been with the Roxton christening gown? How could you trust a person for thirty years and not know her at all?

"Sebastian asked you a question," Tilly said. "Do you love him?"

"Yes." Rowena dug her elbows into her stomach and grabbed her head. Her long, red hair flopped forward like a velvet cape. "God help me, yes. I can't remember a time when I didn't. But neither of you were meant to know. No one was ever meant to know. I was taking my secret to the grave, Tilly. You must believe that, you must."

"Shh, darling." Sebastian wrapped himself around her. And something struck Tilly. Why had she never noticed before? They were the same height; they balanced each other out, and as they held on to each other, Tilly tried to avert her eyes. But couldn't.

"And Isaac?" Rowena broke away from Sebastian. "What will you tell Isaac?"

"That's not your concern." Tilly sounded as calm as she felt—hollowed out, scraped clean of emotion. "We've been best friends for over thirty years and you never let one thing slip. Never even hinted. How could you be that cold?"

"Because it was too awful to admit." Rowena sobbed, and Sebastian reached for her again. "I couldn't risk losing you, Haddy. You and Isaac are all that I have. I would cut out my own eyes before I would hurt either of you. What choice did I have? Haven't you ever buried a secret so awful? Haven't you, Tilly?"

Rowena couldn't have inflicted more pain with a switch-blade.

Tilly covered her mouth, trying to stifle the keening that escaped from deep inside, trying to force back the memory. She had thought that if she locked the truth away, never let it out, she would be safe. James and his truth. What did he know about a truth like hers? He would tell her to confront it, drag it to the center of her thoughts and keep it there until her mind lost interest and strayed. But how could anyone confront the horror of that last sentence spoken to a husband? The only promise she had ever broken.

I won't leave you, my love. I swear, I won't leave you.

But then she had fallen asleep and had awoken abruptly, her pounding heart deafening her to the bleeping technology of the hospital.

The panic, the fear—she recalled both, how they tasted acidic, how they stung at her like fire ants under her skin. And the terrible need to call a taxi, to go home and watch Isaac sleep, to reassure herself that unlike her husband, her child would wake the next day. She had followed her instincts, too strong to ignore, had chosen motherhood over everything else. And now motherhood was all that she had left. Because in that one hour, in those sixty minutes that she was gone, David had died. Alone.

Tilly shot back up, gulping for air, then retched into the tub of geraniums.

"Haddy!" Rowena rushed at her. "Christ, are you okay?"

"Not especially. I just threw up the last of the Bombay Sapphire." Tilly used an elbow to shrug off Rowena, then wiped the back of her hand across her mouth.

"Please, Tilly. Please forgive me." Rowena glanced at Sebastian.

"Let's get her sitting down." He walked over and wrapped an arm under Tilly's.

"Stop fussing, the pair of you," Tilly said, but let Sebastian guide her onto a chair. "I've been drinking on an empty stomach. It's my own fault."

She put her head between her legs and listened to her rasping breath. When did breathing become so hard?

"Look, you two are consenting adults." Tilly dragged up her head—why did it feel so cumbersome? She longed for darkness, for dreamless sleep, for oblivion. No one to listen to, not even herself. "You don't need my blessing."

"No, but we'd like it." Sebastian held out his hand to Rowena. Had he ever looked at Tilly that way? She screwed up her eyes and tried to remember how it felt to be loved by Sebastian, but there was nothing except a prick of pain above her right eye.

"I want to be happy for you." Tilly hung her head. "And I will be, once I get over the freak-factor. Just give me some time. And you guys must have a lot to talk about. Why don't you go, take the lasagna."

"Goodness. What's going on out here? I was on the phone when I heard a scream." Tilly swiveled toward her mother's voice, but too quickly. Multicolored lights swam before her eyes. She clutched at her head, trying to keep the world steady.

"Hmm. Something smells good." Mrs. Haddington hopped through the French doors and beamed at Sebastian, unruffled by the desire in his eyes as Rowena wiped dirt from his chin. Tilly frowned at her mother. She had known, her mother had known all along. "Hello, Rowena dear. Have you been cooking that delicious pheasant lasagna again? That was Sari, by the way. On the phone."

What phone? Tilly hadn't heard the phone. She hadn't

heard anything beyond her body expelling the truth, along with the dregs of her duty-free gin.

"Darling? Are you all right?"

Tilly laughed. "Too much reality and too much gin. Sebastian and——" She watched as Rowena's arm found Sebastian's waist, and he mirrored her movement. Sebastian and Rowena: two halves of a whole. "Sebastian and Rowena are leaving," Tilly said. "And I'm going to lie down. I feel a migraine coming on."

"Poor you. I'll make this quick, then. Sari says not to worry," her mother continued. "She's taken down the porch swing, put the garden art and outside furniture in the garage——" Mrs. Haddington checked off items on her fingers as if running through a shopping list "——dragged all your pots under the deck. And boarded up the basement window. If the phone lines go down, she'll contact you when she can. And she's sorry she didn't call earlier, but they didn't discover the storm had shifted until they turned on the morning news and then the excrement, I believe, hit the fan." Mrs. Haddington wrinkled her upper lip.

"What are you blathering on about?" Tilly mumbled, holding her head.

"Hurricane Evelyn," her mother replied. "The eye is projected to pass over the Triangle."

"Hurricane Evelyn? But it pounded the coast of Florida and then petered out across the Atlantic. They were talking about it yesterday on Radio 4."

"Evidently things changed during the night. It picked up strength over the ocean and veered northwest. Made landfall at Wilmington as a category three. But Sari said it's been downgraded to a category two." Her mother gave her best-foot-forward smile, when her lips disappeared into a thin line and the dimples on either side of her mouth became so pronounced she looked ridiculously girlish. "Not too bad, then."

No, not to someone who remembered rationing, but then her mother hadn't cowered in the basement listening to apocalyptic cracks and booms as Hurricane Fran had toppled sixty-foot oaks like giant bowling skittles. And that was before Tilly had the greenhouse. Bugger. How did you protect a structure made entirely of plastic sheeting?

Inside the house, Monty barked. That ruddy dog. Would he never shut up?

"What did she say about the greenhouse? Has she—" Tilly gave a halfhearted laugh and forced the pads of her fingers into her temples. Clearly, she was the one having the breakdown after all. An episode of delirium, no doubt, generated by stress and blue gin. Had to be, because the tall, scowling man striding around the side of the house with matching luggage was, at this precise moment, disembarking from a plane in North Carolina.

"Either this is a really bad migraine, or I'm ready for the cuckoo shack." Her voice sounded scratched, like a worn-out record. "You here for the floor show?" she asked the James doppelganger. "'Cos I've got to tell you, we're putting on one helluva performance tonight."

He dropped his duffel, swung his suit carrier off his shoulder and unhooked his backpack. "They kept us in the departure lounge for hours delaying the flight in thirty-minute increments until they could confirm the path of the hurricane it was hell Tilly." Normally James spoke slowly, but he sounded breathless, as if he were dashing to force out his words before speech failed him. "It was hell. Then they canceled the flight and told us to come back tomorrow but I can't, Tilly, I can't get on a plane." He glanced at her mother. "I'm a nervous traveler," he said, and began twisting his hair.

Adverse weather and travel delays were triggers for his OCD; Tilly knew that. It was all about control, he had explained once. But surely life was a big ol' crapshoot no matter who you were.

James fastened his gaze on Tilly and blinked through a constant rhythm of anxiety; Rowena and Sebastian stared at her, waiting for absolution; swallows searched for insects with a soft collective whistle that seemed to say, *We need, we need.* Everyone needed, and everyone would have to wait. She'd reached the end, hit her wall of concrete.

Tilly tented her fingers and stared inside. The shape she'd created was a tepee, a place to hide from the demands of others, a place from which to watch the amber sunshine leak through the clouds.

A thought lambasted her, and she let out an exclamation. Her mind had gone straight to the greenhouse, but what about the two-hundred-year-old oak that dangled over David's studio, the tree that was dying? If it fell, what would happen to the shelves behind David's desk, his high altar stacked with journals and books filled with his words, his theories, his passion? Why hadn't she called the tree surgeon before the hurricane season started? Because of some ridiculous ideal about the sanctity of the tree's life. And now she would pay.

Her face confirmed what he knew. He shouldn't have come back. Why, why had he come back? Because, like a homing fucking pigeon, he could think only of returning to Tilly. Either way, he was screwed. Couldn't leave, couldn't stay.

Had to do this alone; couldn't do it without Tilly.

Don't hate me, please, don't hate me.

His head jerked like a short-circuiting robot, and his arms shook. He had to stop trembling. But he couldn't; he couldn't control the anxiety.

Rowena smiled at him, and he tried to smile back. She was—arm in arm with Sebastian? She'd told him? Good for her, good for her. But that meant…Sebastian wasn't in love with Tilly? How could that be? Sebastian had loved Tilly his whole life. Rowena had said that was why his marriage failed, why his wife had the affair. Sebastian wasn't in love with Tilly? God Almighty, poor Tilly. He should go to her, try and help, try and be…what? The consolation prize? How could he help anyone? He couldn't even help himself. He was shaking; he couldn't stop shaking.

Get a grip, James, get a grip. Virginia was staring at him, must think he was an escaped lunatic. *As good as, Virginia, as good as.* He had to twist his hair, had to twist his hair because tomorrow he had to get on a plane. He had to force himself to get back to Heathrow tomorrow and get. On. A. Plane. And if he didn't twist his hair, the plane would crash and he would die. He would die, without telling Tilly how much he loved her. How he had messed up. How he should never have walked away. How he could never walk away from Tilly.

"That's it. Shoo." Tilly flicked her hand. But she didn't mean him, right?

Of course she does. You're a troll; she hates you.

"I'm serious, here." Tilly raised her voice. "Leave. I need to call Sari while she still has phone service. All of you, scram, before I get nasty."

"Even me?" Isaac appeared and bobbed under Tilly's arm. He squealed, "James!" and tried to break free, but Tilly secured him in place. She wasn't even going to let Isaac near him? He needed a hug so bad, and Isaac gave the best. *Please, Tilly.*

"No, Angel Bug. You're the only one who belongs. Sorry, Mum. Other than you."

"But—" James said, his fist still buried in his hair.

Sebastian picked up James's duffel. "Come on, mate. I think she means it."

Twenty-Eight

Empty windows framed the night and gable ends pointed into the sky like the rigging on the *Marie Celeste*. The stone hull of the Dower House was a roofless shell of history, nothing more. Tilly tugged on Monty's lead and headed away from the ruin. There was no pain in her head now that she had doped herself with Imitrex, just the residue of a weak migraine and the fog of mental white noise. She could almost believe she was numb. Almost.

Halfway around the world a hurricane was tearing up her life, the one she had finally decided to keep, but in the fields surrounding Bramwell Chase, the air was still with a slight nip that promised dew. The moon glowed the color of goldenrod and the starless sky was turquoise, an opaque tone that reminded Tilly of sunlight absorbed into her neighbor's artificial pond. Alongside her, The Chase reached forward and backward like a never-ending tear.

At Creeping Cedars there was no bright twilight such as this, but nothing could compare to the wonder of a clear Piedmont night, when the sky became a magician's cape embroidered with stars of white gold thread, stretched across the stratosphere. How she loved to sit on the porch swing and search for shooting stars in her private planetarium above the treetops. If one treasured object survived the storm, something on which to hang her hope, let it be the porch swing.

Tilly turned left at the estate road, leaving the lights of the village and the sporadic drone of traffic behind. Her Doc Martens squelching on the tarmac, she made for the gamekeeper's cottage and the shooting lodge. Once she had passed both, she would be out in the open, exposed on the estate road to Manor Farm. On a clear day, you could see across two counties from up there.

The sky lost its luster, but Tilly strode on, finding calm in the descending darkness. Nighttime had a way of stripping life to its essentials, of lending perspective as it swept away distractions, including the apology she owed her mother.

Good one, Tilly.

To start an argument with Mrs. Haddington was to finish an argument with Mrs. Haddington, which meant she would wait up for Tilly, even if Tilly stayed out until dawn. Dumping on her mother had been stupid and self-defeating, but the throwaway comment—*I suppose I should find an estate agent. After all, they won't want two homes, will they?*—had shoved Tilly over the edge. Along with the let's-make-the-best-of-it smile that had landed in Tilly's stomach like a right hook. *They.* Already Sebastian and Rowena had become *they.* Suspecting *they* were a couple when Tilly hadn't talked to Sebastian in ten years had barely left a bruise. But witnessing his declaration of love for her best friend after weeks of sifting through her own feelings for him, with said *best friend,* felt like an emotional gutting. Okay, so despite her best intentions, not numb. But come on. How many years had she and Rowena loved the same boy, the same man? And in all that time Rowena hadn't found one opportunity to sneak in a quick "I have a crush on your ex"? Not even after Tilly married and skipped the country?

Why did she feel cheated? Rejection, hurt, even anger, Tilly could understand, but she sure as hell didn't want to own this childish feeling that insisted she had lost when she should have won. After all, she and Rowena were hardly ten years old, competing against each other for blue ribbons in horse shows.

Of course, she could start finger-pointing to explain away these eddies of emotions. Maybe Sebastian had encouraged hope; maybe Rowena had tricked him into a secret tryst. Her relationship with Rowena had been the cornerstone of Tilly's life, had guided her through death not once, but twice. And it had flourished on secrets. Had it also been built on lies? Where did you run to when the past was pitted with more sinkholes than the future?

Duped, that was how she felt. Clearly, she was the only person not to realize Rowena and Sebastian had the hots for each other. She could have scraped the lust off the patio with a trowel, not that it seemed to bother anyone else. Isaac didn't blink when he saw them draped around each other; James showed no surprise whatsoever. Had he known? Had Rowena trusted him and not Tilly?

A muntjac barked, an eerie call that frightened Tilly even though she'd grown used to the cry of coyotes. She shivered, grateful for the snuffling noises as Monty shoved his muzzle into a rabbit hole, oblivious to the hedgehog lumbering across the road. Lucky hedgehog. Two minutes earlier and Monty would've pounced. See, even spines couldn't protect you from the inevitability of death. When your number was up, you could only pray to go quickly, unlike David. No, she didn't want to think about this, not now. Her best friend had punched her to the floor; her childhood sweetheart had kicked her; a hurricane had stomped on her; she was going to leap up and ask for more?

Evidently, she was.

As a child, Tilly loved the comfort of repetition, loved using the same Spirograph cog to create an identical pattern over and over, always going inward, always getting smaller. And yet she was still shrinking, still circling back to the living will, to the five days David hung on, to her broken promise. How could anyone punch through so many layers of guilt? Or was this darker than guilt? Had this become obsession?

Panic tasered her with memories she didn't want to own. She was going under...no air...only pain. And James's voice, deep and soothing: *Concentrate on your breath, Tilly. Breathe in through your nose. Fill your abdomen, then your chest—*

Not helping! She clawed at her scalp, trying to tear out the image of David's body violated by the breathing tube. What had James said about fighting intrusive thoughts? *Think, Tilly, think.* Aha! Cultivate detachment, that was one trick. Been there, done that—sort of—for three years. Monumental failure. Okay, what else? Logic! Right, now she was getting somewhere. Why was she convinced that David had changed his mind about the living will? Simple, because he'd hung on. But why? Simple again, because he couldn't leave her. But what if she flipped that thought. What if he had hung on because *she* was the one who couldn't leave? Suppose, oh God, suppose her presence had tethered David to the nothingness he had dreaded?

Tilly cried out and Monty whirled around, taut with guard dog instincts. Panic swelled, and her eyes burned with tears. And again, she thought of James. If he could confront his fear, so could she. She must stay in that hospital room, she must comb through the memory, because buried in it, somewhere, there had to be forgiveness.

Use the gifts James gave you, Tilly. Use logic. She breathed slowly. First, she would focus on David's personality, on his love of grand gestures. No one ever accused David of thinking small. And just suppose that had led him to the ultimate sacrifice—a desire to save her from the moment of his death. That was as honorable as giving up the last life vest, and so utterly David.

Good, now she was getting somewhere. Her fear thermometer was dropping. But there was a problem with this scenario. David would never choose to die alone. He hated being alone, needed people in attendance always. Hell, he couldn't even stay at the house by himself. Although, that was due to his fear of nature. When he was holed up in the studio with hypotheses, he drowned out the forest with R.E.M. or *Law & Order* reruns. Tilly smacked her head. Of course! That was it. The panic disappeared as abruptly as a twister pulling back into the clouds and left behind a nugget of fact: When David needed focus he isolated himself. He would laugh and say her presence distracted him, and then he would seek out seclusion.

For five days she had been so determined to guide him through the final seconds of his life, so determined to be with him as he took his last breath, that she had never considered how death, like grief, was a journey you took alone. And if that were true, then maybe the person she needed forgiveness from was not David, but herself.

Tilly spread her arms and spun until she was dizzy. "Whoa." She stopped and opened her eyes. Dawn was coming, she could feel it. Finally, a daybreak she welcomed.

The ancient humps of ridge and furrow in the fields below

rose up to greet her. Tilly loved it here, under the beech trees that lined the end of the estate road. Her lost spot, she used to call it—the place she had come to escape her sisters, a live-in best friend, hordes of pets, and later, the demands of Sebastian's devotion.

A red fox dashed across one of the fields below, so different from the gray fox that sauntered through her front yard with the attitude, "I'm takin' ma own sweet time." She sure was looking forward to seeing that Southern fox again.

Her body hummed with energy as if she were warming up for a race. No more spinning with flight but not direction. Tomorrow was today, and there was so much to do—pack to go home, plan the future of her business, paint her bedroom red if she so wished. No, sod the paint, she would put down rugs!

"I love you, David," she yelled. "And I'm sorry, but the library has to go. The MGB, too. And I'm buying rugs for the bedroom." The air snatched up her words and carried them toward Manor Farm, where lights blazed on the ground floor. The naked sash window in the kitchen was flung open, and a tall figure was braced against the frame. So, he hadn't slept, either. Had he been keeping vigil for her?

Tilly held her breath. James couldn't see her from there, couldn't hear her, but could he sense her, sense that connection they had shared from the moment they had met, the feeling that had terrified her? Had that been love? Had she gambled and made the wrong choice, chosen Sebastian when she should have chosen James?

Tilly gazed into the moon until her eyes throbbed from the brilliance of its halo. No, she hadn't been scouting for love. She had been groping toward reconciliation with the pain of love past—holding on instead of letting go. When David was alive she could walk into any room, see him and know she belonged. Without him, she had felt invisible, which was a pathetic state of mind.

James had guided her to this moment of revelation, to the knowledge that she mattered. But the pull of his demands was too strong. He was a magnet that attracted and repelled her, and she needed an emotional lull, not a lovefest akin to scaling Mount Everest in a blizzard. She didn't want to feel a big empty space when James wasn't around, to become invisible again. She screwed up her eyes and hoped that he could hear her thoughts:

If I could pick a point in the future and jettison myself into it, I'd want you there. But the future's a scary place, and I'm going to rest in the present for a while.

She kissed her palm, held it toward James, then headed back to her life.

Sebastian and Rowena had disappeared up to the Hall, leaving him alone at Manor Farm. Rowena had clucked around him, insisting he join them, but she'd waited over twenty years for tonight. Only a prime asshole would gate-crash that kind of a party. In the end, she'd settled for making up the Farm's guest bed for him, despite his announcement that he had no intention of sleeping. Not even a horse tranquilizer could knock him out. He'd already taken twice the usual dose of Clonazepam, and it had merely nibbled the edge off his anxiety.

After pacing the upstairs hallway, James had retreated to the stark, functional comfort of a farmhouse kitchen with its sensorial memories of his mother's baking. She'd given him his first cooking lesson when he was five. They made French toast that had tasted sweeter than anything imaginable. And afterward—James touched his cheek—she gave him the biggest kiss, and declared it to be the best French toast in the world. A lifetime of awards and achievements, and yet no compliment had ever trumped that one.

James tugged open the huge sash window and filled his lungs with early-morning air. Once again, he was at a crossroads of his own making. Once again, he had alienated anyone who dared to care for him. He had orchestrated another spectacular cock-up—a word stolen from Rowena that sounded ugly enough to fit his mood.

Returning to Chapel Hill would be too painful. Maybe he never would. He could always sell the house and live in Durham or Raleigh until the Duke trials were over. In the meantime, he would run back to Illinois and the company of dear friends, until he could muster the strength to visit Daniel.

Tomorrow, he would fly to O'Hare, despite the reel of horror in his mind: images of the plane falling from the sky; images of the plane smashing into the ground; images of an explosion; images of crackling flames consuming everything, including him.

James sighed and stared into the dawn. Tilly was out there, close but further away than ever. Even on the ride to the airport, he'd nursed a ridiculous dream that she would follow him, had conned himself into believing that ultimately, she would pick him over Sebastian. But this had never been about Sebastian. She had rejected James for herself, not for another man, and that was a blow that exploded his heart and slung the pieces to the outer rim of the galaxy. Game over. Game fucking over.

In his fantasies, he'd been dueling for her affection. But now he had no one to fight, other than himself, of course. If only he could have stepped back and given her space. Or if he'd walked away when she'd first said, "I can't help you." And yet, that had never been possible. Not when he, silly romantic James, had believed that she was his destiny. Crazy thing was, despite all that had happened, he believed it still.

For once he wasn't trapped in doubt; he was adrift in certainty. He knew what he wanted, and it would never be his.

James picked up his iPod and clicked through the settings until he found "repeat-one." Music was his drug of choice these days, and right now, he needed dark lyrics that spoke to him of passion and heartbreak. He selected The Airborne Toxic Event and scrolled down to "A Letter to Georgia." When he reached the two lines that lumped fear, truth, love and pain together, James began to cry. But the despair that split him open and lacerated his soul had nothing to do with a failed love affair.

This was his third round with grief, and he would never recover.

Twenty-Nine

"Hey, handsome. Want a lift?" Tilly held open the passenger door and squinted into the Saturday morning sunshine. The world beyond the interior of the Yaris was too sharp and too bright. Too intense. Of course, that could be the result of a strong cocktail of sleep deprivation and a pre-breakfast tête-à-tête with a lush-looking Rowena.

James yanked an earbud free and scowled into the car. "Sorry?"

The roar of a village cricket match rose from the rec field. Sebastian was playing today, Rowena cheering him on. Which meant it was time to get out of Dodge.

"I have wanderlust." Tilly inhaled the smell of freshly mown grass. "Care to join me?"

"Why not." His coldness unnerved her, gave her doubt when five minutes earlier she had been so sure of her plan to find James and explain.

A boy skipped out of The Corner Stores and, with a screech, dropped his iced lolly into a clutter of sickly begonias. *Begonias! Buy One Get One Free!* the chalkboard announced.

Tilly fingered the car keys. In the time James took to settle—goodness, he could faff for all eternity—she could run inside and tell them to rewrite the sign so that it read, *Free Plants Need Good Homes*. Bugger. She was mutating into her mother, trying to live someone else's life when she could barely live her own.

"What're you listening to?" *Radiate bubbles of happiness, Tilly. Keep it light.*

He placed one of the earbuds in her ear, and Tilly had to choke back the shock. Of all the songs he could have chosen. She extracted the earbud and returned it to James, but kept her eyes on the dashboard. "'Stuck in a Moment' by U2. My grief song."

"My OCD song. Musical therapy for when my thoughts get stuck." James wound the earbud cord around two fingers, pulled out the small aluminum case and black twisty tie from his backpack, and secured the bundle. "I was coming to find you."

"Yeah?" The air in the car thinned.

"I've heard from a friend in Asheville. According to the news there was one confirmed tornado in Wake county, and twenty-one thousand homes in Orange are without power, but the damage is nothing like Fran. I'm sure your house is fine."

It wasn't the house she was worried about, though. "Thanks." She glanced over her shoulder and pulled out onto the High Street. "Staying up at the Farm?"

"How did you know?"

"I was out walking most of the night. Saw you in the kitchen."

James gave a wan smile. "Where are we heading?"

Good question. "How about the historic market town of Olney? It's a great place to mooch, and I feel like mooching."

James didn't answer.

"Cowper, the poet, lived in Olney, and so did John Newton. He wrote 'Amazing Grace' while he was the curate there." *Shut up, Tilly.* "And it's the site of the Olney Pancake Race, a mighty sporting event dating back to the fifteenth century. Housewives race around the town tossing pancakes on Shrove Tuesday. That's the day you give up fat and dairy before Lent. Sort of English Mardi Gras without the carnival."

"My father was Irish Catholic, Tilly. I know what Shrove Tuesday is."

"Right." Tilly's hands slipped around the steering wheel. She rubbed one hand, then the other, along her thighs. "There's a fabulous kitchen store you might like and a wonderful Oxfam bookshop." Why was she telling him this? "Historical fiction's my true love, but I'll grab anything that takes my fancy." Crap, that sounded so inappropriate. "How about you? What do you read?"

She glanced at James as he turned away from her. "Fantasy," he said.

"What was your favorite novel, as a teenager?" *Let me guess,* The Hobbit.

"*The Hobbit.* Yours?"

She checked the speedometer before driving under the speed camera. "*Green Darkness* by Anya Seton. It's about past lives and unresolved issues. Ironic, huh?"

He picked up a scrap of paper from the dashboard shelf and folded it in half, then into quarters. When he was done, he sharpened the crease with his thumbnail before returning the paper to the same place. He paused, then pushed it a fraction to the left.

"I'm sorry about Sebastian and Rowena." For the first time since he'd got in the car, she heard friendship in his voice.

"Yeah, well. I have this theory, a Tilly-ism. Want to hear it?"

He shrugged, and Tilly swallowed her sigh. There was so much to say and only one chance to get it right. "Bad things are like the summer hail that covers my deck in minutes," she spoke slowly and carefully, trying to ignore the sensation that her heart was performing Olympic-standard gymnastics on an imaginary trampoline. Why the sudden attack of nerves? This was James. Her friend, her ally, her…what? "Then the storm blows through, the ice melts and the air feels cleansed. It's a respite from the heat, an unexpected gift, like dogwood days."

"Dogwood days?" James sounded bored by his own question.

Bugger, this had sounded so much better when she'd practiced it in front of the bathroom mirror.

"Indian summer in reverse, when the dogwoods are blooming and a cold snap drags you back to winter. The correct phrase is dogwood winter, but I like to put my own spin on things." She offered him the biggest grin she could muster; he didn't respond. "Spring is gorgeous in the Piedmont—brings out the inner gardener in everyone. Plant sales boom, business explodes. A snow day can seem like a gift. It forces me back inside, gives me the chance to goof off and concoct wacky planting ideas." She paused. "I guess that's where I am now, entering my own personal dogwood days. Stepping aside from my life, giving myself a breather."

"Did you not see this coming? In all your years of friendship?"

Damn, right to the core. "No. But you did, didn't you?"

"Her flamboyance reminded me of how handicapped people adapt. I assumed she was overcompensating. And then the night before your date with Sebastian—"

"James, that was a courtesy call to tell me about Woodend, not a date."

He smirked. "We got drunk together that night. Didn't

take long to establish we were seeking oblivion for the same reason."

"You didn't think to mention any of this?"

"Would it have made a difference?"

Aftershocks of the previous night's headache crowded her. "I guess not."

They had moved beyond the vision of the speed cameras, but Tilly continued to drive at 30 mph, hugging the edge of the road. "Turns out they had a drunken grope to 'Nights in White Satin' at some party before Sebastian and I met. Ro, who was drinking by twelve, remembered enough to know she was smitten. All Sebastian remembers, or so I'm told, is his first hangover." She sighed. "Ro was at boarding school then, so we wrote letters. She'd been rabbiting on about Mystery Boy, and then I met Sebastian. When I introduced them, he didn't recognize her. Can you imagine how that made her feel?"

It also explained the only fight she and Rowena ever had, after Tilly scratched Rowena's copy of "Nights in White Satin." Tilly stole the boy and then trashed the soundtrack. Whereas Ro had sacrificed everything and betrayed nothing. And Tilly had never loved her more than that morning, when Rowena stood in the great hall, hands clasped behind her back, feet firmly apart, chin raised and declared, "It's bollocks, because I love him beyond measure, but one night is more than I ever dreamed of. Go ahead, ask me to give him up." And Tilly said, "So you don't want my blessing?" And then they both cried. Since meeting James, she'd cried a lifetime.

"Sebastian and I were merely flirting with the past. Besides, a relationship right now—" she'd reached the point she needed to make "—*any* relationship, would complicate the decision I've made about the business."

"Expanding?"

"Yup. But not into landscaping. I'm thinking retail nursery. James, I—"

"It's okay, Tilly. It's okay. I've cut myself open, shown you my blackened, burned-out heart. The rest is up to you. I won't crowd you, but I will hope that one day you'll pick up the phone and say 'come to me.' And I will." He swiveled around to study her profile, and a tiny part of her wanted to throw her arms around him and never let go. Which was beyond potty, since she was behind the wheel of a car.

"I'm a little confused here. You said you wouldn't wait for me."

"I was trying to push you into a corner, but you outsmarted me."

"No, I believed you." Tilly gave a feeble laugh. "You surprise me constantly."

"Interesting. I think I'm boringly predictable. I'm also a persistent bastard, which is why I left. Or tried to. I had to walk away before I repeated my past, before I forced you into a decision you may have regretted for the rest of your life."

"Meaning?" she murmured.

James circled his lips with his index finger. "When I was fifteen, my father fell in love and I forced him to choose— her or me. Needless to say, I won. She left the area and got married. We didn't know this for years, not until Dad bumped into her on a street corner in Chicago. Can you imagine the chances?"

Yes, she could. How was coming together with James any different? Their lives crossed and they recognized each other. All that remained was to separate.

"My relationship with my father was so tenuous at that point." James leaned forward and slid the control on the air vent one way, then the other. "Seeing her again was enough to shred what was left, and he died before we reconciled." He slumped back into his seat. "I lost one person I loved to hate. I couldn't live through that again. Not with you."

"I assumed you and your father drifted apart because of your OCD."

"OCD began the process…my temper finished it." James scraped back his hair. He held it, for a moment, then let it bounce free. It had grown so much over the summer, long enough now for a ponytail. "Tilly, I want to be with you— every day for the rest of my life. I have no doubts. But you have to want the same thing."

She turned the wheel and they followed a curve. Soon they'd be back on the A5, the Roman road that launched itself at the horizon without curves, without detours.

"Half of me wants it, James. That's the problem."

"But I want it all, and you can't give me that. Can you?"

The sun was shining, the road was straight and she knew where she was heading.

She shook her head. "I'm not ready."

"I fly out tomorrow." He lowered his voice and added, "If I can get on the plane."

"What happened yesterday, at the airport?"

James hesitated before answering. "I've decided to bypass Chapel Hill, give my contractor a break. No doubt he's the only person in the Triangle thrilled to be incommunicado. I fly to Chicago for a week, then on to Seattle for an extended visit."

So, he was shutting her out. Could she blame him?

"I need to spend time with Daniel. Until my father's funeral, we hadn't spoken in ten years. I want to repair our relationship—" James tapped his leg twice, then twice again "—and meet his fiancée, the woman who's carrying my grandchild."

"A grandchild? Wow! Congratulations." Tilly wanted to

say more, but she'd barely processed the existence of Daniel. What would James confess to next, a ménage à trois?

"I wanted to tell you, but vanity got in the way." James twizzled an ear stud. "And since I've screwed up fatherhood, talking about becoming a granddad felt like a jinx. God, Tilly, if you really knew me."

"I do, James." Why did she ever question that?

"No, you don't. You know what I've allowed you to know."

"Then tell me the rest. And I'll promise to respect you in the morning." She paused, but he didn't follow her cue. Yes, she could leave him be, let the unspoken truths fizzle out between them, but that wasn't her way.

There was only one thing left to do. It was a cheap shot, but it would work.

"If you love me—" goose bumps erupted on her forearms "—you'll tell me everything."

James sighed. "My son suffered from clinical depression as a teenager. I thought if I could handle my monsters, so could he. I offered tough love, and Daniel had a breakdown. Amazing how little I've learned from my behavior. Take us, for example. I wish we could start over. I'd get it right, make it perfect from the start."

"I don't want perfect. Perfect is boring. I like messy with lots of flaws. I like us, James. I like that we're two damaged people who understand each other. I've learned so much from you, about fighting back, about trusting myself. Now it's your turn to trust me. Tell me what happened at the airport. Let me help."

"I don't want to discuss it."

Tilly pulled into a lay-by and shut the engine. James glared at her, defiant.

"Isn't that avoiding your fears?" she said. "Exactly what you've taught me not to do?"

"I've hit rock bottom. I listened to the OCD and now the cycle of anxiety begins again. How much worse can it get?"

A soft-sided lorry belted past and the car shook.

"You got me through the hospital, I'm getting you through this. Like it or not, James, we make a kick-ass team when it comes to fighting fear."

"I will not relive what happened at the airport." His voice was quiet but guttural, the warning clear. "Don't make me."

Tilly laughed silently. Did he think he could scare her off? She draped her arm over the steering wheel and leaned into his space. She owed him, and it was payback time. She breathed in the scent of him—cedar, honey and the mystery ingredient that was James—and felt her purpose take root. "What were you frightened of?"

"Stop, Tilly. Please, stop."

"No. Not till you tell me what you were frightened of."

He raised his hands as if to fend off approaching danger and curled his fingers into talons. But Tilly didn't flinch.

She grabbed his thigh and squeezed hard. "Whatever foxhole you're diving into better be big enough for two, because I'm coming in. You're not shutting me out. Not this time."

Fingers still rigid at the air, he began rocking. Back and forth, back and forth. "The plane, the plane crashing. Crashing and exploding. Fire, fire everywhere. Flames. I was burning. But that wasn't the worst part. The worst part was knowing that you couldn't hear me calling your name, knowing that I would die without tasting you, knowing that I would die without hearing you cry out in pleasure that I had given you. Me, not David, not Sebastian. Me." His voice cracked. "How could I face death terrified that you would never love me?"

Without warning, he thrust himself at her. His mouth—

cold, hard, impenetrable—crushed her lips into her teeth and the force of his kiss jammed her head into the headrest. She squirmed, desperate for air, and he fell back. A thread of saliva joined them for a second, then disintegrated.

"I'm sorry," he whispered. "I'm sorry."

Tilly touched her throbbing lips. No one had ever hurt her with a kiss before.

James grappled with his T-shirt and started rocking again. "People think OCD is a joke, Tilly. That we're screwy because we line things up in the fridge. They have no idea. No idea what it's like to be haunted by your own thoughts, always running but never escaping. Of being so exhausted by the effort of dragging yourself through the checking, the rituals, the fear, that some days you don't think you can make it. I can't get off the ride, Tilly, I can't. As a child, nightmares filled my days. At eleven I couldn't go to a movie…I was convinced the theater would burn down with me trapped inside. At fifteen I thought every man I met wanted to rape me. At sixteen I believed *I* was the rapist. By seventeen I was so stoned I no longer cared. Then I learned to hide my fears, learned that people wanted to glide by, their lives uninterrupted by my darkness. *My* darknesss, the horror of *me.*" James closed his eyes. "I'm frightened of life, Tilly, of death, of love. And failing. I'm a failure. The OCD is right. I'm a failure."

He had knotted his hands together, but Tilly pried them apart and held one against her face. A long sigh leaked from his mouth and his fingers molded to her cheekbone. For a moment she forgot who was comforting whom.

"Why, my love?" she said. "Why are you a failure?"

"Because I can't plant one fucking plant. The OCD is telling me that I'm a failure because I left before you showed me how to plant. See how it adapts, how it contorts and perverts? It used to tell me not to garden, that if I did I would die. Now it's saying I'm a failure because I didn't conquer my fear."

"Okey-dokey." Tilly returned his hand to his lap. She started the engine, and they shot across the road in a squealing U-turn.

"What are you doing?" James's voice was weak.

"What are *we* doing. We started this together, James, and we're ending it together. We're going to the Hall and staying until you've buried your hands in dirt. This is my gift to you. And you're not leaving without it."

Tilly crouched behind James, swaddling his body. Her legs gaped around his thighs, and her right arm rested along his like a snake sunning itself. One hip was numb, the other had begun to cramp, but she couldn't risk moving. Not yet. They inhaled in unison and she wound her bare fingers over his gloved ones, tightening her grip until his hand was clamped to the trowel. Before he could exhale, her hand sprang, shoving the trowel deep and then yanking it free with a scoop of soil. He breathed hard, each inhalation rattling through her body, and then he began to quiver. Small tremors in his hand at first, but as she forced him to dig a second and a third time, his entire body convulsed.

He mumbled an incantation, but Tilly didn't listen. She filtered out the world around her—his voice, the birdsong, the peaty smell of earth, the dying sunlight heating her shoulders. She blocked it all and visualized her border up by the road, the garden that had given them both hope. The garden she had created out of grief, out of a need to find order in chaos.

She would not lose focus, she wouldn't doubt they could do this. James had talked about being trapped in a burning building. Well, he wasn't staying in there alone.

She reached for the nicotiana plant, shaking potting soil from its roots. Then she placed it in his gloved palm and cupping his fingers from underneath, fused their hands into one. Together, they eased the roots into the hole, brushed loose soil around them and waited. Only one task remained, a task she could complete in seconds, without thought. But those seconds could stretch into a lifetime of horror for James. Was this how a field surgeon felt operating without anesthesia?

Tilly held her breath. She had coached James, prepared him for what would follow, but could she inflict that much pain on another person? Could she force him to touch, to feel, to confront the one thing that terrified him beyond all reason? She could never pet a snake. Hell, she couldn't even pick up a worm.

Part of her wanted to reassure him, tell him he didn't have to do this. But that would be a mistake. If she retreated now, she would skew his story to fit her point of view, to see his path through her eyes. And that was shortsighted and wrong. She knew what James wanted and the role he hoped she would play. He'd told her as much every day since they'd started work in the garden, just as David had done with the living will. All those years, she had understood what David expected of her if the unimaginable happened, and when it did, Tilly had known instinctively what to do. As she knew now.

You can do this, James. I know you can.

James released his fingers, like a coil snapping free. But she was quicker than he was. Throwing her weight against his back, she grabbed his right wrist, clamped down, and with her left hand, yanked off his glove.

He gave a strangled cry, more animal than human, but Tilly refused to stop. She shoved his palm into the soil and held it there, pressing the plant into its new home, forcing

James's exposed skin into the soil until she was convinced he had left his mark.

"We're done," she said, and let go.

He collapsed into her, and her bottom smacked onto the gravel. A shockwave of pain ran up each vertebra, but she held on as he juddered into her—from relief or tears she didn't know and didn't care. His accomplishment was their accomplishment; she felt it in every muscle.

She tugged him closer, gripping him to her chest, and closed her eyes until she could see neither the past nor the future, just the present.

"This is better than sex," James said. He and Tilly had shared something more intimate than making love, and when he was dying, this was the moment he would retreat to. This was the moment he would hold on to as his last spark of consciousness. This was the reward for three hours of planting.

"The orgasm of gardening?" Tilly smiled. "I like that."

"You knew all along I could do it, didn't you?"

"Failure wasn't an option." She chinked her beer bottle against his. "Besides. You overcame your fear of holding hands to help me at the hospital. You got on two planes—"

"Also for you," he said.

"The cause doesn't matter, only the result. You really are the bravest person I've ever met. I think you're incredible."

Her leg flopped against his, and James draped his wrist across her knee. Everything he did with this woman felt so right, even if it was just sitting side by side on a mossy path, legs pulled up as the two of them leaned back against an old stone wall. And tonight they were bathed in the nocturnal perfume of the nicotiana that he—he!—had planted.

James sipped from one of the bottles Sebastian had brought

them, but even warm beer couldn't poison his euphoria, the incandescent joy exploding inside. He had never experienced feelings this pure. Never. Is this how it felt to be happy, to live without fear? Had normal finally entered his repertoire? As if.

OCD would always shadow him; he wouldn't delude himself about that, but today he was victorious. Today, he had learned that he could wrestle fear into a corner and keep it there. Today, he had learned that he could take control of his life; he could win. And if he'd done it once, he could do it again. This time, repetition really was the answer.

After thirty-five years, he'd also learned he didn't have to do this alone. He took another sip of beer and forced himself to swallow. "I hate warm beer," he said.

"I just hate beer." Tilly took a long gulp.

"Sebastian didn't know that?"

"I guess he did—once." She picked at the label on her bottle. "How quickly men forget."

"I won't, Tilly." James's head lolled against the wall. God Almighty, he could never forget a single thing about Matilda Rose Haddington.

"No. I don't suppose you will." Tilly inhaled. "Mmm. Smell that? It's the Gloire de Dijon, that buff-colored rose." She pointed with her bottle. "Isn't it fabulous?"

Tonight was fabulous. His whole life had been leading up to this scene of quiet celebration. There were no fireworks; there was no champagne. There was dirt, warm beer, the scent of roses and a man who was deeply in love. James had always worried that the best part of himself had died with his mother, but Tilly had proved him wrong. Just looking at her, he knew he could love as fiercely as his dad had done. He, too, was capable of sacrificing his own happiness for that one person who meant everything. And he would. Tilly had visited hell for him, and he wouldn't ask for a repeat performance. He was going to let her off the hook. Set her free. But not without a proper thank-you.

James jumped up and used his wrist to brush the hair from his face. "You are, without doubt, the best. Up." He tugged her to her feet. "Since we met you've asked me for only one thing, and I denied it."

"A lift to the breast clinic?" Her smile flickered. Clearly she was unsure of where he was going. God Almighty, she was beautiful. No makeup, her hair a mess, a froth of beer on her upper lip.

"Other than that." His arms slid around her waist, and he sighed. He had held her once and it had felt so good. Twice was even better. "You asked me to do something that I've fought against since I was ten years old, since fear hijacked my life.

"You asked me to willingly live in the moment." He bent toward her. "To enjoy doing so." Her body stiffened. She snatched back her head and stared up at him, but he continued. "You asked for a kiss that led nowhere. A kiss without expectations."

Her chest was moving rapidly. "James," her voice squeaked. God, she was adorable. "You're on a roll. You need to keep going, get on that plane tomorrow. If you don't, the OCD wins. A kiss will only complicate things, for both of us. I—"

He shushed her then stepped back. There would be no rationalizing, no listening to doubt. There would be nothing but instinct. "You talk too much, and I think too much," he said. "Enough. I want to meet you at eye level. Jump."

She did, and he caught her. She weighed so little. Not much more than air. Slowly, she raised her eyes.

"Why are you trembling?" he said.

"Why aren't you?"

"Because…" He paused. "I'm at peace."

She wrapped her legs around his hips, and he tightened his arms under her.

Would it be a first kiss or a last kiss? And did it matter? He knew only one thing: He wanted to live in the moment. Their moment. He didn't know when he would see her again; he didn't know if he would see her again. He would slip her a scrap of paper with his cell phone number and his son's address and that would be his only concession. The rest was up to her.

Sometimes you had to take what life offered. Sometimes you had to dare yourself to be happy and damn the consequences. And sometimes all you needed was a kiss.

She pulled herself farther up his body, and he smiled as his lips stroked hers.

"If we do this, how can I let you go?" she said, and he felt the vibrations of her words.

"You will. And you'll find me again, when you're ready. Take as long as you need."

He swallowed her breath and tasted hops and the sweetness of ripe strawberries. He whispered her name, even though he longed to scream it into the night.

For this woman, he would get it right. For this woman, he would be the person he always wanted to be: the son his dad could be proud of.

Thirty

Tilly ignored the scrabbling as Monty interred the decapitated rabbit he found earlier under the raspberry canes. She bent down and picked up a tuft of rabbit fur—soft, white, pure—and nudged it around her palm. There was no blood, no hint of violent death. Strange, how deceptive the outward face could be, how easy it was to look at a place, a person, and see what you wanted to see. A garden, for example, might appear to be a gentle place of harmony, but while you weren't looking snakes gulped down frogs, praying mantises hoovered up insects, and foxes munched the heads off baby rabbits. And a man like James might appear successful and confident, but inside he was battered and torn, a well-kept secret.

Rooks flapped on their way home to roost, marring the robin's-egg sky, and undernourished apples that had tumbled before their time crunched and splattered under her clogs. Tilly stepped sideways, grinned and stomped on another faller. Squelching apples was way more fun than jumping into puddles.

Apples meant Halloween and Isaac's favorite time of the

year. And then they would roll from one holiday to the next. Maybe this year they would stay home for Thanksgiving, instead of schlepping up to New York to be with David's sister. And maybe they would have a Hanukkah tree decked out in blue lights and dreidels. Maybe they'd start some new traditions this holiday season. Maybes were good. She liked their promise of uncertainty.

Tilly circled the lilac tree and dialed. Finally, a connection. She'd forgotten how little patience she had for the frustrations of life in Woodend and poor phone service was top of the list. She flopped to the grass, her heart beating so hard she felt each pulse in her throat.

"Sari, it's Tilly! I've—"

The answer phone screeched, and Tilly jerked the receiver away from her ear.

"Tils! Hang on!" Sari yelled. "I was about to call. Phone and power back on within an hour! Jesus, I'm so excited I could lose my *Ann Coulter Eats Babies* bumper sticker and not bawl. The house is fine, greenhouse—not a scratch. Garden's a bit flattened, but nothing you can't fix. It's so good to hear from you."

Tilly smiled. "Is everything okay with Aaron, the boys? Your house?"

"All tickety-boo, as you Brits say."

Tilly knew what was coming. She could hear it in what Sari wasn't saying. "The old oak fell, didn't it?"

There was a pause. "Smashed into the studio, hon. But the books are fine, which is a miracle. And Aaron clambered up on the roof to secure a tarpaulin." Sari sighed. "My hero."

Balancing the portable phone between her shoulder and her cheek, Tilly yanked a Biro from behind her ear. Then she fumbled in the back pocket of her jeans for a small, spiral notepad. Damn, her first to-do list. How grown-up was that?

"Brilliant." Tilly drew flowers down one side of the pad and kept on doodling until there was no room left to write. "If a tree's involved, my homeowner's insurance will cover it."

"Tils? You're scaring me. You're still coming home, right? Because I'm a sneeze away from going postal. I need a hot stone massage and serious shoe retail therapy. Hey, want the kids to box up the books, move them to the house?"

"No, thanks. I'll deal with them. It can be my exposure." She was using her James language, words that made sense.

"Sorry, hon. No idea what you're talking about."

"I've made a decision." Tilly chewed the end of the Biro. "I've studied your five-year business plan and I agree about turning Piedmont Perennials into a retail nursery with the studio as an office. But the plan needs revising before I talk with the bank. You can start by contacting the county planning department. Find out if we need to upgrade the site plan review. Oh, and ask about parking."

Sari gasped; Tilly continued. "I see mail order as a stage two expansion. Mail order nurseries have a life expectancy of fifteen years, so I want everything on solid ground before we throw in a catalog. Packing and shipping plants? Dicey at best." Tilly paused. "You can jump in at any time."

"I c-can't. I'm in shock." Sari sniveled. "What changed your mind?"

Tilly slipped off her clog and fondled a clump of clover with her toes. "I want this. And I can't remember the last time I wanted anything just for me." She took a deep breath. "I'm selling David's MG, too. Investing the money in the business."

"Now that's a fucking smart move."

Wo-oo-oh a pigeon called from the paddock, and Tilly's mind drifted to James. She pictured him leaning against the doorjamb at Manor Farm, watching as she walked backward to the car. He flicked his mess of hair from his face, threw out a smile meant only for her and held up his hand in a solitary wave. And after she pulled onto the estate road, she turned for one final glimpse and realized he was watching the space where she had been.

"And this has nothing to do with the cute James." Sari's voice was heavy with irony, but quiet, as if she were thinking aloud.

Cute. What an inadequate word to describe James. Tilly turned the page on the pad, wrote *quote for studio,* and then dropped it to the grass. Suddenly, she was cold. Freezing, in fact.

"He's in love with you, isn't he?" Sari said.

Tilly hugged herself. She was still reeling from the feel of James, remembering his tongue gently exploring her mouth, then his lips, greedy for more, moving down to her neck and her chest and back to claim her mouth. And afterward, he closed his eyes and mapped her body like a blind man reading Braille.

"Yes. He's in love with me." She was surprised at how comfortable the admission sounded. *He's in love with me.* Tilly arched against the lilac tree. The bark grazed her right shoulder blade, and she winced. Her back was wrecked from all the planting with James, but the pain had purpose. It had led to the kiss of a lifetime, a kiss she was glad she had waited for because in that one moment, she and James had wanted the same thing—each other. "I've never met anyone like him, Sari. He's smart, quirky, compassionate, and he gets me."

"Sounds like Aaron. Maybe we should make up a foursome one night."

Tilly stood and brushed off her jeans. "James isn't going to be around for a while. Right emotion, wrong time and place. But dinner...you and me...might be nice?"

"I'd like that," Sari said quietly.

"Sari, can I ask you a really embarrassing question? I ran the washing machine yesterday without any clothes in. Have you ever done anything as loopy as that?"

Sari guffawed. "Oh, hon. Wait till perimenopause. I don't lose the car keys, I lose the goddamn car. I reported the Passat as stolen from the mall the other day. Turns out I'd parked by one entrance, exited from another. Jesus."

Tilly laughed. "Any chance you could pick us up from the airport next Thursday?"

"You mean flight AA173, arriving at 4:10 p.m.? Already on the calendar, hon."

Tilly waited until the thrush began its dawn chorus and then crept downstairs, avoiding the stair that creaked. In one hour she had to wake Isaac, say goodbye to her mother and leave. But first, she needed to force herself to do something alone.

Monty eyed her with suspicion when she entered the kitchen, but rose and padded to the back door. She let him out and followed. Damp grass tickled her feet, a pigeon cooed in the cherry tree and the air smelled of lavender.

She would never return to Woodend. She knew that now. Sebastian would move into the Hall and Woodend would pass to a stranger. And maybe that was easier. A clean break with no backward glance.

Tilly ambled around the garden she had loved since she was a little girl, committing every flower, every shrub to memory. She stopped to bury her nose in the sweet peas, to stroke the Lucifer red crocosmia flowers, to admire the spiky leaves of a huge acanthus, a plant famous for inspiring Corinthian columns in Ancient Greece. She came to a small bed, half-hidden in the shade of the summerhouse, and stopped. Matilda's Rose Garden, her father had called it, despite the lack of roses. Her mother had encouraged her to find a sunnier spot, explaining it would be easier for a first garden. But Tilly had refused to listen. She had set her heart on shade. Even as a child, she knew what she wanted.

She practiced a few of James's yoga breaths and then began reciting words she memorized ten years earlier from Ecclesiastes. Words she had last spoken at her father's funeral:

"'To everything there is a season, a time for every purpose under the sun. A time to be born and a time to die; a time to plant and a time to pluck up that which is planted.'"

And a time to go off script.

"A time to move on—" she turned around to face her childhood home "—and a time to say goodbye."

Thirty-One

"Dad!" Daniel shouted up the stairs. "C'mon! We'll be late."

James glanced at his watch. No, they had three minutes. Daniel definitely had a touch of OCD, but they'd had a good conversation about that—one of many centered on anxiety, depression, the whole genetic shebang. James had even shared his recent journey through the world of exposures, although, if he were being honest, that was a poorly disguised excuse to talk about Tilly. Thankfully, Daniel had suspected nothing. James was torn between his desperation to keep Tilly present in his daily life and a dread of answering questions about their non-relationship. If he had to explain his feelings for her out loud, he would crack. Five weeks and six days since he'd heard her voice, but every time he spoke her name, he kick-started his heart.

"Give me two minutes," James called back. He sat on the bed in his son's guest room, phone pressed to his ear, resisting the urge to twist his hair. Was Saturday night a bad time to call?

"Virginia!" He shot up when she answered the phone. "James Nealy here."

"James! What a delightful surprise. How are you, my dear?"

"I'm well, thank you." As he should be—running every day, pushing his body until the exhaustion in his limbs melted away and his need for Tilly dulled to match the ache in his lungs. September in Seattle had surprised him with endless warm, sunny days, but he'd hoped for gray skies and rain. Weather that spoke to him of Tilly.

James cleared his throat. "I'm afraid this is a quick call, since my son and I are going to the movies."

"How lovely."

James smiled. He missed Virginia, although maybe not her psycho dog. And he missed Woodend. He had never been as happy, or as desolate, as he'd been in that house—thanks to the torture of love, or rather his love for Tilly, which was unique and exquisite, and killing him cell by cell. His only link to her these days was the twice-weekly phone call with Rowena that had become his means of watching over Tilly and Isaac, of reassuring himself that they were safe and happy. That knowledge was invaluable.

James cleared his throat. "Rowena tells me Sebastian has decided not to buy Woodend."

"Indeed. Heaven only knows what took him so long. I gather she proposed?"

"And he accepted." So, Virginia wasn't surprised that he and Rowena had stayed in contact. But then again, Virginia was all-knowing. "Do you have a new buyer?"

"James." Virigina sounded like his tenth grade Spanish teacher, the one who spent an entire school year turning his name into a reprimand. "I won't sell Woodend to you."

"Not even if I begged?" Or doubled her asking price, which he could do if he sold his never-lived-in mansion.

"You don't need Woodend to win my daughter's heart. Have a little faith."

Yesterday Rowena had told him the same thing, but he was almost out of faith. He was almost out of everything. Tilly had given him back his life, but without her, what was the point? Without her he was empty.

A ragtag tropical storm had answered Tilly's gardening prayers with three inches of rain and seventy-degree warmth. Scarlet salvias spilled into coleus the colors of stained glass windows, and the giant leonitis and castor bean plants had stepped, surely, from the pages of *The Lorax*. Had her main bed ever looked this good?

Tilly tried to relax into her Sunday afternoon and enjoy the music of her forest: the melody of the thrush, the hammer of the scarlet-headed woodpecker, the cry of the hawk seeking its mate. The sunshine was soft and the air flavored with wood smoke, yet the pinched feeling in her stomach tightened, stealing her joy piecemeal.

She concentrated on the memorial dogwood, its leaves of copper and crimson marking the end of another year without David. But this year's end was different. She was different. Images of the breathing tube protruding from David's mouth—a stake through both their lives—still haunted her, but she no longer struggled to recall David's voice nor fought to convince herself that he was merely waiting for her out of sight. And thanks to James, she anchored memories of David with laughter, not remorse.

Tilly grinned, conjuring up the day her mother had visited David in hospital. Groggy from jet lag, Mrs. Haddington had pulled the wrong cord in the bathroom and a battalion of nurses had barged in to rescue her mid-flush. Tilly and

Isaac had laughed until they'd ached. David would have been laughing, too. Their last family joke.

A pair of hummingbirds chittered over her candy corn cuphea, and the memory evaporated, replaced by the ache of words unspoken, but not to her husband.

Twenty-three hours earlier she had called James's iPhone, the phone he kept with him always, and had reached his voice mail. Sick with nerves, she had been unable to leave more than a brief message. How could she have been so sure of him, of them, and been so wrong? But yesterday was over, and she didn't have to accept his silence. Tonight, she would explain to Isaac that Sari was coming to stay, and then detail the school carpooling schedule she had jury-rigged while he slept. Her brain spun with the favors she'd owe when she returned.

Would Isaac cheer or cry at the news that she was running after James? How would James react? And what would his son think? Okay, so she might make a fool of herself, but living with regret was far worse. She should know.

A mob of cyclists whooshed by on Creeping Cedars Road, and an acorn clonked down the roof through the web of a fat, russet spider. Cyclists, acorns and spiders—the next month belonged to them. And, if she could convince him, James and Tilly.

"Mom...." Isaac kicked over a large stone and scoured underneath for skinks. She smiled at his stained T-shirt, his untied sneakers, his bangs falling into his eyes now that he had decided to grow his hair as long as James's. "When can we put up the Halloween decorations?"

"This afternoon?" *Great, Tilly, bribe him.*

"Awesome!" He plunked the stone back in place and moved on to the next one. "Don't we need a new crashing witch this year?"

"Already bought one." Damn, that was meant to be a surprise.

"You have? Wow-zee. You're the best, Super Mom."

"That would be me." Super Mom had always been enough, but not today. Tilly flopped back and splayed her arms, crucifixion style, over the steps.

The phone in her hand shrilled and she leaped up, her spine tingling. *Let it be James. Let it be*— She clicked the talk button. "Piedmont Perennials."

"Hello, Tilly." Was this the voice Sebastian used to coax clients through tough financial decisions? Or had he created a special tone for the ex-lover best friend to the love of his life? That had to be worth a session or two on the psychiatrist's couch. Not that Sebastian would ever consider visiting a shrink.

"Hey. This is…a pleasant surprise," Tilly said. Why couldn't it have been James? Was it so hard to answer one phone call? Was he avoiding her?

"How's the business?" Ice chinked on the other end of the phone line, even though it was way past English cocktail time.

"Expanding. Sari, my partner, pelts ahead with a vodka tonic in hand. I prance along behind with the gin." The humor worked; the maelstrom in her head dissipated.

"Jolly good, then."

What, no reprimand for mixing business and alcohol? "Want to tell me what this is about?"

Sebastian made a sucking noise, as if he'd tasted something sour. "That obvious?"

"You? Spitting out what you want to say on the first attempt?"

"I'm a changed man. All touchy-feely."

"Yeah, I can imagine." Although she preferred not to. "How's Ro?"

"Christ, she's amazing." Sebastian's voice filled with the awe of a child watching fireworks. *Yukety, yuk.* Tilly pointed a finger into her mouth. Isaac gave her a quizzical look, and she shooed him away.

"And the kids?" Tilly pushed her hands into the small of her back. She was stiff from a day of standing in the greenhouse, and there was so much left to do, especially now she'd added Halloween decorating to the afternoon's activities. "How're Archie and Sophie adapting?"

"You mean to their father becoming a love-struck teenager?"

Not exactly what she meant, but close enough. Tilly bent down and rubbed her fingers over the leaves of her scented agastache, then sniffed. *Hmm. Anise, delicious.*

"Sorry," he said. "You probably didn't want to hear that."

"Nonsense. It was nauseating, but sweet. I'm happy for you both, really."

More ice chinked and Sebastian took a gulp of something. All summer she had tried to figure out what his favorite tipple was, but Sebastian had become a man without a cocktail preference, a social chameleon who drank what everyone else did. The realization was oddly irritating.

"The children are fine, better than fine. They adore Rowena. It's not them I'm worried about."

Aha, so *that* was his problem. "If Ro's still beating herself up, tell her not to."

"I have, I do, but it's not enough. I want to give her a present for our third-month anniversary. A special gift." Tilly rolled her eyes as Sebastian spoke. "You."

"Me? I may be short but I'm impossible to gift-wrap. And shipping's prohibitive. Jewelry would be cheaper."

"Very funny."

Except he wasn't laughing. God, how did Rowena have the patience?

"I have to fly to Washington at the end of October," Sebastian said. "I thought I might bring Rowena and then fly down to North Carolina for a weekend. Or would that be too awkward? Lousy idea, huh?"

"Are you kidding? That would be fab. Hey, Isaac! What d'you think about Ro and Sebastian trick-or-treating with us?"

Isaac gyrated his limbs in opposing directions—part crazed soccer fan, part disco diva. Was it too much to hope that he would accept her news as happily?

"Isaac concurs. Come whenever."

"Brilliant, bloody brilliant." Sebastian blew into the phone. "There is one other thing." He sipped his drink. "You won't give us separate bedrooms, will you? It's just that we can't bear to sleep apart."

"Oh *puhleeeease*." Did he really have to say that?

She shivered. Sebastian and Rowena were sharing bed-rooms, bodies, probably even a sodding toothbrush. They were creating a future together, doing everything that she wanted to do with James. A yellow oak leaf spiraled to Tilly's feet and she stared at it. Her admiration for Rowena doubled, tripled, quadrupled. Ro had lived with this yearning for twenty years; Tilly wasn't sure she could make it through twenty-four hours.

"How's James?" If Sebastian were aiming for casual, he failed. Clearly he hadn't forgiven James for bunking with Rowena.

"On walkabout." Tilly worried at a rose thorn in her finger. Finally it had risen to the surface; one tug and it would be out.

"Rowena thought he might be back by now."

Terrific. Rowena and Sebastian had been discussing her love life. "Me too, which pokes a big fat hole in the sanctity of female intuition. His house is done, though. You should see it." Tilly snapped open the butterfly clip that scraped back her hair. "Well, you wouldn't be able to, since you'd never clamber over the gates and hike up the drive."

"You *tres*passed?"

"I just wanted a quick butcher's for garden possibilities. James wouldn't care. The house is stunning, with lots of sharp angles and long thin windows." Speaking his name, *James,* made Tilly want to turn herself inside out and howl. She was where she had never wanted to be again—in love. And it was the worst feeling in the world.

"Tilly. Why don't you admit that you love him?"

Love advice from Sebastian. How bizarre was that? She must have been really messed up over the summer if she'd believed they could make the whole friendship thing zing. Her best friend's husband, on the other hand, was a role they could both handle. Civility without strings. She resecured the butterfly clip. "I reached the same conclusion, about being in love. So I called, left a message, but he didn't respond. We had this agreement, you see, that he would wait for my call. Only he didn't live up to his end of the bargain."

Tilly pinched a dead leaf from her red cascade rose. All spring she had struggled to train it up a trellis, but while she and Isaac were away it broke free. Now it wove wherever it fancied, and the effect was stunning. Next year she wouldn't interfere.

An unexpected thrill pounced, a longing for the surprises of spring when tender plants poked through the soil in defiance of hardiness ratings, self-seeded annuals popped up in unexpected niches and perennials died without explanation, leaving gaps for new plants. Her garden was a place of death, rebirth, and change, and like her life, would continue to evolve whether James loved her or not. She would go after him, she would confront him, and if he rejected her, she would walk away. Some things were worth the fear of heartbreak.

Sebastian cleared his throat. "Ring him again. Messages get lost...mobiles break."

"Not in James's world. Nuh-huh. He got my message. The only question is what he chooses to do with it." The rest of the story was hers. Sebastian didn't need to hear more.

"You didn't get this from me, okay?" Sebastian's voice was muffled, as if he'd turned away from her. "Village rumor has a wealthy American buying Woodend."

No! Her mother would have told her. Wouldn't she? Tilly squinted up through a visor of fingers and watched a cumulus cloud scud across the sky. *Where are you, James?*

"Mom?" Isaac touched her arm. "Are you sick? You look kinda odd. Wow!" He jumped away from her. "Did you see that? Down there by the creek."

"Tilly?" Sebastian sounded concerned, or was that irritated?

"Sorry. Isaac's pointing at something. Probably a snake."

Sebastian gave a verbal shiver. "How can you cope with all those snakes?"

"They live here, so do I. I can't throw a conniption every time I see one." One of the many things she'd learned from James. He wasn't even here, might never be, and yet he was embedded in her life.

They'd exhausted the conversation. It was time for Sebastian to say goodbye and Tilly to return to her day. She winked at Isaac but he frowned back, motioning her to join him. And that's when she spotted the copperhead. But what the hell was Isaac doing? He had spun around and was sprinting—as if fleeing an army of ogres—in the opposite direction.

Her hand flew to her mouth, and she stifled a weak *omigod.*

"Tilly?" Sebastian said. "Are you—"

She tossed the phone onto the mulch pile and ran after her child.

A tall figure dressed in black and wearing red sneakers strode down the driveway swinging a huge, black duffel. A black leather backpack hung from one shoulder, a black suit carrier from the other. The black cord from his earbuds flapped over his chest. His grizzled hair was brushed into a smooth ponytail, exposing the raw beauty of his face— the sharp cheekbones, the sculpted chin, the huge almond-shaped eyes.

Tilly halted at the edge of the driveway. She couldn't move, couldn't speak. She had left a three-word message, "We should talk," and he had jumped on a plane—two, at least, given his route. He'd changed planes for her, and he hated changing planes. That had to be good, right?

James pulled out his earbuds as Isaac slammed into him. "You're just in time!" Isaac squealed. "There's a copperhead down there!"

"Go keep an eye on it." Isaac tried to pull away, but James gripped his shoulder. "From behind the well. Let me say hello to your mother, and I'll be right there."

"Gotcha," Isaac said, and skittered off the second James released him.

Her child had disappeared to ogle a venomous snake, and she did nothing. Squirrels chased up a tree, yammering as their claws scrabbled for purchase on the bark, claws that excavated her plants, and she did nothing. Deer padded through her woods, grazing on her shrubs, no doubt, and she did nothing. Paralyzed by apprehension and desire, all Tilly could do was breathe.

"Your hair," James said.

"Frightful, isn't it?" She tugged the butterfly clip loose. "Growing like a weed. Yours, too." Oh crap, had she just insulted him? "Where's the Alfa?"

"In town. I took a taxi from the airport." James walked up to her and stopped.

He lined up his luggage, then extracted his iPod from his jeans pocket and handed it to her. "You wanted to talk?"

"You couldn't pick up the phone like most people?" Panic lodged in her throat. She was ruining everything. He wasn't like most people, and she didn't want him to be. She wanted him to be James. A dog howled through the woods, and Tilly heard the beat of her heart.

James frowned. "Why? I told you I'd come if you called."

"Hurry up, slowpokes!" Isaac yelled.

Spooked, the deer bounded away, snapping branches as they took flight.

"When you didn't call back I panicked. I…I was coming to find you. Booked flights and everything." Tilly reached out with her free hand and laced her fingers through his. "I wanted to tell you that I've decided to take on a garden design job. Just one. And only if you still want me. I mean it's okay, if you don't feel the same anymore." The first time they had touched, his handshake had been so loose, so fleeting. Today his grasp was firm, but he didn't clutch at her. It was as if he were holding back. And then she understood: whatever happened next was up to her.

In her right hand she felt his iPod, passed to her without hesitation, and in her left hand his palm, surprisingly cool and slightly damp. She imagined her hands balancing out her future, repeating what she already knew.

"Actually, no. It's not okay," she said. "It's far from okay, because even though I've waited six weeks, and I'm sure you've met some buxom beauty in that time, here's the thing—I'm in love with you. And not just a little oh-he's-hot. Which you are. We're talking crazy in love. Nuts for you, really." The sound of her words rushed in her ears. She darted at him, kissed his cheek and jerked back, overwhelmed by the scent of him—so familiar, so comforting. So predictable.

"Buxom beauties? And I thought I was the one with the overactive imagination." His eyes glistened with humor, and the dimple in his chin became more pronounced. "How long will this garden design job of yours take?"

Her muscles had frozen. Nothing worked in her body except for her sweat glands and her heart, both intent on pumping toward shutdown. She stared into his eyes and saw herself.

"The English author H.E. Bates said that a finished garden is a dead garden." She held his gaze and sensed the ebb and flow of her breath matching his. "It'll take a lifetime. A garden's a work in progress without end."

Reaching out with their linked hands, he ran a finger down her cheek. "Are you sure about this? I'm high maintenance," he said, with a hint of sadness. Or was it honesty, pure and naked, handed to her out of trust?

"Are you buying Woodend?"

"Do you want me to?" His face transformed, his eyes wide with terror.

"No. I don't need Woodend anymore."

"Thank God. Because your mother refused to sell it to me." Tilly gave a smile and James mirrored it.

"Ask me what I do need, just as you did on the day we met." Her voice grew more solid with each word.

"And what is it, Matilda Rose, that you need?"

"I need—" she savored his smile as it grew "—you."

"Hurry up!" Isaac sounded more persistent.

"Be right there!" James shouted. Pinning Tilly's arm behind him, he nuzzled her ear. "You had until Thanksgiving," he whispered, "and then you were mine."

Desire tore through her, and her heart swelled with adrenaline and joy and an unexpected shot of fear.

James pulled back but tightened his grip on her hand. "Are you scared?"

"A little."

"Do you know why the taxi dropped me by the road?" he asked.

Tilly shook her head.

"I thought walking down your driveway might stop my legs from shaking."

"Did it?"

"No. Seeing the woman I love did." Then he blew her a kiss so slight that his lips barely moved. Someone who didn't know him as she did, who hadn't studied his face until every line had etched itself into her memory, might have missed the gesture.

"Come see the snake with us," James said, and led Tilly slowly forward.

★ ★ ★ ★ ★

✑ *Acknowledgments* ✑

It took a transatlantic village to write this novel, and I would like to extend thanks to people on both sides of the pond for sharing stories and expertise: Caroline Crawford, Dee Crump, Coleen Miller, Carol Sazone and Carol Young at www.youngwidow.org; Deborah Smith, Rose Stone, Eileen Ingram and Sharon Ireson for information on breast cancer treatment in England; Pam Baggett, Sharon Snider and Karen Suberman for all things gardening; Aaron Burris at Piedmont Wildlife Services (also thanks to the Piedmont Wildlife Center); Robert Cain and Charlotte Dunn for help with English inheritance laws; Jonathan Boyarin for critiquing the Brooklyn accent; Jeremy Packer for his expertise on mobility; Mike Edwards, Teresa Parsley Edwards and Donna Gilleskie for helping me figure out careers I don't understand; Daniel Hanbury Higgins for taking me through the workings of an English estate; Stephen Piercy for explaining banking to someone who will never get it; Patty Rich and Charles Rose for medical advice; Jennifer Leaf in the planning department of Orange County; and Harry Rose, Jack Rose and Carolyn Wilson (the original Petal) for answering miscellaneous, pesky questions.

Many readers and writers gave generously of their time to offer feedback or advice. Special thanks to Joyce Allen, Elizabeth Brown, Bernie Bro Brown, Marcy Cohen, Sheryl Cornett, Cathy Davidson, Therese Fowler, Ann Weibel Jarvie, Sharon Rothspan Kurtzman, Martin Langfield, Joanne Rendell, Maureen Sherbondy, Caroline Upcher, Densye Woods and Anne Gentry Woodman. Big hug to my language guru, Dan Hill.

A world of thanks to Dr. Pat Gammon at the Duke Child and Family Study Center and to Dr. Mike Gammon, who gave my family the tools we needed to defeat the OCD monster.

Thank you to everyone at Spencerhill Associates and MIRA Books. Eternal gratitude to Nalini Akolekar and to Miranda Indrigo for believing in Tilly and James and for making the final leg of a long journey to publication so easy.

Thanks to my mother, Anne Claypole White, research assistant extraordinaire and chief cheerleader, to my sister, Susan Rose (walking, talking encyclopedia of the English countryside), and to the Grossbergs—Al, Mike, Linda, Jeff, Sharon, Andy, David, Karen, Miriam and Edie.

To old pals Jocelyn Piercy and Carolyn Wilson, thank you for never giving up hope despite the first manuscript. Thanks to Julie Smith, Catherine Parker and Jill Sugg for becoming Team Barbara, to flag-wavers Hannah and Hugo Piercy, and to Danlee Gildersleeve, Chuck Whitney and Ellen Wartella for keeping my menfolk sane. Love and gratitude to all the friends—old and new—who've been supportive along the way.

Tears of appreciation for beta reader Leslie Gildersleeve, who has been behind me, alongside me and ahead of me from the beginning, who listened to the first idea and the last idea and critiqued every draft in between. What would I do without you and Friday afternoons?

A kiss to my husband, Lawrence Grossberg, without whom, nothing. Thank you for encouraging me to chase dreams, for tolerating uncleaned bathrooms, for not throttling me when I said, "Can you read this one more time?" and for understanding that a woman needs her garden, even if she is kvetching about deer, voles, whitefly and drought.

To my award-winning poet son, Zachariah Claypole White, you are my hero. Thank you for keeping me in smiles and giggles, for knowing when to blast U2 in the car, for showing me what it means to be loyal and brave, and for reminding me constantly of the beauty of words.

Last, but never least, to my father, whose death inspired me to write *Dogwood Days,* which became *The Unfinished Garden*: "Look what I did, Daddy."

*James's comment about children and oxygen masks comes from *When Children Grieve* by John W. James, Russell Friedman and Dr. Leslie Matthews.

1. How is gardening used as a metaphor in this novel? Do you believe in the healing power of gardening?

2. James is an unlikely hero. What do you think draws Tilly to him?

3. Do you have a favorite moment, scene or line in the book?

4. What roles do trust and mistrust play in the characters' relationships?

5. Why do you think issues of control appear repeatedly throughout the novel?

6. Is it reasonable for Tilly to cling to guilt after carrying out her husband's final wishes? What role does Isaac play in helping her navigate her feelings?

7. What are the parallels between Tilly's guilt and James's fear?

8. How does the parent/child relationship impact other relationships in the novel?

9. In what ways do you think Sebastian and David have played important but different roles in Tilly's life?

10. Finding the balance between closing yourself off and opening your life to others is an important theme of the novel. Discuss.

11. In the final chapter, Tilly says that she needs James. In what ways do you think Tilly and James need each other?

12. How do you think Tilly's relationship with James will differ from her marriage to David?

13. How has Tilly changed from the beginning of the book to the ending? What events have caused her to change?

14. What obstacles, if any, do you see for James and Tilly in the future?

What was the inspiration for *The Unfinished Garden*?

The Unfinished Garden is a personal story on many levels, and, like Tilly's flower beds, evolved over time. The original idea came from watching my mother navigate life as a new widow and thinking, "What if that were me?" I was a stay-at-home mom with no income of my own and no citizenship of the country in which I lived. I'm English, but my husband is American—a renowned academic who loves to joke that I killed him off in my novel. (He's nothing like David, except for his attitude to bugs and his philosophy of pizza toppings.)

I always knew my heroine would be a gardener, since gardening is my therapy, but I wanted to understand why she made the decisions she did after her husband died. I read a wonderful book called I'm Grieving As Fast As I Can *by Linda Feinberg and interviewed a group of young widows. Before long, I found Tilly.*

Finding James was a more difficult journey and took several years. My original hero was a grieving dad, but as I sought escape from our child's obsessive-compulsive disorder, James appeared. I rewrote my hero, and yet I held back, avoiding his dark corners. And it showed. I put the manuscript aside, researched and wrote another story, and became involved with a nonfiction project about parenting and OCD.

But James, being a good obsessive-compulsive, got stuck in my head and refused to leave. Finally, I caved. As I rewrote the manuscript to give James his true voice, I wanted to show the side of OCD I saw every day. Popular culture often portrays obsessive-compulsives as victims, serial killers or people to ridicule, but I see only compassion, empathy and the courage it takes to fight unwanted thoughts. James really is the bravest person Tilly knows.

Many teenage girls have scoliosis. Is there an autobiographical element to Tilly's curved spine?

Yes. My spine is gloriously S-shaped, and serious gardening can wreck my back! (Does it stop me? No.) Like Tilly, I'm always lying on the bedroom floor with my legs in the air. I was diagnosed when I was twelve or thirteen and wore a spinal brace as a teenager. Nasty instrument of torture it was, too. But it did start my lifelong love affair with scarves. (I wore a scarf every day to conceal the metal frame around my neck.) I may, actually, be a little obsessive about scarves....

Are there any resources you would recommend for individuals and families living with OCD?

I urge anyone battling obsessive-compulsive disorder to contact the IOCDF at www.ocfoundation.org for a list of support groups and psychologists versed in the language of CBT and exposure therapy. Not all psychologists are created equal, and OCD is highly individualized. Connecting with the right specialist is vital. I also found useful information through the English group OCD-UK.

I joined a support group for parents of obsessive-compulsive kids about a year ago and have no idea why I waited so long. My son is an OCD success story, but stress and exhaustion can always trigger an episode. I love being able to share with people who understand the simple phrase, "He was checking." Our group starts each meeting with tears but finishes with laughter. Find a tribe. It's a blessing.

As for reading material, I recommend anything by Dr. John March and the following memoirs: Devil in the Details by Jennifer Traig; Rewind, Replay, Repeat by Jeff Bell; and Nowhere Near Normal by Traci Foust.

Do you have a favorite scene in *The Unfinished Garden?*

The scene in *The Chase* has always been my favorite. The setting is loosely based on Badby Woods in Northamptonshire, which dates back at least seven hundred years. The woods are carpeted with bluebells in spring and magical year-round. My sister lives nearby, and every time I step into that forest, I'm transported into another world. As James and Tilly head deeper into *The Chase*, everything strips away until we see just the two of them. They've already begun to trust each other, but this is where their relationship truly begins.

If I had a second favorite scene, it might be when Rowena and James are sitting on the floor at Bramwell Hall, after Rowena quotes Sir Winston Churchill's "Keep buggering on." I wrote the whole scene around that phrase.

Did anything in the manuscript surprise you?

Once I unleashed James, he surprised me constantly. For example, it was a shock to discover everything went back to his father, not his mother. I had been so convinced his mother was the root of everything. And the scene where he takes off running through *The Chase* came from nowhere—with a sound track. ("I Wanna" by All-American Rejects.)

Why did you choose to set the novel in both England and America?

I needed to see Tilly *in both environments to figure out which garden she would ultimately choose—the one that belonged to her childhood or the one she had crafted out of grief. A garden can become such an important part of someone's history and emotional well-being. (Did I mention I'm a gardening addict?) The question is, can grief be transformed into love?*

The Unfinished Garden is your first published novel. Have you written any other novels?

The Unfinished Garden was the second novel I wrote. The first is hidden in the closet where it belongs. However, a fascination with mental illness keeps drawing me back to messed-up characters, so my current manuscript is another love story with damaged people. The romantic in me always wants to believe those who need each other will find each other.

What is your writing process?

I start with a "what if" question, lose myself in research and follow my instincts. This part of the process includes interviews, reading autobiographies, photographing settings, building character profiles, etc. I have way too much fun with research and have to wrench myself away. I love to connect the dots between ideas, and I love to people-watch to steal quirks.

At some point I start writing, and when I do, I have the first and last scenes in my head, but everything in the middle is a journey and can change many times. I believe in the Anne Lamott theory of shitty first drafts, and I rewrite endlessly. I also use stream of consciousness writing as a tool to go deeper and deeper into the same scene.

I'm not a great plotter—wish I were—but after the first draft, I create a working outline and force myself to be somewhat analytical, even though my brain doesn't function that way. As I type this, I'm staring at character goal/motivation/conflict charts and lots of colored sticky notes plastered over my office wall. That's the closest I come to being logical.

I write every morning between two fifty-mile round trips to school and back. (My son is gifted, and we were fortunate to find the perfect school for him. It is, however, quite a trek!) On the weekends, I work in my jammies before breakfast, while the house is quiet. If I've fallen behind on my schedule, I work at night, but that's never a great option for me or for my family. If I'm not heading to bed with a novel by 10:00 p.m., I'm just plain nasty.

How did you become a writer and what was your road to publication?

As a child, I wrote stories and poems and dreamed of becoming a novelist, but as a teenager, I gravitated to fashion journalism. After a detour through history at York University—I studied mainly women's and medieval history—I ended up as a public relations person in the London fashion industry. I was fortunate to work for some of the world's premier designers, including the amazing Vivienne Westwood, and wrote as many press releases as I could. (Writing is still writing!) Everything changed after I met my husband at JFK Airport and moved to a small Midwest college town, with a resume no one understood.

I started a fashion page on the local newspaper, and I dabbled in fiction writing. Then I landed a soul-sucking marketing job, which practically killed my ability to function outside the office. I didn't return to my manuscript until I was a stay-at-home mom in rural North Carolina with a son in preschool. I soon developed a dirty little secret—writing when I was meant to be cleaning the house. But it wasn't until I stumbled into an evening class at the local arts center that I found the courage to say, "Hi, my name's Barbara, and I'm a writer."

I lost some years to my son's OCD but eventually learned to cut out time each day to write. I finished my first novel and started what would become The Unfinished Garden. As my son grew and OCD no longer held our family hostage, I went to conferences, networked, entered writing competitions and read authors I admired. Like most writers, I started querying too early, so lots of rejection followed. But I refused to give up and kept adapting and rewriting. I queried more selectively, the rejections improved, and I started getting requests for pages. One Friday morning, after two weeks of polishing my query letter, I sent a submission to Nalini Akolekar. The following Friday, a day I will never forget, she called. And was completely unfazed by my lack of intelligent remarks. (I think I said wow over and over.) Nalini made everything so easy from the get-go. Three months later, I had a publishing deal.

Who are your favorite authors?

I tend to have favorite books, not authors, and my reading goes all over the place—from nonfiction and memoir to psychological murder mysteries, women's fiction, historical fiction, YA, Victorian classics...and thanks to my son, who has won national awards for his poems, I am rediscovering the pleasure of poetry. My favorite novel is Jane Eyre, and authors I consistently enjoy are Kate Atkinson, Eoin Colfer, Dave Eggers, Therese Fowler, Tana French, Jennifer Haigh, Kristin Hannah, Angela Huth, Marian Keyes, Barbara Kingsolver, Carole Matthews, Kate Morton, Jodi Picoult, Karen White and Denyse Devlin/Denyse Woods. And I think Terry Pratchett is a genius.

What do you like to do when you're not writing?

Other than avoiding housework, I love to be home alone with my family, to potter in my woodland gardens and to read. My favorite thing in the world is to clamber into bed at 9:00 p.m. and read until I can't stay awake. I have a weakness for hanging out with girlfriends (cocktails, heart-to-hearts, shopping...I'm not that fussy), and I live for our annual beach holiday with dear friends Chuck

*and Ellen, and Ken and Cathy. My husband would add, with a
sigh, that I have a weakness for plant and book sales and indulge in too much retail therapy at my favorite boutique in
Chapel Hill, LARK.*

*If you have any other questions, feel free to contact me at
bclaypolewhite@gmail.com.*